Freedom Town

a novel

By
CB Florence

Order this book online at www.trafford.com
or email orders@trafford.com

Most Trafford titles are also available at major online book retailers.

© Copyright 2011 CB Florence.

All rights reserved. No part of this publication may be reproduced, stored in a retrieval system, or transmitted, in any form or by any means, electronic, mechanical, photocopying, recording, or otherwise, without the written prior permission of the author.

The views expressed in this work are solely those of the author and do not necessarily reflect the views of the publisher, and the publisher hereby disclaims any responsibility for them.

Printed in the United States of America.

ISBN: 978-1-4269-2571-9 (sc)
ISBN: 978-1-4269-2572-6 (hc)

Library of Congress Control Number: 2010900325

Trafford rev. 08/15/2011

Trafford PUBLISHING® www.trafford.com

North America & international
toll-free: 1 888 232 4444 (USA & Canada)
phone: 250 383 6864 ♦ fax: 812 355 4082

Chapter 1

The Birthing

The sound of the slave driver's whip, ripped through the cool October air, as the grunts and groans followed. "I done told you slaves, it ain't going to be no playing, dis year," the slave driver shouted, with his harsh Cajun voice.

EVERY WORD THAT BEGAN with the letters Th, exploded from the Cajun's mouth led by the sound of a taunting D. And he kept that forever haunting pause, which appeared to be a warning, which stated, a new flood of words were well on their way. And the words, do you hear me, came with a roar, as he popped the whip, which cost some poor gator, its very existence.

"I want dis here cotton, out of deese fields in two weeks," he yelled, as his horse galloped through the sea of white bowls.

With no fiscal control from its rider, the horse went exactly where the slave driver wished for it to go. It was as if the man from the Bayou was controlling the animal with some kind of hoodoo, or a monkey's foot that had to be safely tucked away in one of his pockets.

"Two weeks," he shouted once more, as if the slaves were unable to hear him the first time.

The thought of two weeks, created an enormous amount of fear in the slaves, as they knew their deadline was an impossible task. But like always, the slaves pushed on, hoping for a miracle or two, from the man up above.

Another painful crack of the whip, which was followed by a loud groan, that hung in the air like a high flying bird. An old slave called Mae, picked a fist full of cotton, and quickly laid it in a young slave boy's sack.

"Old one, you's better keep yo's cotton," the child whispered.

But it was the boy who needed saving, and the old slave was trying her best to keep him from the whip. Yet she also stood at the threshold of pain, which would surely come from the green gator's skin. But still, the old female did not want to see the child get the whip, on his very first day.

"Hush child, you's here to pick," old Mae whispered. "And don't you's look up," she said with a trembling tone.

"Yes um," the boy replied quickly.

Like lightning striking in the same place twice, the boy caught a case of bad luck. For no sooner then he spoke, the slave driver's horse came to a complete stop. It was as if everything in the universe had lost its will to move, just to please the man from the Louisiana Bayou. For even the flies, which courted the animal's ass, appeared to be frozen in mid air. Yet when time took to moving again, the slave driver's head turned ever so frightening, giving old Mae and the boy a full view of his serpent colored eyes. And the two slaves knew the green geams saw them as well. Yet the white man's eyes, wasn't the most frightening thing that caught the two slaves by surprise. For when the horse began to turn, causing the Cajun's body to rotate in line with his head, the man appeared to be something that crawled out of the Louisiana swamp. And before the young slave could figure out that the horse's actions, was no more than a Cajun trick, the white man's eyes seem to disappear right out of his head. Yet old Mae knew it was only the Cajun's slow smooth movement, which made the trick work so well.

But neither old Mae nor the boy knew what was to come, after the horse had flexed its nostrils. For the green balls reappeared, as if to signal the slaves that Hell was on its way. And Hell charged forth with a strong gallop, forcing the slaves to hold their breath, as they waited for the horse to run the boy down. And as a few of the captive souls shut their eyes in fear, the animal quickly came to a stop, with its nose resting less than an inch from the boy's face. Yet the young slave didn't feel lucky, as he stood nose to nose with the stout brown beast. But it was the horse that gave out an arrogant snort, which commanded the boy to lower his head, as it did the same, giving way for the Cajun to dismount. And in dismounting, the Cajun brought his long skinny leg across the front of the beast, and fell from his saddle.

"Let me see what you got dere, boy," the tall slim man said, as he snatched the sack from the child's hand. With one green eye on the boy, and the other peering into the sack, he grunted, and said, "It ain't much, but it'll do for starters."

Hearing such a thing, the boy quickly felt at ease. But before the youngster could breathe a sigh of relief, he found himself getting an eye full of the thing he feared the most. For the slave driver was shaking his whip as he spoke.

"You better keep picking like dis, or you too, will feel da love of dis here whip," the man growled.

The young slave gave a trembling nod, as he uttered the words, yes sir. But just when the boy thought he couldn't be any more afraid, things took a turn for the worst. For the slave driver had started in and on old Mae.

"You better show dat boy how to pick dis here cotton, or it'll be da whip for you as well," the man from Cajun country yelled.

"I's trying, sir," old Mae respectfully replied.

The boy felt bad for the old female, as he saw her situation to be that of an impala, caught between a cliff and a pack of hungry lions. And just like the impala, there was no where for old Mae to go, as she stood with her back up against the cotton. But what the boy didn't know, the old slave had been there many times before, and came out smelling like a beautiful black rose. Yet something in the air said the old female had only dead daisies, hovering over her head like a bunch of flesh eating vultures.

As the slave driver got back on his horse, he started to laugh. He laughed, because like many white men, he took the source of old Mae's problem to be a joke. But if it was a joke, then it had to be a cruel joke, played by evil men. For the so call joke, was just greed trying to make a last ditch effort to control its bottom line. For when ever a slave owner felt a female slave had become too old, to handle the harshness of the fields, they would place her back in night rotation. That way the slave owner would get his last dollar out of the female, while gaining a new life, born in to the damnation of slavery.

For Mr. Arnold, the owner of the Big A plantation was hoping that would be the case with his oldest and best picker, even though he had yet to lose any money on her. But the blood thirsty slave owner felt the old female time was growing short, and he was getting tired of waiting for her to keel over and die. And being one of the few slaves her master had no intentions of selling, old Mae braced herself, for the even darker days to come. For the short, fat, unsightly slave, had every intention of making the white demon wait for the pleasure of watching her die.

Old Mae and the young slave went back to picking their master's cotton, as the slave driver moved on, while shouting, with every step his horse took. And the old female quickly picked another fist full of cotton, and once again, she placed it in the child's sack. Yet the boy didn't say a word, as he just shook his head, while looking at her with sad eyes.

"Don't look, pick" old Mae whispered.

"Yes um," the boy said rather quickly.

"And don't talk, cause I's uh done told ya, you's here to pick," the old slave whispered strongly.

The old female was doing her best, to get the young slave to understand that his life had only one meaning. He was a slave, brought and paid for, just like the mules that pulled their master's wagons. Yet the mule had the ability to make the white men beg for their labor, when the boy had no such liberty.

"What's wrong?" the boy asked, as old Mae held her side.

"Hush child, and pick," old Mae replied, as she hated the thought of bringing another child into a world of hardship and hatred.

When they reached the end of the row, old Mae winced, while stretching her tired back. And as she did so, the old female noticed the boy's fingers. They were covered with blood, as he did his best to pick what little cotton that he could. But old Mae knew she had to do something, or the child would surely get the whip. So while holding her sack open with the left hand, she instructed the boy to do the same. Then she showed the child how to hold his fingers. And like all good instructors, the old female went at a ball of cotton, to show the boy how it was done. And when it was time for the boy to give it a try, he cried something about being told, to pick with two hands.

"Child, if n you's don't get masa Arnold cotton, you's gon get that whip cross yo's back," old Mae said, as her voice held an enormous amount of fear.

A fear that told her, the boy would surely be getting the whip, if he didn't do exactly as she said. And with her pain growing stronger with every passing minute, the old slave didn't believe she could deal with the child's fear much longer. Then like a bolt of lightning, the sound of the slave driver's whip, came across the air. Yet before the groan could reach their ears, the boy was doing exactly as the old female had instructed him to do. And seeing such a response, the old slave tilted her head upward, as if she were thanking the Lord for his intervention.

By the time the Cajun had brought his shouting to an end, the slaves took to getting as much cotton as humanly possible. For they knew the Cajun was still watching, as he sat up on his horse, looking over the field as if he were a bird of prey. And like such a bird, the man was waiting to pounce on the first thing that moved. But just as mother earth saw fit to blow the heat from their backs, old Mae gave the boy another bit of advice.

"You's start at the top of that there cotton, and pick ya way down. Then go to that one younder, and pick yo's way up," she said.

"Up, down. Down, up," the boy replied, as he took aim on another fluffy white.

Old Mae grabbed her side, and said, "I's uh make uh cotton picker out of ya yet."

About half way up the next row, old Mae tried to strike up a conversation with the plantation's newest arrival. "Where you's from?" she whispered, but getting no answer. "When you's got here?" she asked, only to receive another round of silence. And not being one to give up rather easily, old Mae tried once more. "Ha old you's is?" she asked.

Seeing that the boy wasn't going to do any talking, old Mae did something she had only done with her fifteen babies. The old slave leaned over and whispered in her native tongue, which made the boy throw his arms up over his head, as if he were about to be struck.

"Child, you's gotta pick, or you's gon get that whip," the old slave whispered franticly.

But old Mae's warning, did nothing to alleviate the boy's fear, as he sat in a crouching position, looking as if he were about to strike out running. And that told the old slave, she had to do something, before the boy's fear got the best of him. So with fear in her eyes, old Mae quickly filled her hands with cotton, and placed it in the child's sack. Yet the old slave's efforts, wasn't enough to get the boy back to picking, as he went on looking like a rabbit, being stalked by a bobcat. Then just like before, the old slave received a gift from an unlikely source. The driver roared at a slave name Isabella, thus bringing the boy back to his feet, forcing old Mae to thank God and the Cajun for helping her through another desperate moment.

With the boy back on his feet and picking, old Mae smiled, hoping it would make him feel a little better. But with her smile looking like a Jack O lantern, that was carved by a one arm blind man, the old female, may have been doing more harm then good.

After the boy had made his way through two more rows of cotton, and a number of unbearable smiles, he spoke. "I's uh not say that," he whispered.

"No child, you's can't say um here," old Mae whispered as well, while pointing to her mouth. "You's say um here, and here," she said, pointing to the side of her head, then to the very large breast that covered her heart. "Every night, fo you's go to sleep, you's say um, till you's can't say um no mo, if n you's wanna make it," the old slave cried.

"Yes um," the boy replied, as he took aim on another fat ball of cotton.

The day some how moved to its slow tedious end, which landed the slaves back on the chain. And as they headed for the main yard, the boy kept flipping his eyes from old Mae, to his bloody fingers, as he could tell with every step they took, the old female was finding it hard to deal with her pain. And even though the boy wanted to let the old female lean on him, he was too afraid to do so. Yet he couldn't help but to feel at any moment, his new friend was going to fall dead.

But despite the child looking for the worst, old Mae made it back to the main yard, alive and kicking.

At the far end of the main yard, the slaves stood in a line, to receive their evening meal. And when the young slave got his portion of grits and shortening bread, he went and sat at the foot of a large tree across from old Mae. And as he ate, the boy could tell by the way the old slave picked at her food, something was desperately wrong with the aging female. Yet the boy knew there was nothing he could do, while he went on eating the meal, that wasn't enough to fill the belly of a small child. And when he was done gobbling down the tiny morsel, their master called a meal, the boy got up to take his pan, to the slave girl who was to wash it. But before he could make two steps, old Mae stopped him.

"You's take it up yonder, for me?" old Mae asked the child.

As the boy took the pan, he could see that old Mae had barely touched her food. Feeling she needed to eat, the boy tried to give the over size female her pan back. But old Mae just pushed the pan back to the boy, along with a jester for him to eat it, leaving the youngster to shake his head no, as he tried once again, to give the old slave her food. But when the large female grabbed her side in pain, the boy stuffed the left over grits and shortening bread in his mouth, and darted off.

Upon the young slave's return, he sat back down in the same spot.

"Oh no, child, you's can't stay here," old Mae cried in fear.

The old slave quickly got up and took the boy by the wrist, then led him over to where the other male slaves were sitting. The large structure was unlike anything the boy had ever seen. And after giving the building a good hard look, the boy sat down on the ground in the mist of the other male slaves. And with his back to the large building, as well as the other males, he could feel their eyes crawling over every inch of the flesh, their master claimed to own. But the boy wasn't thinking of their staring, as he wondered how could so many, allow themselves to be controlled by so few. Yet the boy didn't have to wonder long, as he himself, sat trembling with fear. Then all at once, the sound of a deep heavy voice came creeping over the air, bringing an end to the boy's shame.

"Ya first day here, boy?" the voice whispered rather fast.

He tilted his head, to see where the voice was coming from. And when the boy saw that the slave was just as large as his voice, the boy's mind went back to its first thought. And as he thought, the boy's facial expression changed several times over the course of a few seconds.

"I's reckon, Mae baby, came out tall like masa cotton," the heavy voice said.

The boy listened, as the other male slaves laughed. Yet he couldn't help but to wonder, how the slaves could find room to laugh, when their lives were no different than his?

"You's mind Mae na, cause she knows them there fields, better then that old masa," the heavy voice slave said, then raised his shirt, allowing the young slave a good view of the future. "You's see this? This is what slaves get, when theys don't get masa cotton. So you's learn good, boy," the large slave said, as he showed off the five long scars that ran across his back.

As quick as the large slave spoke, he became silent, while pulling his shirt down. And a long with his shirt, the large slave lowered his head, as the others quickly did the same. And being just as afraid, the boy bowed his head as well.

"You, you, you, and you, come on," the slave driver said. "Make haste, I ain't got all night," he yelled, as if the slaves were moving rather slowly.

But the four slaves were already moving like jackrabbits across the yard, toward a much smaller building. A building that had wooden shutters, which were open for the white men, that gathered around them, as if something was about to happen. And the boy wondered if what they were waiting for, had anything to do with the slave girls, who were standing in the middle of the building. But when the boy heard the slave driver say you first, to a slave called Eat Um Up, he felt sorry for the small male. Yet when the new comer saw what was to be the slave's fate, his sympathy quickly turned in to envy.

For Eat Um Up, and the female Isabella, were taking their clothes off, as the white men cheered them on. And when her dress was removed, the boy couldn't seem to take his eyes off of Isabella, as Eat Um Up took her down to the dirt floor. And just like the white men, the boy watched with a starving anticipation, as Eat Um Up crawled on top of Isabella, and inserted his stiff dick in her hair covered pussy.

But unlike the white men, the boy could only wish it was him, who was snaking his dick in and out of Isabella's furry wet box.

With his eyes closed, the boy tried to capture the stale smell that flowed from between Isabella's legs, as he could still envision the fuzzy black hairs that covered every inch of her fat hanging lips. But his thoughts were quickly brought to an end, when he heard a voice shout look here boy.

With his head flying in the direction of the voice, the boy eyes faithfully went toward the ground. But the white man rudely placed the butt of his whip under the young slave's chin, and toyed with the underdeveloped throat muscle, like a cat toying with a mouse. Then like the cruel animal that he was, the white man manipulated the boy's fear, by slowly raising his head with the brutal instrument. And as the boy's head was being raised, his eyelids drifted downward, until all he saw, were the black whip, and the white hand which held it.

"Look at me, boy," the white man said with an anger that was so deeply rooted, it had to come from the depth, of his dark hollow soul.

The boy slowly raised his eyes, as the chain master was becoming impatient with his fear.

"If you want some of that over there, you got to get me more cotton then you got today. You hear me, boy. A whole lot more cotton. I want all of you boys, to get me a whole lot more of that cotton," the chain master growled.

"Turn dem around," the slave driver bellowed, as he walked their way.

"You boys heard the man, now move," the chain master shouted, as he gave the Cajun a short envious glance.

As the man from Louisiana spoke, the chain master ran the chain through the slaves's rings. For every slave on the Big A plantation, had a metal ring, which was held by a band that lived on the ankle of their right leg. And the band would be there, until their flesh was ready to be placed in some cold damp hole. And the hole would claim their bones captive, as if it were another form of slavery.

"You see dat?" the slave driver yelled. "Dat is what you get, when you get my cotton. And dis is what you will get, when you don't," he shouted, while cracking his whip.

The young slave jerked against the chain in fear, as he moved about like a caged animal. And just when the chain master was ready to give the boy a firm smack, the slave driver caught his wrist.

"Dere will be plenty of time for dat, Mr. Bernard," the driver said, as he locked eyes with the chain master.

The look in the two men eyes, said they would never be friends. Yet something in the air, said there would be trouble, if the two men were ever to lock horns.

When the pleasure taking was over, the slave driver gave his last order of the day. "Lock um down," he yelled, while walking away with a young slave girl.

The four male slaves were chained to the female they had did their business with, and locked in the small shed.

"Alright, you boys know what to do," chain master Bernard said as if he were speaking to a group of trouble making abolitionist, who needed to be given a good old fashion Southern beating.

As the male slaves were being led into the large building, a chain master name Lamar went to bragging intensively about the slave with the heavy voice. He bragged about how large the slave's tool was, and how well the slave used it. He went on and on, until Bernard couldn't take it any more.

"Will you shut up," Bernard yelled.

Just like everyone knew he would, Lamar didn't speak another word, as he passed the chain that held the slaves captive by their rings, through the hole on his side of the wall. And Bernard was going to do the same with his end of the chain, on the opposite wall. And there would be a man waiting outside of each wall, to wrap the end that he would be given, around a tree, which sat on each side of the building. And every night, the men locked their end of the chain with a big black lock.

As the young slave laid his head back, he heard the squeaky hinges, signaling that the doors were being closed. And as the two doors drew closer together, they took to drawing the light from the building. But to the slaves, it was more then just the doors closing, and the light being removed. For it was also a bold statement, which said, all who is held captive behind these doors, shall never be free. Night after night, that dreadful feeling would haunt them for the rest of their lives. Here you are, and here you shall stay, until life leaves your hopeless bodies, it silently shouted to each and every male slave. And when the two doors were finally closed, and the light was gone, the silent shouting had become a taunting darkness. And like everyone else, the young slave could hear the metal bar that was being placed across the doors. Then there was the dreadful sound of the locks. Click. Click. Just like the chain that mocked their thoughts of freedom, the locks challenged the slaves to escape.

By the time the young slave found himself lying on the dirt floor, he was peering through a small hole in the roof. And while his thoughts fell on a place he would never see again, a flood of tears ran from his eyes. Over, and over, he said to himself, the words old Mae had whispered to him earlier. And as the words ran through his head, like he once ran under the pretty blue sky of Africa, the young slave thought of home. And some where between the words, his tears, and the thoughts of a home he would never see again, the boy drifted off to sleep.

While the boy slept, old Mae was on the other side of the slave yard. With her bare feet steeping into a small structure that had been standing long before she was captured, old Mae said a silent prayer. A prayer for herself, as well as the small run down woodshed, that was being used as a birthing place for the female slaves. And seeing the place for the fifteenth time, old Mae painfully made her way down to the floor.

"You's all right, Mae," Ella asked?

Ella was a young female slave, with an extremely gifted body, and a face to match. Her skin was smooth as the finest silk, which did wonders for her short hair. Her breast still claimed most of its firmness, even though she had been a mother several times over. And Ella's gentle sounding voice, made her perfect for the duties of a birthing mother.

"I's uh all right, child," old Mae replied, as she sat on the floor. "Old Mae is just fine, this here old night," she mumbled, as her breathing told a different story.

When old Mae was well positioned on the floor, Ella placed a small piece of wood in her mouth. The old female then closed her eyes as she began to breathe deeply. Then like all females giving birth, the old slave tightly clinched her fist, and prepared herself for life's awful punishment. And biting down on the stick, old Mae gave her body one good hard push. But for some reason, the old slave's body, refuse to cooperate, as she found herself breathing like a slave that had been running on the tracks of that unseen railroad, trying to find freedom. Yet old Mae's fight wasn't with freedom, as she said to herself, the words she whispered to the boy, which made him curl up like a snake.

And with the words said, the old slave tried it again, yet her baby still did not come, which started Ella to worrying. And as old Mae appeared to have stopped breathing, while lying perfectly still with her eyes closed, Ella quickly paniced.

"Mae, you's dying, Mae," Ella cried, as she laid her hand on the old slave's large shoulder.

With her eyes still shut, old Mae spoke decisively. "You's hush talking bout dying, cause this here child, is trying to live," the old slave said, as her spirit caught fire.

Seeing that she had gotten Ella back on the side of the living, old Mae dug deep into her Angola pride, thus bringing forth a powerful drum beat that had to be heard around the world. So with the few teeth her mouth still possessed, sunk firmly in to the stick, old Mae pushed with a vicious determination. And seeing the old slave's renewed sense for victory, death went crawling back into the depths from which it came.

"Come on Mae. Don't you's let that old masa beat ya. Masa just trying to beat ya, Mae, but don't you's let him. You's hear me Mae. Don't you's let old masa, beat ya," Ella cried, as the tears fell from her eyes.

But old Mae didn't drop a tear, as she went right on pushing, while letting out an awful yell. And when the loud crack was finished, there wasn't a sound to be heard. For even the crickets chirping had came to a halt, as if all of the little critters had fallen dead. Yet it was old Mae who stood at death's door, pounding on it, as if she were dying to get in. And the old female would have rushed into Lucifer's burning embrace, if it were not for her suffering a far greater pain, then the demon could ever administer. So with Lucifer shaking in his shoes, old Mae went back to fighting, as the African drums held her like an avenging spell. And when the drums were beating as loud as God's thunder, the baby eased out into Ella's hands.

With the baby in her control, Ella quickly tied and cut its life line, thus forcing the infant to make it on its own. Ella then held the baby up by its little legs, and gave its bottom a good firm slap. A slap that was no different then the one a white baby received upon its arrival. Yet old Mae's baby wake up call, said it was born into a world, fueled by greed and hate. And as life exploded from its little mouth, the baby knew not of the words, slave or freedom.

After laying the baby on the fat part of old Mae's arm, Ella wiped the sweat from her friend's face, as she cried, "You's done it, Mae. You's done it."

"Yea child, we's done made it through another one," old Mae said, as her week trembling voice, told the story of the near death experience.

Ella was crying both tears of joy and sorrow. For she was happy, her friend had made it through the ordeal alive. Yet Ella couldn't help but to feel, that old Mae, may not make it through the night. "I's uh gon go na, Mae," Ella whispered, as she pressed her face up against the old slave's jaw. And on the way out of the door, Ella whispered, "You's rest, na Mae, you's hear."

As Ella closed the door, old Mae looked at her baby as it cried, and said, "You's hush na, cause the worst is over."

Then the old slave whispered those secret words to her baby, as it fought to capture the art of nursing.

Once her baby had quieted down, old Mae laid her head back, knowing she needed to get some sleep. Yet she wondered, if her old body would still be around when the cock crowed, signaling the start of a new day.

When Ella finally made it back to the female shed, she felt her long night had gotten longer. For chain master Bernard, the meanest white man south of Mr. Arnold, was up against the door, sleeping like a baby. And Ella could have smelled the whiskey on his breath from the neighboring plantation, which was more then a mile up wind of the man. And as she stared at the empty bottle that sat between his legs, Ella knew it would earn her a stern kick, among other things. Yet Ella didn't know what to do, as she stood in a state of fear. So like a tired dog on a cold night, Ella curled up on the ground at Bernard's feet, and prayed for the whiskey to stay with him through the night.

While Ella made her bed under the stars, she started crying just like the baby, old Mae brought into the world. For the beautiful black female was thinking of the two babies she had out in the fields. The same fields, old Mae would be returning to in a matter of hours. And the twenty four year old mother couldn't help but to worry about the old slave, as her mind fell on the six babies that she pushed out into the world of slavery. But Ella knew one of her six efforts would never have to work for a master, nor anyone else for that matter. Yet she often prayed at night, for God to give it a better life then it would have gotten as a slave. As for the other five, Ella could only wonder where they were. And as she wondered why some slaves were allowed to keep their babies, while others had to live with the painful scars of separation, Ella wiped the tears from her eyes, knowing she couldn't afford to lose a moment of sleep, over things that was never going to change. So the pretty black female closed her eyes, and said a silent prayer, while ending another day under the cruel banner of slavery.

Chapter 2

A Reward

Like always, the cock crowed before the sun was ready to show its face. Yet old Mae knew she still had to get up, even though every inch of her body reaped with pain. And as the old slave opened her eyes to the darkness, she could smell the haunting stench of after birth, mixed with her baby's first bowel movement. Yet, old Mae knew she didn't have the time to trouble herself with such matters, being that there was so much to do, before heading out to the fields. For the old slave had to clean her baby, as well as herself. Then she had to clean the half broken down crate, her master called a birthing shed. And when all of that was completed, the old slave still had to get the things that would be needed to care for her baby out in the field, while hoping to catch the food line before the feeding came to an end.

AFTER TAKING A DEEP breath, old Mae tried to pull her tired, weak body up off of the floor. But to the old slave's surprise, her body didn't respond, and she quickly became frighten. And in her state of fear, old Mae went straight to the special words, which she held so dear. And after mumbling the words a few times, the old slave tried to lift herself once again, only to be faced with the same results. A result, that left old Mae crying for the first time in sixteen years. For the old slave hated to think she had carried her child nine long months, endured a whole day of labor, while tarring in the field, only to suffer the worst birthing of her fifteen pregnancies, just to die. But old Mae had no intentions of giving up, as long as there was life left in her body, even if it was draped with pain.

With Ella's sleep being brought to an end, by the noise from chain master Johnson opening the doors to the female shed, the young birthing mother was quickly caught off guard. And being that she wasn't in any pain, Ella took a quick look around, but Bernard was nowhere in sight. So after thanking the white man's God, Ella stood up, and did her best, to rid herself of the dirt, which she acquired from spending the night on the cold hard ground. And as she did so, Ella watched the females, as they stumbled out of the shed one after the other, looking at her as though something was desperately wrong. But before Ella could shake off the females disturbing stares, she heard the slave driver's voice, and took off running.

"Sir, sir," Ella cried, as if the cotton fields were on fire. "Mae done had her baby, sir."

"Finally," the slave driver barked, as he began to fill his cup with the steaming hot coffee, which sat over a small fire. "How is da old goat?"

"It tore her up awful bad, sir. Awful bad, it did," Ella cried sadly.

"Well I guess, she won't do us any good today," the Cajun said to Lamar. "Go tell da old girl, to hang around dis here yard, and get her rest. But come cock's crow tomorrow, I want to see her ready to go. Now you go tell da old girl what I said," the slave driver barked.

"I's uh tell her, sir," Ella said, then immediately started to put her feet in motion.

"Hold up," the slave driver said firmly, thus bringing Ella to an abrupt stop. "What did da old girl have?"

"A boy, sir. It's a boy," Ella shouted joyfully, giving credence, to the old slave's first victory, out of her sixteen tries.

Both the slave driver and Lamar watched, as Ella's round ass shook beneath the old dress with delight, while she ran off to tell old Mae the good news. And from the look on the slave driver's face, Lamar knew right away, what the man was thinking.

"Remind me, to try dat one, tonight," the slave driver said to Lamar, with a gleam in his eyes.

With old Mae finally up off of the floor, and cradling her baby ever so gently, she was ready to try and make it to the door. But before the old female could take one step with her badly aching body, Ella nearly took the door off of its hinges, as she yanked it open.

"Mae, he said, you's can stay her today," Ella shouted with joy. "You's hear me Mae? He said you's can stay here," she reiterated, right before disappearing from the doorway.

Even though it was still dark out, the open door gave old Mae just enough light to see her way out of the shed. And after slowly placing her feet on solid ground, the old slave shuffled over to the fire, which was burning a few yards from the shed.

"Well we's done made it through the storm," old Mae lied, as her bottom lip trembled, from a great deal of pain and fear.

In fact, the old female knew things were about to get worst. So with one foot knee deep in the grave, and the other coming up lame, old Mae found herself, faced with a seven pound cast iron pot. And to make matters worst, in an attempt to help her old friend, Ella filled the pot to the rim with water. That made the pot even heavier, while it sat over a strong fire, getting hotter with each passing moment. Yet the old slave looked up on her death sentence, knowing what had to be done.

After laying her naked new born on the cold ground, old Mae picked up the poker. But before she could use the iron rod, old Mae heard the slave driver's voice.

"I don't dink, you need to be doing dat," the driver said, as he came up on the old female.

With the poker in his hand, the slave driver plucked the pot from over the fire with ease. He then placed the pot on the ground, and replaced it with a fresh pot of water. The funny talking white man then used his handkerchief, to carry the hot pot while speaking kindly.

"Come on old girl, let's get you back inside," he said.

The two walked silently back to the birthing shed, with the driver appearing to be in too much of a rush, to wait on old Mae. So when he reached the shed, the Cajun sat the pot just inside the doorway. The man from Louisiana, then leaned against the weak building, and waited for old Mae to catch up. And when she reached the shed, he looked the old slave in the eye and gave it to her straight.

"I got to have you back out dere tomorrow, old girl."

"I's uh be there, sir."

"It's not like we have a choice, now do we?" the driver said, then headed for the food line. "I'll send a boy to fetch dat other pot," he shouted while still walking. "And make sure you put some salt on dat floor," he shouted after taking a few more steps. Then he stopped and turned around. "Oh yea, be sure and get plenty of rest," the Cajun shouted with a kind tone, then preceded to go about his business, as if he hadn't said or did anything that would raise so much as a touch of suspicion.

Old Mae didn't have the time to think about what had taken place, as she crawled into the birthing shed on her right hand and knees. With her baby clutched safely in her left arm, the plantation's oldest picker struggled along like an old crippled grizzly.

After finding a safe place, to have a talk with himself, the Cajun smiled, as he mumbled the words, the old girl had a boy. The driver spoke, as if he were proud of the old female. He then took his hat off, and gazed up at the half lit sky, and began to speak with a gentle softness.

"Deir fait is in your hands now, so I just want you to know, I have a job to do, and I got to do it. And you know if I were one of dem others, she would be marching out to dem fields, so it's up to you old boy. You got to take care of da old girl, for dat baby sake. Now I know you hear me, because you're always listening. You got to deal her a better hand, den you dealt me," the slave driver said, while looking toward the Heavens, as if he were waiting for an answer.

Seeing that his little talk with God didn't go exactly the way he planned, the Cajun went about starting his day. And as the slaves marched toward their daily dish of abuse, the boy looked around for old Mae. But the old slave was nowhere to be seen, and the boy quickly feared she had died during the night. Yet he went right on looking, refusing to give up on his new friend. And while looking back for the old slave, the boy stumbled and nearly fell.

"What is wrong with you boy?" the slave driver shouted, as he rode up on the youngster in a flash.

But just as the horse reached the young slave, he fell into a crouching position, ultimately bringing the line to a hault.

"Look here boy. I see you looking around for Mae. But don't you be worrying about her, because da old girl is fine. Now you need to get your mind on dat cotton, or you will be getting a taste of dis whip," the slave driver shouted. "All of you hear me, and hear me good. Mae is just fine. Da old girl done had dat baby, and she's going to work around da yard today. So dat mean da rest of you, need to get her share of dat cotton. And if you don't, I got a little some ding for you," the slave driver shouted, as he cracked his whip. "So boy, you need to walk straight, and put your mind on dat cotton," he barked at the youngster.

When the picking started, the boy found a spot off to himself, and tried his best to remember everything the old female had taught him. For the boy knew he had to stay focused, in order to stay one step in front of the slave driver's whip. So with his mind on their master's cotton, the boy silently said the words old Mae whispered to him the day before.

About mid morning, the boy's sack began to take on a bit of weight, thus creating another problem for the child. And as he towed the sack through his master's cotton, like a mule pulling a plow, the boy caught the slave driver's attention. But the man from Louisiana didn't break in to his shouting mode, as he eyed the boy with disappointment. Yet he gave his horse a swift kick, which sent the animal into a gallop.

"Pick up dat sack, and toss it," the slave driver said, as his horse came to a stop behind the young slave.

Filled with an enormous amount of fear, the boy never noticed the slave driver's tone. Though stern, the Cajun's voice lacked aggression, yet the young slave never took notice of that, as he grabbed the sack, and gave it his best shot. And to say the boy's effort was far below dismal, would have been more then kind.

"Well I guess, dat's a toss to you," the slave driver barked, as he leaned forward in his saddle.

As the boy went back to picking, the slave driver felt he would give the young slave something to think about.

"If I catch you dragging deese sacks again, I'm going to put you in night rotation," the Cajun said with a smart tone.

Hearing the strange threat, the other slaves quickly took to laughing at the boy's possible punishment. But the young slave felt he didn't have time to think about the white man's words, or his fellow slaves laughing, being that he only cared about staying on the topside of the whip. So while the others enjoyed their laugh, the boy went right on picking.

When the boy finished picking the cotton that sat around the sack, he tried to toss it again. And just like before, the sack went no where, causing the slave driver to shake his head.

"Well if you ain't some ding for nu ding, den you ain't nu ding for some ding," the driver said, looking disgusted.

Chain master Bernard sat on his horse, wondering when the man from the Bayou, was going to break out the whip, and teach the boy a lesson. But what Bernard failed to notice, should have been obvious to the average slave handler. The young slave had far more cotton in his sack, then all of the day before. And with that type of productivity, the slave driver saw no reason, to break the boy's rhythm, so the Cajun used his head, and called out for Eat Um Up.

"Show dis boy, how to toss dat sack," the slave driver said, as Eat Um Up came running with his sack.

"Yes sir, I's uh do that, sir," Eat Um Up replied rather quickly, while dropping his sack.

"Don't do it for him," the driver shouted, before Eat Um Up could take hold of the boy's sack.

"Yes sir, I's uh show him good, sir," Eat Um Up replied, as he went about doing as the man from Louisiana stated.

Then with out further ado, Eat Um Up set out to get the young slave to mimic his every move. And when the sack was gripped, and the knees were bent, the boy tossed his sack right along with Eat Um Up. But just like before, the boy's sack went about as far as his feet.

The slave driver looked down on the boy, wondering what to make of him, as he said, "Well I guess you got to start some where." Then the Cajun told Eat Um Up, he wanted the boy tossing his sack by the day's end. And as Eat Um Up got down to giving his usual reply, the Cajun felt the need to leave the two slaves with something to think about. "Den we won't have a problem," he said, while moving on.

Though only in his early twenties, Eat Um Up had been around long enough to know what the slave driver meant, by his last statement. It was get it done, or get the whip, and Eat Um Up had no desire to taste the white man's whip. And for the little slave who knew how to pick big, Eat Um Up had became a wiz at avoiding trouble. For one of the slave's best secrets, was to always answer rather quickly, when ever a white person spoke to him. The young slave learned that from the same man, who had given him, such a crazy name. It was a short burly man, who called himself, the best damn slave ship captain in the world. The captain told Mr. Arnold, he gave Eat Um Up the name, because every time he dropped food down to the captives, the little shit would always come up eating. Thus, born the name, Eat Um Up, and Mr. Arnold saw no reason to change it.

By the end of the day, the boy was a little shy of having picked two full sacks of his master's cotton. Yet he was one full sack ahead of his previous outing, and that would surely keep both him and Eat Um Up from the whip. But the young slave still wasn't satisfied with his achievement, as he stood at the edge of the field, stuffing his sack with even more cotton. And as he did so, the slave driver watched him like an evil predator, looking for something to destroy. Then like a bad dream, all of the boy's efforts were about to be lost, as he struggled to get the heavy sack on to the back of the wagon.

"You filled it, now get it up dere," the slave driver growled, as he readied his whip.

Seeing that he was about to be struck, the young slave tried desperately to do as he was told. Yet no matter how hard the boy tried, he couldn't bring himself to lift the heavy sack.

"Don't just stand dere, Eat Um Up, give da boy a hand," the slave driver shouted.

Eat Um Up grabbed the sack, and tossed it on the back of the wagon with ease, thus causing the slave driver to slap his horse with its tie down strap. And like the man from Louisiana knew it would, the animal was on top of the short slave, faster then a mountain cat could pounce on a rabbit.

"Da next time I tell you to help him, and you do it for him, you will be getting his taste of my whip. Now line up," the driver snarled.

When the slave driver's crew got their food, they were given a little extra portion of grits and shortening bread for their hard work. And just like the night before, the young slave got his food, and went sat at the base of the tree across from old Mae. And once there, a strange expression came over his face, as he gazed at the baby sapping on old Mae's tit.

"Who that for?" the boy asked nervously.

"Hush child, and eat ya grits, cause you's ain't got all night," old Mae said, as she was taken back, by the boy's lack of knowledge.

For it told the old slave, the boy hadn't been in their cursed world long enough to lose his innocence. But it also made the old slave fear more so for the boy, as she felt he wouldn't make it. For she knew if he didn't learn fast, the child would parish under the weight of the white man's cruelty. Too many times, old Mae had seen her kind come to the plantation, fresh off of the slave ship, only to perish in a matter of weeks.

"I's uh ain't gon be feeding no baby ain't mine," old Mae said with a touch of harshness, as she sought to harden the child up.

"I's uh sorry, I's ate ya food," the boy said, holding his pan out for old Mae to take some of his grits.

"Child, I's got my own."

"But they's gave me uh heap," the boy said, as if old Mae couldn't see the white man's generosity for herself.

"Well you's better eat it, cause you's ain't gon get uh lot, come morning," the old slave assured the youngster.

"I's uh done like you's told me," the boy said, as he scooped up a mess of grits with a piece of bread.

"Well you's ain't gotta worry bout that whip, cause I's heard you's done mighty fine," old Mae mumbled, still feeling weak from giving birth.

The boy smiled on the inside, as he went back to eating his food. But the look on his face, told the old slave, he was happy to hear her words of praise, as he was clearly thinking about something. And as she waited for him to look up, old Mae could tell, the boy was making an effort, to keep his head down.

"What you's thinking bout, child?"

After working hard all day, and placing everything on the driver's word, the boy wasn't afraid to tell old Mae what was on his mind, as he pointed to the small shed.

"Na you's listen to me, child. If n you's wanna keep that old whip off of yo's back, you's uh stop worrying bout that over yonder. Cause that old shed, ain't gon get ya nothing, but that whip cross yo's back. And that old slave driver, he's uh put it on ya, shows I's sitting here," old Mae said with fear. "Na you's gone eat ya food," she went on with a bit of frustration.

With his head hung in shame, the boy mumble, "Yes um."

But if the young slave had no intentions of looking for a motherly figure, he some how forgot to relay his sentiments to old Mae. And from the way she spoke, the old female didn't give a fist full of cotton, on how the boy felt about the matter, or the small shed. For she had spoken, and that was all to it as far as the old slave was concern.

Even though the old slave had spoken, the boy still sat with anticipation, as he watched the white men began to gravitate toward the small shed. Yet it was the same four slaves from the night before, who were called up on for entertainment. And when the boy saw that he wasn't going to be chosen, the youngster wondered why, as he turned his back to the activity that was about to take place. But even with his back to the action, the boy could still see the females in all of their glory. For he had their bodies tattooed in his mind. And even with his eyes fixed on the back wall of the large shed, he could still see their thighs parting, like gates to some Heavenly reward. A reward, the boy could almost taste, as Isabella's scent began to fill his nostrils. And how could he forget the long fat nipples, which dressed the short girl's tits.

By the time the boy was staring deep into the large shed, his dick held and aching erection. And before he knew it, the boy could see the females in his mind, as their asses shook and trembled, from the pounding they were receiving.

While the white men enjoyed the four slaves taking their pleasure, the driver walked the grounds as if he were in search of something. And as the man continued to walk, while striking fear in every slave that crossed his path, the Cajun did so, until he came up on a young slave girl, who wore the name Sistah. Sistah was born without the grace of being normal. And if the young female had been born white, her inability to reason, would have been an asset. But being born in to slavery, she was expected to work just as well, and just as hard as any other slave.

Taking the female by the hand, the slave driver led the poor girl around, as if she were a piece of livestock. He even stopped off to have a slave girl to wash her up a bit, which was a sight in it self. Every time the female tried to touch Sistah, the near normal slave would start fighting. That is, until the slave driver cracked his whip.

When chain master Lamar saw the slave driver with Sistah, he sought to remind his boss of their earlier conversation. "I thought you wanted me to remind you about Ella," he said.

"Dat has already been taken care of, now go get me da new boy," the driver said, never laying his eyes on the man.

Lamar didn't ask any questions, he just went over to the large shed, and began to take the boy off of the chain. And as he did so, the chain masters heard the driver call for the slaves to be locked up. Lamar quickly wondered why the driver was making such a call, when he had told him to take the boy off of the chain. But not being one to question authority, Lamar did as he was told, and brought the boy to the driver.

With the butt of his whip under the boy's chin, the slave driver spoke firmly. "Dis is only because you got my cotton. But if you don't do better tomorrow, you will get a taste of my whip," the driver said, as his green eyes held a hellish flame. "Now chain dem to dat tree, and give dem a couple of blankets," the man from Louisiana said, while departing.

Hearing the Cajun clearly, Lamar suddenly felt a growing need for the outhouse, as he feared word would get back to Mr. Arnold, about his participation in such an act. But fearing the Cajun just as bad, Lamar decided to go with the lesser of the two evils. For if bad came to worst, Lamar knew he could always place the blame, squarely on the Cajun's shoulders.

With the order carried out to the fullest, Lamar laughed, as he checked the chain, to make sure the boy had enough slack to do his business. "I recon, you ain't never been with a girl before," Lamar said, touching the boy's face. "Na you watch her, boy, because this one here ain't much in the head, but she can be a real hell cat, if she get the notion," he said laughing. "Now you give it to him good, girl, because you don't pick worth nothing any how," Lamar went on, as he held tight to his smile.

Seeing Sistah with the look of an angry woman, Lamar removed his hand from the young slave boy's knee. And after rising to his feet, Lamar headed for the chain master cabin. Yet before disappearing around the backside of the female shed, he took one last look over his shoulder. And to the man's dismay, Sistah was still watching him, as if she had the where with all, to give the chain master a piece of her mind, which made Lamar think twice about his selfish desires.

When the boy was sure they were alone, he made his move. And with his weapon fully erected and ready for a frontal attack, the teen ran his hand across one of Sistah's nice round tits. But the boy was greeted with a bit of discipline, as his hand received a light, yet disappointing slap. But the boy wasn't about to let a little slap, deter, him from getting his first shot of pleasure. So with sleep in his eyes, and sex on his mind, the youngster, prepared himself to go at it one more time. And as the bulge in his pants would not allow him to give up, the young slave tried a different approach. With his hand on Sistah's leg, the boy tried to raise her dress for a little peep. But like a cat bringing its paw down on a wounded bird, Sistah's hand fell on her dress, thus crushing the boy's dream.

With no more then escaping the whip for his reward, the boy laid back wishing he was in the large shed. And as he turned his back to Sistah, the young slave knew there would be nothing extra for what was a hard day's work. So he closed his eyes and said those same special words, and tried to get some sleep. Then like a child wanting attention, Sistah laid her arm across him. She than placed her hand on his stomach, and slowly ran it down to his firm erection. And even with all of her short comings, Sistah could understand the boy's need, as well as feel his desire, pulsating in her hand, as she gripped his dick tightly. And the size of the youngster's tool, was as frightening, as the whip it self.

Knowing the danger that awaited her, Sistah gently tugged on the boy, until she finally got him on to his back. And while the cool night air chilled their flesh, she immediately went to undoing the young slave's breeches. And once the buttons were undone, she straddled him, and pulled the pants down to his knees, giving the moonlight an opportunity to display the youngster's enormous gift. But unfortunate as she may have been, Sistah was no fool. The young female had no intentions of allowing the boy to have his way with such a large weapon. So with the massive dick under her control, Sistah carefully placed the beast at Heaven's doorway.

With what little mind she had focused on the challenge at hand, Sistah slowly worked the dick's large head between her lips. And already being wet from the tease, her doors gently parted, allowing the large head to enter like a welcome guest. But with her right hand being the only thing that stood between her, and an enormous amount of pain, Sistah held the dick tightly as she rode it seductively. And as the misguided female closed her eyes and enjoyed a small portion of the boy's firm erection, she moaned from its pleasing satisfaction. A satisfaction, that was unlike any other, as she and the boy reached an early climax. Then like a well season female, Sistah descended down on to the large chuck of flesh and muscle, seeking the pleasure that could only come from a perfect mixture of passion and pain. And even though the boy's throbbing ejaculation ended peacefully, the two knew it was something special, as they fell asleep wrapped in each others arms.

Just before the cock crowed the next morning, Sistah laid sleeping with her back to the boy. Yet before the feathered bugler could open its eyes, the boy went in search of more. And as he squeezed Sistah's breast, she began to awaken with a moan. But Sistah was still too much asleep, to realize she was in a dangerous position. For the boy had maneuvered her body forward, and the head of his massive dick, was already sliding between her hairy wet lips. And when his right hand went from Sistah's breast, to draping over her left shoulder, it was far too late for the girl. For the boy, had Sistah, and with or without her approval, she was being forced to take every inch of his giant shaft.

By the time the chain took to rattling, Sistah was already crying out in pain. And as she struggled to free her body from the unbearable pain, Sistah mistakenly placed herself in a far worst position. A position that had Sistah on her knees, while her head laid flat on the blanket. And with his hands firmly planted on her waist, the boy humped inside of Sistah, as if he were losing his mind. But how could the boy control himself, being that Sistah's pussy was so warm and wet, just begging for him to get deeper into its wetness. And the way the boy continued to drive his body deep into Sistah's cabin, all who had ears, could hear her pain.

When the boy had finally calmed down form his violent explosion, Sistah found herself lying flat on the ground. Yet she didn't want either of them to move a muscle, as the boy laid on top of her. And while feeling his pelvic hair on her ass, Sistah began to breathe softly, as the boy's dick took to shrinking inside of her wet walls. Yet such a feeling made Sistah reach back to play with the boy's ear, while whispering her own special words to him.

Shortly after the cock crowed, Lamar came to release the two young slaves from the tree. And approaching them, the man wore a big bright smile.

"Don't you be looking shame now girlly, because we all heard, you. You gave it to her good, didn't you boy," Lamar said, looking at the two young slaves.

But neither Sistah nor the boy said a word, as Lamar went on sporting his big bright smile. And the way he held the boy's flesh in a state of aw, made the two young slaves wonder, what was running through the white man's head.

No sooner then the boy got his grits and shortening bread, he ended up across from the old slave once again. Yet the old female didn't have a moment to spare, as she had to eat, and feed her baby at the same time. And the old slave's baby was already hard at work, sapping on her left breast without a care in the world. And as she sat looking down on her only son, in sixteen tries, the old female had two flour sacks, and a long strip of cloth resting on her large thigh. The strip of cloth was taken from a cotton sack, which had seen its better days a few years back. The two sacks would be used to make the baby's diapers. And the long strip of cloth was the baby's new temporary life line, as it would keep him safely connected to his mother. But if old Mae were to collapse for what ever reason, the baby's life would most likely be short lived, which challenge the thought of being safely connected.

When the slaves had finished eating, they were quickly assembled for their daily march to the fields. As for old Mae, she stood at the front of their line, where the slave driver had placed her. And while the old slave stood waiting, she clung to her baby with fear. For chain master Bernard, with all of his evilness, was headed her way. And the old female knew the white man would kill her baby just for the hell of it, if he got the notion. But the old slave was dead set on keeping her baby alive, until their master came for him.

"Why is she on dat chain?" the slave driver asked of Mae, while dismounting his horse as it came to a stop behind Bernard.

"I thought, we were taking her out," Bernard replied, while running the chain through Sistah's ring.

"Take her off of dat chain, before you get any more bright ideas," the slave driver said with a touch of anger.

"Why?" Bernard asked, as he stood up.

The slave driver didn't speak a word, as he stood staring at Bernard, like a gator watching its prey from a far. And having a feeling that the whole situation was about to turn bad, Bernard quickly broke the silence.

"It's my job to chain them up," Bernard said.

"Den I suggest, you run dat chain, through da rings, of da ones dat can run," the slave driver barked, while still staring at Bernard with bad intentions.

Bernard removed the chain from the rings, and started all over again. And just like the slave driver demanded, he ran the chain, without adding old Mae to the equation. But the old slave knew in her heart, the man with the funny accent had condemned her baby to an early death. And if he himself didn't hurry up and leave the Big A, Bernard would surely introduce him to death as well. Yet something told the old female, the driver was no stranger to men like Bernard. But she was hoping the tall slender man from Louisiana could handle himself, when the devil decided to make his move.

Upon reaching the field, old Mae got Isabella to help her with the baby. And Isabella quickly tied the long cloth around the old slave's upper body, just before all hell had broke loose. For old Mae had given Sistah the baby to hold, and the misfortunate slave was refusing to give the child back.

"Mine," Sistah said, as Isabella reached for the baby.

"Sistah, you's give that child, that baby," old Mae cried.

But the old slave's greatest fear was already up on them. The slave driver's horse stood with its head down, as if it was praying for the poor lost souls, and for what they were about to receive.

"Give dat girl, dat baby," the slave driver bellowed.

With her head bowed and crying, Sistah gave the baby to Isabella. But Sistah still didn't move, as she continued to watch the baby like a hungry hound waiting for table scraps. And Sistah went right on staring, as Isabella slid the baby between the cloth and old Mae's breast. Then with a gentleness that even Sistah could understand, Isabella placed the flour sacks behind the baby's back for support.

"We's gon go na, Mae," Isabella said, as she took Sistah by the hand, and led the crying female away.

But as Isabella led Sistah across the field toward their friends, the misguided female couldn't stop looking over her shoulder at old Mae and the baby. And as she treaded on the line of defiance, Sistah mindlessly tracked over her master's cotton, until she got a word of encouragement.

"Watch dat cotton, girl," the slave driver yelled, sending Sistah running, as she left Isabella behind.

With the day well on its way, and the slave driver had yet to yell once, old Mae had nothing to take her mind off of the pain she was forced to suffer. So once again, the old slave found herself mumbling those special words, as she began to think of the boy. The old slave had never seen anyone learn to pick cotton as fast as the boy, and she was dying to find out how he did it. But before old Mae could enjoy the thought of the boy staying one step ahead of the whip, her pain quickly took over. And like a vengeful enemy, the pain quickly smothered her thoughts, as if it were sucking the life out of a helpless child.

But if old Mae's pain had killed her thoughts, then what she heard come across the mid October air, massacred her fleeting will.

"What you looking at, boy?" the slave driver shouted, after watching the young slave for a while.

The man from Louisiana couldn't help but to notice how the boy kept looking toward the old slave. And feeling that the old girl needed all the help she could get, the man saw no reason to keep the two hardy workers apart.

"You want over dere boy?" the driver shouted.

With his head pointed toward the ground, the boy nodded, while uttering the words, yea sir.

"Den pick up dat sack, and get," the Cajun said, with some what of a humorous tone to his voice.

As the boy gathered up his sack and ran, the slave driver smiled a good smile.

With the boy finally where he wanted to be, the youngster quickly started picking like the day before. Yet old Mae just looked at the boy, as she continued to suffer through her pain. But when the young slave picked a fist full of cotton and placed it in her sack, the old slave's pain increased two fold. And even though old Mae found the boy's generosity to be heart warming and courageous, she knew he needed to keep his cotton, to stay that all important step in front of the whip. And the old slave also knew, a few fist full of cotton wasn't going to help her none. Yet that didn't stop the boy, as he went right on giving his friend a bit of cotton, with every new row he started, which prompted the old one to speak up.

"You's better keep yo's cotton, if n you's want Sistah tonight," old Mae said, only to see the boy shake his head no. "You's ain't like Sistah?" the old female asked, while having second thoughts, about all the hollering and screaming she heard.

With a cat like grin, the boy nodded swiftly, revealing to the old slave, that her first assumption was the better choice.

"Well you's better keep yo's cotton," old Mae said, realizing the boy was no different then any other male.

Shortly after the boy returned from filling his first sack, he dropped another hand full of cotton in the old slave's sack. And as the boy did so, the slave driver saw him, and tied another knot in his horse tie down strap. For the slave driver hadn't missed a single contribution, the boy had made to the old female. But there was something sinister about the Cajun's stare, as he glared at a group of slaves picking to his left. And while he tried to figure the boy out, the slave driver gave his horse a jerk, and the animal headed for the small group of slaves.

When the boy saw that the slave driver was preoccupied, he quickly whispered the word Pleasant.

"What's that you say, boy?" old Mae asked softly.

After placing another hand full of cotton in the old female's sack, the boy repeated himself. "They's call me Pleasant."

"Land sake, child, what kind uh name, masa Arnold done gave ya?" old Mae barked, as if the boy had a choice in the matter.

But slavery had broken the boy, who had been born to a strong and proud tribe, just as it had broken the others. And no matter how much the boy wished for his former life, he had to face the fact, there will be no brighter tomorrow.

When Pleasant saw the Cajun get off his horse to confront Sistah, he bent over and quickly scribbled something on the ground. And after staring at the work of art for a brief moment, old Mae shook her head, revealing to the boy, she didn't quite understand the symbol. And seeing that the old slave was confused, Pleasant quickly rubbed the symbol out, and drew it again.

"Sixteen," old Mae said, after recognizing the number she hadn't seen in years. "You's sixteen," she whispered.

Pleasant tried to say the word a few times, but then quickly put it to rest, as he went back to picking. As for old Mae, the aging one went back to dealing with her pain, never letting on how she learned how to count.

Chapter 3

Pleasant

With the sun hanging at a forty degree angle, the slave driver shouted for old Mae to change her baby. And with the baby's diaper being wetter then a river, the slave driver's words were like music to the old slave's ears. But old Mae had only one problem. The flour sacks needed to be cut, and no matter how hard the old female tried, she couldn't tear the confounded thing with her teeth. And as Pleasant watched old Mae struggle with her burden, a feeling came over him like a dark cloud. For it was a cloud of shame, that came from not being able to live up to a tradition, which had been in his tribe, long before he was born. For in his tribe, it was customary for the young ones like himself, to help the old ones with their daily hardship. But slavery had taken that, which once made the young boy proud, leaving him with only hopelessness and shame for his code of honor.

WHEN THE SLAVE DRIVER caught wind of old Mae's dilemma, his horse immediately started charging her way. And when the man from Louisiana reached the old female, he did something that was uncommon around the Big A plantation. He got off his horse, and helped old

Mae with her problem, which brought about a disturbing look from Bernard.

Pulling that thing he called a knife, which looked more like a adolescent sword, dying to be grown, the slave driver sought to cut the sack. "Hold it," he said, as the blade glistened beneath the gleaming sun. "Where you want it cut?" he asked, as old Mae held the sack. "Watch your fingers," he warned the old female, after she had marked the flour sack with her lips.

Then like a hot knife cutting through a warm breeze, the razor sharp blade sliced through the sack with ease.

Still clinging to the part, which old Mae had intended on using to cover her baby, the Cajun got back on his horse. He then said something that sucked the air right out of the old slave's body.

"Give him to me," the Cajun said, leaning forward on his horse.

Old Mae forced herself not to panic, as the shades of her past, came rearing its ugly head again. And as she laid her only son out of sixteen tries in the slave driver's awaiting arm, the old lioness was truly ready to give up on life. But just as the driver's horse turned to walk away, Pleasant took his friend by the hand, and guided her back to the cotton.

As the old slave tried to get back to her picking, she heard the slave driver call out for Sistah. Looking up, old Mae saw Sistah running with her sack. And the poor girl looked like a baby doe, trying out its legs for the very first time. Her every move, was as awkward, as two left feet, living inside two oversize right shoes. And when the unfortunate female reached the driver with her sack no where close to being half full, she stood scared and confused, not knowing what to think.

"Drop dat sack," the slave driver said mildly.

When Sistah finished doing as she was told, the driver got off his horse and gave her the baby, along with the make shift diaper. But being that the poor girl was far from normal, she immediately accepted the baby as a gift. And when Sistah took to bouncing the baby in her arms, as she smiled joyfully, the slave driver was forced to spring in to action.

"Change dat baby," the driver growled.

Sistah dropped to the ground, and laid the baby long ways on her legs. And as she smiled, while occasionally spouting a dysfunctional laugh, Sistah appeared to be taking a great deal of pleasure, in dealing with the very smelly diaper. Yet Sistah's extra care for the infant was a bit more then the Cajun had expected, when he called upon her to do old Mae's dirty work.

"Hurry up," the slave driver shouted, bringing the baby's sleep to an end.

With one crack of the baby's voice, the man from Louisiana knew he had made his second mistake of the day, in only a matter of minutes. And while the court was still out on what may turn out to be the man's biggest blunder, it had already rendered its final verdict on his latest miss step. And from the sound of the baby's voice, the slave driver had no other choice, but to throw himself on the mercy of the court.

"Mae, what is wrong with dis baby?" the slave driver shouted, as he watched Sistah flap her arms like a drunken parrot.

The old slave calmly mumbled to herself, "You's hush that fuss, cause the worst is over."

Like two misbehaving kids responding to their mother's voice, both Sistah and the baby quieted down. But that only left the slave driver's problem half solved. He still had to deal with Sistah's reactions, to the baby squinting from the sunlight beaming in its little face.

"Turn around," the slave driver said rather softly.

Sistah proceeded to turn, until her body was able to block the sunlight from the baby's eyes. She then went back to pinning the baby's diaper, before carefully pulling herself up off the ground. And once back to her feet, Sistah totally ignored the slave driver, as she grabbed her sack and tried to leave with the old slave's baby.

"I guess dat baby, is going to help you pick dat cotton," the driver said, which started the other slaves to laughing.

But Pleasant didn't crack a smile, as he went right on picking, leaving old Mae to wonder, what to make of him. For even old Mae had to laugh at the slave driver's joke. But what really had the old slave wanting to laugh, was the fact that Sistah had never reacted to the driver's voice, one way or the other. For the misfortunate female just went right on walking, as if the white man hadn't uttered a word.

"Girl, if you don't give me dat baby," the slave driver said, still not getting a reaction out of Sistah. "Sistah," he said firmly.

Sistah turned around, showing the slave driver just how happy she was to have the baby in her arms. And at that very moment, the driver wished he could have allowed the girl to keep the child, but the Cajun knew it wasn't his to give.

"Give it to me," the slave driver said, reaching his hands out.

With Sistah's gut telling her, she was about to be awarded a taste of the man's whip, the teen reacted rather quickly. But seeing that the slave's understanding fell far short of her beauty, Sistah ended up digging herself deeper into an already bottomless pit.

"Here sir," she said, while trying to give the slave driver the soiled diaper.

"Give me dat baby," the Cajun said with his teeth firmly together.

After giving the slave driver old Mae's baby, Sistah walked away crying, as if she had been beaten down by the man. And when the sad female reached the spot where she had stopped picking, Sistah found her self all alone. But that was just fine with the dysfunctional female, as she wiped the tears from her eyes. Yet when she heard the slave driver tell old Mae to wash her baby when they get in, Sistah angrily uttered the words, my baby.

The way Bernard shifted in his saddle, said Sistah wasn't the only one harboring ill feelings of jealousy. For Bernard held a feeling so vile and so contempt, he could have choked on it. And as the man spat, he wished it was the Cajun, rather then the ground, his tobacco juice had landed on. But Bernard weren't known for tangling with white men, like he was famous for beating slaves. In fact, the man's reputation was just the opposite. And he had two white men who unfortunately met their demise, when his blade caught them napping. And Bernard was planning on being just as lucky, with the man who had taken his job.

As the man from Cajun country sat thinking about the bonus he hoped to earn, he kept a close eye on Sistah and Isabella. For in his crew, the two females were the weakest links, and he was finding it hard to get at their weakness. But like all Cajuns, the man from the Bayou loved a good fight. And for that, the Louisiana native was determined, to make good pickers out of every slave under his command, including Sistah. But the Cajun knew everything was still centered around, the old slave, who's problem he was hoping to solve.

Just about an hour before the slave driver were to give his call, Pleasant completed his second sack. But for some reason, the teen didn't take the sack up to the wagon and trade it for an empty one. Instead, Pleasant gave old Mae a jolt, when he started filling her sack with his cotton.

"You's can't do that," old Mae cried fearfully.

Pleasant didn't seem to be troubled by the old slave's warning, as he went right on stuffing her sack, with every fist full of cotton that he picked. And he went right on defying old Mae, even after the call had came out, for them to bring their sacks to the wagon.

"Child, we's gotta go," old Mae cried.

Young and naïve, Pleasant held on to the sack, unaware of the danger he was dragging the old slave into. But the young slave was hoping the same trick that gotten him, his first shot of pleasure, would help the old slave get by, without having to taste the driver's whip.

"Don't talk, pick," Pleasant said, while never taking his eyes off of the cotton.

Feeling she was about to take the last beating of her life, old Mae went back to picking like the day had just started. But the old slave found herself being weighed down, by the very reason she worried the most. And old Mae knew if she didn't do something with her baby, Pleasant might end up dying as well. So seeing that she had no other choice, the old slave called out for Sistah.

"Gone," the driver said to the girl, as he wondered what the old slave could possibly want with such a lost soul.

When Sistah reached old Mae, things became clear to the Cajun, as well as Bernard. For the old slave quickly passed Sistah her baby, so she could pick a little better with the time they had left. And seeing that his foe, was inching closer to the two weeks deadline, Bernard went to thinking.

"Don't just stand dere Eat Um Up, you and dat boy, take Isabella over dere and give um a hand," the Cajun shouted, as he could feel the slave's eyes calling out to him.

By the time Eat Um Up, Isabella and the large slave reached old Mae and got to picking, Bernard had came up with a plan. And knowing he had to act fast, the disgruntal chain master didn't waste any time.

"If those sacks don't get up here, it's going to be the whip, for all of you," Bernard barked, hoping to put an end to the slave driver momentum.

The large slave grabbed Pleasant's sack, and headed for the wagon with it, as he kept his eyes on Bernard. But as for Eat Um Up, he wasn't so lucky. As the young slave tried to pull the drawstring to old Mae's sack, he found Pleasant's right hand, to be a menacing foe. For Pleasant had beaten Eat Um Up to the punch, with another fist full of cotton. But no sooner then Pleasant got his hand out of the sack, Eat Um Up was off and running with the old slave's best efforts.

When old Mae finally shuffled up to the wagon, she saw the driver push the wagon slaves aside. Then just like Bernard and the other slaves, old Mae got the shock of her life. The slave driver tied the sack, and let it fall, signaling that it was full. He then got down from the wagon, and shouted for the slaves to line up. But Bernard had a hold card, which he quickly played.

"That boy, there, is suppose to get the whip," the envious chain master grumbled.

The driver didn't open his mouth, as he stared at Bernard, like a swamp Queen's pet coon. And the feeling that he gave off, left Bernard, as well as the slaves, wondering if the man had a personal relationship with the Devil himself.

"So tell me, Mr. Bernard. Why am I going to give dat boy dis whip?" the driver asked, when he finally got around to speaking.

"You told him last night, before you chained him to Sistah, that he had to get more cotton. And all he got, was the same two sacks," Bernard replied rather nervously.

Even though he stood in fear, Bernard felt the slave driver was no better off then an outlaw, caught between a posses and the scalp hunting Indians. For the man knew perfectly well, the boy had done what was commanded of him and then some. Yet Bernard was truly banking on the slave driver giving old Mae the whip. For if the old slave were to take a beating, she would surely die, causing the slaves to slow down, which would result in Mr. Arnold losing another bet. And Bernard knew that would send the new slave driver humping his way back to Louisiana.

With Bernard's well hatched plan being obvious to the Cajun, the man was still willing to play alone. But before the Cajun saw fit to give Pleasant a taste of his whip, he sent a shot across Bernard's bow.

"Dat is not what I asked you, Mr. Bernard," the man from Louisiana spat, as he held the look of an angry gator.

The air suddenly became thick with a deathly silence, as Bernard couldn't bring himself to speak. For the not so brave chain master, saw the slave driver's words as a warning, that left him feeling naked, as his manhood rested some where south of childhood. Yet the chain master tried to keep a stiff upper lip, as he waited for Pleasant to receive his fair share of abuse.

"Take dat shirt off, boy," the Cajun said nonchalantly.

Pleasant's eyes fell on Sistah, as he started to undo one of the two buttons that held his shirt closed. And as he undid both of the buttons, there wasn't an ounce of emotion on his face.

"Don't just stand dere, Sistah, get dat shirt," the driver snapped.

Scared to no end, Sistah saw fit to give old Mae her baby, before taking the shirt from Pleasant. And with the tattered cloth in her hand, Sistah stood next to Pleasant, looking at the garment, not knowing that she was in the driver's line of fire.

"Mae, get dat girl out of my way," the driver grumbled.

Old Mae quickly grabbed Sistah by the arm, and snatched her off to the side. Yet with her limited mind, Sistah still appeared to be unaware of what was happening around her, as she watched old Mae's baby, while it went on nursing peacefully.

The words grab my saddle boy, rolled out of the Cajun's mouth, as he snaked his whip. And when Pleasant turned around to take hold of the well crafted saddle, old Mae nearly dropped her baby. For the old female, couldn't believe her eyes, as she stared at the mountain of scars, which rested on Pleasant's back. And even the slave driver himself, had to adjust his hat, after taking notice of the boy's flesh, before giving him a taste of the whip.

"Alright, let's try it again," the Cajun shouted in anger. "Line up," he went on to say, while putting his whip to rest.

With the man from Louisiana being madder then a blind coon, that had just spent the night with a skunk, Bernard took it up on himself, to inform the Cajun of the plantation's long standing whipping policy.

"They usually get five lashes, for being short," Bernard complained.

"You need to keep in mind, Mr. Bernard, usually don't run dese slaves, I do. And while you're holding dat, Mr. Chain master. Try to remember, you are not sitting on my shoulder."

Unfortunately, the slave driver wasn't calling Bernard a parrot. For he was referring to the chain master, as one of the monkeys, that were often seeing, sitting on a hoodoo master shoulder. And seeing that Bernard was far from being the kind of monkey he would want, the slave driver saw fit to put the man in his place.

"Do I make myself clear, Mr. Bernard?"

"Very," the chain master replied.

"Den I suggest you run da chain," the Cajun snarled.

Feeling it would not be wise, to challenge his boss, without the other chain masters to back him up, Bernard did as he was told. But as he ran the heavy chain through the rings, Bernard took to plotting his next move.

All the way back to the main yard, the slave driver expressed his anger. Up and down the slave line, the man from Louisiana shouted his every word. "I don't know what to make of dis bunch. You act, as if you can't live with out your beloved Mae. But when you get her back, you still ain't worth a coon's tail, on a rat's ass," the slave driver shouted, as he stared at Isabella. "One slave is not going to get dat cotton."

The Cajun paused for a moment, as he eyed old Mae. For the old slave's baby was crying up a storm, and there seem to be no stopping it.

"Come tomorrow, I want to see all of you, getting dat cotton, or you will get dis whip," the slave driver shouted, while looking at the old slave and her baby. "Mae hush dat baby up," he growled, right before riding his horse toward the back of the line.

"I's uh trying, sir, but he's won't stop," old Mae cried, hoping the man would not allow his anger, to carry over to her child.

Even though the white man had been good to the old slave thus far, she knew her luck could change with the blink of an eye. And with her baby crying even harder, old Mae didn't know what to do.

"Will you give it some milk, before he wake da dead," the Cajun shouted from the back of the line.

"I's uh tried sir, but he's won't take it."

"Den give him to Sistah, so she can take dat wet diaper off of him," the Cajun said, as his voice came down a notch.

"But he's ain't wet, sir."

Hearing that the child was neither hungry nor wet, the slave driver paused to regroup his thoughts. But before the white man could even think about what might be troubling the baby, he noticed a difference in the air. Other then the rattling that came from the chain hitting against the rings, there wasn't another sound to be heard. That left the man from Louisiana feeling a little out done, as he casted his eyes on the baby and grunted.

When the slave driver's crew finally made it back to the main yard, he marched the slaves right on up to the feeding line. There, he told Bernard, to remove the chain, while the slaves stood waiting to eat.

"There will be no pleasure taking tonight," the slave driver said forcibly, after raising more then a bit of hell, when a server didn't give old Mae enough extra grits.

"Well I guess, we got to work our girls a little harder," chain master Johnson said, while looking at a server.

"I said! Dere will be no, pleasure taking. Now if you don't own one of dese slaves, den dat means you," the slave driver shouted with a far greater deal of force.

Understanding the slave driver a little better, the chain masters were looking just as sad as Eat Um Up and his three friends. But neither the free, nor the enslaved could do anything about the Cajun's decision, as they stood in silence. But when Eat Um Up and the heavy voice slave got to the girl who did the serving, they received a bit of consolation for their lost reward.

"Give dem extra, as well," the slave driver said.

After nearly receiving the Cajun's whip, for not giving old Mae what the driver considered to be suitable, the slave girl didn't make the same mistake twice. Yet when the driver told her to do the same for Isabella, then Sistah, the girl thought the white man had gone crazy. For everyone knew Sistah and Isabella couldn't pick a lick, but the girl didn't let that stop her from giving Sistah two extra scoops of grits.

"Well you do know how to change a baby," the slave driver said, while giving Sistah a comforting look. "How many you had?"

"I's uh ain't got none, sir," Sistah said sadly.

"Well I guess da Man up dere, know what he's doing," the Cajun replied sympathetically.

The slave driver didn't appear to be the same angry man, who marched his crew home in a state of fury. But the Louisiana native was still far from being a cuddly gator, ready to be house broken.

"Hey you dere," the Cajun called to the slave girl at the end of the table.

"Yes sir," the girl said, as she came running.

"What are dey eating over dere?" the slave driver asked, referring to the chain master's table.

"You's got fried chicken, butter beans, and corn bread. Oh, you's got cake, to sir?" the slave girl said trembling.

"Go over dere, and get me some of dat chicken."

"Yes sir," the girl said bowing.

The girl darted off, and returned without ever being missed. "Here sir," she said, holding three pieces of chicken in a red and white plaid napkin.

After opening the napkin, Mrs. Arnold had grown tired of seeing on her table, the slave driver carefully surveyed its contents. Then with a touch of Louisiana flare, the Cajun caught everyone by surprise, when he told the girl to give old Mae the breast. But the man from Louisiana shocking personality didn't stop there. The Bayou native also told the slave girl, to give Eat Um Up and Pleasant, who he referred to as the boy, each a leg. But knowing how their master felt about what the man was telling her to do, the slave girl couldn't bring herself to move. So she just stood in front of the slave driver, as if her feet were deeply rooted in the ground, like an old oak tree.

"Did you not hear me?" the driver shouted.

The young girl didn't know what to say, as she stood praying for the white man's God to help her. Yet something told the girl, the white man's God, wanted no part of her situation. So the girl closed her eyes, and hoped for her master to come strolling by.

"Girl don't make me put dis whip to you," the slave driver shouted, while raising his right hand, as if he was about to strike the child down, thus sending her to Hell, for all eternity.

Feeling it would be much better to avoid the whip that was before her, the girl quickly did as she was told. But when the girl gave old Mae her piece of chicken, it brought about an unfavorable response from Bernard and the other chain masters. For the white men took to mumbling among them selves, as they watched their precious pieces of chicken, being handed over to slaves. But the driver had no intentions of listening to the men complain over nothing, as he walked away unnoticed.

"I don't care what they do down in Louisiana, but around here, slaves don't eat like good white folks," a chain master name John said.

Even Lamar, who everyone took to be rather weak, had to speak out against the slave driver's action. "It ain't right, for him to feed them like us," the white man mumbled to himself, while looking at the heavy voice slave.

"Well I'll be a horse's ass, if that don't beat all, I have ever seen," another chain master complained. "I reckon, Mr. Arnold don't know about this," he went on to say, with a bit of frustration in his voice.

One after the other, the men voiced their disapproval of the new man in charge. And like the serpent looking for a kill, Bernard sought to take advantage of their anger.

"If you boys want to see a thing or two, you need to stick around, and see what that old goat do, when she finish eating," the envious chain master hissed.

And just like Bernard expected, the men ran to his deception with out giving it a second thought. But no matter how hard the men tried to get Bernard to share his little secret, their former boss, would not give in.

"You boys are going to like this one," Bernard said with a snake like smile.

But when old Mae finished eating, there was no change to her routine. The old female went directly back to her stump, and waited to be locked up, as if she were some kind of prisoner. And as the old slave sat on the stump holding her baby, Bernard felt she needed a bit of reminding.

"You better get up, and go do what that slave lover told you to do, before I put this whip to your fat ass," Bernard said, right before spitting a lump of his tobacco juice in the old female's face.

Feeling more inhuman then ever, old Mae found herself standing before the Devil's handyman, knowing that she didn't have a moment to lose. So the old slave shuffled off with her baby, while waiting for the whip to come crashing across her back. But the whip never came, and that started old Mae to thinking, as she took to counting her steps. For the old slave knew Bernard's extra attention, came from the lost of his top position. And with the new slave driver doing things different, it had Bernard looking to kill something. But old Mae had no intentions of letting Bernard kill her baby, in the same manner, in which he killed Ella's. So while looking down on her baby with a fear, only a mother could relate to, old Mae spoke softly.

"Yo's ma ain't gon never drop ya. I's uh ain't gon let you's die like that," the old slave cried. And while her tears took on the look of a fast moving stream, old Mae's voice spun in to something different. "We's ain't gon blame poor Ella, cause she's just couldn't do no better. She's was young, so we's ain't gon blame her. We's gone blame that devil, cause he's put that whip to her," old Mae said with distain, as if the baby understood her every word.

By the time old Mae finished wiping Bernard's spit from her face, she caught sight of the slave driver. He was sitting on a stump, in the very spot, where she was to give her baby a bath. That put the old slave's mind to wondering. Why was he so dead set on making Bernard hate her, more then he already did? The old slave felt trapped, as she came upon the man from Louisiana.

"Dere you are, old girl," the slave driver said, as he rose to his feet. Then with a puzzled look on his face, the Cajun gave old Mae a little piece of cloth. "Dat dere is a little something special. After you wash your baby, put it in some hot water, and wash your self," he said.

"What it do, sir?"

"It's going to help with your healing, old girl," the slave driver said. "Mind you, it's going to burn a bit."

"I's uh ain't gon mind, sir."

"Na don't you go dinking I'm soft, because you earn dat, and every ding else you got from me. You showed dat boy how to get dat cotton pretty good, and I like dat."

"I's uh tried, sir,"

"You did a bit more den try, and I always take care of dose, dat take care of me. Now I got to get back," the driver said, as he walked away.

"You's see this. This is gon make that devil kill us," old Mae said to her baby, after seeing the slave driver cut in front of the storage shed. "But we's gotta stay out of his way, till masa Arnold come for ya," the old slave cried.

When the man from Louisiana reappeared on side of the male shed, he still went unnoticed. And as he stood watching Lamar lock the females down for the night, his Cajun eyes caught sight of Ella. She was standing off to the side, looking as frighten, as a newly captured slave. And being that the man from the Bayou knew what he was up against, his Cajun instincts, told him to move in for the kill.

"Mr. Bernard," the slave driver called out with a chilling tone.

"Everything is locked up," Bernard said, as he walked away with his arm around Ella's waist.

"Dat is not why I called you," the slave driver said, as his arms came unfold. "What I want to know is. Why dat slave is not locked up with da other females?"

After being chilled to the bone, by the slave drivers question, the other men wasted no time, separating them selves from Bernard. And with Lamar moving faster then the others, it was obvious to the Cajun, the man, had no desire to involve himself in Bernard's problem. But it didn't take the others long to pick up their pace as well, after hearing Bernard say, he was taking Ella with him for the night.

"I guess, I didn't make my self clear," the slave driver said before pausing, to look at Bernard's feet. "Now put dat slave where she belong," the Cajun barked rather harshly.

"I am not a slave," Bernard snapped.

"And you don't own one, so I suggest, you leave her be," the driver replied, as his voice still hung soft and cold, like a empty shallow grave.

With his point made, the slave driver took hold of his knife, while Bernard moved his feet about like the dancing bear, the Cajun had seen in a dime circus. But unlike the bear, Bernard wasn't getting any applause, as he tried to come up with some type of a response, to the man's statement.

"Well we'll just see, what Mr. Arnold got to say about this," Bernard squawked.

"You can do what ever suits you, but da girl stays," the Cajun said, as he stepped out of the shadows with a disturbing swagger.

A sense of danger slithered through the air, and wrapped it self around Bernard like a giant snake. And as the defiant worker stood staring at the Cajun, he began to rub his eyes. For a brief moment, Bernard thought his eyes were playing tricks on him. The unruly chain master could have sworn he saw a moss covered creature, standing in the very spot, where the slave driver stood. But seeing that he was on his own with the man, Bernard had no intentions of waiting around for the creature to reappear. So being the devil that he was, Bernard flung Ella to the ground at the slave driver's feet, and started for the mansion.

"Get her up," the slave driver said, in a tone that was fit for killing.

"What?" Bernard asked.

"I dink you heard me."

"I don't help slave, and I damn well don't love them," Bernard said, as he rounded his shoulders.

Then like a soul that had caught fire, Bernard slowly made a move for his musket pistol, as if he were ready to bring the unsettling matter to an end. But when the slave driver's left hand, made a quick move toward his faithful Bowie, Bernard had a sudden change of heart. And with his hand no longer reaching for the pistol, Bernard took hold of Ella's arm, and began to lift the slave with a bit of roughness.

"Gently," the slave driver said, as he gripped the handle to the large knife.

Feeling the Cajun was just one step away from slinging his massive blade, Bernard quickly sought to oblige the man. But no sooner then the chain master got Ella back to her feet, he was off and running toward the mansion. And the man didn't stop, until he reached the back door to the Arnold's, giant pride and joy of a home.

Breathing like he had just come from the furthest end of the plantation, Bernard stopped at the foot of the steps to catch his breath. And as he stood bent over, sucking the chilly night air deep in to his lungs, Bernard never noticed the eyes that were watching him from beneath the steps. Nor did he catch sight of the sharp ten inch stabbing tool, which rested close to the peering eyes. In fact, Bernard never noticed anything, accept his desperate need for air.

When Bernard was able to pull himself up the steps, he gave a soft knock on the backdoor. In no time at all, the old slave Jeremiah was greeting Bernard with words so well spoken, the man felt it to be criminal. Yet Bernard knew better then to lash out at Jeremiah, before making sure the coast was clear. So that is what Bernard did, as he poked his head in the back door, to scan the room. And after seeing that the mingled gray headed slave was alone, Bernard entered the house as if he were in charge.

"Get out of my way, you old fool," Bernard spat, knowing that Jeremiah would never speak a word to his master about the incident.

"And what can I do for you tonight, sir?" Jeremiah replied.

"Go get Mr. Arnold, boy, and be quick about it," Bernard said, as he clinched his fist.

It was obvious to Jeremiah, that Bernard was feeling a bit sprier, so he left the room without saying another word. Yet when Jeremiah returned with Mr. Arnold, the slave saw a totally different white man, standing before him and his master. And rightly so, because like everyone else, Bernard knew how Mr. Arnold felt about Jeremiah. For it was said, there were only three living souls that Mr. Arnold cared for, and Jeremiah stood smack dab in the middle of the trio.

"What is it now?" Mr. Arnold asked, with Jeremiah on his heels.

It was a common thing, for Jeremiah to be with his master, seeing that he had always been by the man's side. From the day Aaron J. Arnold was born, he had not lived a single day without his Jeremiah. Jeremiah was there to catch little Mr. Arnold, when he took his first steps. And when Mr. Arnold started school, Jeremiah went along to carry his books. Yet that wasn't enough for the young spoiled slave owner. He had to have his slave in the classroom with him. So the elder Mr. Arnold made his son wish a reality, despite the school master's disapproval.

But Jeremiah education didn't stop there. When the day came for young master Arnold to leave for College, Jeremiah had to have a whole new set of clothing. And just like his young master, Jeremiah found the art of higher learning, to be both exhausting and rewarding. Yet nothing was more troubling to the slave, then his master's marriage. For that, should have been the day, when Jeremiah's life took a sharp turn. And the tall gray headed slave saw no reason to dispel his master's belief. So Jeremiah let Mr. Arnold go on believing, he knew everything the wealthy slave owner had in his head, except for the flesh, of the new Mrs. Arnold. So it was normal for Jeremiah to be there, while his master conducted business with white men, or the white women, he often sought for amusement.

"I'm sorry, Mr. Arnold, sir, but it's that new slave driver, sir," Bernard said politely.

"Then I suggest, you go talk to him," Mr. Arnold said, as he pulled on the belt to the red and black robe, that covered his day clothing.

"We can't talk to him, Mr. Arnold, sir."

"Do you speak for everyone?"

"Everything is going wrong out there, sir," Bernard said, never answering the man's question.

"Things like what?" Mr. Arnold snapped.

"Well sir, he is not using the whip. And you know we got to use the whip, if you want to get your cotton out of those fields on time," Bernard explained, with his voice still as polite, as a school boy.

Before Bernard could think of what he wanted to say next, Mr. Arnold violently struck the kitchen table, sending Jeremiah's coffee for a wild ride. And as the coffee ran across the table, and down to the floor, Mr. Arnold took Bernard to task.

"I'm not paying you men for excuses," Mr. Arnold yelled. "Now if you can't do the damn job, then I suggest, you get the hell off of my property," he continued to shout.

After hearing the man she married, dabbling in a bit of language that was beneath her, Mrs. Arnold left the parlor for the comfort of their bedroom. There, she would separate herself from one of her husband's favorite hobbies. And even though there was a litany of things, Mrs. Arnold found appalling about her husband, she stayed with him just the same. Yet Mrs. Arnold wasn't the average good Southern wife. Though she had no intentions of breaking a long standing Southern tradition, Mrs. Arnold was growing tired of her ungrateful husband bad habits. And how could the man be grateful, when the Southern way of life was built on power and exploitation. But what wore on Mrs. Arnold the most, was how the Southern men held such a great contempt for their wives. It was as if there were no difference between the wives, and the slaves, the men often laid with. But on that particular night, Mrs. Arnold just wanted to close the door to their bedroom, and get back to her reading.

While Mrs. Arnold headed for the spiral staircase, Bernard tried to find a way out of the hole, which he foolishly dug for himself.

"It's not us, sir. It's the new slave driver, Mr. Arnold, sir. He's giving them meat, sir, and you said we should never give them meat."

"Did you tell him that?"

"I couldn't, sir. I tried to tell him about using the whip, and he didn't want to listen, sir."

"What do you mean, he didn't want to listen?" Mr. Arnold asked, staring Bernard straight in the eye.

"He said, he ran things around here, and that, I should never forget it. And he ain't put the whip to that Sistah, yet. And she, ain't never picked worth a lick, sir," Bernard said, laying it on thick. "And that old devil didn't pick at all, yesterday, sir."

"Are you trying to tell me, he haven't whip, not one single slave?" Mr. Arnold asked.

"He gave that new boy two lashes, that wasn't worth spit. I've seen you beat slaves better then that, when…," Bernard caught himself, before he spoke of his boss ability to drink a little more then he should. "Now Mr. Arnold, I ain't trying to tell you how to run your place. But I ain't never seen a slave, fear a man, that didn't put the fear of God in him. But the way he's doing things, we'll never get your cotton out of those fields, sir."

"You go and tell Mr. Duval, I want to see him. And I mean tonight," Mr. Arnold growled.

Bernard gave the wealthy plantation owner a hardy yes sir, followed by the word goodnight. But by the time Bernard placed his hand on the doorknob, he thought of one last thing.

"Oh, Mr. Arnold, sir, I was going to take the girl Ella to bed with me, but he told me that I couldn't."

"Did he give you a reason why?"

"He said, no one on this plantation, would be taking pleasure tonight, sir."

If Bernard thought Mr. Arnold bought his last statement, then the arrogant slave owner silence said other wise. And as Mr. Arnold stared at the spilled coffee, growing cold on the kitchen floor, the chain master, got the feeling he was being ignored.

"Well I guess, I'll be going," Bernard said, as he stood at the door, wondering what to make of the man's silence.

"Well Jeremiah, I think it's going to be one of those nights," Mr. Arnold said, after watching Bernard closed the door behind him.

"Yes sir, I do believe you are right, sir," Jeremiah replied, as he held the door, for Mr. Arnold to leave the kitchen.

When Mr. Arnold finally made it back to the parlor, and found that his wife had gone, he became intensely frustrated. "I think, I need a cigar," Mr. Arnold said, as he took a seat in front of the fireplace.

"Right away, sir," Jeremiah replied.

The tall slave picked up the box of expensive cigars from the table, which sat next to his master's chair. And once he opened the box, Jeremiah held it, until Mr. Arnold found a cigar to suit his taste. And when Mr. Arnold was done removing the tip from the smoking delight, he spat the unwanted portion into Jeremiah's hand. Then like so many times before, after receiving the unwanted tip, Jeremiah struck a match, and placed it to his master's imported treat.

"Leave me," Mr. Arnold said, after pulling on his cigar. "Oh Jeremiah," Mr. Arnold called out softly, before the tall slave could reach the door.

"Sir," Jeremiah replied peacefully.

"You might want to get one of those girls, to clean up that mess."

"Yes sir," Jeremiah replied, right before leaving his master to think, while enjoying his cigar.

And think, Mr. Arnold did, as he took a long pull on the fat cigar. And as the man stared at the portrait of his late father, he began to feel somewhat inadequate. But the powerful slave owner was determined not to allow his father's ghost, nor his defective childhood, control him or the plantation he inherited. For Mr. Arnold could hear his mother's voice, telling him how proud she was, to have such a good strong son. And he could see her standing in front of his father's portrait, smiling down on him, as if she were still alive and well.

Chapter 4

The Firing

Upon returning to the slave area, Bernard found Duval eating in front of a small fire. With his nerves slightly shaken, Bernard adjusted his pants, while taking a good look around. But it wasn't as if the man had expected to see the other chain masters rushing to stand at his side. But if the truth were to be told, Bernard was trying to muster up enough courage, to carry out Mr. Arnold's order.

"Mr. Arnold wants to see you," Bernard blurted out, after taking a deep breath.

Duval didn't say a word, as he just stuffed his mouth with another spoon full of beans. And as he started to chew the well cooked beans, the man from Louisiana held a dangerous look about him. And the look made Bernard uncomfortably nervous, as he waited for the man to give him some type of a response.

"Are you hungry, Mr. Bernard?" Duval asked, while never raising his head to look at the man.

"No, I had more than enough," Bernard, replied, feeling he had taken the Cajun down a notch.

"Den you best, be getting along, while you can," Duval said, as his green eyes appeared to turn blood red.

Feeling that the Cajun's advice was worth adhering to, Bernard politely moved on. But no sooner then Bernard felt he was at a safe distance, the cowardly man repeated his statement. "Mr. Arnold said, he wanted to see you tonight," Bernard mumbled, as if he truly didn't want to speak.

"I heard you da first time," Duval said, sending Bernard rushing off to the chain master shack.

Duval shook his head, as he stared at the off breed dogs, sitting silently, waiting for the next bone to come flying their way. "At least ya'll are not afraid of me," Duval said to the dogs. Then with the playfulness of a little boy, the Cajun stood up and stumped his foot, sending the dogs scattering like crows, fleeing from a cat. "Wrong again," the man said after he grunted.

When Duval approached the same back steps, Bernard had used earlier, he asked old Pete how he was doing. And out of the darkness, came an old, but vibrant voice.

"I's uh doing mighty fine, sir," old Pete said.

"Dat's good. Now you stay warm under dere, you hear."

"Old Pete, is always warm, sir."

"Good," Duval said, standing on the steps looking at Jeremiah through the kitchen window.

"Good night, sir," Jeremiah said, greeting the man from Louisiana, as he opened the door, before Duval could knock on it.

"I'm afraid, dey has never been any ding good about a hurricane, old boy," Duval replied, as he entered the house.

"I hear, they are mighty bad, sir."

"Dat dey are," Duval said, while nodding shyly, to a young slave girl on her knees, cleaning up the coffee, that had been victimize by her master's earlier conversation.

And even though Duval had seen countless of slave girls in his life time, there was something about the teen, which made the man think. But the Cajun's thoughts weren't that of the selfish nature. In fact, they were as far from sex, as a man's thoughts could get. For there was some thing about the girl, that appeared to be between fourteen or sixteen years of age. And even though he couldn't put his finger on it, the man from Louisiana wondered if the lump in her belly was for a white man or another slave.

"He is waiting for you, sir," Jeremiah said, breaking Duval's thoughts of the very pretty, yet very pregnant girl.

Being forced to pull his eyes away from the girl, Duval gave her one last thought. With the parlor door in his sight, the Cajun knew the girl couldn't have stood much taller then the doorknob in Jeremiah's hand, yet some one felt she was large enough to carry the burden of pleasure taking. Once again, Duval found himself shaking his head, as he passed through the doorway, which brought him face to face with Mr. Arnold.

"I hear you wanted to see me," Duval said, feeling he was walking into a hostile situation.

And the way Mr. Arnold went on the attack, told the slave driver, his Cajun instincts were working just fine. He watched as the thirty five year old slave owner, took a long pull off of his expensive, yet worthless cigar. Then like some dying breed of arrogance, Mr. Arnold blew the smoke out of his mouth.

"Why am I hearing, you are not worth the money that I am paying you?" Mr. Arnold asked angrily.

Unimpressed by Mr. Arnold's lead up to his question, Duval showed a little arrogance of his own. "I didn't know you were paying me, for what you hear," he said with more then just a touch of defiance.

"Don't you be getting smart with me, because I'm not afraid of you, nor that knife of your's," Mr. Arnold shouted, as he leaped from his favorite chair. "Now we had an agreement. But if you're not going to live up to your end of the bargain, then you won't be getting one dollar, from me."

Seeing that he was only killing time, Duval ignored the man's little threat, rather then carve him up like a pig at a Cajun cook out.

"So it don't matter, you have more cotton out of dose fields today, den you had last year, dis time?" Duval asked.

After hearing Duval's good news, Mr. Arnold sat back down in his chair. But when the man heard how much of a gain the Cajun was talking about, he was back to his feet in a flash. And even though Mr. Arnold was giving up about a foot in height, he was ready to do more then stare in to Duval's eyes.

"Calm down, we've only been picking for four days," Duval said, appealing to Mr. Arnold's knowledge, rather then his common sense.

There was a moment of silence, before Mr. Arnold felt the need to back away from the Cajun. And with a bit of distance between the two of them, Mr. Arnold took a quick look at his cigar, before shooting Duval another question. "So tell me. What is this I hear, about you sparing the whip?"

"Deir haven't been a slave born, who can pick cotton, while running from a whip," Duval stated with some assurance.

"You care to explain that," Mr. Arnold growled, as he sat back down in his chair for the second time.

Knowing that his boss held the same stupid ideas as Bernard, Duval felt no amount of explaining would ever change the man's mind. Yet for the sake of his money, and Mr. Arnold's life, the Cajun proceeded to do just that. "When a slave is in pain, it can never work up to par. Dat mean it pick less. Now I don't claim to know much, but I do know dat don't help da bottom line."

"And what about those stubborn devils, who refuse to work?" Mr. Arnold asked, while puffing on his cigar.

After walking over to the fireplace, Duval said, "Dere is two dings all creatures fear, death, and dat which brings death."

Mr. Arnold swallowed, just before speaking with a slight trimmer in his voice. "Just remember, I have a lot riding on you. Now what is this, I hear about you giving them meat?"

"I do what it takes, to get da job done."

"I don't see how you can get the job done, when my best picker, is not picking."

The Cajun was a little surprised, but not amazed, in how Mr. Arnold slid into his next question. But like all good creatures from the Bayou, Duval was well prepared. "I take it, you're talking about Mae."

In a heart beat, Mr. Arnold was back to his feet, shouting. "Damn right, I'm talking about that old devil. And I'll tell you this. If you are trying to destroy me, then you need to remember it's a long way back to Louisiana."

While Mr. Arnold stood fuming, Duval placed his foot on the base of the fireplace. The two men locked eyes, and it didn't take Duval long, to find out that his boss was a far better man then Bernard. But without breaking his stare, or bating an eye, the Cajun spoke as clear, as any Cajun could.

"I did it, because she had her baby. And da last ding, any fool would want to do, is to go running around in the Bayou, after dark."

"She's not the first slave to drop a baby," Mr. Arnold yelled, while ignoring Duval's counter to his threat.

"But dey all, don't get tore up, like she did."

"Don't you go feeling sorry for that old bat, because she's as evil, as they come," Mr. Arnold said, feeling some what defeated.

It was plain to see, Mr. Arnold didn't know much about his new slave driver. For the Cajun had a heart that was blacken by pain, which had given birth to a hate unlike any other. And he held his precious hate, as if it were a long lost love, worthy of the ultimate sacrifice.

"If I felt sorry for her, she would be dead," Duval grunted. "Dat baby nearly killed her."

When Duval finished speaking, the room didn't appear to be the same. And as Mr. Arnold took another puff on his cigar, he began to ponder the warning, which the man's father had given him. For the wealthy slave owner could hear the words, my son has been in the belly of the hurricane, and he only live to hate the living. And having no idea, of what the strange statement meant, Mr. Arnold found him self hiring Duval, despite the mind boggling warning. But just like that stormy night when he heard the strange statement, Mr. Arnold saw the Cajun to be a bit disturbing. For that was the night, when Mr. Arnold witness Duval's handy work. For Duval and a gentleman, disagreed on how a spilled drink should be cleaned up. And when the disagreement was over, Duval held the man's guts in his hands. And just like that night, Mr. Arnold felt his supper coming back on him.

"What did that old devil have?" Mr. Arnold asked, while trying to get away from the past.

With an empty look in his green eyes, Duval said, "I have dealt with da Devil, and I don't dink he is planning on being a slave."

Just as fast as Mr. Arnold tried to get away from that awful night, Duval had quickly pulled him back in to the storm. And while Mr. Arnold was back to thinking about how peaceful Duval looked, when he had finished killing the man over nothing, a chill came over his body. And as the sudden touch of cold air wrapped around the wealthy man, just like it did Bernard, Mr. Arnold found himself trapped in his own mind, drifting back to that rainy night, when Duval displayed a need to kill, to satisfy some growing hunger that held him captive.

"Is dere any ding else?" Duval asked, bringing Mr. Arnold back from the dead.

"Tell me about the boy," Mr. Arnold said, as if there was something caught in his throat.

But there was nothing wrong with the man's ability to swallow. It was Duval's eyes that made Mr. Arnold speak in such a manner. There was something about the way the flame, danced in the cat colored gems, which the Cajun carried around for eyes. And the more Mr. Arnold stared into the doors of darkness, the more it appeared as if the flame was burning deep inside of Duval's body, which brought another chill over Mr. Arnold, as he tried to keep his wits about him.

"What about him?" Duval asked.

"I hear you are being soft, with him."

"I don't call two sacks a day, soft. Now move on."

Ignoring Duval's request, Mr. Arnold stayed with the present topic. "So he did, pick cotton before."

"Your lead mule, showed da boy how to get dat cotton," Duval said, as if he had a bitter taste in his mouth.

The Cajun's rude response, along with his tone, told Mr. Arnold, he was getting under the man's skin. And being a born agitator, Mr. Arnold gloated over the turn of event, as he mistook the sudden change, for more then it was worth.

"Now back to that old goat. You find me a slave to replace that old bat, before I start feeding her, more then she's worth."

"I don't dink, I can find a slave anywhere, to replace dat old goat, as you call her. So I suggest you stop trying to kill her," Duval said, as he stared at a portrait of Mr. Arnold's father.

"So what am I suppose to do with that old bitch?"

Standing in a moment of silence, Duval noticed how old Mae went from being a devil, to a goat, a mule, a bat, and most of all, a bitch. And as he prepared to answer the man who paid him, the Cajun wondered what other titles, the man had for his best picker.

"What you have always done with her, now dat she has some ding to live for."

Duval was banking on the words of the only woman he had ever loved. And if the truth were to be told, the Cajun was still in love with the woman, even though she had been dead, more years then they had spent together. Yet in those ten short years, the love of his life, had taught him everything he needed to know about females. And the one thing, that haunted him every night, charged out of his past, like a beautiful black mare.

"So you're trying to tell me, that old goat, can make another five years in those fields," Mr. Arnold said, while looking at his cigar.

"She can do dat, and more," Duval said with confidence.

"Man that devil is old, and no amount of chicken, is going to keep her alive."

"Dat old slave, know how to work dose fields, better den any I have ever seen. Now with da right lure, we can get a lot more den five years out of her," Duval assured the wealthy man.

"And how do you suppose to do that?"

"A pregnant woman, once told me, dere is no love greater, den dat of a mother, for her child," Duval said with a ghostly sadness.

Mr. Arnold went from calm to chaotic in a blink of an eye. "No!" he shouted, springing to his feet, while violently throwing the cigar toward the fireplace. "That thing will be leaving here, just as soon, as I can find a buyer for it," the man continued to shout. "It's bad enough, I had to buy that Sistah back, and I'll be damn, if I give in on this one," the man said in anger, while filling the room with confusion.

At that very moment, Duval thought about, how his father use to warn him about certain gators and snakes. He could hear his father's voice, as if the man was standing next to him at that very moment, saying, don't you go messing with dat old gator, boy. But just like so many years ago, when he was a little snapper, Duval felt the need to ignore his father's warning.

"What Sistah got to do with dis?" Duval asked.

"You just make sure, she suffers out there."

"If you want to do my job, den I'll be leaving at first light. But I done asked you, what Sistah got to do with dis?"

Feeling he had made a mistake in hiring the Cajun, Mr. Arnold knew there was no way he could get out of answering the man's question. "She's that old devil's daughter," Mr. Arnold said with a strange and regretful tone. "But don't you go telling that old snake, or I will be forced to kill the both of them," he vowed, after falling back into his chair.

After hearing Mr. Arnold's threat, Duval felt he was ready to start taking his father's advice. And even though the Cajun didn't seek to further their mind disturbing conversation, he couldn't help but to wonder about his boss. For Mr. Arnold had become preoccupied with the flame burning in the fireplace. And as the man appeared to be held captive by the flickering flame, Duval studied his face carefully.

"If that old devil, ever find out that Sistah is her Honeybee, so help me," Mr. Arnold said, then paused, as if he were at a lost for words. "I will put a pistol to that invalid's head, and kill her right in front of that old witch," the man growled, as he stared intensely at the crackling fire.

"You and your slaves, can go gator hunting in da dark, for what I care. All I want is my money," Duval barked.

After spouting his remark, the man from Louisiana started to leave the room, but stopped. "How you handle your family business, is no concern of mind. But I will tell you dis. Da day dat old slave dies, you are going to need a miracle, to keep dis place a float."

"You hold up there, mister," Mr. Arnold said, as he once again, regained his voice. "Now I'll deal with that old devil's dying, when the time comes. But what I need to hear from you, is will my cotton be the first crop heading east?"

"Dat is up to you, and your lead mule," Duval said convincingly.

"I guess you're still talking about that damn baby?"

"It's your money," Duval said, as if he was planning on getting his payment, one way or the other.

"She can keep it. But if you don't get my crop to that market before everyone else, I will make that old bitch, dig her own fucking grave," Mr. Arnold said, with a horrifying look in his eyes.

Putting Mr. Arnold's words behind him, Duval sought to solve his last problem. "What are you going to do about Bernard?" he asked.

After walking over to Duval, Mr. Arnold spoke decisively. "Don't let Bernard, be the reason, for my cotton not making it to that market on time. Now if there is nothing else, you need to talk about, I am going to go to bed," Mr. Arnold said, as Jeremiah held the door open for his master, so the man could leave the room.

"I guess, she had another girl," Mr. Arnold said, as he stood in the doorway.

"Only a boy can tear a female up like dat," Duval said, as if he had seen Mother Nature at her best, many times before.

"Well I'll be damn. Now ain't that something. After fourteen splits, she finally got it right," Mr. Arnold said, before disappearing, leaving Jeremiah to see the Cajun out.

Duval entered the chain masters shack, holding a lantern. "Get up," he said, standing over a sleeping Bernard.

The befuddled chain master cleared his eyes, as he anticipated good news. But the Cajun wasn't the type of man, who went around giving good news to his enemies.

"Get your stuff together," Duval said firmly.

Unable to believe the words that shot through his ears, Bernard ran his ten fingers through the dark brown shoulder length hair, which the slaves knew all too well. And while the long frizzy hair made the man look sinister, Bernard was everything but courageous. For Bernard took a great deal of pride, in taking advantage of the weak, the injured, and the drunk. But being faced with a foe that was neither, Bernard suddenly felt the weight of his ill doings coming back on him.

"Dere is a horse, waiting for you at da front gate," Duval said, as he tossed an old tobacco pouch full of coins on the table, which sat by the stove.

"How much did you take out for it?" Bernard asked, regarding the horse, as he stared at the dirty white pouch.

"No man should leave a job walking, when he has given it more den a year of his time," the Cajun replied.

When Bernard had finished saying his goodbyes, Duval watched him walk to the front gate. And after seeing the man mount the horse and ride off, Duval returned to the chain master shack. Standing in the middle of the floor, Duval asked the remaining chain masters, if any of them had a problem with the night's proceedings. One by one, the men gave their reply. There were three who said no, one not me, a single, I don't care, followed by, it's not my business, which came just before a nasty sounding, same here. That left Duval feeling good, as he waited for Lamar, to give, what would be the final word on the matter.

"Now that he's gone, can I get some sleep?" Lamar asked, as he pulled the wool blanket over his head.

Duval felt the last remark, was something they all needed, so he said goodnight, and left the men to get their sleep.

With the long day finally behind him, Duval entered his shack and lit the lantern. To the man's surprise, he found himself slipping. In the mist of the confusion, he had forgotten to lock Ella down. The female slave, men saw as having the perfect ass, was lying across Duval's bed in the most seductive manner. And while Ella's nice round ass elucidated its superior rating through the blanket, she glared up at Duval with a longing hunger.

"I's uh been waiting for ya, sir," Ella said, as she reviled her dark naked body, which had a burning desire to be blanketed with the man's pale white flesh.

Duval's green eyes quickly went to the cold black hair that covered Ella's well worn pussy. And no matter how much the Cajun tried, he couldn't stop himself from thinking of its sweet taste.

"Dere won't be any pleasure taking to night," Duval said, as he sat on the bed, with a throbbing erection.

"Did I's do something wrong, sir?" Ella cried.

Yet before Duval could answer the beautiful black slave, she was up on her knees, crawling toward him. And by the time he began to speak, Duval could feel the nipples that sat proudly upon Ella's tits, pressing against his back.

"I need you to be still," the Cajun said reluctantly.

Ella fell back on to the bed, with a burning desire, that could only be cooled by more of what she had been given the night before. But the man from the Bayou had spoken, and there was nothing the poor slave could do to change his mind. Yet she watched as he stood up after kicking his boots off. And Ella's eyes stayed with him, as if there was nothing else to see. And while he washed the dirt from his not so hairy body, Ella went right on watching the man with a great anticipation. But when it came time for Duval to crawl into bed, he just waved his hand, thus sending Ella toward the wall.

"Night, night," Duval said, as though, Ella was a little girl.

Yet Ella felt it was impossible to fall asleep, with her left nipple resting between Duval's fingers. And having his severely erected penis against her ass was driving Ella out of her mind. Yet the luscious black female laid perfectly still, thinking about how Duval was the only white man who cared enough to make her cum. And cum Ella did, as she creamed twice during their first encounter, followed by three explosions from their second go around. But on that night, poor Ella had to come to grips with a man who always stood behind his word.

After finally falling asleep, Ella's eyes were forced right back open, as the rooster called out for the sun, to grace the territory with its gleaming light. And while the bugler shouted it was the start of a new day, Ella laid into a long stretch, until it hit her. The butt naked female, quickly realized she was alone, and immediately went wild. With her feet kicking and her arms flapping, Ella laughed a joyful laugh, until she was near exhaustion. But exhausted or not, Ella wasn't planning on allowing anything to ruin her day, as she rolled out of the Cajun's bed. And how could she, after spending the night in a white man's arms, without having to spread her legs, or having her mouth filled with a million little swimming seedlings. Ella felt she had been given a nice big slice of Heaven.

With her emotional cup running over, Ella darted out of the shack, looking to get a jump on what would be another long hard day. But the overly excited female came to a complete stop, when she heard Duval's voice. And looking across the yard in the direction of the female shed, Ella could see Duval standing on the night watchmen's stump. And as she listened to the way he laid out his new rules, Ella knew the white men would surely be disappointed.

After quailing all of the complaining over his new whipping policy, Duval continued to disappoint the chain masters. "Dere will be no more taking of pleasure during da day," he said, causing the men to look at each other.

If the men were unhappy about the new rule, they weren't showing it, as everyone did their best to keep from laughing. For it appeared, the Black Smith's son had forgotten that a slave handler's day start, long before the crack of dawn. And seeing the young man holding his sagging pants with one hand, while clutching to a pan of food with the other, as he shuffled up to Duval, had the chain masters a little speechless. Yet the white men did notice, the boy looked like a lost sheep among wolves, as he waited for his scolding.

"Lamar, I would like to have a word with you," Duval said, walking away from the kid, everybody called Biscuit.

Yet the teen bared no resemblance to a small piece of well baked bread, as he stood larger then life it self. But being that the teen's first name was hard to pronounce, everyone was happy to call him Biscuit, even though his mother dreaded the awful word.

After ignoring Biscuit's lack of punctuality, and trading three of his best pickers to Lamar, Duval was ready to start the day. But before the man from Cajun country could march his group of slaves to the fields, he had to get Biscuit to run the chain. And as the young man ran the chain, Duval stared at Sistah with unbelieving eyes. The man, who was resting everything on old Mae, found it hard to believe, the old slave could bring forth a child so beautiful in every way.

"All right, let's move out," Duval shouted, after Biscuit had finished running the chain, and the two were sitting comfortably in their saddles.

As each slave on the chain shuffled pass the nose of Duval's horse, Sistah kept her head down. But that still didn't stop the misfortunate slave from feeling the white man's eyes up on her. And like all slaves, misfortunate or not, Sistah feared the extra attention, feeling she had done something wrong. Yet Sistah didn't allow herself to look the white man's way, as she marched in time with those who had the misfortune, to be in chains, while living under the flag of freedom.

When Duval finally got his crew to the spot where they were to pick, he gave old Mae the good news first. And hearing, that she was going to keep her baby, the old slave stood speechless. But then it struck old Mae. The white man had forgotten to tell her what to call the child.

"Sir," old Mae cried in fear.

"Yea, old girl," Duval replied looking at Sistah.

"What masa Arnold, gon call him?"

The next words out of the Cajun's mouth, told old Mae, it was official. She was going to keep her baby.

"Well I guess, he's going to call him, what ever I call him," Duval said, then called out for Sistah.

As Sistah came running, the old slave wondered what the Cajun wanted with the misfortunate female. And when Duval told old Mae, he was going to try something new, she couldn't see, Sistah having anything to do with it.

"New, sir?" old Mae asked.

"Don't worry, it won't hurt a bit," the man said with a smile. "Now where I'm from, da slaves work together. When a female have a baby, all da females in her family, get together and help with it."

"I's uh ain't got, no family, sir," old Mae replied, feeling lost and alone.

"Dat's all right, old girl, we'll just use Sistah," Duval said, knowing full well, he was placing old Mae and her two children directly in the path of death.

"But she's can't pick, sir," old Mae cried, as Duval took the long cloth from her hand.

Old Mae couldn't help but to feel sorry for Sistah, as she stood trembling with tears in her eyes. And as the old slave was once more faced with the painful memories from days gone by, she hoped it was all a bad dream. But old Mae knew at the end of the day, it would be poor helpless Sistah, taking the whip for her, just like Pleasant.

Feeling the deep sense of fear in the old slave, Duval sought to bring old Mae a little comfort. "Don't worry old girl, Sistah is going take good care of dis here baby," Duval said, as he took the baby from old Mae's hands. "And I don't speck, she's going to hurt us none, with her picking," the Cajun assured old Mae, while giving her a wink.

But neither the wink, nor the Cajun's soft voice, could bring the old slave any comfort, as she continued to worry about the misfortunate female. And as old Mae slowly walked away, she wiped a tear from her eye, knowing that Sistah was doomed. But when the old slave heard Duval call out to her, she was hoping the man had thought twice, about condemning Sistah to the whip.

"I's uh coming, sir," old Mae replied while turning around.

"I dink, you're forgetting some ding," Duval said, as he pointed to the three slaves he got from Lamar. "I need you to show dem, like you showed dat boy," Duval said, as he climbed on his horse.

After taking one look at the three slaves, old Mae knew right away, they weren't worth the money her master had paid for them. She also knew, each one of the three slaves, had been on the Big A for more then two years, yet they still couldn't pick their way out from under the whip. Nor could the female that stood between the two males, find a way to pick her way out of night rotation. Just like Isabella, the poor female was shuffled off to the small shed, to be used just like the very sack, she couldn't seem to fill. And knowing the three slaves like she did, old Mae was beginning to think, Sistah had gotten the better end of the deal.

"Come on," old, Mae said, as she walked away with the three slaves following her like little ducklings.

With everything as it should be, Duval sat in the saddle, with his Cajun instincts on high alert as usual. And if the man from the bayou could spot a mosquito pissing on a frog, it was safe to say, he saw Biscuit chewing like a grazing cow. And if old Mae thought she could help the three slaves by whispering, then the old girl was wrong. For every time the old slave whispered, don't do that, you's gotta do it like this, and who's showed you that? The Cajun heard her loud and clear. Yet the man from Louisiana didn't move a muscle, being that he knew everything was going to be all right. That is, until Duval spotted something he truly hated to see.

For it was Pleasant. And the young slave had the cotton sack close to his chest, as he foolishly ran through the sea of white bowls.

With the first day jitters having him as jumpy, as a bug dancing in a hot skillet, Biscuit immediately took aim on the young slave. But Duval quickly raised his hand, halting the young man from firing. And as the other slaves held their breath, knowing that death was among them, Duval quickly evaluated the situation. For he had never seen a slave, make a run for it with a sack. And if that was to be the case, then Pleasant would surely be a first.

But when Pleasant came to a stop at Sistah, he left both Duval and Biscuit a little baffled. And when the young slave pulled an empty cotton stalk from the ground, and trimmed it down to a twig, Duval thought the boy had lost his mind. But after Pleasant carefully placed his creation in the top of Sistah's sack, forcing it to remain open, Duval immediately understood what the boy was trying to do. Yet the Cajun saw the boy's effort to be no more then a waste of good picking time, as he signaled Biscuit to lower his weapon.

With his extremely ill advised act completed, Pleasant quickly returned to his original spot, and went back to picking. Biscuit on the other hand, didn't know what to make of the whole situation, as he sat feeling relieved. For the young man would have found it very hard to face his mother, after taking a life, slave or other wise.

Allowing himself, to be guided by his past, the Cajun waited before taking action, on what most would call an act of disrespect. But Duval wasn't the average white man. For he, was a Cajun. And like all Cajuns, the man walked a different path. But his years of experience, told him, the young slave's efforts wasn't going to help Sistah one bit. But just for the hell of it, the man kept his eyes on the misfortunate female.

"Drop dat sack, boy," Duval spat, as the shadow of his horse, fell over Pleasant.

The Cajun had seen Sistah's productivity increase three fold, in a matter of minutes, and he wasn't about to look that gift horse in the mouth. Yet the man from Louisiana was planning on teaching Pleasant a lesson.

While Pleasant did as he was told, the other slaves kept one eye on the action, while doing their best to keep picking. Yet, the poor captives couldn't help but to hold a great deal of concern, for one of their own.

"What you's think gon happen, Mae?" the female whispered.

"Child, you's can't worry bout that, cause that old slave driver got plenty enough whip to go round," old Mae whispered in return, as she steered the three slaves back to picking.

If there was one thing old Mae knew about the white man, it had to be, never to show him any emotions. With all the weapons in the white man's arsenal, his opponent's emotions, was the most powerful one of all. And old Mae knew that all too well, as she feared for Pleasant more then anyone. Yet the old slave went right on picking, as her young friend stood one step shy of the whip.

"Go get dat sack from Sistah, and be quick about it," Duval said strongly.

With his fear quickly taking control, Pleasant went racing toward Sistah like a charging leopard. And while every muscle in his body exploded with thunderous contractions, he propelled himself through the tall cotton with a great deal of urgency. Yet, when Pleasant heard Duval shout, come on boy, we ain't got all day, he dug deep down within himself, to come up with a little extra burst of speed. But it didn't take the young slave long to figure out, that his speed was about to deliver him a much bigger problem. For Pleasant was moving so fast, when he came up on Sistah, the poor boy had to make a looping pass around the female, in order to keep his footing. And as he did so, Pleasant never took his eyes off the sack, as Sistah held it out from her body.

By the time Pleasant completed his soaring loop around Sistah, he had plucked the sack from her hand, like a hawk would a mouse, sitting on top of a dried out ant hill. And as he did his best to make a hastily return, Pleasant gathered the sack up in to his arms. But before the young slave could take comfort in the fact that Duval was still sitting on his horse, he heard the Cajun's voice once again.

"Sistah, if you don't get over here with dat baby, you're going to find me to be an awful man," the Cajun roared.

With a brief look over his shoulder while still running, Pleasant saw Sistah shuffling her way through the sea of white bowls. And the way the young female looked, took Pleasant back to his days of running free in Africa. For Sistah looked like that old broken down female, who often passed through their village. And Pleasant could see the woman's face, as Sistah laid bent over, for her precious cargo sake.

"What's your name, boy?" Duval asked firmly.

"Pleasant, sir," the young slave said with his head down.

"Well I guess your name, can't do no more for you, den mine could do for me," Duval said, watching Sistah walk up behind Pleasant. Leaning back in his saddle, Duval gave the two petrified slaves a bit of bad news. "Now I ain't going to tell you dis but once. From here on out, you better make sure she get her share of dis here cotton, or it's going to be da whip, for da both of you. And boy, you better make sure, you get me more then two sacks. Now put another twig in dat sack, and get back to picking," Duval growled.

After condemning Pleasant to the whip, Duval moved on to old Mae and her three struggling trainees. And in his usual way, the Cajun came up on the slaves, and inquired about their progress.

"Theys doing fine, sir," old Mae said, stretching the truth a bit.

"Good, because I need dem to be like dat boy," Duval said, looking at the girl.

"I's uh try, sir, but it's that whip, that got him scared," old Mae said honestly.

"Now I tell you, old girl. Who ever, cut dat boy up, did a mighty good job of it," Duval said, as he stared across the field at Pleasant.

Then without saying another word, Duval rode off, as if he had some where to be in a hurry. And when the Cajun's horse came to a stop, it was standing over Isabella. The poor female quickly started praying, while preparing herself for a taste of the whip. But rather then use his whip, Duval just tried to shout Isabella through her frustrating slow down.

Chapter 5

A Deadly Gamble

After an auspicious start to what had the makings of another long day, Duval prayed for a bit of peace and quiet. But when the Cajun heard a voice he quickly took, to be that of an angel, the Louisiana native felt old Gabriel had finally came to take him home. And with his Cajun eyes looking toward the Heavens, Duval waited for his savior to lift him up to the waiting arms of his maker. But the only thing Duval saw hanging from the Heavens above, was a bright blue sky, dressed with pretty white clouds.

"WELL I'LL BE," DUVAL said, realizing the most beautiful voice to ever touch his ears, was coming from a slave.

And not just any slave. For Sistah's head, was as empty, as a busted pail, which left Duval wondering how the girl knew how to stay on key. And even though he heard it, Duval couldn't bring himself to believe the all mighty, would give someone like Sistah such a remarkable gift. But what shocked the man the most, was how Sistah had the presence of mind, to change octaves and the tempos at the same time, without missing a beat. It had to be the baby, Duval thought to him self, as he began to fall into some type of hypnotic trance.

Without knowing how he got there, Duval found him self looming over Sistah in a state of euphoria. And as Sistah transformed her singing into humming, just like his horse, Duval didn't move a muscle. The man and his beast were captured, like two flies in a web. But unlike a spider, Sistah posed no threat to her victims.

With Sistah's little bundle of joy sleeping peacefully, the slave used that time to give her voice a break. And unhappy, as he may have been, Duval knew he needed a break as well. So the Cajun shouted he was going to check on the other chain masters, as his horse broke in to a strong gallop.

Upon returning to hear more of Sistah's singing, Duval found Pleasant dragging a full sack to the wagon. The driver wasted no time, riding over to the struggling young slave, and dismounted. And after grabbing the ass end of the sack, Duval gave Pleasant a stern warning.

"You're going to learn how to tote dese sacks, or you're going to get a whole lot of trouble out of me."

"Yes sir, I's uh do that, sir" Pleasant replied without ever taking his eye off of the ground.

With the sack on the wagon, Duval got back on his horse and rode over to Biscuit. "I guess dat girl, is slowing him down," Duval said with a bit of disappointment.

Not knowing a thing about slaves or their picking habits, Biscuit was left with a blank look on his face. But when Duval explained that Pleasant should have completed his first sack long before then, the young man was more then willing to talk.

"The boy took his sack up, a while back," Biscuit said, as if he were a lot older then Pleasant.

"Are you telling me, dat was Sistah sack?" Duval asked.

"Yes sir," Biscuit replied, like the well mannered boy, his mother and father had raise.

With Biscuit's answer ringing in his head, Duval's Cajun instincts went to crawling like an army of greedy ants. And that left the man trying to figure out, the strangeness that Sistah and Pleasant had about them, which couldn't be explained. Yet the man from the Bayou, was determine to figure the two slaves out, no matter what his father said about leaving well enough alone.

"How long da old girl, has been feeding her baby?"

"About an hour or so, sir," Biscuit replied.

Duval rode off in the direction of old Mae, quickly giving the three misfit pickers, the indication he was coming for them. And as the horse trotted closer, the three trainees became desperately nervous, being that they were still working on their first sack. But to their surprise, when the horse came to a stop, the man acted as if they weren't even there. Instead, Duval inquired about the baby, leaving the three slaves, to nervously pick their master's cotton.

"Is he still sucking?" Duval asked of the baby's nursing.

"He's sleeping, sir," old Mae replied, while picking.

Before the old slave could say that the baby needed changing, Duval had called out for Sistah, while dropping out of his saddle. But before the man could get the long cloth off of old Mae, Sistah was upon them, pawing at the baby like a wolf, trying to get a rabbit from beneath a log.

"Na Sistah, you's wait," old Mae cried, hoping to slow the misfortunate female down.

Yet Sistah went right on reaching for the baby, until she had him in her grasps, long cloth and all. Then like a falling rock, she fell to the ground, and immediately began to remove the wet diaper from her baby's gentle bottom. Yet neither Duval nor old Mae was prepared for what Sistah did, when she finally got the soiled diaper off of her baby. The twisted slave opened her mouth, thus allowing a line of saliva to run down on to the baby's genitals, until they were good and wet. And like a good mother, Sistah took one end of the long cloth, and wiped her baby dry.

With the first order of business completed, Sistah returned to Pleasant, while Duval went back to sitting on his horse. But before the man could get comfortable, he noticed Sistah reaching over her shoulder to touch the baby. Yet there was no need for the Cajun to be alarmed, seeing that Pleasant was doing his job for him. The boy quickly gave Sistah a light tap on the head, thus sending her back to picking. But just like all females, even the twisted ones, Sistah had to have the last word, as she poked her tongue out in defiance, which brought a smile to Duval's lips.

That night at feeding, Sistah sat next to old Mae, just like the night before. But on that night, Sistah sat so close to the old slave, there weren't a spec of light between the two of them. And old Mae knew Sistah wasn't going to eat, as long as she kept her eyes on the baby.

"Na Sistah, you's eat," the old slave said firmly, hoping to strike a bit of fear in the young female.

But Sistah couldn't eat, with the baby holding every bit of her attention. Nor could the poor slave think beyond the sight of the baby. For Sistah was so caught up in looking at the baby, she never noticed the slave driver, as he snuck up behind her. And as Duval stood over Sistah for a moment or two, the man wondered if he had made the right decision, tying the poor girl to the baby.

"If you don't eat dat food, you won't be giving dat baby its washing," Duval said, as he stood looking down on the half wit slave.

Sistah took to eating like a hungry hog at feeding time, as she foolishly stuffed the food in her mouth. And when she was done shoveling grits, and choking down the shortening bread, Sistah rushed off to take her pan up.

"Gimme Mae. Gimme baby," Sistah said, as she ran up to the old slave, trying to talk with a mouth full of grits and shortening bread.

Old Mae looked up at Sistah with sympathetic eyes. And there was no mistaking it. The old slave's heart was heavy, as she watched Sistah move about like a little child in need of a slop jar. But all old Mae could do, was to spread her arms and watch, as Sistah gently took hold of the baby.

When Sistah got the baby from old Mae, she cradled it in her right arm, just before proceeding to do the impossible. For the misfortunate slave took out one of her tits, and tried to breast feed the baby, as if it had came from her own womb. And not knowing any better, the baby did its best, to draw milk from the empty well.

In his effort to ignore Sistah, Duval cranked up a conversation with old Mae. "I don't really know what to call dat little Cowayne, oh girl," Duval said, while forcing himself not to look in Sistah's direction.

Before the old slave could react to Duval's statement, one way or the other, Sistah had already given the child its name.

"You's hear that, Cowayne?" Sistah said, smiling at her and old Mae's baby.

Sistah had no idea the man was using the word, as a derogatory remark, for the baby disturbing his temper tantrum the day before. To Sistah, it was a name, and she wanted to keep it, for all that it was worth.

"I's uh reckon, you's done gave him uh name, sir," old Mae said, as she was more then willing to accept the name, in which Sistah had chosen.

"I guess, I did, oh girl," Duval said, as he watched Sistah head off to go give the baby a bath.

When the slaves were fed, the chain masters were given a female for the night. But when it came time to give the slaves who earned it, their rewards, Pleasant wasn't among the four that was chosen. And once again, the young slave found himself, disappointed. So when he saw Duval walking toward him, Pleasant quickly did the first thing that came to mind, which was to lower his head.

"Pick one of dem girls, for your pleasure?" Duval said, as he pointed the butt of his whip, at the three female slaves, who were standing to the left of the small shed.

With his head still down, Pleasant replied, Sistah. But Duval had to tell the young slave, because of his efforts, Sistah had earned the right not to take pleasure on that night. Then the Cajun told Pleasant once again, to pick one of the females that were standing across the yard. But the young slave just pointed at the large shed instead, making it obvious to the Cajun, he much rather do without, then to share his seeds with another female. So with his hat pushed back, Duval walked off, feeling he had once again, made a bad decision.

With another stroke of bad luck, Duval ran in to Sistah, as she was returning from giving old Mae's baby its bath. And the way, the misfortunate female had the baby wrapped in a bunch of rags, as if she was hiding something, made the Cajun a little scared. But the way Sistah said the baby's name with a great deal of joy, as she repeated it over and over, told Duval, the girl would never harm the child. And while Duval sought to take a look at old Mae's baby, as he pealed back the rags, the man could feel Sistah squeezing the child closer to her body.

"I want hurt da old girl's baby," Duval said softly.

"Mine," Sistah said, as she turned away with the baby.

Duval may or may not have been a slave lover, but at that very moment, the man didn't have the heart to tell Sistah the truth. For the baby was, and would always be old Mae's child.

"Now I want you to hear me, and hear me good," Duval said as Sistah appeared to be focusing her entire attention on the baby. "You don't have to do it, if you don't want to. But remember, dat boy is da one who helped you get dat cotton," Duval went on, as Sistah continued to play with the baby. "Now he wants to take pleasure with you," the Cajun said, but not getting a response out of Sistah, one way or the other.

As Duval and Sistah came upon old Mae, who was sitting in the same spot, the twisted slave stood in silence. And after kissing the baby in which she declared to be her own, Sistah sadly gave the little wonder back to its rightful mother. Sistah then wiped her hands on the dusty dress that she was bound to wear, until it fell from her well shaped body. And like a young maiden about to be burned at the stake, Sistah took a deep breath and let it out. She than looked at the Cajun, as if to say, I am ready for what ever is to come. And after marching Sistah over to where Pleasant was sitting, Duval told Lamar, to chain them to the large magnolia tree, which sat near the west fence. And when Lamar had finished doing as he was told, he left the two slaves alone, to enjoy their night beneath the large tree.

When the plantation had finally taken on its nightly stillness, Pleasant and Sistah gave each other a look that said it was time. And as she hastily came out of her dress, Sistah was more then determine to stay in control of the situation. Yet before the twisted female could lay her dress in the dirt, Pleasant had stripped his pants down to one leg, and was moving in for the kill. And with a handful of her breast, he quickly pulled Sistah to him. But armed with the determination of a sparrow fleeing for its life, Sistah gave her lover, a firm slap on the leg, thus slowing him down to a complete halt.

With Pleasant some what subdued, Sistah immediately went about charting herself a safer course. And like a good lover, she placed his hand between her thighs, so he could feel the soft wet hairs that were waiting to be parted. Then like so many females that had walked the earth for thousands of years, Sistah placed her head on Pleasant's shoulder, as if she was ready to be submissive. And the age old trick worked just fine, as Pleasant pushed Sistah closer to the edge of her climax, with his gentle stroking of her wet moist split. But Sistah wasn't quite ready for their big moment, as she ran her index finger across the top of Pleasant's dick. And as she could feel a few of his escaping seeds, Sistah caught an idea, which sent her head beneath the wool blanket, where the misfortunate female began to nibble on Pleasant's nipples.

By the time Sistah had made her way to Pleasant's belly button, she could smell the stench flowing from his pelvic. And even though the odor loomed some where near intoxicating, Sistah still sought to give the seeds, their much needed release. But as the warmth of her mouth took in the dry salty skin, which covered the steely erection, Sistah went about the task for a reason.

"Why you's pick me?" Sistah asked, from beneath the blanket.

"Cause I's, want ya," Pleasant replied, like a typical male.

Knowing she had the upper hand, Sistah played her cards accordingly. "You's want me to do it some mo?" she asked. And after watching Pleasant nod his head, Sistah asked the not so wise male again. "Why you asked him for me?"

"Cause you's mine."

With Pleasant's second reply, being no better then the first, Sistah decided to set the matter straight. "I belong to Mr. Arnold," she said, while mounting him.

And when Sistah had finished making Pleasant cum faster then a young rooster, she once again found herself trembling in the dark. Yet while lying wrapped in his arms, Sistah relished the fact, her trembling, was the result of a mind numbing climax, rather then a mountain of pain. And as she desperately wanted more, Sistah knew such an act, could bring the whip crashing down on the both of them. So with nothing on her mind but Cowayne and Pleasant, Sistah slowly floated off into a deep relaxing sleep.

The next morning while eating, Pleasant thought about the statement Sistah had uttered seven hours earlier. The words, I belong to Mr. Arnold, stuck in the boy's gut, like an old rusty knife. And the way it was so boldly stated by the twisted female, tore deep into

Pleasant's soul, yet he still took to plotting against the other male slaves, with hopes of keeping Sistah all to himself. But first, Pleasant had to make sure she continued to get her two sacks of cotton. That way, the two slaves would elude the whip, while keeping Sistah out of night rotation at the same time.

With his well laid plan in mind, Pleasant finished off what few grits he had left, and called out for the water boy. And when the little pail lugger reached him, Pleasant grabbed the scoop out of the bucket, thus bringing up a nice cool drink of water. But unlike the other slaves, Pleasant didn't just use the water to quench his thirst. For the young slave moved rather quickly, as he used his eyes, to locate each and every white man that stood among them. And while he did so, Pleasant carefully hid the chunk of left over bread from his morning meal.

With the cool water in his belly, and the shortening bread safely tucked away for later, Pleasant took the nearly spotless pan to the wash girl. Then like a good obedient slave, Pleasant went to the chain line ready for work. But if the young slave thought his little move was a success, then he had clearly underestimated the old slave. For old Mae had been watching the young slave, and was wondering, what he was up to, as she set out to have a word with him.

"Alright, let's move out," Duval shouted, just as old Mae reached Pleasant.

Hearing the driver's words, old Mae became dreadfully fearful, as she felt the young slave was planning to escape. But knowing that she had a child to care for, old Mae couldn't afford to risk her life for a foolish slave, no matter how much she cared for him.

When the crew made it out to the picking sight, old Mae quickly helped Sistah with the baby. Then like a mother with a troublesome child, she tried once again to have a word with Pleasant. But before the old slave could reach the teen, Duval called her.

While old Mae stood listening to the white man talking about the weather of all things, she noticed Pleasant talking to Isabella. And right away, the old slave felt at ease about her friend trying to escape. For she took to believing, Pleasant was trying to move beyond Sistah, to a more experience female. Yet the old slave knew Pleasant was going to need a lot more cotton, if he was planning on out doing Eat Um Up.

"I guess dat boy, is looking to see what Isabella got," Duval said, as he abruptly changed his conversation from the weather to Pleasant.

Like everyone who had crossed the Cajun's path before her, old Mae had begun to wonder, if the man had eyes in the back of his head. Yet her words didn't reflect what her eyes had already told the strange man from the Bayou.

"They's all the same, sir," old Mae said of male slaves.

But some how, the old slave felt the white man knew she was referring to all males in general, enslaved, or other wise.

After sending old Mae to her three bumbling slaves, Duval climbed on his horse, and watched Pleasant as he returned to Sistah. And the man had no doubt, things were going to get a bit interesting, before the morning dew, left for greener pastures. And before the man could finish his thought, Sistah had given Pleasant a firm stare. Then like a typical female, Sistah cut her eyes toward Isabella, who was off picking by herself. And seeing that, Duval wondered, what would he gain from Pleasant's, recent act.

With his father's favorite phrase on his mind, the Cajun spent his morning waiting to catch the next phase of Pleasant's plan. And as he waited, Duval sat enjoying Sistah's singing, while imagining the two females in a cat fight. He could see Sistah ripping Isabella's dress off in a matter of seconds, as she bellowed some twisted sounding scream. And poor naked Isabella would have no other choice, but to pull Sistah's dress off to even the score. Oh what a fight it would be, Duval thought to himself, as he felt his erecting flesh, growing harder with each passing moment. And just when Duval's dick took to throbbing like an aching heart, a blanket of silence came over the air, which sent the Cajun's daydream crashing in to a pit of reality.

With a perfectly good naughty thought left some where hanging in the clouds, Duval looked around for who or what was the cause of his frustration. And the moment he saw Pleasant struggling with his first full sack of cotton, Duval knew the boy was the reason for the sudden state of silence. And as he watched Pleasant fight to balance the large sack on his head, it struck Duval for the first time. The Cajun quickly wondered how he could have missed such a thing, seeing that it was so obvious. For Isabella was sitting directly in the path of the wagon, and that started Duval to wondering. Did the boy know Isabella was going to be in that very spot, when he completed his first full sack, or was it just a strange coincidence? The Cajun was dying to know, as he went back to playing possum.

After laying the heavy sack on the wagon, Pleasant headed back toward Sistah in good fashion. And while clutching the empty sack, as it hung from his shoulder, Pleasant kept his eyes on the man who commanded the whip. For it was he, that stood between the young slave and his well thought out plan. Yet the boy knew his plan would be nothing, with out the empty sack that the white man so eagerly wanted him to fill. But for one short moment, Pleasant was planning to use the sack in the same manner, in which his tribal warriors often used their shields. Yet Pleasant knew there was no room for a mistake, seeing that he would be dragging Isabella down with him.

With his eyes still on the Cajun, Pleasant sent his left hand disappearing inside the old shirt. And when his hand reappeared under the protection of the empty cotton sack, it held the left over shortening bread. Yet the bread wasn't for the young slave's consumption, as he held it with the tip of his fingers. And while passing in front of Isabella, as she stood bent over picking, Pleasant stuffed the chunk of bread in her mouth.

With his scheme deemed a success, Pleasant returned to Sistah and went back to picking. But the young slave's blundered move was everything but a work of art. For all Pleasant succeeded in doing, was fooling old Mae, who had been religiously watching the boy all morning long. But when it came down to the Cajun, the man's eyes were all over Pleasant, the moment he left the wagon. And from beneath the rim of his hat, Duval watched Pleasant, as he suspiciously carried the empty sack on his shoulder. And when the time came, Duval saw the crumbs fall from Pleasant's fingers, as well as Isabella lips. Yet the man from Louisiana did nothing. Instead, Duval focused his attention solely on Isabella, wondering if the gift would help the girl any.

But as Duval watched Isabella slowly chew the dry sweaty bread, he decided to put a touch of fear in the young slave. So with one thump of his heals, Duval sent his horse galloping straight toward Pleasant. And when the horse came to a stop, Duval called out to the little slave boy that towed the water, telling him to give Isabella a drink.

At the sound of Duval's voice, the little slave boy that was sitting on the wagon, immediately sprung in to action. And after removing the lid from the barrel, which held the slaves water, the child grabbed his scoop. Yet before the child could put one drop of water in his old dying pail, Duval's voice roared across the air once again.

"Just a scoop," the Cajun growled, while looking down on Pleasant.

But the young slave didn't panic, as he went right on working like a true picker. Yet Duval couldn't say the same for old Mae's baby, as it appeared to wake up with a huckleberry in its diaper. And as the baby took to screaming its little head off, Sistah released her secret weapon, thus saving the Cajun from another shameful defeat.

When Sistah's voice had finally calmed Cowayne down, and sent him back into a deep sleep, it apparently did the same with Duval. And the Cajun would have probably enjoyed his state of rest a bit longer, if it were not for a male hawk flying above. For the love sick bird, was desperately advertising his availability, to any and all females that would listen. Yet the only creature the sex hungry bird was able to arouse, didn't seem to fancy it's mating call. And Duval would have killed the horny bastard, if it were not for a strange sighting in the field.

After rubbing his eyes to clear the sleep from its shinny green balls, Duval took another look. And upon taking that much needed second look, the sighting stayed the same. Isabella had picked right on through her much anticipated slow down, which gave the female a remarkable opportunity. For the first time in her life, Isabella could end the day with two full sacks of cotton, thus awarding the female a good night's rest.

"I'll be right back," Duval shouted to Biscuit, as he rode off.

But the Cajun didn't ride away without thinking of what Pleasant may have had on his mind. But at that very moment, all the man could see was his money, and all that it would buy. And if Pleasant were to run off, Duval was sure to give the boy something far worst then any whip he had ever felt.

Returning to the field, Duval gave the slaves a chance to witness one more of Mr. Arnold's commandments, be laid to rest. For Duval had returned with a bundle of freshly cooked shortening bread, ready to be handed out. And as he walked his horse through the tall cotton, giving each slave a nice chunk of the soft warm bread, Duval called for the water boy once again. But when the Cajun saw the boy's first stop was in front of a male slave, the man from the Bayou responded very unkindly.

"Boy, when I tell you to give dem water, you better go to da females first. Now go give old Mae some water," the man from Louisiana shouted angrily.

"Yea sir," the boy said, as he rumbled away with the heavy pail.

After handing the last slave his portion of bread, Duval shouted, Sistah give dat baby to old Mae, so she can give it some milk. Then without ever noticing the angry look on Sistah's face, Duval rode off once again, with out telling Biscuit where he was going.

By the day's end, Isabella had turned Duval's speculation in to fact. The poor unproductive female had picked her two sacks of cotton with time to spare. And Isabella couldn't have been happier, as she hoped Duval would hold true to his word. Yet the well worn female didn't say a thing, as she stood quietly picking at her fingers, while Biscuit ran the chain through their rings.

"Well I guess dere won't be any pleasure taking on you tonight," Duval said, while looking down on Isabella from his horse.

To Isabella, Duval's words sounded far better then any song Sistah had ever sung. For the female had often prayed for the ability to pick as well as the others, yet day after day, and year after year, she found herself crying with disappointment. But on that day, after six long grueling years, Isabella had finally seen her prayers answered. And as she proudly marched back to the main yard, Isabella knew there would come a day, when Pleasant would seek his payment. And when the young slave call on her, Isabella felt the Devil himself, would not be able to stop her, from giving Pleasant, all that she had to offer.

Duval's two weeks deadline came a day late, yet the Big A was still able to lay claim, to being the first plantation to reach the market. And the Cajun didn't just beat the other plantations by a matter of hours. The man from Louisiana, reached the market days before the second place plantation showed up, and that made Mr. Arnold a very happy man. In fact, Mr. Arnold was so happy, he told Duval, the day was his, to do with as he saw fit. But Duval didn't need a whole day, for what he had in mind.

While Mr. Arnold went about collecting his winnings, Duval threw the slaves a feast. And the slaves royal meal, consisted of peas, rice, cornbread, and chicken for his special pickers. Yet no amount of food could have made Isabella as happy, as the gift that Pleasant had given her. For Isabella was no more a night rotation regular, seeing that she had the ability to earn her own extra bread.

"Thank you," Isabella said to Pleasant, while sitting next to Sistah as they ate.

The young slave didn't say a word, as he went right on stuffing his face with peas and rice. Yet as Isabella continued to watch him, she could tell from the way Pleasant looked at Sistah, the unfortunate female was the only one he wanted. Yet Isabella couldn't bring herself to feel happy, despite the fact, that Pleasant had erased her debt from his memory. For Isabella wanted someone to feel about her, the way Pleasant felt about Sistah. But the best Isabella could come up with, as she looked around at the other slaves, was a faded old memory.

By the time Isabella found herself thinking about the precious memory, Sistah's voice sailed across the air, rushing her back in time. And Isabella could see herself in the back of that beautiful white carriage, as Lamar drove it over the grass covered hills. And when Lamar commanded the white horse to stop, the first thing Isabella noticed was Bernard. Yet before her fear could set in, she heard the man angrily tell Lamar to hurry up.

"Pick your berries," Lamar said softly, as he turned his eyes to the basket, sitting on a blanket.

Young and naive, Isabella crawled out of the carriage with no idea of what was about to happen. The only thing the young female knew about her trip, was that she had to pick some berries. Yet the young slave didn't understand why she had to be wash so clean, and placed in such a fine dress, just to pick berries. But Isabella wasn't going to worry about it, seeing that berry picking was such an easy task. And as she went about picking the berries, Isabella looked around for the white people, who were in need of berries with their meal. And seeing no one, the young slave felt it would be wise, to complete her task, before the white people returned.

When Isabella had no more then a fist full of berries in her basket, she heard the sound of horses approaching. Call it slave's intuition, but something told the girl, to prepare herself for the worst. And no matter how hard the young slave tried, she couldn't stop her hands from trembling, while trying to pluck the berries from their bush.

"Hey you there," a soft female voice shouted, after commanding her horse to stop.

Isabella turned to find herself, being eyed by two beautiful smiling white females. One of the girls had long blond hair, which ran far beyond her shoulders. The other, though just as beautiful as the blond, had her shiny black hair, carefully hidden beneath a fancy yellow and white hat. But what took young Isabella by storm, was the way the two females stared at her with a curious strangeness.

"Yes um," Isabella replied.

"What are you doing, there?" The blond asked, with her Northern accent.

And the accent was just as much of a problem for Isabella, as the brunette's staring.

"I's picking berries, ma'am," Isabella replied fearfully.

"Do you own that berry bush?" the black haired female asked.

"No ma'am, I's uh don't own nothing, ma'am," Isabella said, as her trembling voice, told the two women, the matter needed to be investigated a bit further.

"Then you will have to pay for your thieving ways, you sweet little slave, bitch," the brunette snarled, while getting down from her horse.

The blond licked her lips, while her partner in crime drew closer to Isabella. And when the ready for sex female reached the young slave, she took a berry from the basket, and popped it in her mouth.

"Is it sweet?" the blond asked.

The brunette took another berry, and placed it in her mouth as well. She then gave Isabella a kiss. And being that it was the first time the young slave had ever been kissed by a female, she took to trembling like a cold wet pup. Yet Isabella was too young to know, that her trembling would only add fuel to the woman's hot burning fire. And as the brunette's tongue probed Isabella's mouth with a savage desire, her fire began to burn out of control, as she sought to satisfy herself even more. And with Isabella's left tit in her right hand, the white woman's breathing became that of a wild animal.

"I take it, the bitch is sweet," the blond said, as she dismounted her horse. "Come here, bitch," she commanded Isabella, while walking toward the blanket.

When Isabella reached the blanket, she could clearly see the fur, which covered the woman's pussy, was just as blond, as the hair on her head. Yet something told the young slave, she was in for a lot more then just a good look at the woman's delicious hairy treat.

"Lay down, bitch," the brunette ordered Isabella.

Knowing she didn't have any say so over her own being, Isabella didn't hesitate to follow the white woman's command. And no sooner then Isabella's head hit the blanket, she found the blond straddling her face, which made the girl's eyes quickly filled with tears, as the smell of the woman's stale pubic hair invaded her nostrils. And when Isabella bottom lip took to trembling, it struck a chord in the blond, which caused her to ride the poor slave's face with a vicious yearning. A yearning, which had to be hidden some where deep, far beyond the thick blond hairs that covered her sweet wet pussy.

"Put your tongue in me, bitch. Put it in me. I got to have it," the blond cried, as she took to trembling as well.

"You heard her, bitch. Now lick her pussy, or it will be the whip for you," the brunette snarled, as she took a break from sucking on her friend's breast.

Hearing the brunette's threat, Isabella ran her tongue deep inside the woman's walls, thus causing the pussy to surrender its juices.

"I'm cumming," the blond cried, as she viciously rode Isabella's face. "Oh, it's so good. It's so fucking good. Oh shit, this bitch is good," the blond cried, as she enjoyed the most satisfying climax of her lilly white life.

"Give her to me, bitch," the black haired beauty said with a seductive anger, as she fancied the blond's tit.

Lying on the blanket exhausted, after falling off of Isabella's face, the blond watched as her brunette friend took charge.

"You are not good, until I say you are good. Now kiss me, bitch," the brunette demanded, as her finger slowly moved in and out of Isabella's pussy.

Feeling that the brunette was the worst of the two women, Isabella sat up, and prepared herself for the kiss. And with her trembling lips slightly parted, Isabella accepted the uninvited tongue, hoping to avoid what ever punishment, the woman might see fit to administer. But in a flash, Isabella knew her kiss had fallen short of the woman's expectation. Yet the beautiful black slave, had no idea, how good her punishment was going to be.

With her hand around Isabella's throat, the brunette forced her back down on to the blanket, while shouting, "I want your tongue, bitch. Now give it to me."

"Maybe I need to show her how," the blond said, as she sat up, raring to swap spit with the brunette.

"Stay," the brunette said firmly, while pointing her ridding crop at the sweet luscious blond.

With her command obeyed, the brunette proceeded to educate Isabella in the art of kissing. And as the brunette sucked Isabella's tongue in to her mouth, she began to moan seductively. "Ooo, I love the way you taste," the brunette said, as she licked Isabella's lips, while coming out of her dress. "Lick me gently, bitch," she said softly, after mounting Isabella's face.

As the brunette slowly moved her pelvic on Isabella's tongue, the young scared slave felt the blond tugging at her dress. But Isabella had nothing to fear, seeing that the woman was only looking to give her a little something in return. And when Isabella felt the cool wind blowing on her pussy, as the blond's tongue ran up her left thigh, she became both scared, and aroused at the same time.

"Ooo bitch, your pussy is so pretty," the blond said, as her tongue moved closer to Isabella's furry split.

And when the blond slowly ran her middle finger between Isabella's furry lips, something in the young slave snapped. Before Isabella knew it, she was eating at the brunette's pussy like a wild dog.

"Ooo you little bitch, you have been holding back on us," the brunette said, as she began to ride Isabella's tongue, as if it were a large pink dick.

"You're wet," the blond said, looking down on Isabella. Then without a moment of hesitation, the blond ran the cream covered finger in her mouth. "Do you want me to lick your pussy, bitch?" she asked, with the finger still resting in her mouth.

Not knowing if Isabella was nodding yes, or going crazy with lust, the brunette took it upon herself, to repeat the blond's question. "Do you want her to eat your pussy, bitch?"

"Yes um," Isabella said with a tremble in her voice.

While firmly gripping Isabella's hair, the brunette slapped the young slave's face, then angrily said, "That is not how we answer each other, bitch."

"I say, we punish, the bitch," the blond whispered, as she brushed her face up against the brunette's long slinder jaw.

"Don't you move, bitch," the brunette said to Isabella.

With Isabella frozen stiff, she received a punishment that nearly drove her crazy. And when the two punishers were done biting, squeezing, and licking Isabella's tits, the blond asked her question again.

"Do you want me to lick your pussy, bitch?"

"Yes, bitch," Isabella said, as she truly hungered for the white woman's tongue.

"Now that, is the way, a good bitch, should answer such a question," the brunette said, as she nibbled on Isabella's neck.

As Isabella moved her body in the blond's face, she could feel herself rushing toward a lustful climax.

"You like that, don't you, bitch?" the brunette asked Isabella, as the two of them watched the blond satisfy her starving hunger.

"I's uh love it, bitch. I's uh love it," Isabella cried, as she nearly went crazy, from the blond savagely eating at her pussy.

And while the blond held a burning desire to eat Isabella alive, the brunette enjoyed the slave's nice young tender breast. For Isabella was receiving an induction, fit for a queen, and that was why, she enjoyed every kiss, lick, and fucking finger that she rode, until darkness had forced the three females into the shack.

After a day and a night of wild female sex, Isabella once again, found herself feeling two emotions at the same time. For the young slave was full of excitement, and lustful satisfaction. Yet Isabella felt empty, knowing she would never touch or taste another female, the way she and the two lovely bitches did. And as Isabella got herself ready to go back to being a slave, there was one thing she vowed never to forget. The young slave would always remember the sweet taste, and gentle touch of a woman's body. For Isabella, that would always be her true meaning of freedom.

"Well don't just sit there," Lamar said, as he pulled up in a buckboard.

"Isabella. Isabella," Sistah whispered, causing Isabella to snap out of her trip to the past.

"All right, to the shed with you," Lamar said, as Isabella stood up.

"What's wrong?" Duval shouted from across the yard.

"I reckon, she's a little tired," Lamar replied.

"We all are, now get on with it," Duval said firmly.

"You heard the boss," Lamar said, pointing the way.

Isabella smiled inside, as she headed for the female shed. And while taking a quick look at the small building, Isabella silently uttered the word bitch. For the female's life was truly a bitch, seeing that she didn't have a bitch to love her.

Chapter 6

New Arrival

With Cowayne surviving one of the coldest winters ever, the other females wondered why Sistah was still dragging him around like he was a new born. And they often whispered about how much of a burden it had to be on old Mae, being that she was still having to breast feed the baby, while tirelessly toiling in the fields. But Sistah didn't care about the whispers, or the stares. Nor did the misfortunate slave worry herself with all of the talk, about how she was stealing old Mae's baby. For the retarded female, just went on pinching away at the old slave's share of the baby, as she waited for the day, when Cowayne would no longer fancy his mother's milk.

AS TIME MOVED ON, Sistah left all of the talk behind her, along with the cool temperatures of spring. For with the long hot days of summer, came the blood sucking mosquitoes. And the little critters drove Sistah crazy, as she tried to keep them from getting to her baby. Yet old Mae found a bit of poetic justice, in having the mosquitoes around. The old slave watched as Sistah struggled to do her work, while trying to keep the varmints at bay. But when Duval lashed out at Sistah for her lack of productivity, the old slave quickly sprung in to action, thus rescuing the misfortunate female from the whip.

"You's rub this on him, fo you's take him to them fields," old Mae said, giving Sistah some creamy concoction.

With the mosquito problem solved, Sistah was able to keep her baby all the way up to picking time. For that was when Duval told Sistah, she had to leave old Mae's baby behind.

"Mine," Sistah mumbled, while clutching Cowayne to her face. "My baby," she said, turning away from the man.

Not wanting to put the whip to the female, Duval called out for Pleasant.

"Yea sir," Pleasant said, as he came running.

"Get dat baby, and take him to Ella," Duval said, holding the butt of his whip.

Pleasant humbly went over to Sistah, and took Cowayne without any trouble. Yet that didn't stop the mindless female from falling to the ground, where she began to cry, just like her baby.

"Na Sistah, dat boy is too heavy, to be riding your back," Duval said firmly.

Getting up off the ground, Sistah ran to old Mae, only to throw herself back down in the dirt. "Baby Mae, baby," Sistah cried at the old slave's feet.

Old Mae didn't know what to tell Sistah, as she looked at Duval, then her eyes fell on the other slaves.

Even though the slaves had waited for the day, when Sistah would have to give the Devil his due, they took no pleasure in watching the misfortunate female suffer. But with the truth hanging in the air like a shifting cloud, Sistah no longer held the slaves interest, being that they had already found another female to talk about. For there was a young half breed slave girl name Ethel, who carried in her belly, what was to be Mr. Arnold's second round of bragging rights. For Ethel was pregnant for Big Willie, Mr. Arnold's most prized possession. For the large slave, was Mr. Arnold's one and only fighter? And what a fighter Big Willie was, with his large body, and even a larger punch to boot. And from where the slave's stood, Sistah's little problem was no match for Ethel's pregnancy.

Two weeks and two days after Sistah was forced to accept reality, Ethel came face to face with the cruel destiny that awaited her. And if the Devil had ever added insult to injury, he did so on that stormy night. And with every bolt of lightning, which demanded the earth's respect, Ethel's fear grew stronger and stronger, until it left her soul without an ounce of hope to lean on. And as the fourteen year old mother to be, laid on the floor in pain, she knew there was only one answer to her problem. And no sooner then the name left her lips, Sally, the young slave girl who had the privilege of cleaning up Jeremiah's coffee, that was victimize by their master just over a year ago, darted out of the birthing shed.

"Mr. Duval, Mr. Duval," Sally shouted, as she banged away on the slave driver's door with her fist.

"Who dat?" Duval barked, with a sleepy tone.

"Me, Sally, sir."

"What are you doing out in dis rain?" Duval asked, standing in the doorway, covered only by his long johns.

"It's Ella, sir. She's said Ethel, need Mae."

"What on earth, she need with da old girl, in dis kind of weather?" Duval asked, as he backed out of the doorway.

"Ethel is hurting, mighty bad, sir, and she's crying for Mae," Sally cried.

"Well don't just stand dere, come in here, and get by dat stove," Duval said, as he grabbed his pants.

Sally didn't even take the time to give the proper response, as she closed the door, and made a mad dash for the stove. And while standing in front of the black heat dispenser, soaking up what little warmth it had left, the young slave took a long hard look at Duval's bed. She tried to envision Ella lying next to the white man feeling free. But before the girl could get warm, or envision Duval's head between Ella's healthy thighs, it was time for her to face the rain once again.

With Duval in front of her, clutching a cold lantern, Sally followed the white man through the mud, right on up to the female shed. And for the first time in her seventeen years of existence, Sally saw how the mass majority of her master's slaves were put to bed. And the long steel bar that rested across the doors, sent chills rushing through the girl's body. But it was the two large black locks that frighten Sally, far worst then her master's shouting. And when the door was finally opened, Sally followed Duval into the chilly dark damp piece of hell, the female field slaves called home. A place with a stench that was so strong, it grabbed Sally's breath, while nearly knocking her out cold.

After listening to the man fumbling around in the dark, Sally was greeted to a burst of light. And even though the match gave Sally full sight of Duval, and he of her, it didn't provide enough light, to prepare the two for what they were about to see.

"My lord," Duval said, after standing up with the burning lantern held high above his head.

As both Sally and Duval stood staring at the strange and unusual sight, neither knew what to think. For old Mae slept in the middle of the floor with Sistah and Cowayne next to her. And five pregnant mothers formed a circle around the three. And after the pregnant mothers, there were flowering circles of mothers with their young babies. The last two circles were made up of lone females. But what shocked Duval the most, was the females who weren't a part of any circle. They laid long ways against the walls, as if they were some kind of attack group.

"Well don't just stand dere," Duval whispered to Sally.

With her dress and coat dripping water everywhere, Sally carefully made her way through the maze of sleeping bodies. And as she did so, Sally wondered how the females were able to sleep, in such a fowl smelling place. But being some what of a house pet, the young slave had never worked hard, a day in her life.

"Mae, Mae, you's gotta get up, Mae," Sally said softly, as she tried her best to shake the massive hunk of flesh, which covered old Mae's bones.

"Child, what you's doing here?" old Mae asked, as she immediately became very fearful.

"It's Ethel, she's gon have her baby," Sally cried, as she felt like throwing up the beans and corn bread that lined her stomach.

The fear in Sally's eyes, told the old slave, that something was seriously wrong. And when she heard Duval's voice, telling her to hurry up, the old slave finally looked toward the lantern, as she rolled over. But as she attempted to get up off of the floor, the old female made a terrible mistake. For old Mae had forgotten how close she slept to Cowayne and Sistah. And while moving her massive body, she disturbed the child just a bit too much.

Seeing that Cowayne was wide awake, and already crawling on Sistah, old Mae felt she had no other choice, but take the toddler with her. "Come on, boy, I's uh reckon, you's had to wake up," old Mae said, as she took Cowayne up in her arms.

"Are you trying to kill dat child?" Duval growled.

I's uh gotta take him, sir, cause he's gon cry, when we's leave," old Mae said, knowing her son almost as good as Sistah did.

"Get dat boy," Duval said to Sally.

Sally quickly moved to do as she was told, but Cowayne wasn't for socializing with the strange slave. And just like that, Duval was instantly reminded of their first encounter. For the baby turned away, while letting out an awful screech, which left the man from Louisiana with only two other options. He could wake Sistah, or take the baby from his mother.

With Cowayne wrapped in old Mae's blanket, and the latter option in full swing, Duval darted out into the rain. Sally on the other hand, weren't able to move so smoothly, seeing that her ring was properly completing its second main function. For the large ring, assured Mr. Arnold, he would not be losing any slaves to the method of running. Yet as Duval looked back at Sally shuffling her feet through the mud, he caught another flash back. The man was quickly reminded of how easily Pleasant was able to run with the heavy ring, as if it weren't on her leg at all. And as he reached the birthing shed, Duval had already made up his mind, to pay even more attention to the puzzling slave, his boss called Pleasant.

Moments after entering the birthing shed, Duval watched as Sally drug her wet body through the door. And while her ring carried more then its share of mud, Sally went and stood next to Ethel. As for old Mae, the large slave still had a good ways to go, before she would reach the old broken down structure.

"Well I guess, you girls don't need me any more," Duval said, after watching old Mae fight her way into the small, damp, squeaky building.

With Duval gone, and Cowayne safely in her arms, old Mae tried to stare down a house slave name Effie. On top of being the only slave to have a closer voice to Mr. Arnold's ear then Jeremiah, Effie was also Ethel's mother. And that was the young slave's problem. Just like Ethel and Sally, old Mae knew Effie was totally loyal to the man that fathered her child. And the lack of concern on the arrogant slave's face, told old Mae, Effie wasn't there to give her motherly support.

"You's hold on, child, every thing gon be all right," old Mae said, with out ever taking her eyes off of Effie.

"You's gotta push, na Ethel, you's hear. You's gotta push, if n you's want yo's baby to come," Ella cried.

With the stick already in her mouth, Ethel took a deep breath, right before attempting to do what she considered to be virtually impossible. And while attemping the great feat, Ethel took a quick look at her mother. And not seeing a speck of pity, in the vesicle that carried her everyday of nine months, Ethel took to crying. And the poor child went right on crying, as she squeezed old Mae's hand with all her might, while trying to push another life into Hell's open arms.

"Ethel you's gotta stop crying, so you's can push harder," Ella said, as if it was easy, as shelling peas.

For the last thing Ethel wanted to hear, was for Ella to tell her, she had to stop crying. Nor did Ethel have any desire to push harder, for a baby that may not be what her master commanded. And being only fourteen and scared, not even the tender touch of old Mae's hand, could free Ethel from the unbearable pain and fear that held her like some dying curse.

"Na Ethel, you's can't pay that no mind, cause you's gotta have yo's baby," old Mae said, as she placed a hand over the girl's eyes.

With Ethel no longer able to see her mother's haunting stare, she took another deep breath, and went back to work. And when the young mother felt her baby breaking its way into a world unlike any other, she took hold of the old slave's hand. Then with a look in her eyes that only an Arnold could possess, Ethel snatched the old slave's hand from her sight. And as she stared at Effie, Ethel didn't make a sound, while her baby forced its way into a life it would live to hate.

"It's a girl," Ella said with great joy.

Ethel's heart nearly came to a complete stop, when she heard Ella give credence to her failing effort. Then like a dam bursting, Ethel's tears began to fall like the rain that was pounding, the dilapidated shed. There was no hope for the child, as she thought of all the things, their master had done to the slaves, who saw fit to disappoint him. And in her downward spiral, Ethel sought the help of the innocent.

"You's see the baby, Cowayne," Ethel cried with a trembling voice?

Like any toddler, Cowayne became excited, when his eyes caught sight of the new life. And Cowayne's excitement of the baby, gave Ethel an open door to run through. With a few choice words, Ethel tied Cowayne to a life long commitment, while escaping her fears for a brief moment.

"You's see our baby, Cowayne. I's uh always want you's to take care of our baby, you's hear. You's take care of our Clora Lee," Ethel said as she cried.

And Ethel continued to cry, as a lone raindrop fell through the leaky roof, thus striking her on the forehead. And while the raindrop added a splash of insult to her torment, Ethel went right on clinging to Cowayne, as if the baby were some type of shield, which would deflect their master's anger.

"Na Effie, you's knows that child is scared," old Mae said, as she stared at the preferred slave, standing against the wall.

The old slave's words didn't seem to have an affect on their master's beloved sex provider, as she stood like a monument to self absorption. And while Ethel's whaling baby pronounced its arrival into their world of slavery, old Mae saw fit to give Effie a few choice words.

"Na Effie, you's knows, masa Arnold ain't gon look kindly on that child, for not bringing him uh boy, like Big Willie."

If the old slave was looking for sympathy from Effie, she didn't get it. For the high pollutant slave, just stared at old Mae with an emptiness, which said her job there was done. And to make her point understood, Effie gave Sally a look, which sent the girl running out of the door. But old Mae was far from being finished with the arrogant, well dressed slave.

Stepping in front of Effie, old Mae said, "That there, is yo's. And that baby, is yo's to. Na who's they's gon turn to, if n they's ain't got you? You's knows, the Misses uh kill um both, if n she's get the notion."

"I am not here to listen to your slave yard chatter, now get out of my way," Effie said in her most refined white woman's tone.

"You's ready, Effie," a male slave whispered.

Seeing that Effie was dead set on being a good slave, rather then a loving mother, old Mae grudgingly moved out of her way. Yet that didn't stop the two slaves from giving each other the eye, as Effie placed the low hanging shawl on her head. Then like old Mae knew she would, Effie opened the door all the way, and stepped out in to the rain. And with the male slave holding a quilt over her head, Effie sashayed back to the large white house, without ever recalling what it felt like to wear one of those wretched rings.

By the time daylight had rolled around, old Mae was still counting raindrops. And as the rain continued to fall in buckets, the old slave stood steadfast to her conviction. The aging female had no intentions of closing her eyes, for fear of Ethel doing the unthinkable. Yet old Mae would not have held it against the child, knowing the fate, Ethel may have to face before the daylight turn to dark again. But to the old slave, there were a lot of bad things in the world, yet none worst then death. And if Ethel were to try and make a run for it, father or not, the child was just as good as dead. So the old slave sat with her back against the door, to make sure no one came in or out of the shed.

"Mae!" Sistah yelled, as the large slave fell in her arms.

"Na Sistah, you's help me up," old Mae growled, while holding on to the doorway, trying to keep herself from falling out of the shed, on to the muddy ground.

"I's uh trying, but you's too heavy."

Hearing Sistah's voice in his sleep, Cowayne woke up and raised his head, yet he could not see his loving mother. But once Sistah grunted, Cowayne knew she was near, and struggled to get at her, while ignoring the one who carried him in her womb.

"Ma-ma, ma-ma," Cowayne said, as he tried to get around his birth mother.

"Na Cowayne, you's get back," old Mae said firmly.

Hearing old Mae's tone, Sistah suddenly found the strength to push the large slave back into the shed, as she spoke rather strongly to her old friend.

"Mae, you's stop fussing at my baby."

With old Mae back in the up right position, Sistah grabbed Cowayne before entering the shed. And while tracking mud on the bloody floor, Sistah walked over to see the newest arrival.

"I's uh could have her, Mae?"

"Na Sistah, you's gotta baby, so leave that child baby be," old Mae said softly.

But the old slave might as well had been talking to the rain that was falling for miles, seeing that Sistah was already in the process of putting Cowayne down. And after finding a place to set her baby, that didn't have a drop of blood, mud, or water, Sistah went straight for Ethel's baby. Then like a bird giving thanks for a new day, Sistah took to humming. And the look in Sistah's eyes, told the old slave, there was going to be trouble.

Even though old Mae told Sistah, she couldn't have Ethel's baby, three days later the misfortunate slave got lucky. When Sistah got in from the field, she found Ethel with Clora Lee cradled in her right arm nursing, while Cowayne rode her left hip. Yet with all of that going on, Ethel was still trying to balance a hot skillet of corn bread. So without thinking, Sistah ran up and grabbed the two babies, and darted off with them.

"Mae, I's, need diapers, Mae. Mae I's need diapers," Sistah cried, as she couldn't seem to keep still.

"Isabella, go get Sistah dem diapers, out dat shed," Duval shouted.

"Na Sistah, I's uh done told ya, you's can't take that child baby," old Mae said, as she reached for Clora Lee.

"No! Mine," Sistah said, as she turned away from old Mae.

"Leave her be," Duval said firmly, as he walked up. "Did Ethel say you could hold dat baby?"

"It's a girl, sir," Sistah replied cheerfully.

After shaking his head, Duval told Sistah to go sit down. He then called out for Pleasant. And when the helpful slave reached him, Duval took Pleasant up to the front of the food line, and had the girl to give the slave two pans of beans and some shortening bread.

"I don't know how dat girl is going to eat, but take dat food over dere to her," Duval said to Pleasant.

"Yes sir, I's uh do that sir," Pleasant said, repeating the response he stole from Eat Um Up.

When Pleasant reached Sistah, it didn't take Duval long to see how things were going to work out. With Cowayne standing between Pleasant's legs, Sistah was able to hold Clora Lee, feed herself, and her baby as well. And when Sistah wasn't stuffing food in Cowayne's mouth, Pleasant was doing the honors. But little did the man from Louisiana know, he once again, had given Sistah too much rope to play with.

As the rising and setting of the sun moved the seasons along with perfect timing, Ethel saw Sistah inching deeper and deeper into Clora Lee's life. Yet there appeared to be some sort of unspoken agreement between the two slaves, which said, Sistah would only fill the roll of a play mother. But something told old Mae, what ever agreement Sistah and Ethel may have made, it would surely work out to the misfortunate slave's benefit. And the old slave was just waiting for the day, when Sistah would have Clora Lee, lock, stock, and barrel, just like she had Cowayne. But until that day, old Mae was going to keep her eyes on the three way mix up, that would surely end one way or the other.

One morning while Duval and Biscuit were enjoying Sistah's singing, the boy pointed to his father, who was riding their way, with a full head of steam. Right away, the two slave handlers felt something was seriously wrong, back at the main house. But when Buscit heard his father tell Duval, he was wanted back at the mansion, the boy no longer feared that something was wrong with his mother, as he watched the Cajun ride off in a cloud of dust.

"Come in, Mr. Duval," Mr. Arnold said while firmly holding a cigar between his teeth.

Rather then telling the foolish slave owner he was already in the room, Duval spent his time scanning the area between the four walls. And what the Cajun found, made him think, of something his father said many years ago. Something about how a group of flies could be sitting on a pile of shit, feeling rich.

As Duval caught sight of Mr. Arnold sitting high in his old chair, it reminded him of an old Mardi Gras King, he saw many years ago. But Mr. Arnold weren't as bad, as the woman sitting next to Mrs.

Arnold. For the woman held the look of a hungry gator, as her eyes walked up and down the Cajun's long slim body. And if the man standing in front of the fireplace had the misfortune of being her husband, then Duval knew there would surely be a bad moon rising. Yet, the man from Louisiana had seen his kind many times before. For the man would surely talk loud, but never answer the challenge to a duel.

After standing, Mr. Arnold spoke rather proudly, as he said, "Let me introduce you to my brother in law Richard. Richard Norris."

"I have heard much about you, Mr. Duval. I hope, I get the chance to see you perform a few of your miracles, while I'm here," Richard said, as he held his hand out, in an attempt to give Duval a firm shaking.

While looking out the window at a slave chopping wood, Duval ignored Richard, as well as his well groomed hand. And knowing what kind of man he hired, Mr. Arnold stepped across Richard's waiting hand, and took Duval by the shoulder.

"Mr. Duval, before my husband get to talking, let me introduce you to my sister Ruth," Mrs. Arnold said.

"Woman, will you let me handle this," Mr. Arnold barked.

Knowing that a gator fight can get pretty nasty, Duval moved quickly, before the swamp became a resident of chaos. And after side stepping his boss, Duval walked over to Ruth, and properly introduced himself.

"Excuse my manners, madam, I go by the name, Duval," the Cajun said, with a touch of Louisiana charm.

"Is that your first or last name?" Ruth asked, as her eyes spoke a language of their own.

"It's my name," Duval said rather nonchalantly.

"Well in that case, I guess we will have to find you another one," Ruth teased, while holding her hand out, as if she wished it to be kissed.

"Then I bid you, and your husband good day, ma'am."

Feeling he had served his boss well, Duval offered up a gentleman's bow, catching everyone off guard. And as he headed for the door, Ruth, as well as the others, sat clueless on their lump of shit.

"Aren't you forgetting something?" Mr. Arnold asked, rather boldly.

"Your horses will be waiting," Duval said, standing in the doorway.

Just like Ruth, Mr. Arnold had been blindsided by Duval's Cajun wit. And while the man of the house was left to find a way to save face, his wife was enjoying every minute of Duval's shrewd, yet bold mannerism. In fact, Mrs. Arnold found it hard to keep from laughing out loud, as she sat hiding her face with Ruth's clean white handkerchief.

"I can see, that man needs a bit of a shaving," Richard said, looking at his wife.

"I wouldn't want to be the man, to try such a fool hearted thing," Mr. Arnold uttered, as he stood with his back to everyone.

After three days of meeting and greeting, Mrs. Arnold and Ruth had grown tired of their husbands. And like all women, the two sisters knew exactly what to do. The women sent their husbands out to play. And as the two men headed out of the door, Ruth suggested they go hang out with Duval for a while.

With their husbands gone, Mrs. Arnold decided to show off her collection of paintings. "And this is a little jewel, I picked up in Paris," Mrs. Arnold said, while pointing to a painting at the top of the spiral staircase.

Ruth took one look at the large tree that sat in the center of the autumn painting, and imagine her self being a part of the canvas. The sex crazy woman could see her hands flat against the dark brown bark, while she stood firmly bent at the waist. Her dress and undergarments were thrown among the red and yellow leaves, along with Duval's boots. She imagined herself stock naked, as Duval stood behind her, working his staff like a prize bull. Ruth's body began to moisten, as she could feel the cold wind on her pale white skin, while wrestling with the Cajun's violent hunger. And just as Ruth imagined her hot pink walls creaming all over Duval's firm hard erection, she was rudely interrupted.

"What on earth, are you thinking about?" Mrs. Arnold asked, as she stood staring at Ruth, toying with her breast.

Ruth cleared her throat, and walked away, as if she didn't hear the little spoiled brat, that just so happen to be a woman, a wife, and a mother.

Mr. Arnold and Richard flanked Duval, as the three men came upon Lamar and his crew. And as the crisp October wind danced through the Southern trees, Mr. Arnold proudly looked out at the bountiful crop, which continued to bring him great wealth. But before Mr. Arnold could start his boasting, and long before Richard could assess anything about Duval's system, the visitor sought to give the Cajun a few pointers.

"I think you would fair a lot better, if you were to work all of the slaves together," Richard said, as if he wrote some sort of owner's manual, on how to properly work slaves.

With no desire to comment on Richard's unwanted advice, Duval rode off by himself, leaving the man to give his brother in law an inquisitive stare. And just like Duval's action, Mr. Arnold found Richard's look to be a bit disturbing, as the two proceeded to catch up with the Cajun. And while Mr. Arnold called out to the man who ran his massive plantation, the Cajun pretended not to hear him. Yet the man from the Bayou knew he had no other choice, but to wait for the two men, as he brought his horse to a stop.

When the unlikely pair caught up with the Cajun, Richard spoke with a touch of brass. "Sir, must I remind you, that you are in the employment of my brother in law?"

While looking at Richard's fancy riding boots, Duval tried once again, to drag the visitor into the swamp. "No more den you have to remind me, dat skunks and snakes, don't make for good company. Now if dere isn't any ding else, I have work to do," Duval said, as he could feel his bad moon rising.

With his point made, Duval rode off again, hoping Richard would give chase. But when the Cajun saw he wasn't being followed, the man from Louisiana grunted with disappointment.

"I see, I will have to take him down a peg or two, before I leave here," Richard said, as he squeezed the handle to his pistol.

"Then I suggest, you get your affairs in order," Mr. Arnold uttered, while checking his cigar, as he held a suspicious smile.

That night when Duval entered his shack, he abruptly stopped at the door. The sight of Ruth sitting at the small table, that was a part of the east wall, sent signals running through the Cajun's head. And as he stood in the doorway, Duval noticed Ruth's undergarments resting on the vacant chair, along with her right leg. And on the table, sat an opened bottle of brandy, waiting to fill the empty glass that found no comfort in courting Ruth's tapping on the table. For it was a sight that would have started a fire in the average man, yet Duval stood staring angrily at the woman, as she teased the half filled glass, which she held in her left hand.

"You like to play cards, Mr. Duval?" Ruth asked, while seductively moving her leg from the chair, and placing it on the table, next to the man's deck of cards.

With her leg resting a little higher, Ruth flashed Duval a card. It was the ace of hearts. Ruth then looked at the card with a smile, as she slowly manipulated her petticoat.

"Do I disgust you, Mr. Duval?"

"Where is she?" Duval asked, in a demanding tone.

Ruth stood up and took her slow sweet time walking over to the doorway. And once there, she placed the glass to Duval's lips, while toying with her breast.

"Why Mr. Duval, who on earth could you be talking about?" she asked, while undoing the top button to her dress.

Without saying a word, Duval took Ruth by the arm, and led her out in to the darkness. He then went back into the shack, and closed the door behind him.

"Oh," Ruth said, as she took a step back.

When the door, came flying open again, Ruth could clearly tell, she had rubbed Duval the wrong way.

"You married him, now deal with him," Duval said, as he placed the brandy, along with the empty glass, and the clean white undergarment in Ruth's arms.

Duval then went back into the shack once more, and closed the door behind him, leaving Ruth alone in the dark. And after picking her ego up off of the ground, Ruth downed the rest of the brandy she had been sipping on, right before starting, what would be a long dreadful walk back to the mansion.

On her way up the spiral stair case, Ruth spotted Mrs. Arnold sitting alone in the dark, with nothing but the fireplace lighting the room. Knowing that her little sister was born hating the dark, Ruth started back down the stairs.

"When did you start sitting in the dark," Ruth asked, while standing over her baby sister.

Shifting her drink from one hand to the other, Mrs. Arnold spoke angrily. "Do you have any idea, where our husbands are?"

"I tend not to worry about my husband, and the things he use to entertain himself," Ruth replied, while pouring herself a drink.

"Well you should," Mrs. Arnold barked. "And where have you been?"

"Out for a worthless walk," Ruth snapped, then took a sip from her glass.

"You were always too loose, for mother's comfort," Mrs. Arnold said, looking up at her sister.

"I wouldn't be too quick, to tell some one what mother said, seeing that it was her and grandmother, who taught me everything that I know," Ruth said, as she left the room, still clinging to her drink.

After thrusting her glass into the fireplace, Mrs. Arnold shouted, "I forbid you, to speak ill of our mother, and grandmother, in my home."

"Why you poor little thing you, you have so much to learn, before you leave this old world," Ruth said with sass, as her slow southern drawl, made the statement sound almost contemptuous.

"What so ever I learn, you can bet, I won't end up a harlot," Mrs. Arnold shouted from the bottom of the stairs.

"Better wet, then dry, I always say," Ruth shouted, then let out a wicket laugh, while closing the bedroom door.

Left with only the darkness for company once again, Mrs. Arnold sat at the bottom of the stairs, looking lost and bewildered. For the woman was so torn by her sister's statement, she didn't see Effie lurking in the dark. And that meant, the lady of the house, didn't see the disturbing look in Effie's eyes. A look which said, the slave held thoughts of ill intent. Nor did Mrs. Arnold see Effie appear to vanish in to thin air, just moments before the sound of horses trotting on the cobble stones came rumbling through the house.

After spending three nights alone, Duval came to the conclusion, Ruth had persuaded her husband to purchased Ella from Mr. Arnold. And as he entered his dark shack, Duval tried to come up with a suitable replacement, to take Ella's place along side him at night. That girl I took from Lamar, might be worth a try, Duval thought to himself, as he picked up Ruth scent in the small shack. Duval then tried to focus his eyes, on what appeared to be water sitting in the middle of the floor, as he grabbed the lantern from the wall, and put a match to it.

"Are you lonely, Mr. Duval?" Ruth asked, while lying across the small bed like a whore. "As you can see, Mr. Duval, I have a way of getting what I want, when I want it," Ruth bragged, as she sat up in the bed.

Duval turned his head away from Ruth for a moment, to take a look at the tub of water that was waiting for him in the middle of the room.

"It's just the way you like it," Ruth said, while toying with the ribbon on her dress."

"You have no idea, of what I like," Duval replied.

"But the one who prepared it, does," Ruth confessed, as she fell back down onto the bed, holding some what of a dead smile.

"Stand up," Duval said firmly.

Ruth quickly pounced to her feet, holding the thought, she was about to remove Duval's clothing from his Cajun body. But she was quickly taken back, when the man from Louisiana uttered the words, down on your knees.

"Pardon me?" Ruth grumbled, as if she couldn't believe her ears.

"You heard me," Duval replied, as his eyes walked down Ruth's well shaped body.

Ruth had a good deal of breast, and her ass, sat well and round, as if she were a white slave, waiting to be mistreated.

"And then what?" Ruth asked boldly.

"Then you will crawl, to me."

Ruth laughed, as she couldn't believe the man had the audacity to say such a thing to her. For it was she, who held the line of control, and Ruth wasn't about to give it up.

"Go back to your husband," Duval snarled, as he made a move toward the door.

"Wait," Ruth shouted softly, in a near state of panic.

Duval stopped and sighed, as if he had grown disgusted with the woman. He then cut his Cajun eyes in her direction, and waited for his demand to be met. And like the man from Louisiana expected, Ruth went down on her knees. Yet it wasn't the fact of what she did, as much, as how she did it. For Ruth grudgingly lowered her body to the floor, while never taking her eyes off of Duval. And the look that covered the woman's face was unbecoming of her, as she hoped to please the man, who was nearly impossible to satisfy.

"Is there anything else, you would like me to do, while I am down here?" Ruth asked, after crawling for the first time in her adult life.

"You can wash my back," Duval said, as he began to take his shirt off.

Ruth stood up and looked around, as if she didn't know what to do with herself. The woman who took pride in making men beg for her attention, found herself on the wrong side of the painful experience. And as she watched Duval take his long johns off, Ruth began to have second thoughts about tangling with the Cajun. For the man's dick hung as long, as any slave Ruth had ever wrestled with. She swallowed, and prayed for Duval not to be one of those men, who like to force feed women, all of their long hanging club. For if the Cajun was that kind of man, Ruth knew she was in for a long hard night.

When it came time for Ruth to wash Duval's back, the woman found herself trembling like a fresh cut virgin, trying to hold on to her virginity. Yet that didn't stop Ruth from putting the towel to Duval's chest, before washing his back. And as she stood behind him, stroking the two humps that sat between his throat and his log cabin mid section, Ruth stared at what was to be her evening meal. A meal, that would surely, fill her up, no matter, how she feasted on it.

It was nearing mid night, when Ruth stood in Duval's doorway, kissing his hanging dick goodbye. Yet the way Ruth's mouth pulled on the limp joint, told Duval, the woman would surely stay, if he asked her to. But the man from Louisiana was no home wrecker, and he always remembered the things his father taught him. And the ones that always stuck in his head, had something to do with women.

And no matter how hard he tried, Duval couldn't stop himself from thinking of the one that often made him smile. And in no time flat, he was saying the statement in his head.

"And what are you thinking about?" Ruth asked.

"Nothing," Duval replied, as he could here the words, another man's trash, is no treasure, for it is just more trash for you to deal with.

"Then tell me, Mr. Duval. How does it feel to lose?" Ruth asked, pulling the man away from the old saying.

Seeing that Ruth was the one on her knees, Duval took the time to set the record straight. "Dere's an old saying in da Bayou. Da man who give's a woman what she wants, will get some ding in return. But da man, who can make her crawl, will get all dat she has to give."

Ruth understood every word of the old saying, as she took hold of the wall, to support her effort to stand. And when Duval tried to help her up, Ruth angrily refused his act of kindness. For the woman felt, she had given the man from Louisiana more then her all. And Ruth surely didn't open herself up, just so he could talk down to her, as if she were some common field slave. So while being choked by an unfamiliar emotion, Ruth backed away from Duval, trying not to show the pain, which she felt deep with in her soul.

As the man from Louisiana closed his door, the Bayou blade slinger knew, he had struck a bad chord on Ruth's piano of life. Yet Duval couldn't bring himself to feel sorry for a wife, who was hell bent on being a loose woman. Nor did the Cajun forget how hard he had tried to avoid, what may be Ruth's only defeat, in her little game of seduction. But knowing the woman would never allow herself to face the truth, the Cajun felt he had no other choice, but to reveal the true loser, in a game, women have been dominating, long before men started wearing shoes.

When Ruth found herself on the train bound for home, she pretended to be reading a book. And as she sat by the window enjoying the breeze, Ruth's mind was as far from reading, as she was from being an angel. Yet the woman went on staring at the second page of chapter one, while feeling their trip home, was a lot like her marriage, too long and cumbersome. And no matter how hard she tried, Ruth couldn't stop thinking of the man, who filled her mouth with his salty seeds.

"Are you reading something that I should know about?" Richard asked, while watching his wife, lick her lips.

Ruth didn't utter a word in return, as she slowly withdrew her tongue back into its hiding place. Nor did the woman care to cast her eyes upon the half worthless piece of shit, she were doom to spend the rest of her life with. For Ruth felt sick, knowing that her life was built around a marriage of convenience, to a man who happens to be worthless and weak, not worthy of her body, nor her time.

With Ruth well on her way home, Mrs. Arnold stood staring out of the parlor window, refusing to believe the things she heard about her family. But most of all, the woman was not about to believe the things she heard about their mother. And feeling she had no other choice but to write their mother about the matter, Mrs. Arnold headed for her bedroom. There, she could sit in the chair by the window, and write her tattletale letter.

> Dear Mother:
> I am well, how are you? I am writing this letter, as a matter of concern. Concern that ill words has been falsely laid. My dearest sister Ruth, in her hastens to help me, has miss spoken the truth. She told me it was you and grandmother, who taught her how to be the woman that she is. Mother, I find that hard to believe, being that you and grandmother are such virtuous women. But mother, you must be honest with me. Are these things true?
> Love Always
> Agnes

Mrs. Arnold prepared the letter for transport, just before returning to her chair by the window. And as she stared out across her husband's land, that was well over four square miles, Mrs. Arnold saw Effie. The well dressed house slave, was walking pass the other slaves, as if she were not one her self. Needless to say, the sight of Effie strolling across the yard, made Mrs. Arnold feel a tad bit more then sick. And in a flash, the women wished Effie would fall dead. But Mrs.

Arnold knew her husband would only replace that ungodly creature with another, and there was nothing she could do about it. But while Mrs. Arnold thought of Effie's neck and an axe, she spotted a young slave boy name Jonathan. And through the boy's dirty cloths and uncombed hair, Mrs. Arnold saw something hidden. Something that said Ruth may not have been as ill, as one might have thought. And as Mrs. Arnold wondered what the boy would look like, if she were to give him a bath, and a set of clean cloths, a yearning came over the woman, like nothing she had ever felt before. For Mrs. Arnold had to turn her head in shame, as she found herself with thoughts, which was far from being that of a lady.

By mid summer, Mrs. Arnold had gotten a response to the letter she wrote her mother. It came in the form of five feet, and four inches of female flesh. For the woman felt such matters, should never be discussed through the art of letter writing. So with hopes of keeping her secrets intact, the woman made an unannounced visit to the Big A plantation. And with her every step, were two beautiful black females. The lovely African beauties were in their late twenties, and very well dressed. And behind the two beautiful females, stood three powerfully built male slaves, loaded down with suitcases and handbags.

"Mother," Mrs. Arnold shouted, as she bolted down the stairs, like some over active child.

With her arms stretched out like a goose ready to take flight, Mrs. Arnold ran up to the big bosom woman, begging to be hugged. But no amount of joy and jubilation could cut through the woman's look of disgust, as her eyes fell on Effie, who was standing in front of the parlor door.

"Where is daddy?" Mrs. Arnold asked, with a great deal of enthusiasm.

In a tone, cold enough to send chills up a polar bear's spine, the woman said, "Your father is busy, dealing with those meddlesome fools from the North."

"But I wanted to see him," Mrs. Arnold cried.

"Will you grow up, and take control of yourself," the woman barked, while still staring at Effie. "I thought you would have gotten rid of that wretched slave by now."

Mrs. Arnold turned to see Effie walking away. "I would give anything, to rid myself of that filthy witch."

"Some times, you must fight fire, with fire, my dear," the woman said, as she led Mrs. Arnold toward the staircase, with her two beautiful black beauties, following them step for step.

"I see we have another visitor," Mr. Arnold said, standing by the parlor door, giving the women, the indication he had just walked out of the room.

"And I can see, the winds of change, have yet to blow low," the large breasted woman said, as she made her way up the circling stairs.

Feeling that her bedroom was a personal place, Mrs. Arnold looked at the two female slaves, as if they were intruding. But before she could speak a word, her mother quickly took charge.

"There is nothing sadder, then a lady who has no control," the woman said, looking at her girls. "I don't know which is worst. A lady who think, she is in love, or one who desire to be loved, and can never find it," the woman went on to say, as she held a look of disgust on her face.

And seeing the look of complete and utter stupidity in her daughter's eyes, the woman sought to make her point a little clearer.

"That ungrateful son of a snake, can no more love you, then he could that slave, that the both of you seem to fancy," the woman growled.

"But what am I to do?" Mrs. Arnold asked.

"You must learn how to love your self, my dear," the woman replied arrogantly.

"And how am I to do that?" Mrs. Arnold asked, looking confused.

"Girls," the woman said, while staring at her daughter.

When the two female slaves began to kiss, and feel on her mother with a great deal of passion, Mrs. Arnold nearly lost the well cooked breakfast, she ate nearly an hour earlier.

"Mother, how could you do such a thing," Mrs. Arnold cried, while turning away in disgust.

"Because I will always love my self, before I love anyone else. And my girls are more then just my eyes and ears. And if you want to make that son of a dog suffer, then I have a friend, who has two young females that will serve you well."

Not wanting to hear what her mother had to say, Mrs. Arnold went to her chair by the window and cried. But if the spoiled child, thought her actions were going to change the big bosom woman in any way, form, or fashion, then she was sadly mistaken.

"Ruth was right. Your father has made you weak. And that is why your husband, will forever march over you like the army of Jericho," the woman said, as she tried to talk some sense, in to her husband's most favorite child.

"I don't care, I will never lay with a female, slave or other wise," Mrs. Arnold said, through her crying.

"Then get yourself a male. Or better yet, maybe you need to give that Mr. Duval a try. I hear, he has everything, a good night can offer a lady."

"I am not Ruth."

"Nor, are you satisfied. Now I will be in town, if you should need me," the woman said, turning away.

"But I thought you were going to stay here," Mrs. Arnold cried, as if she were still the little girl, who clung to her mother's every move.

"I would love to oblige you, my dear, but I never sleep alone," the woman said, as she pulled the two beauites close to her body.

While responding to her daughter's unkindly stare, the woman spoke, after taking a brake from kissing one of the girls. "I have been doing this, long before you were born, and I am not about to stop, not even to please your father. Now there is nothing, I can't ask my girls to do, yet you can not, say that about your ungreatful husband."

Mrs. Arnold watched the bedroom door, as it slowly closed behind her mother and the two female slaves. And when she found herself alone, Mrs. Arnold took to pacing the floor. And she continued to repeat the same five steps, while pondering the things her mother had said. But the spoiled young woman had her self respect, and she was not about to throw it away, no matter what her mother and Ruth did, to get even with their husbands. For Mrs. Arnold was dead set on living a monogamous life. But after returning to her chair, the lady of the house had to wonder, why she held a certain fascination for the young slave boy. And why did he have to appear, when she had so much to think about.

"You's need anything, ma'am," a slave girl asked, while standing in the doorway.

Before she knew it, Mrs. Arnold found herself standing with her back against the window, looking at her chair, as if she couldn't remember leaving it. And after taking a deep breath, before clearing her throat, Mrs. Arnold then turned back to the window. "What is that ungrateful slave's, name?" she asked, while pointing at Jonathan.

"Jonathan, ma'am," the girl said, after walking over to the window, and casting her eyes on the slave.

Mrs. Arnold just stared at Jonathan, as if there was something on her mind. Something that made her softly mumbled the words, why should I love myself.

"Ma'am," the girl asked, as her ears could not capture Mrs. Arnold's statement.

"Leave me," Mrs. Arnold said, as she stood like a woman, trying to hug herself.

While the slave girl humbly did as she was told, the poor female was unaware, that Mrs. Arnold asked her what was Jonathan's name, rather then saying, what do my husband, call him.

Chapter 7

The Change

The next five years, brought the Big A plantation many things. A few months after Clora Lee's first year, she had stolen her first kiss. The bold little slave, toddled over to Cowayne, and took hold of his hair. Then with all of her might, Clora Lee pulled his head back and laid her wet lips to Sistah's struggling baby. And no matter how hard Cowayne fought, the little pleasure seeker held on to him, until Duval intervened.

"I DONE TOLD YOU, GIRL, you can't be taking pleasure, until I tell you to," Duval said, after pulling Clora Lee off of her unwilling participant.

No sooner then Cowayne made it to his feet, he rumbled pass old Mae, and went straight to Sistah for protection. But the damage was done, as he stood between Sistah's legs, clinging to the look of a petrified possum. And while everyone enjoyed a good laugh, the old slave looked at the children, as if something was eating at her soul.

While time took Cowayne from the horror of his first kiss, to allowing Clora Lee to lip lock him at will, their's, as well as the fate of the wealthy plantation owners, appeared to be already carved in stone.

One by one, the plantation owners rode into town, to discuss their latest problem. And with the Big A being the largest, and the most profitable plantation in the valley, that meant everyone had to wait on Mr. Arnold. And like always, the arrogant slave owner had to be the last one to arrive.

"I guess, God had to take his time again," a gray headed old man whispered to a much younger gentleman.

"God, I was thinking more on the line of Devil," the younger man whispered in return.

"I am getting sick, of conducting business, with that got damn slave in the room," a man standing behind the two gentlemen uttered softly.

"I wonder if that old slave is there, when he bed down that young wife of his," the younger man said under his breath.

"Some one has to ride that pretty little filly," the old man whispered, causing the two younger men to chuckle.

"I didn't know we came here to socialize," Mr. Arnold spat, while standing next to the Mayor.

The room became silent for a moment, paving the way, for the meeting to start. Yet there was really no need for the gathering, being there was only one way for the men to vote. And as the plantation owners knew all to well, how things were going to turn out, the men still cast their ceremonial vote just the same.

When the men finished taking their symbolic vote, they headed for the saloon, to carry out the often disturbing, yet equally important, second half of what had to be an ugly tradition. For it was time to give those who had no tomorrow, their final farewell.

As the wealthy slave owners, slowly entered the saloon, their presence sent a pair of everyday patrons shuffling to the far side of the room. And even though the men walked across the hard wood floor with their noisy shoes, you could barely hear their footsteps, as they headed for the bar. For it was the bar, which would speak without saying a word, as it often told the bartender, all that he needed to know. And yes, the man would surely tell his evening crowd about those who didn't walk away, until they were sloppy drunk. For those would be the ones without a future.

After finishing their customary drink, the men left the saloon in the exact same manner, in which they entered it. But unfortunately for the rich plantation owners, they had to leave one of their own behind. For it was the old gray headed man, that found Mr. Arnold's grand entrance, as an act of arrogance. And while downing his second drink the man had to face the fact, that Mr. Arnold would be the one most likely to buy him out, lock, stock, and barrel.

"Leave it," the old man said, referring to the bottle of whiskey that sat on the bar.

Backing away from the bar, the bartender knew the man would finish the bottle off. And if the nearly full bottle of whiskey didn't do the job, then the bartender would surely be giving the gentleman a second bottle.

The next morning, while Mr. Arnold sat eating breakfast, Jeremiah entered the dinning room and whispered in his ear. The selfish slave owner dropped his eating utensils, and before taking a sip of coffee, from the very expensive cup, he told Jeremiah to get their horses ready.

"Is something wrong?" Mrs. Arnold asked, as she went about cutting the strip of meat, which sat in the middle of her plate.

"It appears, I'm going to get that old goat's land, a lot cheaper then I thought," Mr. Arnold replied, as he stood finishing off his cup of coffee.

The wealthy, self centered slave owner, was so caught up in the opportunity at hand, he never noticed the look on his wife's face. For the woman held a look that said, she was more interested in cutting the thin slab of meat, then anything the man could spew from his ugly mouth. And while her husband went about putting on his coat, Mrs. Arnold continued to cut away at the meat, as if she was trying to saw clean through the high dollar plate, which had been in the man's family for years. And as Mrs. Arnold watched her husband leave the room with his most favorite slave, she quickly bought the knife to a rest, and got up from the table.

By the time Mr. Arnold returned home with the deed to the man's property, as well as a leg up on his rivals, he was not prepared for what was going on in his home. And as he ran through the giant house, shouting for his wife, a slave name Obdi, told him, the lady of the house was up stairs.

Filled with excitement, Mr. Arnold bolted up the staircase. And with every step he took, the man shouted, as if a mess of Northern abolitionist were invading his lovely home. But to Mr. Arnold's surprise, his wife was nowhere in sight. And when he spotted the young slave girl Sally, coming out of a room, she had no business being in, all hell broke lose.

"What in the blazes, are you doing?" Mr. Arnold asked, as he stood in the doorway of the empty room.

"There is such a thing, call knocking," Mrs. Arnold replied, as she went about washing the young slave girl's hair.

"If you don't send that slave back out to those fields, I'll…"

"You will what?" Mrs. Arnold snapped, as she leaped to her feet, denying her husband the right to speak.

The woman's sudden response caught her husband by surprise. And while he stood speechless, his wife decided to inform him about a few changes that were about to take place.

"No matter what you may think, my girls are not a part of your private collection. And under no circumstances, are you to ever speak to them. Now get out, and don't ever enter this room again," Mrs. Arnold yelled.

"Woman, if you think, I am going to let you raise your voice to me, in my home, then your mother, has taught you wrong," Mr. Arnold yelled, as if he were shouting at a slave.

"Then I suggest, you get one of your slaves, to pack my things, because I will be leaving," Mrs. Arnold said, standing her ground.

Before Mr. Arnold knew it, he had raised his hand to strike the wife, who was in her early stages of bearing his second child. But being wise for the first time in his life, Mr. Arnold didn't allow the hand he would undoubtly lose, to come crashing down on the woman. He just stood with his hand suspended, as if it were hanging from the ceiling.

Seeing that her husband wasn't the fool her mother thought he was, Mrs. Arnold some what repeated herself. "We will discuss this further, when I am finish," she said softly, then went back to washing the young slave girl's hair.

By the time winter had set in, Mr. Arnold found himself far away from home, in the Nation's Capital. There was serious talk coming out of the North, threaten to change the Southern way of life, and it had to be dealt with. And who was better equipped to deal with those meddling fools from the North, then the good proud Southern boys, who were hell bent on war. So with fire in their eyes, and hate in their hearts, the proud men from the South, stormed into the District of Columbia, looking to give the Northern trouble makers a piece of Southern hospitality.

While the men strutted around Washington arguing over change, Mrs. Arnold was slowly crafting herself a bold new image. And for the woman Ruth and everyone else took to be weak, there would be no debating her transformation. For the surprise visit from her mother, had been a real eye opening experience for Mrs. Arnold. No more would she wear the word wife, like the slaves wore the bands, which held their rings. No longer would she allow her husband the right of control. From that day forward, Mrs. Arnold vowed, to control her own life. And that meant, no more reporting her every move, to a man who was far from deserving of such a privilege. For Mrs. Arnold was a new woman, who no longer cared, about what people thought of her?

As Mrs. Arnold plan took shape, she became some what of a tyrant. The once soft mannered woman, walked through her home, armed with a riding crop. And knowing the woman rarely sat a horse, the house slaves saw the tool for its one true purpose. For it was a weapon, which Mrs. Arnold had every intentions of using? The slightest twitch, from even the smallest of slaves, would bring about a most disturbing response from the woman. And there was no mercy to be found in Mrs. Arnold, or the way she used her new toy.

With Mrs. Arnold's change, bringing a new form of Hell to the Big A plantation, Duval did his best to keep Clora Lee and Cowayne out of her reach. But with the two little slaves having to take on chores, it was virtually impossible, for Duval to protect them every minute of the day. And on a cold winter's morning, the Cajun's luck ran a ground.

With a small pail of milk in her tiny little hands, Clora Lee waddled across the icy ground, as she headed for the backdoor to the large white house. And from the moment she tottered out of the barn, Clora Lee locked her eyes on Cowayne, who was gathering firewood, just inches from the back steps. The same icy steps, Clora Lee was trying her best to reach. But no matter the task, the little slave still found time to poke fun at her friend. So with a sudden case of the sniffles, Clora Lee called out to Cowayne, like a baby sparrow to its mother. And it didn't take long for Cowayne's dark face to light up, when he saw Clora Lee struggling with the pale of milk. But the little girl didn't mind her struggle, as much as she hated walking across the icy ground, which she was starting to ignore.

By the time Clora Lee reached the steps, the little slave was paying far too much attention to Cowayne, and not nearly enough to the hardest part of her journey. And just as she placed her left foot on the first step, Clora Lee shot Cowayne one more playful look. But things didn't go exactly the way the little slave thought they would, as she shot Cowayne the funny looking face. And before the face could take affect on her friend, Clora Lee had let out a loud scream, while on her way to the cold hard ground.

Standing in the kitchen, dishing out her orders as if she were on a battlefield, Mrs. Arnold couldn't help but to hear the scream. And her reaction to such a scream, didn't take long, as the kitchen door swung open, taking in every ounce of cold air that Mother Nature had stored away for the winter.

"Who is the blame for this?" Mrs. Arnold shouted.

"I's uh made her fall, ma'am," Cowayne said, before Clora Lee could open her mouth.

Some how, Clora Lee didn't hear Cowayne take the blame for her careless mistake. Maybe it was because she couldn't stop staring at Effie, who just so happen, to be standing in the kitchen window. For the first time in her young life, Clora Lee saw the emptiness, that Ethel had often spoke of, as she sat in the wet snow.

"Don't just sit their, gal, get up, and go get some more milk," Mrs. Arnold spat, as she stood over Clora Lee.

If anyone would have asked the little girl, there was no way, she could have told them how, or when the woman had made her way down the steps. For Clora Lee was too caught up in Effie's eyes, to notice anything else.

"And you boy. Take off that coat, and that shirt," Mrs. Arnold said, as if her mouth could spit fire.

While Cowayne proceeded to remove the old tattered coat, which several young slaves had worn before him, Clora Lee picked herself up out of the snow. And while the two little slaves, went about doing as they were told, neither had the courage to look at the other. For both Clora Lee and Cowayne knew what would happen, if Mrs. Arnold were to get her petticoat in a wad. So while Cowayne dropped the coat from his shoulders, Clora Lee grabbed the pail and ran for the barn.

By the time Clora Lee had reached the old faded structure, she was more then ready to look at her friend. So with her body resting between the doors, Clora Lee waited to witness Cowayne's fate. But before Mrs. Arnold ever raised her personal piece of Hell, the little slave disappeared from the doorway.

"I's knows, Sistah done taught ya better," a slave name Thomas, whispered as he dragged Clora Lee from the door.

For Thomas was the old slave, who had given Clora Lee the pail of warm milk, that was growing cold in the snow.

"Come on here, so I's uh can show you's ha to milk this here old cow," Thomas whispered, as Clora Lee struggled to free herself from his grasp. "You's don't need to watch that," the gray headed slave said, as he sat down on the stool, and placed Clora Lee between his legs.

But Clora Lee couldn't help but to watch her friend, being that the wind had blown the doors open again. And from where she stood, Clora Lee didn't only see Cowayne, the little slave saw Mrs. Arnold as well. But it was the sight of Mrs. Arnold's riding crop that made the little slave vow, to get even with the source of her pain, no matter how long it took. And when Clora Lee saw Cowayne offer up his back for sacrifice, she began to tremble like a leaf on a tree.

Seeing that the little slave needed something to pull her attention away from what was about to happen, Thomas placed Clora Lee's hands on the cow's tits, and squeezed them. But no amount of milk, squirting into a thousand pails, could have stopped Clora Lee from hearing the thunderous licks, which her friend volunteered to take in her behalf. And like three bolts of lightning, the licks seared a hate in Clora Lee, she would hold for all eternity.

"You's hush, or the Misses gon knows you's done it," Thomas said, of Clora Lee's crying. "And if n she's knows he's done lied to her, she's uh kill him dead, cause she's uh evil old witch," Thomas warned the child. "Na you's take this here milk, and don't you's ever forget what he's done for ya."

After Thomas used his shirt to wipe the tears from Clora Lee's face, he escorted the little girl to the door. And as he pushed the doors open wider, Clora Lee drew deep into her nostrils, a healthy helping of the frigid air. Then like a bull aiming to kill the matador, Clora Lee violently discharged the air from her body, thus signaling another long fearful journey across the icy ground. And just like before, Clora Lee eyes never left Cowayne for a moment, as she repeated her steps through the snow.

Reaching the menacing back steps for the second time, Clora Lee watched, as Cowayne picked his coat up out of the snow. And as she carefully placed her left foot on the first ice covered step, Clora Lee eyes begged for Cowayne to look at her. But Clora Lee wasn't about to get her wish, as Cowayne kept his eyes on the patch of snow covered ground, which rested before his feet. And feeling that Cowayne was mad at her, Clora Lee felt empty, as she started up the icy steps, looking like a lost dream.

Entering the kitchen, Clora Lee found Mrs. Arnold to be madder then ever. And as she stood listening to the woman's yelling, Clora Lee no longer feared her, nor the black thing that caused Cowayne a great deal of pain. And to prove her point, Clora Lee set out to call the woman's hand. For the little girl stared at Mrs. Arnold with her grandfather's eyes. Yet the little slave's stare was short lived, thanks to Effie. For the special slave had accidentally touched Clora Lee on the shoulder with a hot pot. Yet after jumping, while crying out softly, Clora Lee continued to hold on to the pail of milk.

"You's give me, this here milk," Effie snarled, as she took the pail from Clora Lee's hands.

No longer weighed down with the heavy pail, Clora Lee left the house running. And the little girl didn't stop, until she reached the very last stall in that old faded barn. There, Clora Lee found a pile of hay that was perfectly suited for a little slave, who was in need of a good cry. Yet Clora Lee wasn't the only one crying in the barn that day. For Thomas was crying as well. Yet his tears were falling for a totally different reason. It appeared, the gray headed slave was crying from the shame, which dwelled deep inside of him. And Thomas knew there was no way, he could rid him self of the unsettling shame, that dwelt deep in his bones.

By the time dust had came over the plantation, the field slaves were marching in like a flock of geese, flying South for the winter. And like she had done for the past six years, Sistah rushed off to find her baby. But when Sistah found her Cowayne, she was greeted with a bit of rejection. Yet the misfortunate slave went right on giving her poor performance of a hog, as she grunted her way up to Cowayne. And as Sistah carried on with her joking, Cowayne held steadfast to his corner, while Clora Lee did the same, on the opposite side of the large shed.

Seeing that something wasn't right, Sistah went to her baby, and took a seat next to him. "What's wrong with my baby?" Sistah asked, as she tried to hug Cowayne.

But in the corner of the female shed, Sistah got some what of a startling surprise. Never in her life, could Sistah have dreamed Cowayne would reject her loving embrace. Nor did Sistah notice that Cowayne didn't give his usual reply, which was, I's uh not no baby. But the misfortunate slave did notice how her baby flinched, when she went to hold him, and that sent Sistah spiraling out of control.

With her mind running wild, Sistah scooped Cowayne up in her arms, and dashed out of the shed with him. There was only one place the dysfunctional mother could go, and Sistah didn't stop, until she reached old Mae. But Sistah had no idea, her crazy love for Cowayne, was doing more harm then good. Nor did Sistah notice that Clora Lee wasn't following her.

"Mae! Mae! Something wrong with my baby, Mae," Sistah shouted, as she fell to her knees, while still clutching Cowayne tightly.

"You's let me see him, na Sistah," old Mae said, as she stood in the food line in front of Pleasant.

But Sistah couldn't respond to the old slave's request, as she continued to cry, while rocking back and forward with her precious Cowayne.

Like always, Duval was on top of the problem, faster then a humming bird could flap its wings. "Get dat boy," Duval said to Pleasant.

But if the Cajun was banking on Pleasant closeness to Sistah, then the man was sadly mistaken. For when Pleasant attempted to carry out Duval's order, he was met with a strong resistance. The moment Pleasant reached for Cowayne, Sistah commenced to slapping the poor slave, any and every where she could. And Sistah's wild dysfunctional screaming, didn't help the situation, as Cowayne took to crying as well.

Knowing that he needed to get control of the problem, before it got out of hand, the moment Pleasant grabbed Cowayne, Duval made his presence felt.

"Sistah," Duval shouted, as he violently took hold of her right shoulder.

With one hard jerk, Duval had pulled Sistah back from Pleasant, which ultimately sent her crashing down to the cold hard ground. But in a flash, Sistah was back on her knees, reaching for Cowayne.

"Sistah, don't make me hit you," Duval said, after firmly placing his foot in the middle of the slave's back, thus sending the half wit female crashing face first in to the snow.

Through the whole ordeal, old Mae just stood trembling, knowing that once again, Duval was the blame for Sistah's pain. For it was he, who had given Cowayne to Sistah, now the man was punishing her with the little slave.

"My baby. My baby." Sistah cried out in pain.

"The Misses, beat him," Clora Lee shouted, then ran back toward the female shed.

"Let me have dat boy," Duval said, as old Mae was about to raise Cowayne's shirt.

With Cowayne in his possession, Duval slowly removed the little slave's shirt, thus revealing the three long fat scars that draped the child's back. And upon seeing the scars, Sistah immediately began to claw the earth. But no amount of clawing was going to stop the misfortunate female's pain, as her body laid stretched out on the icy ground.

Even though Duval wasn't at liberty to speak ill of the hand that paid him, he took Mrs. Arnold's action to be a bit cruel. And the Cajun knew, if the man of the house didn't have a talk with the woman, she would surely ruin his life. And for that reason, Duval was willing to stomach the bitch, until her husband made it home from his business in the Nation's Capital. Yet at that very moment, the Cajun had to find a way to keep from putting the whip to Sistah, as she continued to cry over her child.

"Get up, and go get some warm water, so you can wash dis boy back," Duval shouted, as he gave Sistah an encouraging kick.

As Duval walked off with out saying another word, old Mae noticed that the man's kicking of Sistah, was far from anything she had ever received. Yet old Mae couldn't help but to feel the man had did enough damage to Sistah, by tying her to Cowayne. And what poor Sistah was going to do, if their master ever took a notion to sell the boy. Old Mae felt Sistah was doomed, and not even the white man's God, in his giant white Heaven could help her.

"Sistah!" Duval shouted, when he returned holding a small can of ointment.

The bumbling slave came running with a pot of warm water, raring to take care of her son. But with her face, dress, and legs, coated with dirt and snow, Sistah needed just as much attention, as her child did. Yet the misfortunate female cared not for herself, but only of the son, she could not bring in to the world with her own body.

"Mae," Sistah cried.

For after making several attempts to touch the unsightly scars, Sistah realized, she didn't have what it took to do the job. And seeing that Sistah was suffering worst then any slave, who had taken their master's whip, old Mae answered the young mother's plea for help. But as the old slave tried to do what needed to be done, Sistah kept grabbing her hand, fearing the slightest touch, would cause her baby even more pain.

The next day after the female slaves were forced to suffer a night of Sistah's humming, Cowayne chores didn't take him any where near the main house. That meant Clora Lee was on her own, which gave Sistah a greater reason to worry. But she wasn't the only one worrying. For old Mae, Ethel, and Cowayne worried as well. And that kept the old slave burning God's ears, as she went about her work.

While everyone was worrying about her, Clora Lee entered the house, armed with a gift from old man Arnold himself. And as she stood in the kitchen, listening to Mrs. Arnold profess her sour mood, Clora Lee watched the house slaves search frantically for some lost cause. For the slaves were at a total lost, just like their Misses would for ever be, when it came down to possessing the Arnold's hate. For the only way to obtain such a hate, is to be born with it. And that was one thing Clora Lee would always have on the woman, who struck her Cowayne.

Seeing that she had no part in the royal search, Clora Lee placed the basket of eggs on the table, and quietly walked out of the door. And when Clora Lee returned with a pail of milk, Mrs. Arnold was still yelling to high Hell, as if the Devil had given her the keys to his beloved home. But Clora Lee went right on ignoring the woman and her yelling, as she placed the pail of milk at Effie's feet.

"I want it, and I want it now," Mrs. Arnold shouted, as she watched Clora Lee timidly shut the door behind her, while setting out to face the cold morning alone.

When Clora Lee closed the door behind her, she made eye contact with a little slave girl, which had the most peculiar look on her face. And even though the two only stared at each other for a brief moment, Clora Lee could tell the girl was hiding something. But Clora Lee wasn't going to let it bother her, seeing that she was faced with four slippery steps. So the little slave focused all of her attention on making it down the icy steps in one piece, as she could still hear Mrs. Arnold's voice ringing in her ears.

With Sistah's most hated winter being a thing of the past, the plantation was buzzing from the news, that some poor soul had made a run for it. But when old Mae got wind of who the runner was, she took a long hard look at Cowayne.

"What's wrong, Mae?" Sistah asked the old slave, while cleaning the cold from Cowayne's eyes.

"You's hush, bothering me," old Mae replied in a tone, Sistah had never heard her use before.

Though unintended, old Mae threw Sistah for a whirl. And with only the theft of Cowayne on her mind, Sistah quickly dropped her head, as if she were a child, who had just gotten caught sticking its finger in a freshly baked pie. But Cowayne had no intentions of seeing his second mother unhappy. So the little boy wrapped his arms around Sistah's head, and gave her a great big hug. And the hug was all that Sistah needed to bring her a joy, far greater then freedom. She began to flap her arms like a bird, thus bringing a smile to Cowayne and Clora Lee's face. And it didn't take long, for Sistah and her two babies, to end up hopping around like a trio of drunken cranes. And they continued to flap their arms and hop around, while making strange squawking sounds, until Sistah gave out, and fell to the ground. And just like everyone expected, Clora Lee and Cowayne ended up on the ground right along side of her.

"I don't reckon, I have ever seen a slave so happy," Lamar said, to chain master Johnson.

"I guess she don't mind being a slave, as long as she got them young ones with her," Johnson replied.

One morning, shortly after Thomas had made his run for Freedom, the slaves saw a group of strange men riding pass them, as they went about their work. The men were dirty and unshaven. They also possessed a disturbing atmosphere, that hung over them like a low hanging cloud. And their horses moved as if they were going somewhere dark and cold, far away from the living.

Old Mae looked up, just as a chill wrapped around her body like a tattered blanket. And something told the old slave, she didn't want to know the men, as they rode with death for a companion. And the men loved their companion with such a great passion, it was no doubting, they would gladly kill each other, for no more then to smell the vile stench of rotting flesh.

When the men came to a stop, they ended up in the most unlikely place of all. For they had made the unfortunate mistake, of riding up to the Big A front gate. And despite the old slave called Lewis, asking them to turn around and go to the west end of the plantation, the men walked their horses through the front gate, as if the faithful servant had moved his mouth without ever saying a word.

With more courage then any fool should possess, the men rode up to the front porch, and got off of their horses. And while their leader foolishly placed his filthy boots on the Arnold's front porch, they proceeded to remove Thomas lifeless body from their pack mule. And after their leader had banged the door knocker with his dirty hand, he found himself being greeted by Obdi. The man quickly shot his eyes on Obdi's right foot, and immediately went to counting his money.

"Morning, sir. How may I help you?" Obdi asked, as he stared at the object in the man's hand.

"You can go get your master," the slave hunter said, as he toyed with the ring, Thomas had been charge to wear.

Obdi closed the door, giving the men the impression, they were about to be received with open arms. But a moment later, when the door opened for the second time, life was truly different. And while the man stood playing with the bloody ring, as if it were a toy, Mr. Arnold stepped out on to the front porch, gripping a pistol in each hand. And right behind Mr. Arnold stood Jeremiah, who held two pistols as well.

"The hired help is received, at the backdoor," Mr. Arnold growled, while holding the pistol in his left hand to the man's head.

Finding themselves face to face with the death they so desperately loved, the men no longer desired the company of their passion. For the men constant companion had brought them full circle, to a house that took pride, in being perceived as the gateway to Hell.

"Well sir, I think we have something that belongs to you," the leader said, as his voice cracked with every word.

After looking at Thomas dead body strapped across the mule, Mr. Arnold spoke. "You kill something that belongs to me, and you come here seeking payment," he yelled. "Then you shame my home, after being warn. Go to Hell," Mr. Arnold shouted, as he released the bullet from his pistol into the man's head. "I will kill the first ass, to sit a saddle," Mr. Arnold shouted, as the men went to mount their horses. "Now come get this trash off of my porch, and take your dead slave with you," he went on to say, as two of the men slowly made their way up the steps.

The men quickly gathered up their dead friend, and left by way of the west gate.

"Get a few of those boys, to clean that porch," Mr. Arnold said to Jeremiah, as he headed for the parlor.

By the time old Mae saw the slave hunters again, there was no doubt in her mind, the men had been introduce to the Devil himself. And for that, the old slave smiled, knowing Mr. Arnold had given the men a good taste of Hell.

With the North and South inching closer to war, Mr. Arnold and Jeremiah rarely had the luxury of spending time at home. But when he was home, Jeremiah made the best of his time with Clora Lee. But as for Ethel, Clora Lee often had to tell her great grandfather some tall tale, about her mother being too busy, trying to keep up with Matthew. Yet Matthew was far from being the reason, for Ethel avoiding her grandfather. The young mother no longer wanted the old slave's protection. Nor did Ethel want to sneak around the plantation, hiding here and there, trying to learn things she would never get the chance to use. For Ethel no longer saw the white man's education, as the freedom her grandfather often spoke of.

One day while Jeremiah was helping Clora Lee with her learning, she yelled, "I's uh wanna spell Cowayne."

"You keep your voice down," Jeremiah said firmly.

But Clora Lee did just the opposite, as she attempted to bellow her sentiments for a second time. Yet the little girl never got the chance, to display the touch of white blood, which flowed through her body. For a slave named Nelson, put his hand over Clora Lee's mouth, and waited for Jeremiah to give him the signal. And when the aging slave nodded his head, old Pete second born son, quickly disappeared, taking Clora Lee with him.

When Nelson brought Clora Lee back to Ethel, things nearly took a turn for the worst. After Nelson had told Ethel of Clora Lee's behavior, the angry young mother raised her hand to strike the little slave. But before Ethel's hand could reach Clora Lee's face, it was halted by Nelson's strong grip.

"Don't you's hit my baby," Sistah said, as she stood behind Ethel.

By the time Ethel had turned around, Clora Lee was already standing next to Sistah, as if to say, she was untouchable. But Ethel wasn't amused, by Clora Lee's sudden show of defiance. And to make her point felt, Ethel looked down on her daughter, as if to say, their little matter would be taken care of at a later date. And Clora Lee being fully knowledgeable of what the look meant, quickly disappeared behind Sistah's much larger body.

Like a bold warrior challenging its foe, Sistah's eyes fell on the hand, which gripped Ethel's wrist. And seeing Sistah's piercing stare, Nelson immediately released Ethel from her temporary state of restraint. Yet the young mother did nothing to obtain her child, as she waited for Nelson to step between her and the misfortunate female. But Nelson didn't move a muscle, as he stood watching Ethel massage her wrist, while staring at Sistah with praying eyes.

Knowing that Ethel didn't have the stomach to tangle with her, Sistah took Clora Lee, and went about her business. As for Nelson, he faithfully retreated back to Jeremiah, where he gave the old slave a full account of what had taken place.

After being shamed by Sistah's actions, Ethel ran to the only person, she felt would listen to her. And as she sat next to old Mae, Ethel broke down in to tears.

"What's ailing ya, child?" old Mae asked softly.

"I's uh gon have another baby," Ethel cried.

"Lord uh mighty, child, what you's go do that for?"

"It was Big Willie. He's made me do it," Ethel cried. "And he's hurt me, when he's do it," Ethel went on to say of the large slave.

"Na you's knows, he's ain't like you's having a boy for another."

"I's uh know, Mae, but I's uh think, he's gon kill him."

"Na child, you's hush that kind uh talk, cause you's knows he's ain't gon do no killing, till masa Arnold tell him to."

"He's uh kill him, if n he's ask masa Arnold to fight him," Ethel said, as she went on crying.

"Na you's hush that, cause you's ain't got nothing to be scared of," old Mae said to Ethel, as she pulled the young mother close to her.

"But he's hit me, Mae."

"Well you's tell old Pete. Cause old Pete, knows that ain't our way. Na you's hush that crying," old Mae said, as she rubbed the back of Ethel's neck.

Old Mae had said a mouth full, yet it wasn't enough to stop Ethel's tears, nor her fear of Big Willie. Ethel knew Big Willie was going to kill Matthew's father, and there was no stopping him. But what Ethel feared most, is that she felt Big Willie was going to kill her as well. Yet she knew Big Willie would never harm her, as long as she was carrying his baby. But there was something telling the young mother, she was weighed down with another girl, and that made her fear Big Willie even more so.

Chapter 8

War

On October 16, 1859, a Christian zealot, name John Brown brought war to his Nation's front door. For he and his men, stormed into Harpers Ferry Virginia, to boldly ring the bells of war. And word of John Brown's action, brought both praise and scorn, as America braced herself for a war she so desperately needed, yet cared so little for. And as the bells rung out, the United Confederate States welcomed John Brown's call to war, with dry powder and a strong will.

It was a cloudy day fit for sorrow, when a rider came charging through the front gate of the Big A plantation, with orders for Mr. Arnold to fall in and be counted. And knowing that he wanted nothing more then to teach those Northern boys a lesson or two, Mr. Arnold told Jeremiah to pack their things. Mr. Arnold also sent for Duval. He wanted to get his last bit of instruction across, so there wouldn't be any excuses when he got back. For the wealthy plantation owner had it in his head, the war would last, about as long as the Northern picnic. So that left the arrogant slave owner feeling, he would be home before the next harvest.

By mid day, the slaves were standing as close to the cobble stone path way as they were allowed. Everyone but old Mae, watched as their master and Jeremiah, rode off to fight in what the white man called, a Civil War. And even though the slaves didn't know what to make of the white man's war, they cheered their master on just the same. Yet no one told the poor captured souls, they were cheering for the wrong side.

On April 12th, 1861, just twelve weeks and five days after Mr. Arnold had left his lovely home, the war was off to a running start. And while the women on both sides of the war, found themselves worrying about fathers, husbands, brothers, and sons, the slaves were left not knowing what to do, as the white men fought over them, like a bunch of spoil little boys.

With the man of the house, off fighting in the war, Mrs. Arnold spent most of her time in the parlor, reading, or writing letters to the other Southern wives. But no matter how much the women wrote about their proud Southern right, they could still feel the winds of change, blowing roughly through the trees.

By the time the war had endured its first six months of fighting, it brought about a change for Mrs. Arnold and Ruth. For the two sisters, found themselves closer then they had ever been before. And it didn't take the two often bickering siblings long, to become each others crutch, as they prayed for an early resolve to the Nation's dispute. But while the sisters waited through the endless days and lonely nights, they wrote each other constantly. And they wrote about everything, including their deepest and darkest secrets. And the more Mrs. Arnold read of Ruth's wild lustful orgasms, from her unspeakable affairs, the more she desired one of her own.

On a warm sunny day, after not hearing from Ruth for over a month, Mrs. Arnold received a letter from her sister, endorsed with their new secret code names. And like a little girl clutching a new doll, Mrs. Arnold held tight, to the letter endorsed with the name Snow Dove. And after tossing all of the other letters aside, Mrs. Arnold tore open her sister's written words, and began to read them with a smile. But the lady of the house quickly lost her gleaming smile, as she covered her mouth, just before crying.

My Dearest Fried,
These days has found me in the most awful position. For I find my self with a child. Please don't be mad with me, for I did not intend for such a thing to happen. But when the body is good, the mind is cloudy. And I tell you my friend, there is nothing better in this world, then a cloudy mind. So tell me, are you still holding on? If not, then be very careful. For my mind is so cloudy, I am dreading this war's end. For such a thing, would force me to live without my nights of unspeakable passion and pain. And we both know I would not want to go on living, without a good mule, to plow my field.
Your Friend
Snow Dove

"That wretched little bitch," Mrs. Arnold snarled, just before putting a match to the letter. "Leave me," Mrs. Arnold said to her girls, as she stormed over to the window.

With her head down, Mrs. Arnold prayed for Ruth to do the right thing, and sell the baby to another plantation. But knowing her sister like she did, Mrs. Arnold knew Ruth would be foolish, and keep the damn animal close to her.

While she stood motionless in the window thinking of Ruth, something told Mrs. Arnold to look up. And when she raised her head, he was there. Walking with a load of fire wood in his arms, Jonathan was headed for the backdoor. And while staring at the slave that rested in his mid teens, Mrs. Arnold felt a gentle touch in her special place. So before the clock could go from tick to tock, the woman had called out for her girls. And the two chocolate beauties came running, in their fine hand me down Southern bell dresses.

"You's call? ma'am," the girls asked, as they spoke with one voice, as if their words came from the same mouth.

"Go to the kitchen, and get that boy, and bring him to me," Mrs. Arnold said with a sense of urgency.

"What boy? ma'am," the girls asked, as they looked at each other.

"Just go to the kitchen, damn it," Mrs. Arnold snapped.

The girls disappeared from their Misses sight, leaving her alone with only lustful thoughts for entertainment. And Mrs. Arnold had no problem with using her imagination, as she thought of the young slave, with the dirtiest of minds.

The news from the battlefield wasn't good. In fact, it was down right disturbing. Mrs. Arnold called Duval to the parlor, and read him, her husband's latest letter.

After hearing how things were going for the good old Southern boys, Duval felt he wasn't doing the South any good, by sitting around the Big A plantation watching slaves. So before packing his belongings, Duval went to the blacksmith for a talk. For the blacksmith, his wife, and their son Biscuit, were the only workers left on the plantation, other then Duval.

The two men had a long talk, over a pot of coffee that had been touched with a dab of whiskey.

After leaving Biscuit's father with the best tasting coffee that had ever graced his lips, and a clear understanding of what to do, Duval stopped in to see Mrs. Arnold. The talk didn't take long, and both wished each other well. But for some reason, Duval didn't comment, when Mrs. Arnold uttered the words, God speed. He just walked away with a strange look on his face, as though the woman had spoken some foreign language.

Knowing that the war may be the last of him, there was no way Duval could leave the plantation without saying goodbye to his favorite slaves. But Duval didn't just say goodbye to those who held a special place in his heart. In fact, the Cajun called all of the slaves together in front of the female shed, to bid them farewell. Then it was time for him to say goodbye to the ones he would truly miss.

"You Sistah, you're sure some piece of work, I just couldn't figure you out," he said. "But you just keep taking care of dem young ones."

"They's mine, sir," Sistah replied.

Believing the female with every beat of his heart, Duval didn't bother to comment on the misfortunate slave's reply. For he just directed his attention toward old Mae, "What you looking sad for, old girl?" Duval asked with a smile.

"I's gon miss ya, sir," the old slave said, knowing the man had been good to her.

"You just be here, when I get back," Duval said, trying to keep his hopes up.

"Sir, I's done got old."

"My grandpa had a Cowayne, older then you."

Duval hugged Clora Lee, Matthew, and Cowayne in silence, right before taking Pleasant off to the side. "Here, you take dis, and you protect dem babies," Duval said, as he gave Pleasant his Bowie knife.

Without saying a word other wise, Pleasant took the large knife, and put it down in his pants.

"Now you make sure, old Mae and dem others, get some ding to eat," Duval said, as he rested his hand on Pleasant's shoulder.

"I's uh do that, sir," Pleasant said looking down.

"And if I don't come back, you give dat blade to Cowayne, when he is old enough," Duval said, as if he were a proud father, leaving something behind for his son.

"But masa…."

"Don't you be worrying about your master, because if I don't make it back, dere won't be anymore master. Now I done told ya what to do," Duval barked firmly.

"I's uh do it, sir," Pleasant said, still looking down.

"Good. Now go tell Ella, to come here."

Duval took Ella into his quarters, and they said goodbye with a touch of emotion. And what the two did, would forever, keep Ella hungering for the man who treated her like a lady.

Two days after Duval departed the Big A for the battle field, Big Willie commandeered his quarters. And even though Ella wanted to gather up her things, and go back to the female shed, Big Willie kept her, as if she were a part of the shack. That meant, the large slave, had both Ethel and Ella to lay with him through the night. For the master's top, dog, was living high on the hog, yet he was still afraid of Mrs. Arnold, and all of her fury.

Old Mae looked at Ethel combing Clora Lee's hair, and tried to figure out what the young mother was doing. The poor child left eye was nearly closed, and her bottom lip had a slit in it, that had to come from Big Willie's fist. The old slave didn't understand why Ethel, the master's daughter, weren't using her mother's power to rid herself of the worthless hyena.

"Ethel, you's think its right, for that child to be in there with you and Ella?" old Mae asked softly.

"What I's uh gon do, Mae? Big Willie, want her in there."

"Then you's should have yo's boy in there with ya," old Mae said of Matthew, sleeping in the female shed with her and Sistah.

"Na Mae, you's know Big Willie don't want him in there."

"Na you's listen to me Ethel, I's looking after yo's boy, and I's uh don't mind it uh tall. But that child don't need to be round, when Big Willie go to beating on ya, like he's the masa na," old Mae said, as she looked at Clora Lee.

Not knowing what to say, Ethel quickly put Clora Lee's hair in two plaits, and tried to hurry off with her.

"I's uh gon go na, Mae," Ethel said, as she took Clora Lee by the hand.

Standing against an oak tree, Sistah could see the pain in old Mae's eyes, as Ethel started to walk away with Clora Lee. So with her eyes shifting from old Mae to Ethel, Sistah felt she had the remedy to everyone's problem. And after darting out in front of Ethel, Sistah softly whispered something to the poor excuse of a mother. And when she was finished, Sistah knelt down and wrapped her arms around Clora Lee, while looking up at the worthless female.

When old Mae saw Ethel reluctantly hand Sistah the comb and brush, she knew Big Willie would be coming to pay her a visit. But rather then wait for the large slave to come calling, old Mae sent him a stern message. And after receiving the old slave's message, Big Willie assured the plantation's oldest picker, he had no quarrel with her or anyone else.

With Clora Lee clearly under Sistah's protection, she and Cowayne soon became inseparable. The two did everything together. Everyday was a new adventure, just waiting to be explored by the two young adventurous slaves. For if the two slaves explored the main yard, one day, the young couple could be almost anywhere, the next. To Clora Lee and Cowayne, there was no adventure too big, or too small for their liking.

On a warm spring day while hiding in the pecan tree, a group of Rebel soldiers appeared at the front gate. And hearing that the soldiers were among them, Sistah frantically ran about the main yard, in search of her two wondering babies.

"Come on Sistah, we's gotta hide," Pleasant begged, knowing the misfortunate female would gladly give her life, for the two adventurous kids.

"I's uh gotta find my babies," Sistah cried, as she continued to look for her two stolen children.

"But them Reb, gon see us."

"I's uh don't care, na you's leave me be," Sistah yelled, as she angrily pulled away from Pleasant.

Like a hawk swooping down on an unsuspecting prey, Nelson came from out of nowhere, and gave Sistah a good strong punch in the gut. Then like a kidnapper with a well laid plan, Nelson stuffed a rag in Sistah's mouth before she could cry out in pain. But when Nelson tried to lift Sistah, he ran in to a bit of a problem. For Sistah was a lot heaver then she looked. And seeing that Nelson couldn't lift the only female he ever laid with, Pleasant grabbed Sistah and made off with her, like a fox stealing a hen.

When Pleasant found him self safely tucked away under the large dog house with the females, he and Isabella was forced to restrain Sistah. And while Pleasant held his hand over her mouth, Isabella had the daunting task, of holding the misfortunate slave down. And even though the female was half way to Heaven, seeing that the only thing to separate her face, from Sistah's pussy, was an old tattered dress, Isabella still couldn't bring herself to think about the word, bitch. For Isabella feared how Sistah was going to react, if something were to happen to her precious Cowayne.

The next morning by the crack of dawn, the soldiers were up and assembling, signaling, they were ready to move on. But the soldiers didn't leave with the plantation's blessing. For the stinking Rebs, as Clora Lee like to call them, took what little food the Big A plantation had for them selves. And even with that, Mrs. Arnold still believed the men were fighting for their proud Southern way of life. But if it were not for Effie out witting the soldiers in their quest to confiscate every bit of food the plantation possessed, the woman's belly would have gone empty.

When the soldiers had marched over the hill and out of sight, Cowayne and Clora Lee slowly crawled down from their perfect hiding place. And as they did so, the two crafty young slaves were both thinking the same thing. The young slaves were wondering why the Rebs took the plantation's food, as if they were a group of Blue Coats. And seeing that there was no difference between the two armies, Clora Lee and Cowayne were convinced, there could be no friends in war. For there were only enemies, be they blue or gray.

By the time Clora Lee and Cowayne's feet hit the ground, they could hear Sistah calling out their names. And hearing the desperation in her voice, Clora Lee quickly got an itch to play a trick on their make believe mother.

"Come on," Clora Lee said, as she ducked behind the house.

"No," Cowayne replied, as his voice also held a bit of desperation.

"Why?"

Rather then answer his friend, Cowayne took her by the hand, so the two of them could meet Sistah together. And when Clora Lee saw the fear that held Sistah's face hostage, she immediately understood why Cowayne couldn't bring himself to play such a fool hearted trick. And the way Sistah charged toward them with all her might, made Clora Lee feel a sense of guilt, for thinking such a foolish thought. And the way Sistah wrapped her arms around the two adventure seekers, Clora Lee had no other choice, but to let out a laughing cry. And seeing how Clora Lee was enjoying the hug, prompt Sistah to give the little girl a great big kiss, which was followed by a good tongue lashing.

"Where ya'll been?" Sistah asked, while still holding on to her babies.

"We's was up in the pecan tree," Cowayne confessed.

"And we's see'd something," Clora Lee said with excitement.

"I's uh don't care what you's see'd. And I's got a good mind to whop ya both," Sistah threaten, as she released the two children, and raised her hand.

"But we's ain't do nothing," Clora Lee cried in fear.

"You's done scared me half to death," Sistah said in a high pitched voice. "Na I's want you's young ns to stay where I's can see ya."

"We's will," Clora Lee promised.

With Sistah being Sistah, Clora Lee knew she could promise the female the world, and if they should fall short of their goal, all would be forgiven. And that was Sistah's problem. For the childless female loved her babies far too much, to calm the fires that burned deep with in their adventurous souls. But with Clora Lee promising to do better, Sistah was happy again, as she took to playing with her little lost sheep.

"Mat-thew, Mat-thew," Sistah's voice flowed through the air, as sweet as honeysuckle, after a mid summer's rain.

As Sistah, Cowayne, and Clora Lee ran around flapping their arms like birds, for the little boy's benefit, he smiled up a storm, while standing next to old Mae. Yet his nose was all snotty from crying, being that the soldiers had scared the little boy out of his mind. But with Sistah heading his way, the little unwanted slave, knew everything was going to be all right. And just like he suspected, Sistah took her dress and wiped his nose. She then gathered up her unwanted child, and took him for a joyful ride.

"Mat-thew, Mat-thew, who love Matthew? I do. I do. I love my lit-tle Mat-thew," Sistah sang, as she danced around with Matthew high above her head, as Clora Lee and Cowayne sung right alone with her.

The very next day during the early evening hours, the two adventurous slaves came barreling back to the plantation. They had just returned from watching the Rebel soldiers practice their war games. And as Cowayne and Clora Lee watched from a great oak, they were able to see a cannon ball hit the ground, just a few feet shy of their tree. Filled with excitement, the two young slaves quickly crossed their fingers, and prayed for the Rebs to do it again. But the two young slaves never got their wish, seeing that the solders had taken aim on another tree, about thirty yards to the children's left.

After walking the main yard for the fourth time, Sistah found herself angry with her babies once again. And feeling she needed a little help from Pleasant, Sistah made her next stop, the blacksmith shop. And once there, Sistah thought she heard the children arguing. And what Sistah heard, sent the dysfunctional female scrambling around to the far side of the building.

"It is to," Clora Lee shouted, with a small branch in her hand.

"I tis not," Cowayne replied, not having a clue, of what Clora Lee was talking about.

"It is," Clora Lee shouted once more in anger.

"I's uh right here," Cowayne replied, as he slapped himself in the chest.

While using the branch to point at each individual letter on the ground, Clora Lee spelled out the word. "B, o, y, boy," she said angrily, right before giving Cowayne a good whack with the branch.

Before Cowayne could say stop, Sistah was down on her knees, rubbing the letters from the dirt. And when she was finished, Sistah pulled the children to her. And with a fear in her, unlike anything Cowayne had ever seen, Sistah spoke clearly.

"Where did you learn that?" Sistah asked angrily.

"Jeremiah," Clora Lee replied, with a trembling voice.

"You can't teach him that. If master Arnold find out, he know how to read and write, he will kill him," Sistah cried.

"I's sorry," Clora Lee said with tears in her eyes.

Sistah pulled the children to her and cried out, "Help me Lord. Lord, please help me."

Cowayne knew Sistah had to be hurting mighty bad, to be calling on her Lord. For Sistah only called on her Lord, when things had become too much for her to bear.

While Cowayne thought of Sistah and her pain, Clora Lee saw what her friend refuse to see. For Sistah spoke, as if she was a totally different person. And what did she know about writing? And where did she obtain such knowledge? There was something strange about Sistah, and the eleven years old was becoming suspicious of the female.

Through the days and weeks that passed, Clora Lee and Cowayne became very fond of that old pecan tree. For the tree had become more, then just a daily attraction for the two young slaves. And if ever Sistah wanted to find her babies, she would just head for that old tree, which sat on the west side of the mansion. And six times out of ten, she would find the children there, yet Sistah was never able to visibly see the children in their tree. For the tree had to be the best look out spot in the whole valley.

In the tree, the two adventure seekers could spot both the Rebs and the Yanks for miles. The two also would spy Sistah, when ever she was heading their way. And that gave Clora Lee and Cowayne time to scramble from the tree, and meet Sistah, just as she came up on the East end of the mansion. And the children's ability, to meet her in the same place every time, left Sistah wondering how her babies were able to do such a thing. But what Sistah didn't know, there were only two rooms, to have windows that sat directly across from each another. And fortunately for the little slaves, the pecan tree was deeply rooted outside of their master's bedroom. That gave the children a bird's eye view of the female shed, where Sistah spent most of her day. And every morning, when Mrs. Arnold opened her curtains, Effie would open little Aaron's curtains as well, giving the children a clear advantage over their adopted mother.

One day, shortly after Clora Lee had turned twelve years of age, the little slave noticed that her dress was stained with blood. And being unaware of what was happening to her, Clora Lee ran in search of her mother. But Sistah caught Isabella and old Mae off guard, when she quickly cut the girl off, and immediately sent Cowayne away. And as Sistah held Clora Lee in her arms, she along with old Mae, and Isabella, couldn't believe the carelessness of Ethel.

"You's ain't hurt," Sistah said to the child.

"But I's bleeding," Clora Lee said crying.

Taking Clora Lee by the hand, Sistah led her away. And even though the misfortunate slave had never suffered one day of the problem, she still knew what the little girl needed to do. But the moment Sistah got Clora Lee all cleaned up, she quickly took the little baby catcher back to old Mae, for that all important, mother, daughter talk.

"What you's want me to do with her?" old Mae asked.

"You's talk to her," Sistah replied, while moving about nervously.

"I's uh thought, you's was gon talk to her," old Mae said, winking at the other female slaves.

"Na Mae, you's talk to her. You's talk to her, Mae, you's talk to her," Sistah went on, as she pulled at her hair.

Like everyone else, old Mae could see, Sistah was about to lose what little self control, she had stored away for safe keeping. So with that in mind, the old slave softly pulled Clora Lee to her. And as Clora Lee got comfortable, so did Sistah. But before the old slave could get down to the meat and potatoes of Clora Lee's problem, Sistah started crying, as if the girl was about to die.

"Na Sistah, you's hush, cause you's scaring this child," old Mae said, as she gave Sistah that look, which shouted, you better behave yourself.

"I's uh can't help it, cause I's scared," Sistah said through her crying.

"Well you's should uh thought uh that, fo you's run round here, and got all them young ns," old Mae said, as if Sistah was the girl's biological mother.

"Mae, I's could have many babies, as I's want," Sistah said angrily, as she took hold of Clora Lee's wrist.

"Na Sistah, you's leave that child here, so I's can talk to her," old Mae said, looking at Ella walking up.

And after seeing the condition of Ella's face, old Mae knew Sistah had did the right thing, by forcing Ethel to leave Clora Lee to live among the females.

After being told everything she needed to know about what would be a long tedious journey, Clora Lee went in the female shed for a bit of rest. Then for the first time, of what would be many more times to come, Clora Lee felt the pain old Mae had spoken of. Yet the pain of her stomach, twisting and turning, as it tried to reshape it's self in to one big knot, was over shadowed by Clora Lee's thoughts. For the twelve year old, couldn't help but to think about what her absence was doing to Cowayne. But most of all, Clora Lee wondered how he would look at her, once she told him about their problem. And it was their problem. Yet Clora Lee searched her mind, as she tried to figure out a way to keep her new monthly routine a secret, until the time was right, to break the news to Sistah's son.

Waking up to the second full day of being without Clora Lee, Cowayne struck out on his own. And while walking across the yard with nothing to do, he spotted Pleasant and Matthew checking the traps, the four of them made together. Yet the little slave didn't feel much like helping any more, as he decided to go in the opposite direction. But not even avoiding Pleasant and Matthew could make Cowayne feel better, as he ended up by the front gate.

"That's it. I's uh set a mess of traps, outside the main yard," Cowayne said out loud, as if he were talking to Clora Lee.

By mid day, no one had seen hide or hair of Cowayne, and Sistah had begun to worry about her baby. And the poor female walked the main yard, until she couldn't walk any more. And up on taking a break at the blacksmith shed, Sistah asked Pleasant once again, had he seen her child.

"I's uh done told ya, he's went cross that fence at first light," Pleasant replied, as he tinkered around with a broken wagon wheel.

"I's uh done told him, to stay where I's can see him," Sistah said nervously, as she stood looking out across the yard.

Pleasant quickly left the broken wheel Mr. Herren had him working on, and took hold of Sistah. "Na don't you's be crying, cause he's gon come cross that old fence in no time uh tall," Pleasant said, as he tried to convince both Sistah and himself, of his own words.

As the two slaves stood thinking about their love one, they also thought about the shooting that came bellowing from the fields shortly after dawn. But Pleasant wasn't going to give up on Cowayne, even if he heard a lion roaring across those old fields. For he knew the young teen was strong, and his strength would surely bring him home.

With the day nearly gone, Cowayne strolled up to the female shed, looking like he was born of dirt. And the poor boy looked, like he could use a good deal of sleep, after taking anything that would come close to a bath. Yet Cowayne wasn't thinking of water or sleep, as he looked around for Clora Lee.

"You's see'd Sistah?" old Mae asked, as she sat on her stump.

Looking like a lost puppy, Cowayne shook his head no, as he peered into the female shed, hoping that Clora Lee was there. But Clora Lee had spotted her friend coming, and quickly hid against the front wall. And she had planned on staying there, until Pleasant or Nelson close the door.

Sensing that her child needed more then just Sistah's love, old Mae felt it was time for her to resume, that thing called motherly duties.

"Why you's looking like that?" old Mae asked, in her forever soft voice.

"Cause I's made Clora Lee sick," Cowayne replied sadly.

"Child, you's ain't do no such thing."

"Then why she's sick?"

Even though old Mae had anticipated her son's question, she still couldn't find the right words to explain such a delicate conversation. And it was all for the best, seeing that Sistah had shown up, armed and ready for action. For the misfortunate female grabbed her son, and began to violently shake him, as if he was someone she hated all of her life.

"Where you's been?" Sistah yelled, as she continued to shake the boy. "I's uh done told ya, not to leave here," the misfortunate female went on, as her anger quickly turned to sadness.

"I's uh just went into the woods, so I's could set some traps," Cowayne said, as his voice bounced around.

"I's uh don't care bout no traps. And I's uh don't care, if n we's never eat. Theys been shooting, and I's uh don't want ya out yonder, you's hear? I's uh don't want ya out yonder," Sistah shouted, as her shaking of Cowayne came to an end, just to give way to a flood of tears.

"Don't cry Sistah," Cowayne said, while holding his special mother.

"Na Sistah, that child is already scared, cause he's think, he's done got Clora Lee sick," old Mae said, thinking it would calm the bubbling mother down.

"It serves him right, cause he's ain't got no call, to be dragging her all over them fields, like she's some boy," Sistah shouted.

"Na Sistah, I's uh done told him, he's ain't got that child sick," old Mae cried.

"Well you's done told him wrong, Mae. Na he's need to get on to that old barn, fo she's up and die."

Hearing Sistah's words, Cowayne ran of in the direction of the blacksmith shed, leaving his two Mothers to laugh, until they cried.

"Na you's hush that, cause you's wrong," old Mae said through her laughter.

"You's see'd him, Mae? He looked awful bad, to me," Sistah said, as she couldn't stop herself from laughing as well.

"Na Sistah, I's uh thought you's love, yo's boy?" old Mae chuckled.

"I's do Mae, but he's need to stop dragging that child off from here, and I's uh mean it," Sistah said, as she no longer laughed.

By the time Clora Lee five days were up, Cowayne had suffered far worst then a Union soldier, who was fortunate enough, to be tortured by a mess of Rebs. Yet, the boy's torture had to be the best thing, to happen to the old plantation, in a long time. And if everything went as Cowayne planned, the teen knew he and his family would never go hungry again. But most of all, the young adventurous slave wanted to know how Clora Lee was going to feel about him calling her just plain old Lee. And his Lee didn't waste any time, as she literally hit the ground running.

"Come on," Clora Lee said as she ran pass Cowayne, who was sitting on the ground by the large magnolia tree.

With Clora Lee ready to take on another adventure, her first order of business, were to get re-acquainted, with their favorite place. And after running pass the old fig tree, which sat a few yards from the pecan tree, the girl came to a complete stop.

"Come on, so we's can go to the tree," Clora Lee said, walking back toward her Cowayne.

"We's can't," Cowayne mumbled, while Clora Lee stood over him.

"Why?"

"Cause you's gon, get sick."

Clora Lee gave Cowayne a good slap on the shoulder, before voicing her opinion. "If n you's don't stop listening to Sistah, I's ain't gon be with ya no mo," she said, with an angry look on her face.

"But Sistah said I's made ya sick."

"Who's you's gon believe?"

Cowayne got up, revealing to Clora Lee, that she still had the power to make him do what ever her little heart desired. And as the two young slaves ran as fast as their feet could carry them, they saw the most unusual thing. It appeared as if Biscuit and his family were leaving. The two quickly forgot about their special tree, and headed for the blacksmith shed.

"Pleasant! Pleasant!" The two kids yelled, as they entered the old shed.

"What's you's two up to na?" Pleasant asked, as he moved about the place.

"We's ain't do nothing," Clora Lee yelled.

"We's see'd Biscuit, and his ma and pa, and they's leaving," Cowayne swore, while crossing his heart.

"We's ain't making it up, neither," Clora Lee said, in support of her friend.

"I's know," Pleasant replied, without looking at the children.

"You's do?" Clora Lee and Cowayne asked in unison.

"Biscuit told me yesterday, they's was leaving."

"But why?" Clora Lee asked, as she wondered why all of the white people were deserting them.

"Cause they's going back home," Pleasant replied, while checking a wagon wheel.

"But who's gone watch us?" the girl asked, as if they were sheep left unattended.

"I's uh speck, we's uh be watching our self," Pleasant replied, after placing the wheel on the table that sat near the front door.

Cowayne and Clora Lee left Pleasant, to continue his tinkering about the old shed. And as the two young slaves slowly headed for the fence, they pondered their fate. Yet their silence only lasted a few minutes.

"You's wanna see our new traps?" Cowayne asked, hoping to cheer Clora Lee up.

"Yea," Clora Lee replied joyfully, as she placed her arm around his neck.

And just like that, the two were off and running again.

When Clora Lee and Cowayne made it to the first trap, they found them selves with a problem. The trap had snagged a coon, and the animal wasn't about to be taken without a fight.

"Ha we's gon get him?"

Clora Lee's question prompted Cowayne to search for a way to kill the poor animal. But the only thing the two children could come up with, were a few large chunks of dirt. And the two young slaves soon found out, that pitching dirt rocks at a raccoon, was just as bad as pulling its tail. For the more rocks the children threw, the madder that old coon got. And the way the two adventure seekers saw it, that old raccoon was standing on the front end of a bad situation. Yet Clora Lee still saw fit to tell her friend, their plan wasn't working.

"Come on Lee, we's gotta find something better," Cowayne said, as he took off running.

The children quickly ran off, not knowing what they were going to find. Yet the two young slaves had no idea, it would be five dead Union soldiers.

"You's think theys dead?" Clora Lee asked.

"They's dead," Cowayne assured his friend.

The flies, backed by the dark color of the white men skin, told Cowayne all five of them were dead. Yet the two slaves still approached the men, as if they were very much alive. But when Cowayne caught sight of the pistols, he quickly got an idea, as he rushed to retrieve the unwanted firearms.

"Come on Lee, we's gotta get they's pistols," the boy said, after finding a full pouch of powder, and shots, on one of the soldiers.

"We's need to get they's money too, cause we's gon need it," Clora Lee said, as if she had an idea of her own.

"For what?" Cowayne asked, as he ran his hand in one of the soldier's pocket.

"When we's leave here, we's gotta have some money," Clora Lee said, causing Cowayne to look upon her with an enormous amount of doubt.

Clora Lee was thinking ahead, in case the North did win the war. For Jeremiah had told her on many occasions, in order to live free in the white man's world, one will need two things, a good deal of knowledge, and a whole lot of money. So that meant the two slaves would have to keep their eyes open, with hopes of finding many more dead soldiers.

With the pistols, shots, powder, and a few Union dollars in their possession, Clora Lee and Cowayne went back to their coon. And after many days of watching the Confederate and the Union soldiers, Cowayne, as well as Clora Lee, knew how to load a musket. But it was Cowayne who loaded a pistol, took aim, and killed the raccoon dead. Yet the feeling of victory came at a price, as the two slaves stood looking at their first kill with a deep sense of sorrow.

"The next time, you's kill it," Cowayne mumbled.

"Why?" Clora Lee asked, looking scared.

"So we's both, knows ha to kill," Cowayne said, hoping Clora Lee would buy in to his half dead excuse.

When Sistah showed up at the blacksmith shed, Cowayne, Matthew, and Clora Lee were already roasting the raccoon. And having no doubt, the day's meal had come from one of Pleasant's traps, Sistah walked by the children without saying a word. Yet the two young slaves held their breath, until Sistah entered the shed without giving them a second look. Then, and only then, did Clora Lee look at Cowayne, and he at her. And like they often did, the two were thinking the same thing. They were hoping Sistah wouldn't ask Pleasant about their afternoon meal, for he would surely be telling her the truth.

Later that day, as the two young slaves sat up in the pecan tree, Cowayne asked Clora Lee, how did she know, he wasn't the reason for her getting sick. And upon hearing the disturbing question, Clora Lee caught a sudden case of amnesia. The poor girl could feel her body growing numb, as if she had died and gone to slave Heaven.

"You's lie," Cowayne said angrily.

Having no idea of what to say, Clora Lee struck her friend on the shoulder, right before saying, "You's stop that swearing."

Feeling he had been betrayed, Cowayne no longer wanted to be in the tree. But Clora Lee wasn't about to let the boy leave her, while feeling she could no longer be trusted. So Clora Lee followed Cowayne down that old tree, as if he had stolen her one and only soul, and was about to sell it to the Devil.

And when Clora Lee's feet hit the ground, she ran out in front of her friend. "Wait," she said franticly.

"I's uh got uh go, Lee," Cowayne said with a sadness, which came from a broken heart.

"I's uh trying to tell ya something," Clora Lee said, as she stepped in front of Cowayne, before he could maneuver around her. "We's can make uh baby," she shouted, stopping Cowayne in his tracks.

"We's ain't do no such thing," Cowayne bellowed, as if he was mad with the world.

Like all males, Cowayne didn't pay close enough attention to what the better part of his life had said. For the young teen went back to walking, never realizing, he would have to learn a little something about Mother Nature, before gaining the ability to understand anything about a female.

"I's uh ain't said we's did, I's said, we's can," Clora Lee cried.

Hearing the pain in Clora Lee's voice, Cowayne had no other choice but to turn around. And what the poor boy saw, nearly brought his racing heart to a dead stop. For Clora Lee was on her hands and knees crying, as she poured her pretty little quarter breed heart out in a flood of tears.

"What's wrong?" Cowayne asked, after falling to his knees, and wrapping his arms around Clora Lee.

"You's don't wanna be my friend, no mo," Clora Lee replied tearfully.

"Na Lee, you's knows, I's uh gon always be ya friend."

"Then why you's don't believe me, when I's tell ya, we's can make uh baby?"

"If n you's wanna baby, then we's uh go get ya one," Cowayne quickly assured his friend.

But all Cowayne succeeded in doing, was assuring Clora Lee, she needed to cry a little harder. And seeing that their friendship rested squarely on her shoulders, Clora Lee had no trouble with crying, even if it meant she had to cry all day, and half of the night. So without giving it a second thought, the little female turned her tears up a notch, knowing it was going to pull the boy's heart one step closer to her love.

"Come on Lee, we's gotta go, fo Sistah come round here," Cowayne said, as he helped his friend to her feet.

Like always, the two young slaves ended up in the loft of the old barn on their bellies, looking out across the yard. But unlike the many times before, the two weren't as playful, as usual. Nor were they as talkative. Yet Clora Lee would not have preferred to be any where else, but in the loft with Cowayne.

"You's knows where my ma got Matthew from?" Clora Lee asked, as she laid her head on Cowayne's back.

"I's uh ain't gave it much thought," Cowayne replied, looking at Jonathan go in the back door of the mansion.

"He's come out of her belly," Clora Lee said softly.

"I's know that."

"Well ha he's come out of her belly?"

"Don't know."

"The way yo's young ns, gon come out of me," Clora Lee said, right before taking a quick look at Cowayne, to see his fiscal reaction to her statement.

"We's ain't got, no young ns," Cowayne replied, as the look of fear gripped his face.

"We's gon have um, and we's gon have uh heap," Clora Lee said in a tone, that told Cowayne, she was in one of her moods again.

Cowayne knew his friend well enough know, not to argue with her over matters that she cared deeply about. So with the thought of Jonathan entering the mansion still in his head, Cowayne went back to staring out across the yard. And while he stared in the direction of the fields, Clora Lee returned to resting her head on his back. And even though Cowayne didn't know why, he always felt life was much better, when Clora Lee's body was touching his.

Chapter 9

Growing Pains

After spending all day and night trying to figure out the new Clora Lee, Cowayne got up the next morning, and struck out on his own. The poor confused teen, didn't have the desire to check a single trap. For he just went down to the creek, and sat, until life told him it was time to go back and hang out with his Lee. But when Cowayne stood up and turned around, he was facing a small band of Indians. And where they came from, the young teen didn't know. Nor did he know how long they had been standing behind him.

"Y OU SLAVE?" A STRONG tall warrior asked.

"Uh huh," Cowayne replied.

Being that Cowayne had never seen an Indian before, the poor boy was left speechless, as he found himself face to face with about twenty of the strange looking people. Yet the teen didn't panic, as he couldn't seem to be able to take his eyes off of the warrior's feathers. And the feathers made the warrior appear to be larger then life. But what really brought Cowayne jealousy to the forefront, was the fact, that not one of the male Indians wore a shirt. Oh how Sistah would be on them, for walking around without a cover on their bodies, the teen thought to himself.

"You got food," the warrior asked, then looked over his shoulder at the squaws, and the children that were with him.

"We's can go check my traps," Cowayne said, as his eyes fell on the children.

The warrior spoke to the Chief, who was a rather short old Indian. And while the Chief and the warrior spoke to each other in their native tongue, Cowayne noticed the man had something in common with his birth mother. For the old Chief, had just a tooth more or less then his mother.

"We go," the warrior said, after he finished talking things over with the Chief.

The warrior's last two words, were like a call to manhood for Cowayne, the one thing, the white man would not allow him to have. And as he saw their trip to be the ultimate adventure, Cowayne knew it would be something, the white man could never take from him, for as long as he lived. So in a blink of an eye, the teen was off and running with the well built Indian, and two other warriors, as if they had been hunting together for years. And as he ran with the warriors, Cowayne couldn't help but to think of his Lee. She would have loved to see the Indians and their babies, he thought to himself, as he kept pace with the fast moving warriors.

When Cowayne and the warriors returned with what little food his traps provided, the Chief thanked him. Then the warrior told Cowayne, the chief wanted to know, who squaw was hiding in the brush. Cowayne looked to where the warrior and the Chief were pointing, yet he saw no one. He then turned to the Chief, holding a questionable stare. And seeing that Cowayne didn't believe him, the Chief made a motion with his hand, thus, causing Clora Lee to slowly walk out into the open.

"That ain't no squaw, that's Lee," Cowayne said smiling.

Seeing her Cowayne smiling, told Clora Lee, she had been worrying over nothing. Yet the little quarter breed slave didn't know what to make of the Indians, as she approached them with a great deal of caution.

"Your squaw?" the warrior asked Cowayne.

"No, she ain't no squaw, she's Lee. Lee," Cowayne said, as he tried to get the Chief and the warrior to understand, that Clora Lee was his friend.

The Chief uttered something in his native tongue, thus sending two of his warriors over to Clora Lee. And after reaching the teen, the two warriors took hold of her arms. But the fiery young female, wasn't about to let anyone hold her captive. Nor was Clora Lee going to let anyone take her from Cowayne. So she immediately went to kicking, and biting, like a bobcat in a fight with a couple of wolves. And when Cowayne attempted to help her, a group of warriors took hold of him as well.

"Chief say you want to keep squaw, you must fight for squaw," the big warrior said.

Staring at the Chief, as if he wanted to kill the old Indian, Cowayne gave his reply. "She's Lee, and I's uh fight all of ya, for her," he shouted angrily.

With Cowayne's anger fuming, the warriors released him, and the Chief raised his hand. Then like a well plotted plan, their smallest warrior came forward to face Cowayne. And no sooner then the fight started, Clora Lee got the chance to see how much she was worth to her life long friend. For the young slave fought long and hard, but the warrior got the best of him, which left Cowayne on the ground, trying to catch his breath.

"Get up," the Chief said, as he kicked the young slave.

"Don't you's kick Cowayne," Clora Lee shouted, as she violently struggled to free herself from those who held her captive.

While Clora Lee fought to free herself, the big warrior gave Cowayne a few pointers on how to attack, while keeping a steady form of defense. And as Cowayne stood armed and ready with his new knowledge, he and the warrior resume fighting. But with or without the pointers, after nearly thirty minutes of taking and giving a few knees to the gut, accompanied by a lot of rolling around on the ground, the fight ultimately ended in the same manner as before.

"A good squaw, need a strong warrior, so she can give him many young. His people need him to be strong, so he can lead them to good hunting grounds," the Chief said with a great deal of pride.

Cowayne looked at Clora Lee, and for the first time, he saw the woman in her. The change, he had been fighting, was truly a thing of beauty, waiting to be adored. "I's uh understand," Cowayne said, still looking at Clora Lee, but wondered why the Chief didn't speak any English before.

The Chief gave Cowayne a nod of approval, right before signaling his people to move back into the brush.

"Why they's leaving?" Clora Lee asked the tall warrior, as the band began to disappear into the brush.

"Take this. Bent Tree, want you to have it," the warrior said.

"What is it?" Cowayne asked, as he held the large buffalo hide, that was rolled up, as if it were a scroll from some ancient time.

"You will understand in time," the warrior assured the teen, then he to, disappear back into the brush.

On the way back to the plantation, Cowayne was more then ready, to talk about their problem. "Ha you's knows you's change?" he asked.

"Cause I's got these," Clora Lee replied, pointing to the two lumps in her chest that would surely grow larger.

"Ha you's get um?"

"I's uh reckon, theys come up like cotton," Clora Lee said, looking down in her dress, at the two little tits, her and Cowayne often ignored.

And seeing that Cowayne was just as curious about her two little lumps as she were, Clora Lee politely offered him a chance to see the change for himself. And without saying a word, Cowayne quickly peeped at the two not so rosy tits, and more.

"You's got hair, to," he said, revealing to Clora Lee, his eyes had traveled a wee bit further then she wanted them to.

Clora Lee quickly pressed her hands against the dress, thus putting an end to their little event. And as the two friends went back to walking, Clora Lee felt a sense of relief come over her, while clinging to a touch of embarrassment. Yet the twelve year old, wasn't going to let her silly little feelings cause another rip, in what she saw as a perfect friendship. So with her hand in Cowayne's, Clora Lee walked on, as happy as any free female ever born.

By the time the two young adventurous slaves, had made it back to the main yard, they could hear Sistah's voice bellowing across the air. And the sound of her voice, told the children, she was madder then ever, which meant they had to come up with something quick.

"Mae, I's uh gon kill them babies, yet," Sistah said, as she did her best to keep still. "I's uh done had enough of them running off from here," she yelled, while sitting down, only to bounce back to a standing position, before her ass could touch the bench long enough to feel the wood.

"We's ain't run off," Cowayne said, stretching the truth, far more then he should.

"You's get in that shed," Sistah yelled at Clora Lee, as if she were a bad girl.

With Sistah on the warpath, Clora Lee humbly did as she was told, even though her heart desired to spend more time with Cowayne. And when she heard Sistah tell Cowayne to get, Clora Lee couldn't help but to feel, it was all her fault, for growing up. Yet the girl didn't know what all the fuss was about. For if there had not been a war going on, she would have already been taken by some white man, and no one would have had a word to say about it. And knowing that her thoughts were true, the poor girl felt they were all living a lie, as she watched Cowayne head for the old barn, with his feet dragging like a lazy dog.

Two weeks, after Sistah had blasted him, for taking Clora Lee beyond the main yard, Cowayne was still checking their traps by himself. But one morning when he returned with a mess of raccoons, Matthew, who were soon to be eight, ran up to him.

"Can I's go with ya," Matthew asked.

Even though he heard the boy, Cowayne appeared to be miles away. For he was staring at Clora Lee sitting on a stool, looking like her world had came to an end.

"Can I's go, Cowayne? Can I?" Matthew asked over and over, as he tugged on the teen's shirt.

In an attempt to stop Matthew from talking, Cowayne quickly told the little boy he couldn't take him. But before Matthew could express his disappointment, Clora Lee spoke up.

"Why we's can't go?" she asked.

"Cause Sistah gon be mad at me," Cowayne replied.

"But she's ain't gon know, if n you's take me," Matthew said, as if he knew how to out fox the misfortunate female.

"She's uh know," Cowayne assured the little slave.

"I's uh don't need to go, and I's uh don't like ya no mo," Matthew shouted, just before taking off for the blacksmith shed.

Cowayne went after Matthew with hopes of calming the little slave down. But when the teen reached the shed, the first person he saw was Sistah. And as the acting mother stood with her back to the doorway, Cowayne immediately tried to walk away. But before he could make two good steps, his mother's voice invaded the air.

"Where you's been?" the disfunctional female asked softly.

Knowing Sistah's voice better then any other, Cowayne could tell she had been crying. And something inside of the teen, told him, he was the sole reason for her suffering.

"I's uh ain't been far," Cowayne said, just before turning around to catch Sistah trying to eliminate the evidence, which would prove him right. "Why you's crying?"

The misfortunate female couldn't bring herself to answer the son, she so desperately loved. So rather then searching her head for the right words, to answer the beloved child, Sistah walked up to him, and did what any good mother would do. In an effort to alleviate her pain, Sistah gave Cowayne the biggest hug any child had ever received from his or her mother. She then took Cowayne's face in her hands, and gave him a great big kiss on the jaw.

"I's uh don't know what I's uh do, if n I's ain't got you, no mo," Sistah whispered, as she went back to hugging her baby.

Feeling Sistah's tears on his face, Cowayne was forced to ask her again, why she was crying. And when his mother blurted out the words, cause I's uh made ya hate me, the teen felt he wanted to die.

"I's uh don't hate ya, Sistah, I's love ya," Cowayne confessed. "But you's mad at me," he said to the best mother, any kid could ever have.

"Cause I's scared, I's gone lose ya."

"I's uh ain't gon go no where."

"Them white folks gon take ya from me, if n you's keep going out yonder," Sistah said, as she cried.

"But if n I's uh don't go, we's ain't gon have nothing to eat."

"I's uh done told ya, I's uh don't care bout no eating," Sistah said angrily.

"But what uh bout my ma, she's gotta eat. And Matthew gotta eat to."

Cowayne was hoping Sistah's love for his mother and Matthew would get her to see his need, to venture beyond the fence. The fence, that gave her and the other slaves, a false sense of security.

"Don't you's let nothing happen to ya. And don't you's let nothing happen to Clora Lee, neither," Sistah said, as she wiped the tears from her eyes.

"I's won't," Cowayne said, as he held his second mother, for all that she was worth.

While Cowayne and Sistah stood holding each other, Matthew made, what he soon found to be an untimely appearance.

"Why Sistah crying?" the little boy asked, as a sad look came over his face.

"Cause I's happy," Sistah said, as she took a break from crying.

With nothing left to do, but to bring Matthew into their warm embrace, Cowayne and Sistah knelt down, and together, the mother and son gave the little boy, the one thing he didn't care too much for. And while Matthew tried his best to break free from Sistah and Cowayne's hold, things took a turn for the worst. For just a moment before the little boy could start protesting their unkindly act of kindness, he found the right side of his face, being assaulted by Sistah's sweet motherly kisses. And Matthew was extremely glad none of his friends were around, to witness such a horrible act of affection. And feeling he needed to break the hold, before one of his toad catching friends came looking for him, the boy cried out for Pleasant.

The next morning after breakfast, Clora Lee and Cowayne made it their first order of business, to head straight for the pecan tree. For it had been more then a few days, since the two, had rested peacefully in their favorite place. And they were also hoping to catch Mrs. Arnold and her girls going at it again. Yet neither Clora Lee nor Cowayne could figure out, what the three females were getting out of carrying on in such a manner.

When Clora Lee and Cowayne finally made it in the old pecan tree, the two found there had been a slight change, since they last visited their old look out tower. Instead of seeing Mrs. Arnold and her girls, engaging in wild forbidding sex, the two saw the strangest thing. For Mrs. Arnold was with Jonathan. And the poor slave wasn't doing any chores, as he moved about their master's bedroom with out a stitch of clothing on his body.

Clora Lee and Cowayne quickly looked at each other, while smiling joyfully, as if they were happy to see the new twist, in Mrs. Arnold's life. And as the two young slaves thought nothing could get better then watching Mrs. Arnold and Jonathan wrestle around the room with out any clothing, they were soon given a disturbing surprise. For after the two forbidden lovers found them selves on the bed exhausted, Mrs. Arnold rolled over and kissed Jonathan on the lips. And their master's wife didn't stop there, as she took to kissing Jonathan all over his face, chest, and stomach. But when the kids black and white operetta appeared to turn in to a state of cannibalism, Clora Lee laid her head down on a branch. And when Clora Lee gasped, it told Cowayne, his friend could predict the future. Yet Clora Lee's head didn't stay down long, as she returned to watching the deadly game of chance go on with out a care.

As she watched along with Cowayne, Clora Lee didn't understand what females got out of wrapping their mouths around males dicks. But she knew what ever it was, her mother and Ella was getting the same thing from Big Willie. And from the way Mrs. Arnold's head kept going up and down, it told both Clora Lee as well as Cowayne, it had to be something awful good. And the kids knew poor Jonathan had to be in a whole lot pain, being that his eyes were shut tighter then any slave, who had taken a good taste of Duval's whip. Yet the poor boy never cried out from the awful punishment, as his right leg shook intensively, while levitating a few inches above the bed.

By the time Jonathan's leg took a brake from its intense shaking, the teens were whispering about their master, who was off fighting in his Civil War. And before Clora Lee could say the man was going to be more then a bit mad about his wife's activities, the woman was on her way to doing something far worst then the kids could have ever imagined. For Mrs. Arnold straddled Jonathan, and placed his firmly erected cock inside of her juicy wet cut. And right away, Clora Lee was thrown back to her and old Mae's conversation. Yet the girl couldn't believe their Misses, wanted to have young ones for a slave.

As Mrs. Arnold went about riding Jonathan, like she often rode that old white horse, them Rebs stole, like a bunch of thieves, Clora Lee got the feeling they were being watched. Yet as her eyes went from window to window, the teen didn't see a soul looking out at them. And when her eyes returned to the action, Jonathan was on top of Mrs. Arnold, and the woman was clawing his back, the way a cat scratches a piece of wood, or a tree.

"Oh," Mrs. Arnold grunted. "Oh! Oh God! Oh God, this dick, is killing me. Oh God! Ooo shit, God, this mother fucker is good. He's killing me, Godddd!" Mrs. Arnold shouted, as Jonathan had her knees pinned to her shoulders. Work it, Jonny, work it, you big dick mother fucker, work it. Work it, like them good for nothing slaves, worked those fields, or it's going to be the whip for your big dick ass," Mrs. Arnold painfully shouted, as Jonathan stabbed his black dick, deep between her pink walls.

By the time Jonathan's stroking had became that of a violent animal, as he tried to dig deeper into Mrs. Arnold's furry pink love box, Clora Lee knew the show was about to come to an end. And the way he moved, as well as the way she held him, told the kids, the slave had been there a few times before. But as the newly preferred house slave took a brake from his savage stroking, just so he could maneuver Mrs. Arnold to another position, the kids wondered what they would be seeing next. But by the time the woman was on her knees, with her ass shouting, here I am, take me for your selfish pleasure, you big dick mother fucker, Clora Lee was well on her way to climbing higher in that old tree.

"Lee, where you's going," Cowayne whispered.

"To see the floor."

"What you's wanna see the floor for?"

"So I's uh can see God."

"Ha you's know's he's on the floor?"

"Cause I's ain't see'd him, no where else."

Knowing she had only one question to ask the white man's God, Clora Lee wasn't wasting any time in her effort to get higher in their tree. For even if it were to cost the girl her soul, Clora Lee was going to shout to the white man's God, what gives you the right, to say we must be slaves? But after climbing as high as she could, which was more then enough to see the whole floor, the young female still didn't see the white man's God. For after all of her efforts, the only thing she saw, was more of the same old dusty floor. And even though the girl was well hidden, she could have sworn, Jonathan knew they were there, as he winked his eye right before smiling.

"Come on, let's go," Clora Lee whispered, as she began to slither her way back down the tree.

With their feet back on solid ground, Clora Lee and Cowayne headed out across the fence, hoping to find a new adventure. And once in the brush, the two knew they had made another clean get away, as they came out of the dense wooded area, running like a couple of wild horses.

"What God look like?" Clora Lee asked, when their running came to an end.

"I's uh ain't never see'd him," Cowayne mumbled.

"You's think, we's uh ever see him?"

"Maybe we's uh see him, next time," Cowayne said softly, not wanting to disappoint his Lee.

"Where we's going?" Clora Lee asked, as she took hold of Cowayne's hand.

"If n we's gon leave here, we's gotta know ha to shoot," Cowayne said, as he appeared to be focused on something.

The two adventure seekers went and got their pistols, then headed off to practice. And just like the soldiers, there would be no playing around for the two friends. For if the children was going to leave that old plantation, then they had to be ready. And that meant the two would have to practice everyday, if they were going to be just as good as the white man.

When Cowayne and Clora Lee were all out of shots, the two kids were forced to hang around the main yard. And with the traps bringing in only enough meat for one meal a day, Cowayne had begun to second guest his decision to use the shots and powder for practice. But Clora Lee quickly reminded him, that knowing how to shoot was just as important, as eating. And she also pointed out, hanging around the main yard, made Sistah feel a whole lot better, which Cowayne had to agree.

One day while eating in front of the blacksmith shed, Cowayne, Clora Lee, and Matthew saw Sistah barreling their way. And from the way Sistah was running, Cowayne could tell his mother was fighting mad.

"Pleasant, Mae say you's gotta come quick," she shouted, before reaching the blacksmith shed.

"Them Rebs, back?" Pleasant asked, as he rushed out of the shed.

"No, Big Willie took Ethel food," Sistah said angrily.

Without giving the old slave's call to arms a second thought, Pleasant left Sistah and Matthew in the dust, as he, Cowayne, and Clora Lee dashed across the yard for the female shed. And when Pleasant rounded the corner of the old building, he ran up behind Big Willie and knocked him over. With the slave having grown seven inches taller and about forty pounds heavier in the past thirteen years, he was truly a force to be reckoned with. But for Big Willie, it wasn't going to be a fight, being that Pleasant had Duval's knife against the large slave's throat.

"You's ain't gon take nothing, from nobody, no mo," Pleasant growled. "Cowayne, you's get them young ns out uh here. Na," Pleasant shouted, seeing that his young friend wasn't moving.

With the large blade at his throat, Big Willie didn't hesitate to call on old Mae. And the way his eyes fell on the old female, told everyone, the plantation's prize bull was scared. For Pleasant had succeeded in reducing their master's top dog, to a helpless begging pup.

"Let him up," old Mae said, as if she held a great deal of concern, for the worthless excuse for a father.

Pleasant didn't budge an inch, as he kept the knife pressed against Big Willie's throat. For the first time in years, Pleasant was ignoring the old slave, the same way he did, when she told him to keep his cotton. And all Cowayne and Clora Lee needed to do, to end Big Willie's life, were to take the children away, like the helpful slave asked them to.

"You's let him up, na Pleasant, cause we's don't kill our own," old Mae said with a tremble in her voice.

Pleasant had no intentions of honoring the pleading request, as he stared at Big Willie with a deadly appetite, to press the knife deep into his throat. And with Pleasant's nostrils flaring from hate, Sistah knew her friend really wanted to kill the large slave.

"Pleasant, na you's get off him, like Mae done told ya," Sistah said, after hearing Ethel cry out to the old slave for Big Willie's life.

"You's leave me be," Pleasant said with a deadly tone.

Sistah desperately wanted to do as Pleasant asked, yet she couldn't bring herself to stand by, and watch him kill Big Willie in front of the children.

"Na Pleasant, I's uh ain't gon tell ya no mo you's leave him be."

After hesitating for a moment, Pleasant allowed Big Willie to live, but for how long, no one knew. For not even Sistah could guarantee the large slave, he would still be among the living come morning. All the misfortunate female could give the slave that father Ethel's first child, was safe passage back to Duval's shack. And as she stood in front of Pleasant, allowing their master's top dog to dart off in shame, the misfourtunate female cast her eyes on Clora Lee. For the girl held a look of complete and utter disappointment.

By the time old Pete had gotten wind of Pleasant and Big Willie's altercation, the old slave sent for the helpful one. But Pleasant didn't make the trip alone. For Sistah, Matthew, Clora Lee, and Cowayne accompanied their friend to the back of the mansion. And as the five slaves caught sight of old Pete, they saw Effie placing a cup of water in his hand. And seeing such a thing, four of the five slaves, quickly realized, the old slave was blind.

"Old Pete, we's got Pleasant," Clora Lee said, as her and the rest of the group drew closer to the blind slave.

"I's uh see," old Pete said, turning his head in their direction. "I's hear, you's got trouble with Big Willie," old Pete continued, right before taking a drink from the cup.

"I's uh ain't got, no trouble," Pleasant mumbled.

"Then I's uh speck, you's better sit down," the old gray headed slave said.

"We's sitting," Clora Lee blurted out, even though Pleasant was still standing.

"I's uh can't member when, but I's uh member, there was this white man, and he's had a white fighter from a place call England. He's uh called him, the Queen's champion, and I's reckon, he's was. And that Queen's champion, went all over, whipping white folk like he's ain't like um uh tall. And theys ended up down in Louisiana, drinking and yelling up uh storm. Theys said, ain't uh soul, in America, uh beat that old Queen's champion. And they's had uh white man drinking, said Big Willie uh beat him. Then that old England man told him to go get his Big Willie, so that Queen's champion can beat him to," old Pete said, then took another drink of water.

The old slave lowered the cup with a puzzled look on his face. And for some strange reason, old Pete took a deep breath before going on with his story from days gone by.

"I's uh reckon, we's was bout to take them dogs out, when uh rider came through them gates out yonder," old Pete said pointing. "When he's done told masa Arnold what he's come for, I's uh had to put them hounds up. The next thing I's know'd, masa Arnold and Jeremiah had done took Big Willie to fight that old Queen's champion."

Old Pete took another deep breath, as if he was tired, then the aging slave picked up where he left off. "When they's got to Louisiana, masa Arnold told Big Willie to play with that old Queen's champion uh spell. And Big Willie tried to do like masa Arnold, done told him, but when he's hit that Queen's champion, he's fell plum down. And Big Willie would uh killed him, if n masa Arnold had uh mind for him to do so," old Pete assured the small group of friends. "Big Willie is my boy, but he's uh kill any body, for masa Arnold. Na you's mind what I's say, cause you's can't take ya eyes off him, cause he's uh kill ya, na masa Arnold gone."

"He's ain't gon do no such thing," Clora Lee shouted, just before making a mad dash for the barn.

Knowing his Lee would be crying, Cowayne went after her, leaving Pleasant, Sistah, and Matthew, to hear the rest of old Pete's story.

After entering the barn, Cowayne went straight to the loft, where he found Clora Lee laying on what little straw they had left. The pretty little slave was crying, as if the whip had been put to her in the worst way. And being young, Cowayne didn't know what to say, so he just put his arm around Clora Lee, and waited for her to stop crying. But Clora Lee couldn't stop crying, being that Big Willie was already hurting her mother.

"He's ain't, Lee, cause we gon take Pleasant with us," Cowayne said, hoping his words would bring an end to the girl's crying.

After hearing the heart warming statement, Clora Lee sprung to her knees. And without giving the boy a chance to react, she wrapped the poor fellow in her arms, and held him with a passion like never before. And with his face jammed between the two small lumps, that he had gazed up on nearly three month earlier, Cowayne found it hard to breath. Yet the lumps were not on Cowayne's mind, as he tried to turn his head, to catch some air. But the harder Cowayne tried to turn his head, the tighter Clora Lee held him.

"Lee," Cowayne mumbled, as he tried to suck in some air.

"What?" Clora Lee barked, as she sent Cowayne crashing down to the straw, with her on top of him.

And when Cowayne grunted from the impact, Clora Lee found his discomfort to be rather pleasing, as their eyes navigated them toward uncharted waters. And venturing into such waters, would surely bring the two young slaves, a whole lot of trouble from Sistah. But as Clora Lee felt Cowayne's body stiffing beneath her, she felt like ripping the skin off of their friendship, to reveal what was hidden just below the surface. And what better way to start it, seeing that she had Cowayne in the perfect position.

"What you's thinking bout?" Clora Lee asked, as her body tingled uncontrollably.

"I's uh ain't thinking bout nothing," Cowayne replied, as his fingers trembled, while resting on the small of Clora Lee's back.

After using her nose to tease Cowayne's face, Clora Lee got up to go take a look outside, thus putting an end to their little game of chance. And as she stood looking down from the loft, Clora Lee was torn by the fact, her and Cowayne, could never have a baby like Sistah. For Clora Lee much preferred to have daughters to grow up like Sistah, rather then Ethel. And Clora Lee vowed at that very moment, never to treat her children, the way Ethel often treated Matthew.

"You's alright?" Cowayne asked.

While staring out across the yard, the words, I's uh swear to ya, I's uh gon be the best mother, you's ever see'd, stumbled out of Clora Lee's mouth. And there was something about the look in the girl's eyes, which told Cowayne things would be just as his friend stated.

On the first rainy day, after Pleasant and Big Willie had their altercation, Clora Lee and Cowayne were standing in the doorway of the old barn. The two were flipping their hands in and out of the rain, to see which one of them could do it, without making contact with so much as a drop of water. And like always, Clora Lee was keeping count, even though Cowayne was beating her badly, which gave the young female a reason to dabble in a spot of cheating. But to Cowayne, Clora Lee's cheating, was just as welcome, as a clear cut victory. For that was the message, he took from the Indians, after fighting his best fight, only to lose? And from that day forward, Cowayne had never forgotten the big warrior's words. He, who wins, must prepare to fight again. He, who loses, may have fought his last fight. So it didn't matter to Cowayne how his Lee won, as long as she was able to fight again.

As the two laughed, while playing their game, Obdi came dashing through the rain. The house slave was headed to the blacksmith shop, where he would find Pleasant tinkering as usual. And after the Blue Coats last visit to the plantation, Obdi started a daily routine, which had him spending time out among the field slaves.

"Clora Lee, ya ma looking for ya," the slave shouted, as the rain attacked his body, like a thousand shots fired by an army of weeping dead soldiers.

"Where she's at," Clora Lee yelled through her laughter, after tossing a hand full of rain water on Cowayne.

"In front of the female shed," Obdi shouted, as he continued on with his wet journey.

With the old hand me down dress held up around her knees, Clora Lee darted out in the rain after Cowayne. The two were laughing as if the rain was Sistah, tickling them on a bright sunny day. But Cowayne saw Clora Lee's laughter to be more of a hinder, rather then a form of humor. And that was why the teen didn't wait for his friend to catch up. For Cowayne took their situation, as another form of training, that needed to be done right.

"You's gotta catch up, Lee," Cowayne shouted, as he pushed his friend, to make her stronger.

Feeling that the statement didn't need a response, Clora Lee went right on running, as they rounded the chain master shack, bringing the female shed in to their sights. Then like the cunning fox that he was, Cowayne slid to an amazing stop. Yet Clora Lee wasn't so fortunate, as she rumbled toward Cowayne out of control.

"Cowayne!" the young female yelled, as if her life was in danger.

Cowayne turned around just in time, to see his Lee coming at him like a wounded goose.

"Don't you's let me fall or I's uh gon whop you's good," Clora Lee bellowed, through her laughter.

Cowayne braced himself and caught Clora Lee as she ran right into his arms. And after a quick three hundred and sixty degree spin with his Lee, Cowayne safely places her feet back on to not so solid ground.

It didn't take long for the other slaves to start laughing, as they watched the two youngsters at their best. And a smiling Clora Lee was more then willing to give the other slaves a good laugh, as she tried her best to get a punch through Cowayne's well crafted defense. But when Ethel told Clora Lee to go get her stuff, the girl's laughter quickly came to an end.

"What stuff?" Clora Lee asked, finally noticing the bundle in her mother's hand.

"We's leaving, na come on, so we's can go," Ethel said.

Then just like Clora Lee, the other slaves no longer had a desire to laugh, as they watched the girl turn her eyes to Matthew, who was standing next to old Mae crying up a storm. And right away, Clora Lee knew her little brother would not be going with them, which made the girl's heart heavy. For unlike their mother, Clora Lee would rather die, then to leave her little brother behind.

"But I's uh don't wanna go," Clora Lee cried.

"Na Clora Lee, we's gotta go, fo the rain stop, so you's gone get ya stuff," Ethel said, looking at old Mae.

"But ma, I's wanna stay here with Mae," Clora Lee said, as she never took her watery eyes off of Matthew.

"Na Clora Lee, Mae already got too much to worry with, so you's gone get ya stuff."

"But I's uh ain't gon be no trouble, I's promise, I's won't," Clora Lee said, sounding like Matthew and Cowayne.

And Clora Lee wanted so much for Cowayne to make Ethel go away, as her eyes fell on him. But Cowayne couldn't help his friend, as he himself wanted to cry. For Ethel was Clora Lee's mother, and nothing on earth was going to change that. So the boy just stood in the rain, hoping for a miracle that would keep him and his friend together.

"Mae, tell her, I's uh ain't gon be no trouble," Clora Lee said, as she ducked behind Cowayne.

"Na Ethel, you's knows that child ain't no trouble," the old slave said, knowing that she and Sistah were already taking care of the girl.

"But Mae…"

Ethel stopped short of completing her statement, when Sistah came up and stood behind Matthew with an unfriendly stare. And the not so fortunate female didn't have to say a word, for Ethel to know what she was thinking. And that left the worthless mother feeling trapped, as she tried to figure a way out of her unwanted predicament. For Sistah had a pair of breeches on under her dress, and an old Rebel coat covering her upper body. That told everyone, including Ethel, there was going be a rumble in the mud. But before Ethel could say another word, Clora Lee made her predicament a lot more cumbersome.

"I's uh ain't gon go, ma. I's uh gon stay here with Cowayne, cause we's gotta feed Mae and Matthew," Clora Lee cried.

Hearing her daughter loud and clear, while watching Pleasant come up on the opposite side of the shed, had Ethel feeling like death was looking to take her and Big Willie down into its deep dark hole. And fearing the worst, Ethel walked over to Clora Lee and Cowayne with her arms ready to hug them both. And as Clora Lee cried, so did her mother. The two were crying for two different reasons, yet from the same cause. Clora Lee was crying, because she didn't want to leave her one true love. Yet Ethel tears were falling, because she would never have, what had been laid at her daughter's feet. For the departing slave, knew Cowayne loved her daughter just as much, if not more then his own life.

"You's take care of her, you's hear," Ethel said to Cowayne, like she did the night Clora Lee was born.

"I's will," Cowayne said sadly.

"And you's be good to Cowayne," Ethel said crying. "And ya'll look after ya little brother."

"Them young ns drag my baby all over this plantation," Sistah snarled, cutting Ethel off.

Ethel stood back to take her last look at Clora Lee. And as the two stood crying, Ethel tried to muster up a smile, but her pain was far too great for such a feat. She was leaving two of her babies, and that was killing the female from the inside. But what could she do? Big Willie didn't want Matthew, and Clora Lee didn't want her. And that left the young mother wishing, she had never been born. For a life like hers, was far worst then any person, who had never lived at all.

"Will you come on," Big Willie snapped, as he eyed Pleasant standing with both hands behind his back.

Ethel gave Clora Lee one last hug, before walking away with the other slaves. Yet the mother, Clora Lee saw as worthless, couldn't bring herself to stop looking back at the two children she was leaving behind. And with every step that took Ethel further away from her babies, it brought her closer to a pain that would come from seeing Clora Lee and Matthew clinging to each other, as they both cried in the pouring rain.

That night, and many nights there after, Clora Lee held Matthew until he cried himself to sleep. And with each passing night, Clora Lee's anger grew stronger, seeing that she ended up crying as well. Yet Clora Lee would not allow her pain to go unrewarded, as she vowed to hate Ethel for all eternity. And as for Big Willie, Clora Lee knew if she ever laid eyes on him again, he would not escape death a second time.

Chapter 10

Vows

Summer had came and gone, by the time Matthew was able to fall asleep without crying. And during that time, Clora Lee and Cowayne didn't stray too far from the plantation. For the two spent most of their time, teaching the little boy how to be strong. That meant every morning, Matthew got up with Cowayne to check their traps. And it didn't take the little slave long to learn how to reset each and every trap, just the way Cowayne had showed him. But Matthew still had one lingering problem. He had yet to get Ethel and their baby sister out of his head, which drove Clora Lee crazy.

WITH MATTHEW SPENDING SO much time with Cowayne and Clora Lee, Sistah's job had become far too easy. And feeling Sistah had too much free time for her liking, old Mae would often use Matthew, to ruffle the disfunctional female's feathers. And on a fall morning, the old slave sought to do just that.

"Na Sistah, where's yo's baby," old Mae asked the misfortunate slave, after winking at Isabella.

"Mae, you's knows, Matthew's running round here with them young ns," Sistah replied with a bit of frustration.

"Na Sistah, I's uh done told ya, I's done see'd that boy go round yonder, with one uh them girls," the old slave said, as she lied for no reason, other then to get under Sistah's skin.

"Na Mae, you's knows, you's ain't told me no such thing," Sistah said in a state of panic, as she ran off in search of Matthew.

While Sistah went off on another wild goose chase, old Mae and the other females quickly took to laughing like they always did. And no matter how many times Isabella told the old slave she was wrong, for treating Sistah in such a manner, every one went right on laughing just the same. For the slaves may not have been free, but the war had brought them something they never had. And for that, the slaves were thankful, as they often enjoyed their free time with a good laugh or two.

As the slaves found them selves with the ability to laugh, they still didn't know what to make of the white man's war. Nor did the slaves know what to expect, when ever the white men made up their minds, to bring that old war to an end. But there was one thing Clora Lee and Cowayne did know. No matter how or when that old war came to an end, they would be prepared to make their move.

On a day when the sun kept playing tricks with the clouds, Clora Lee and Cowayne ran across, what they took to be Chief Bent Tree and his band of Indians. The two started waving their hands, hoping to get the Indians attention. But to Cowayne and Clora Lee's surprise, the Chief kept his people at a safe distance, while sending a warrior over to check things out.

"What you want?" the warrior asked, in his bold and strong voice.

"We's was saying hello to Chief Bent Tree," Cowayne replied.

"You see Bent Tree?" the warrior asked.

"He's right there," Clora Lee said, as she pointed to the Chief.

"Come," the warrior said firmly, as his eyes never stop scanning the area, to make sure the children were alone.

The two young slaves followed the warrior over to the rest of his tribe. And upon approaching the tribe, they noticed something different about the Chief. He had an age old scar that ran from his right eye, down to his throat. A scar that made it perfectly clear to the two young slaves, the Chief wasn't the friend they were happy to see.

Yet if it were not for the unsightly scar, Clora Lee and Cowayne would have gone right on thinking their friend had forgotten them.

"Them know Bent Tree," the warrior said to the Chief.

"How many moons, you see my brother?" the Chief asked, as his English sounded comfortably better then Bent Tree's.

Having just enough knowledge of the Indian language, to understand what the Chief was asking them, the two teens talked it over for a moment, before Cowayne gave their answer.

"We's saw him last year, round this time," Cowayne said, looking at the children eyeing their rabbits. "Yo's young ns hungry?" Cowayne asked the Chief.

A white woman living among the tribe with her young son, who was half Indian, spoke for the Chief, saying they were all hungry.

Seeing that she and the little boy shared the same problem, Clora Lee asked the half breed child to pick a warrior to fight Cowayne, to save face for his people. And after taking a quick look at all of the warriors, the little boy walked up to Cowayne, and stood ready for battle. But with the child being younger than Matthew, Cowayne couldn't stop himself from letting out a light chuckle.

"Joe Buck," the white woman called out to her son.

Knowing he would not back down if it were him, Cowayne felt it was his responsibility to pick a worthy opponent. So with an unmistakable boldness, the adventurous slave, walked over to a warrior, who was slightly larger, then the one he fought from Bent Tree's tribe, and called him out. Yet the warrior laughed at Cowayne, in the same manner, in which he did Joe Buck. But being that Cowayne didn't have Sistah to act in the same manner as Joe Buck's mother, the teen was able to call his own shot.

"You's laugh, when yo's people go hungry," Cowayne said, then spat on the ground, sending a message to the warrior, telling him, he was unworthy to be a member of the tribe.

With Cowayne's insult guiding his decision, the warrior stepped out and accepted the challenge. But when the competition started, the warrior quickly proved to Cowayne, he had made the wrong choice. Yet Cowayne fought the warrior until he couldn't pick himself up off of the ground, which told the whole tribe, he was hungry to earn his very own feather.

"It is the smart mountain cat, which moves away from the bear," the warrior said, as he stood over Cowayne.

"But it is the bear, who makes the foolish cat stronger," Cowayne replied.

Knowing that Cowayne search ran like a frighten deer, the warriors sat in a circle around him. And each warrior pointed out to the young slave, his every mistake. But Cowayne biggest bit of knowledge came by way of the Chief. For the Chief told the young slave, he should always be sure of what the eyes see, before revealing himself, and his squaw. And Cowayne clearly understood what the Chief meant by his statement. For the wise old Indian was talking about those who may appear to be a friend, yet end up being a foe.

"Who fights like a bear, yet speaks like a rain drop?" Cowayne asked, after standing up.

With the warriors chuckling like crazy, Cowayne realized, he had to work on speaking like an Indian, just as much as he needed to work on his fighting techniques.

"I am call, Tall Tree," the Chief replied, when he finally stopped laughing.

"You's ain't very tall," Cowayne noted, looking at the Chief.

"Him brother, is the short one," an old Indian said, then laughed.

When Cowayne and Clora Lee left the band of Indians, the two were far more excited about Tall Tree and his tribe, than they were of Bent Tree and his group. And the two couldn't stop talking about all that the Indians had taught them, as they ran home to feed their family.

As time moved on at its own set pace, bit by bit, Clora Lee incorporated the things she picked up from the squaws into her cooking.

"Where's you's learn that?" Sistah asked Clora Lee one day, while they were cleaning two coons.

Before Clora Lee could answer Sistah, she spotted Jonathan eyeing her. And even though she knew the rarely seen slave was on his way to see Mrs. Arnold, Clora Lee didn't say a thing about it to Sistah. Yet the teen knew Jonathan would be dead, as soon as their master made it home from the war. And as Clora Lee imagine the slave's body hanging from a tree, she heard the words, don't you go looking at him, come crawling in from out of no where. It was Effie, and the female, quickly made a bad feeling come over the young teen.

"Tell Mae, Pete has died," Effie said, as if she were a white woman.

Clora Lee sat trembling, as she so much wanted to grab Effie and beat her, the way Mrs. Arnold had beaten Cowayne. But all Clora Lee could do, was to think about old Pete, and what he meant to Jeremiah.

"I's uh gotta get back to the house," Effie said, as if she was trying to taunt her grand-daughter.

After telling Cowayne about old Pete, the two set out to go see the last remains of their trusted friend. But by the time Clora Lee and Cowayne made it to the back steps of the mansion, the two found they were too late. For Nelson had already loaded his father's body in a buckboard, and he and Obdi, were on their way to bury him.

"Can we go?" Cowayne asked Sistah, as Nelson and Obdi lead the wagon toward the front gate.

Being that old Mae had already asked the misfortunate slave to go and sing a song for old Pete, Sistah didn't see any reason for her babies not make the trip as well. So with her arms around Clora Lee and Cowayne, Sistah started walking behind the wagon, as she took to humming.

When the buckboard came to a stop, it sat beneath a great oak tree, nearly two hundred yards north of the front gate. And with every one crying except for him, Nelson knew his father would truly be missed. Yet as he gave Pleasant one of the two shovels from the wagon, Nelson couldn't bring himself to think of his big brother, nor the ill deed, which separated the two of them. But by the time he and Pleasant started digging, Nelson had to stop for a moment, to stare at his father's lifeless body, knowing the slave died with a heavy heart. But as for Pleasant, he went right on digging, while never taking his watery eyes off of Clora Lee and Cowayne, as the two appeared to be whispering about something.

With nearly an hour of digging under his belt, Pleasant stopped for the fifth time, to wipe the sweat from his brow. And being eager to try his hand at digging, Cowayne pounced on the opportunity that he and Clora Lee had been waiting for.

"You's want me to dig some," the teen asked, before Pleasant could put the piece of rag he was using for a handkerchief, back in his pocket.

Knowing the boy wasn't going to stop asking, until he got the chance to wrap his fingers around the shovel, Pleasant freely held the scoop out for the taking. And like a young warrior looking to earn his all important feather, Cowayne grabbed the digging tool, as if it was made of gold. But Cowayne strong desire, to tackle the shovel, was not seen as a good thing by Obdi. For with his soft hands and weak back, Obdi didn't wanted any part of the shovel, as he found himself forced to speak up.

"I's reckon, you's bout tired," Obdi said to Nelson.

When the grave was dug, and old Pete was laid to rest, Cowayne had earned one more bragging right. For the teen had worked his shovel, far better then Obdi, and almost as good as Pleasant, as far as Clora Lee saw it. And as the seven slaves stood around the mound of dirt, Cowayne and Clora Lee smiled proudly of his efforts, until they heard shots coming from over the hill. And even though the shots appeared to be coming from the neighboring plantation, which was a great deal of distance from where they were standing, it didn't make any difference. For it was more then enough, to send the slaves scrambling back to the main yard.

By the time winter had set in good, old Pete was just another conversation to help the slaves pass the time. And with food being something they rarely seen, Pleasant and Cowayne had to go a few days without eating, so the females and Matthew could eat. And on those days, Clora Lee would remember why she hated Ethel and Big Willie with every beat of her heart. They were no mother and father to her, and she would never forgive them, no matter what old Mae said. And for the pain of her brother, Clora Lee still clung to the vow, of killing the large slave.

One morning after not eating for two days, Cowayne came back with a fat turkey, and two rabbits. Upon approaching the main grounds, he saw a young slave name Dew Dap. The teen was the only slave Cowayne would spend time with, when Clora Lee found herself confined to the female shed.

"Morning," Dew Dap said, holding a single rabbit in his hand.

"That's all you's got?"

"They's ain't got much out, with it being cold, and all," Dew Dap replied sadly.

Knowing the teen had two other mouths to feed, Cowayne gave him one of his rabbits with out saying a word. And having no doubt, Dew Dap would do the same for him, Cowayne didn't wait around for the boy to say thank you, as they both went their separate ways.

Cowayne ended up at the blacksmith shed, where he gave the second rabbit to Obdi and Nelson. But the teen didn't hang around to dabble in a bit of male chatter, seeing that Clora Lee was waiting for him in front of the female shed. And the moment the boy reached the female sleeping quarters, he gave the large turkey to Clora Lee so the six of them and the females could eat. As for the house slaves, they had to fend for themselves, being that they had never did a hard day's work.

As the winter weather began to break, Clora Lee and Cowayne were back to hunting as a team. A team that was a little stronger, and a little larger. But most of all, the two were a whole lot wiser. For the cold winter days, had given the two a chance to create new plans, and set new goals for themselves. And the two teens most important goal, were to enlarge their hunting grounds.

With the new larger area forged in their heads, the two adventurous slaves struck out one morning just after the break of dawn. And not knowing what they were going to find, the two stayed optimistic. Yet, on their way back to the main yard, with two coons for Sistah to cook, Cowayne and Clora Lee spotted a horse. And just a few feet from the animal, there laid a dead soldier. And from the looks of the dead man, the children could tell that the coyotes had been chewing on his remains for a day or two.

"Hold the horse, Lee, while I's check his pockets," Cowayne said so soft, he was almost whispering.

Nervous and deeply afraid of the animal, Clora Lee prayed for the horse to keep still. And while she hoped her friend would do his job, a lot faster then he had ever did it before, every second still felt like a life time to the young female. But no sooner then Cowayne finished rummaging through the man's pockets, he went for the boots. And after the boots, Cowayne searched the saddle bags, which made Clora Lee internal struggle that much longer. And as Cowayne began to stuff her hands with the papers and other objects that would be of no use to them, Clora Lee felt like giving her friend a good lick up side his head.

"We's got it, Lee," Cowayne whispered, as if they were surrounded by a bunch of Rebs.

The two had hit pay dirt. The soldier had three boxes of shots, and a leather pouch full of powder. But being that she was still holding on to the horse, Clora Lee found her self unable to celebrate their stroke of good fortune. For she just stood nervously, hoping her friend would hurry up and take the damn animal.

"I's uh take him, Lee," Cowayne said, seeing that she was afraid of their four legged means of transportation. "Get on him, so I's can walk ya home," he said, taking the letter and the money from Clora Lee's hands.

Even though Clora Lee was deeply afraid of the animal, she would much rather die, then disappoint her Cowayne. So with her eyes closed, Clora Lee nervously got on the horse. And there she sat, knowing that Cowayne would always be there to protect her. Yet the poor girl wanted so much to load the dead soldier's pistol, and put a shot in that old horse, just so she wouldn't have to ride the stupid animal.

When the two reached the main yard, they quickly took the horse to the hay barn. Then Cowayne and Clora Lee set out to find every piece of rope, the soldiers didn't steal.

"I's found some," Matthew shouted, as he came dragging a role of rope.

"You's keep yo's voice down," Clora Lee said angrily.

"Where you's get it from?" Cowayne asked the little slave, as he knelt down in front of him.

"In masa Arnold barn," Matthew said, with his voice still ringing out like a church bell.

"Theys got mo?" Cowayne asked.

"Theys got uh heap," the boy replied, while nodding his head.

"Hide that with the horse, Lee. Come on Matthew, you's show me where you's got it from."

After sneaking into the barn that once held the Arnold's very expensive horses, Cowayne took to gathering up as much rope, as he could possibly carry. The teen then told Matthew to go keep an eye on Sistah. But before Matthew could reach the door, it began to slowly open with a horrifying creepiness, which left the boys not knowing what to do. And with it being too late for the both of them to hide the rope, and scurry up to the loft, the boys stood frozen stiff. But when Clora Lee eased her body through the slightly opened door like a lazy old cat, Matthew and Cowayne couldn't have felt better, if they had heard a mess of slaves shouting, we's free.

"Lee, you's nearly scared us to death," Cowayne cried, as he watched her softly laugh.

"That's what you's get, for leaving me with that old horse," Clora Lee said, as she felt a sense of satisfaction come over her.

After telling Matthew to go and get the two coons, and take them to Sistah, Clora Lee loaded Cowayne down with a few more rolls of rope. Then like the good mate that she was, Clora Lee placed a roll of rope on each of her shoulders and followed Cowayne back to their horse. And together, the two created a holding area for the horse, which they deemed a work of art.

The very next morning before dawn, Clora Lee and Cowayne went to the make shift corral, and spent about an hour, practicing how to ride their horse. And that became their daily routine, until even Matthew was able to ride the animal with a great deal of ease. Then like always, Cowayne caught a new idea. And after getting a good laugh, from sneaking up on the only father figure they ever knew, Clora Lee and Cowayne were ready to give their idea a try.

"Pleasant, You's knows ha to ride that old mule?" Cowayne asked, with a touch of laughter still lingering in his voice.

"What I's know bout ridding that old mule?" Pleasant asked, while wondering who could have put such a foolish notion in the children's heads.

"We's wanna see ya ride it," Clora Lee said, looking at Cowayne.

"I's uh ain't gon be messing round no mule, unless masa Arnold tell me to," Pleasant assured the meddlesome kids, as he hammered away on a piece of metal.

"But what if n them Blue Coats, beat them Rebs?" Clora Lee asked.

"I's uh ain't got nothing to do, with them that's doing theys fighting. And I's reckon, theys ain't got nothing to with me riding that old mule," Pleasant said, as he carefully inspected the piece of metal.

"But we's wanna see ya ride it," Cowayne said, as he tried to pull Pleasant away from the anvil.

"Na boy, you's turn me lose, cause I's got work to do."

"Come on Cowayne, let's go pick uh fight with the Misses," Clora Lee said, as she ran from the blacksmith shed, with Cowayne one step behind her.

"You's young n come back here," Pleasant shouted in fear, as he watched the children run toward the mansion."Cowayne! Cowayne! Clora Lee! I's uh do it, na you's come back here," Pleasant shouted in fear.

Pleasant was played, and played well, as the children quickly gave up on their fake attempt to pick a fight with Mrs. Arnold. But Pleasant didn't know that, and the slave had no intentions of calling the children's bluff. For Clora Lee and Cowayne meant far too much to both he and Sistah, to risk losing them over some stupid half lame mule.

"I's uh don't know what you's young n, gon get out of me riding this here old mule, but you's better hold that there animal," Pleasant said nervously.

"We's got him," Clora Lee said, even though Cowayne was the only one holding on to the plantation last remaining plow puller.

With his body trembling like the day he was captured, Pleasant eased down from the corral, and on to the animal's back. And he did it all, without taking a single breath, yet the children knew their friend would soon get over his fears. But first, Clora Lee and Cowayne had to make sure Pleasant got comfortable with that old mule, so they took him for a walk around that old coral.

With the impression that his deed was done, Pleasant barked, "Na you's young n stop this here animal, so I's can get off."

"But you's ain't ride him good, yet," Clora Lee cried in fun.

"I's uh swear, you's young n is up to something," Pleasant said, as he nervously sat up on the mule.

"We's want ya to know ha to ride, fo's masa Arnold get back," Cowayne said honestly.

Knowing the child like he did, Pleasant knew that was the only straight truth, Cowayne had told him in a long time. And at that very moment, Pleasant was willing to stake his life on Cowayne's words, as the children led their master's mule around the corral one more time.

With Pleasant's daily riding left in Matthew's hands, Clora Lee and Cowayne went back to shooting their pistols. But on a cloudy day, while trotting home after practicing, things took a turn for the worst. As the two went on and on about how their time spent with Pleasant, was the reason for them not shooting well, they ran into a spot of trouble. A burly, bearded Rebel soldier popped out from behind a tree, aiming his musket rifle at Cowayne.

"Where do you think, you're going, boy?" the Reb spat.

Cowayne and Clora Lee didn't say a word, as the two went about ploting their next move. And armed with his Indian training, Cowayne slowly moved toward the Reb, hoping he could occupy the white man, while Clora Lee made a run for it. But Clora Lee's thoughts were clearly different, right down to the smallest detail. For she was thinking the two of them could attack the Reb, get his rifle and kill him dead.

"Did you hear me boy? I asked you, where you be heading?" the Reb growled a second time.

Clora Lee shied away from Cowayne, while raising her dress just a tad. For the girl was placing her faith, in what she often heard Sistah and the other females said about white men. And from the look on the Rebel's face, Clora Lee knew every word she heard was true.

"Get over there, boy," the soldier spat, as he licked his lips.

Cowayne slowly moved to his right, as his eyes walked up and down the white man's body. The young slave was trying to do like Pleasant and the Indian warriors taught him. He was trying to notice the man's strengths, while hoping to detect a few of his weaknesses.

But being afraid for his Lee, Cowayne wasn't able to think straight. For he just kept hoping, Clora Lee would take off running.

"Right there, boy," the soldier said, when he felt Cowayne was at a safe distance. "Na you come here, girlly, cause I ain't going to hurt you none," the bearded face man said, as he looked at Clora Lee with a burning hunger.

"No, you's gon shoot me," Clora Lee said in a voice, she had been saving for Cowayne.

"Now why would I shoot, a pretty little girl like you?" the Reb asked, with his eyes fixed on Clora Lee's fair colored legs.

Like Eve with a basket of apples, Clora Lee backed up a little further, knowing it would entice the Reb even more. For Clora Lee could tell by the way the man took a quick look at Cowayne, killing him was going to be a lot easier then she thought. But when the Reb laid his rifle down and pointed to it, while stating, he didn't mean her any harm, Clora Lee felt the fool was making it too easy. So with her dress up a little higher, Clora Lee made a deceptive run for it, luring the Rebel away from his rifle. But before Clora Lee could shout in victory, her life began to fall apart.

In as much time as it take for a cat to bat its eyes, Clora Lee realized her and Cowayne wasn't thinking the same thing. For Cowayne had charged the Reb, rather then going for the rifle. And as Clora Lee watched Cowayne strike the man up side the head with a leaping blow, she could have sworn, he told her to run. But Clora Lee couldn't run, seeing that the Reb had caught hold of her Cowayne.

Left with only a sense of urgency for a weapon, Clora Lee didn't know what to do, as a sharp pain shot through her head, thus turning the girl's state of panic, in to one giant Arnold's rage. And while the young female felt she had to do something, to get the Rebel's hands from around Cowayne's throat, her anger was moving faster then a runaway train. Yet when Clora Lee heard Cowayne say, what she felt were his dying words, the dam busted, flooding her body with pure Arnold's hate.

"You's leave Cowayne be," Clora Lee shouted, as she ignored his dying call for her to run.

But the Reb had no intentions of allowing Cowayne to live. For the man knew once he killed Cowayne, the pretty little slave girl was his for the taking. And that old stinking Reb had planned on doing a lot of taking, once he rid himself of his one and only obstacles.

"I's uh told ya, to leave Cowayne be," Clora Lee shouted.

Knowing that he was in full control of the situation, the Rebel smiled and winked at Clora Lee, the same way Jonathan did from Mrs. Arnold's bedroom. But unlike Jonathan, the soldier was a threat to Clora Lee, and all that she held deep in her heart. And seeing Cowayne punches grow weaker with every swing, Clora Lee began to cry, as she picked up the soldier's rifle and took aim.

"I's uh ain't gon tell ya no mo, na you's leave Cowayne be," Clora Lee shouted, as the tears ran down her face.

Without ever feeling her finger move, Clora Lee squeezed the trigger, causing the Reb to grunt. And Cowayne could hear the soldier release his last foul breath, telling the boy that he was dead. But the soldier's death, ended up being just as much of a problem, as his living. For the vastly over weight man, collapsed like a rotten tree, in a bad storm, taking Cowayne down with him. And with no better luck then a blind man in a pissing match, Cowayne ended up on his back, with the foul smelling tree on top of him.

If being trapped beneath the nearly three hundred pound Reb wasn't bad enough, Cowayne also had to deal with Clora Lee's sudden burst of rage. And as she kicked the dead soldier's face with every ounce of energy, her body could drum up from the depths of Hell, Cowayne continued to work his way from beneath the enemy that was no more.

"I's uh gon kill ya, if n you's don't leave Cowayne be," Clora Lee shouted, as she went right on kicking the Rebel soldier. "Do you's hear me, Reb? I's uh gon kill ya. Na you's leave Cowayne be," she shouted, after placing two more kicks to the dead man's face.

By the time Cowayne had squeezed and squirmed his way from beneath the Reb, Clora Lee had nearly kicked the white man back to life. And she would have went on kicking the dead soldier, until old Pete rose from his grave, if it were not for Cowayne.

"He's dead, Lee," Cowayne said, as he took the rifle from her hands.

"I's uh don't care, he's need to leave ya be," Clora Lee shouted, as if she was mad with her friend.

Cowayne took Clora Lee by the hand, as his eyes scanned the area, to see if there were soldiers coming to investigate the shooting.

"Come on Lee, we's gotta go," he whispered.

With the two teens back on the move, as they ran wrecklessly through the dense forest, neither had planned on stopping, until their feet, were safely back on the main yard. But before the two reached the end of the brush, Cowayne thought about Sistah. For the boy didn't want his second mother to catch them breathing hard. So with hopes of out foxing his loving mother, Cowayne brought their running to a stop, at the edge of the brush.

"I's killed him," Clora Lee said, still clinging to that unmistakable Arnold's stare. "And I's uh kill him again, if n he's touch ya. I's uh kill any body, if n they's touch ya. You's hear me, Cowayne? I's uh kill any body, that uh hurt ya," Clora Lee said crying.

Clora Lee didn't have to tell the boy, she would back up her threat. For he knew all too well, the girl meant every word she said. And knowing that his Lee would stand behind her word, Cowayne became frighten. For he couldn't help but wonder, if she would kill his mother or Sistah, if one of them were to strike him? But Cowayne didn't get the chance to ask Clora Lee if she would do such a thing, being that the two heard something moving in the brush.

"Come on Lee, we's gotta get over the fence."

The lovers left the brush, without ever looking back. But if the two young slaves had taken the time to look over their shoulders, they would have seen a deer scamper out of the brush in fear, which may have been an early warning. For someone, or something, was in the brush with them, and the deer had given creedance to that.

By the time Cowayne had laid his head down for the night, the boy found himself with a lot to think about. He nearly lost his Lee, and that scared the life out of him. And the young slave didn't know what he would have done, if the Reb had gotten his hands on Clora Lee. Yet Cowayne couldn't figure out where he went wrong, in his attack on the large white man. Nor could he come to a conclusion, about the sound they heard in the brush. And Cowayne wondered why he always felt like someone was following him. And as he began to drift off to sleep, Cowayne made the hardest decision of his young life. For he had made the decision to leave Clora Lee behind, knowing she wasn't going to like it one bit.

The next morning when Clora Lee opened her eyes, and found Cowayne had set out without her, she became seriously angry. And as she stepped out of the female shed, Clora Lee was determine to give Cowayne a piece of her mind. But in order for her to do such a thing, she had to find the rambling teen. And Clora Lee knew she had to find the love of her life, before a mess of Rebs got a hold of him. Rebs that looked just like the one she killed. The one she would gladly kill again, if he were to put his filthy hands on her Cowayne. And that was the very reason, why Clora Lee had to find her Cowayne, before he ran into another stinking Reb.

After tipping pass Pleasant, who was sleeping on the ground, next to Matthew, Clora Lee headed for the fence. But no sooner then the young female, passed the large magnolia tree, she abruptly came to a stop.

With her feet no longer moving, Clora Lee put her eyes and ears to work, just like the Indians had taught them. The young female was sure something was out there, and it was following her. And when Clora Lee heard a twig snap, just before the night air went silent, she took off running. But where would she go, being that the sound had came from behind her, which meant the girl couldn't go back toward the female shed. So with nowhere for her to go but to the mansion, Clora Lee hastily headed for the large house. And as she ran while constantly looking over her shoulder, the last thing to cross the girl's mind, was Cowayne saying, for the two of them, never to do such a thing.

"What's wrong, Lee?" Cowayne asked, taking hold of her, as she ran in to him.

"Theys after me," Clora Lee replied, with her arms wrapped around his neck.

"You's wait here," Cowayne whispered, while prying himself free from Clora Lee fearful grip.

But if Cowayne thought for one minute, Clora Lee was going to stand alone in the dark, after nearly having the life scared out of her, he was wrong. With her hands gripping his shirt at the waist, Clora Lee was determined not to let Cowayne out of her sight. And as they retraced her steps from the mansion, back toward the female shed, the two ran up on Jonathan, who had the smell of a fresh bath.

"Why you's following Lee?" Cowayne growled.

"What I's need her for?" Jonathan grumbled, as he lustifully eyed the pretty young female.

Jonathan's answer, along with his staring, didn't set well with Cowayne. The young slave had his fill, of males looking at Clora Lee, as if she were a chunk of meat. And with his fingers crunched into a fist, Cowayne was ready for another fight. But before he could attack Jonathan, a white tail deer dashed across the yard, heading for the fence. And by the time everyone realized what had passed before their eyes, the deer was over the fence and gone, which gave Jonathan cause to laugh, as he went about his business.

With the new house boy on his way, Clora Lee and Cowayne stood in the dark watching him, as he walked up to the mansion, and enter the large house, as if he owned the place.

Seeing that everything was all right, Cowayne and Clora Lee headed for their traps, never noticing the shadowy figure lurking in the dark. And with the figure never moving a muscle, as it stood staring at the two young slaves, as if it were waiting for the right moment to strike, made for a disasterous situation. But when a lantern showed up in Mrs. Arnold's bedroom, the shadowy figure sent its eyes in the direction of the light. Yet it only stared at the window for a brief moment, then it to, moved on as well, keeping its intentions hid.

After what had been a long morning, the two slaves walked away from their traps with only five rabbits. The two couldn't believe they didn't net, not one single coon, or a possum, which had Cowayne feeling like a failure, seeing that he wanted more for his family. And Clora Lee killing the Reb, to save his life, was eating at the young male, and the boy couldn't hide it, no matter how hard he tried.

"What's wrong?" Clora Lee asked her friend softly.

Cowayne didn't answer his Lee, as he just kept right on walking, which prompted the girl to put her arm around his neck.

"You's mad at me?" Clora Lee whispered in his ear.

"I's uh ain't mad, Lee," Cowayne replied, as he could feel his body rising, from Clora Lee's lips touching his ear when she whispered.

"Then why you's ain't answer me?"

"Cause I's thinking," Cowayne replied, while wondering why Clora Lee was stroking his face with her nose.

"What you's thinking bout?"

"We's ain't got, no coon."

"We's gon get one, when we's go back this evening," Clora Lee said, knowing that her Cowayne would make it so.

After assuring Cowayne they would get a coon or two, Clora Lee gave him a hug. But the hug weren't just a hug. For the teen was playing another one of her female games, as she checked to see if the little nose play had sparked a reaction in Cowayne's body. And to no surprise, Clora Lee got a resounding yes, as she could feel his firm erection pressing up against her pelvic. But the little game wasn't able to remove Cowayne's ugly feeling of inadequacy. For that was something, only Mother Nature and Father Time, could heal. And like always, the old lady took her own sweet time, about the things that matter the most to males.

With breakfast in their bellies, Cowayne was ready to find Clora Lee, so the two of them could go do some shooting. And not having to look very long, he found his Lee standing in the doorway of the old barn, holding a serious look on her face, as she carelessly leaned against the doorway. And her mood appeared to be somber, as she took a noticeable interest in a tiny branch that had fallen from the magnolia tree, which sat behind the large faded building.

"Why's you's told me to run, yesterday?" Clora Lee asked, before Cowayne ventured in to striking distance.

"Cause I's uh ain't want that Reb, to get ya," the teen replied, while stopping in the doorway.

"I's uh ain't gon never leave ya, and don't you's ask me no mo," Clora Lee said with her eyes still held tight to the tiny branch.

"But that Reb was gon get ya," Cowayne replied softly.

"I's uh don't care, I's uh ain't gon never leave ya, and don't ya ask me no mo," Clora Lee said, nearly shouting.

The barn became deathly quiet again, as the teens could feel the ill feeling that loomed between the two of them. And when Clora Lee used the upper part of her arm, to wipe what Cowayne knew to be a tear, the silence came to an end.

"You's crying?"

"Why?" Clora Lee shouted with anger.

"Cause I's don't want ya to."

"Why you's don't want me to?" Clora Lee shouted once again, as the tears ran down her face.

But Clora Lee knew better then anyone, why Cowayne couldn't bear to see her crying. For she knew the boy loved her from the depths of his very soul. And Cowayne would gladly stand in the jaws of death for her again, if the moment should arrive. Yet he never uttered those three little words, which every woman would sell her soul to hear.

"Why you's don't want me crying?" Clora Lee asked for the third time.

Not knowing what to say, Cowayne went back to the reason he was looking for her, and suggested that the two of them go do some shooting.

"I's uh don't wanna shoot," Clora Lee shouted.

"Come on Lee, we's gotta get our shooting in."

"I's uh told ya, I's don't wanna!"

Knowing that Clora Lee was just mad, Cowayne took hold of her hand, and the two headed for the fence. Yet their walk was far from normal, seeing that Clora Lee didn't have much to say. In fact, the talkative female was down right silent, as they made their way through the thick brush. And when Clora Lee and Cowayne reached the spot where they were to do their shooting, she took her two pistols from him, and dropped to the ground. Then with a soldier like precision, Clora Lee loaded the two pistols and stood up. And without aiming, Clora Lee raised the pistol in her left hand, and fired at a tree they had been using for target practice. And after hitting a branch dead center, she raised the pistol in her right hand and fired it in the same manner, thus striking the branch once more. Yet Clora Lee's practice was far from over, as she went back down on her knees, and reloaded the pistols, faster then any soldier could have ever dreamed of doing. Then like a woman on fire, the angry teen rose to her feet, and repeated the same routine. And after the fourth strike, the branch, the pistols, and Clora Lee's tears, all had something in common. For they all fell rather quickly, as the young love struck female took off running.

"Hold up Lee," Cowayne shouted, as he gathered up the pistols.

While Cowayne was left with the daunting task of hiding their pistols, Clora Lee went right on running. Running like she had never ran before, forcing her friend to do a poor job of hiding their firearms.

After poorly hiding the pistols, Cowayne took off in a state of panic, hoping to catch Clora Lee, before she ran in to another Rebel soldier. But no matter how fast Cowayne ran, all the teen succeeded in doing, was cutting Clora Lee's sizable lead in half. And as Clora Lee flew pass their first marker in record time, Cowayne could only hope for her to quickly tire. But when she did the same to their second marker, as well as the dead Reb, that had became bugs food, Cowayne hopes faded faster then Clora Lee's pace. But Cowayne still had one hold card left in his deck. For Clora Lee had never been able to run all the way back to the main yard at half speed. That gave Cowayne the illusion his friend would give out, before reaching the main grounds.

As the reality of Clora Lee out doing his every prediction sunk in, Cowayne watched as she disappeared out of his sight. For Clora Lee had cleared the fence, and was well on her way to the female shed, when Cowayne had finally exploded from the brush.

"Clora Lee, what's wrong, child," old Mae asked, as the crying teen flew by her.

Clora Lee didn't say a word, she just went right on crying, while lying in the far right corner of the female shed, looking like a forgotten ball. And that angered Sistah, as she got up to check on the girl. But just as Sistah got to the doorway of the old shed, Cowayne came barreling around the corner. And old Mae, as well as Sistah, could tell he had everything in the world to do with Clora Lee's crying.

"What you's do that child?" Sistah asked, as her anger came to the forefront.

"I's uh ain't do her nothing," Cowayne said, thinking about what Clora Lee had vowed, after shooting the Reb.

"I's uh don't knows what you's done did that child, but you's better get," Sistah hollered.

"But I's uh gotta see bout Lee."

"You's gone, and do like Sistah done told ya'" old Mae said, as she looked up on her son with disappointment.

"But ma, I's uh gotta see bout Lee," Cowayne cried, with his eyes still clinging to Sistah.

"We's gon look after her, na you's gone," old Mae said sadly.

Cowayne walked away with his head down, thinking about how Clora Lee had ran all the way home with out stopping, and they weren't even talking about it. But most of all, the young male wanted his Lee to stop crying.

When Cowayne was gone, old Mae called out to Clora Lee. But just like before, the girl didn't answer the old slave, as she continued to hold tight to the corner, as if it were her new Cowayne.

"Now Clora Lee, I want you to come out here, and see what Mae want," Sistah said with a voice so clear, not even old Mae could deny, there was something wrong with the female.

After hearing Sistah speak far better then Effie, Clora Lee staggered to the doorway. And once there, the crying female looked at Sistah, before casting her eyes on old Mae. And as she continued to cry, Clora Lee wondered if any of the other slaves, had noticed the strangeness that haunted the misfortunate one.

"Come on na," old Mae said, as she beckon, Clora Lee with her hand.

Clora Lee slowly walked out of the shed, and over to old Mae, as her left hand and face tried their best to become one. And with the old slave's arm wrapped around her waist, Clora Lee cried a little softer. But not even the comfort of old Mae's large arm, could take away the source of the girl's pain.

"Na tell old Mae, why you's crying," the old slave said with a gentleness.

"Cause. Cause. Cause Cowayne. Cowayne won't tell me, he's love's me," Clora Lee said, which started her to bellowing like crazy.

"Aw Clora Lee, Cowayne love's ya, don't he, Sistah?" old Mae asked the boy's mother.

"Everyday," Sistah replied, hoping it would cheer the girl up.

"I's know Mae, but I's wanna hear him say it," Clora Lee said through her crying.

"He's uh tell ya, every time he's take ya with him. And when he's gone, you's knows where he's be, when Sistah and me don't knows nothing uh tall. And he's tell ya, he's love's ya, when he's make sure you's got some t'eat," old Mae explained.

"I's knows Mae, but I's wanna hear it," Clora Lee cried once more.

"But when he's get to saying it, he's gon say it so much, you's gon get tired of hear it," old Mae said, trying to warn the girl, of what was in store for her down the road.

"I's uh never get tired of hearing it, Mae. I's uh never get tired. As long as I's live, I's uh never get tired," Clora Lee said, as she took to crying harder then ever.

"You's gone and lay down, so you's can rest ya self," old Mae said, as her heart went out to Ethel's daughter.

Clora Lee went back in the shed, to the same corner, and resumed the same position on the floor. And even though she was the most high strung female slave the Big A plantation had ever possessed, that still didn't stop her from being vulnerable to that mysterious thing called love. Yet love wasn't vulnerable to Clora Lee, as it treated her like a helpless little puppy. And like a puppy, Clora Lee would forever follow the little boy that dwells deep within Cowayne's soul.

"Mae, that child got it bad," Isabella said.

Old Mae didn't know what to say, as Clora Lee's crying made it impossible for her to deny Isabella's statement. But there was one thing the old slave did know. For old Mae knew Cowayne had to be suffering just as much, if not far worst then Clora Lee, seeing that the teen nearly died, when the girl went through her first period.

By the time everyone was able to block out Clora Lee's crying, they found themselves draped in silence. And as the females looked at each other, old Mae motioned with her head, for Sistah to go check on the girl. And like always, Sistah had to give the old female that look, which asked the question, why did she, have to be the one, to do the dirty work.

Yet after hitting old Mae with the look, Sistah got up and peeped in the shed. "She's sleeping," Sistah whispered.

Old Mae sighed, and said, "Thank ya Lord."

"But I's uh wanna hear it, Mae," Sistah whispered, right before chuckling.

"Na you's hush, and leave that child be."

"But I's uh ain't tired, Mae, that's why I's uh gon find Pleasant," Sistah said, as she danced in front of the old slave.

Old Mae took a swing at Sistah, as if she were trying to hit the fancy dancing slave on the butt.

"Ha, you's miss me, Mae," Sistah said laughing, as she skipped off.

"You's gone on, something gon stop ya," old Mae yelled.

"You's just mad, cause I's gon hear it, and she's can't," Sistah said, shaking her butt.

"Ooo Mae, I's reckon, Sistah uh burn up summer," Isabella said, while watching their friend shake her ass.

"Mae, I's uh gon send ya boy back to ya," Sistah shouted, as she swung her hips from side to side.

"You's keep on, you's gon get old," old Mae said of Sistah's sashaying.

"But I's young, na Mae, and I's gon hear it, till I's ain't young no mo," Sistah bellowed, then let out a laugh, that told the old slave, Pleasant had better be ready, if he knew what was good for him.

"Mae I's uh tell ya the truth, Sistah walk like she got the itch," a female slave said walking up.

"And I's uh reckon, she's itching for a scratch," old Mae said, which started everyone to laughing.

"What you's doing in here?" Sistah asked Pleasant, as she strolled through the door of the old barn.

"Nothing, I's just looking round," Pleasant replied nonchalantly, as he wondered what storm blew the female his way.

"You's see'd Cowayne round here?" Sistah asked, while looking around as well.

"He's was here a while uh go, but theys went out across that field," Pleasant said of the boy, and Clora Lee.

Then after a slight pause, the slave went on to say, the children would be back in a spell.

"I's uh ain't looking for him, I's just wanna know we alone," Sistah said, as she slid her arms around Pleasant's neck.

"What you's up to?" Pleasant asked, as if he didn't know.

"Well if n you's leave that there be, you's uh find out," Sistah said with a tone, that was clearly understood.

"And if n I's do?" Pleasant asked, while looking over his shoulder at the female, as she backed away from him.

"Then I's uh gon hear it," Sistah replied, leaning against a stall. "Hear what?"

Sistah didn't bother telling Pleasant, what she had planned on hearing. For, the horny female, just made her way toward him, from the very last stall, which sat in the back of that crusty old barn. And when she reached Pleasant, Sistah's hands went to work, as the disfunctional female took to pinching his nipples, causing the slave's eyes to slowly close. But before her lover could say the three little words that Clora Lee so desperately wanted to hear, the two slaves heard a voice ring out from the loft.

"Is that you, Sistah?" Cowayne's voice called out, thus putting a damper on the female's little itch.

"Cowayne, what you's doing up there?"

"You's told me to get."

"Na I's telling ya, to get again," Sistah snapped.

"I's uh gotta talk to Pleasant," Cowayne uttered, as he started down the ladder.

Feeling her son had picked the wrong time for a talk, Sistah clearly wanted Pleasant to hurry up and get it over with. Yet something told the strange acting mother, Pleasant could talk to her child, until the white men stop their fighting, and it still wouldn't do the boy a bit of good. But Sistah was willing to stand down for a minute or two, just so she could have something to use against old Mae. And with the old slave on her mind, Sistah was ready to leave the barn, but not before giving her son a word of caution.

"If n you's playing, I's uh gon get ya good," she said, while heading for the door.

"I's uh gotta ask him something," Cowayne said, as he came down from the loft.

Having a good idea of what Cowayne wanted to talk about, Sistah smiled, while stepping out into the sunlight. And once she found herself standing under the biggest and brightest star, Sistah spoke with a womanish look in her eyes. "Na Pleasant, you's help Mae baby, cause he's need it awful bad," she said, which was followed by a nice hardy chuckle.

"What you's two, up too?" Pleasant asked, after Sistah had left the doorway.

"I's was stopping ya from tell her, bout our horse."

Pleasant acted as if he didn't hear the boy, while holding the most peculiar look on his face. And as he kept his eyes running from Cowayne, to the doorway and back, Pleasant appeared to be looking for something that was hidden between time and space. And as Pleasant facial expression pushed the teen to question his sanity, the helpful slave held tight to what he believed.

"You's alright?" Cowayne asked, looking at his friend.

"You's been round Sistah so long, yo's eyes look like hers," Pleasant said, staring at the boy.

Fearing that Pleasant was becoming like old Pete, Cowayne wondered what more could go wrong in his life. But what the young slave didn't know, was what Mr. Arnold might notice, when he return home from the war. And if the evil slave owner were to notice it, then he would make good on his promise, thus killing both of old Mae's babies right before her eyes.

"Just don't tell her bout our horse," Cowayne said in parting.

"Then what I's pose to tell her, if n she's see it?"

"Tell her bout the eyes," Cowayne yelled, as he ran off.

With Cowayne gone, Sistah strolled back in to the barn, and closed the doors behind her. Then like a female in need, she took her own sweet time getting up the ladder. And by the time Sistah had reached the top of the ladder, Pleasant was standing beneath her, looking up at the only spot of Heaven, he would ever know.

"You see something, you like?" Sistah asked, while looking down at her lover.

Pleasant pulled out his long throbbing erection, and asked Sistah the very same question she asked him. And when Sistah licked her lips, it told Pleasant, he was needed up in the loft. So with his dick looking like a small leg, Pleasant scurried up the ladder, dying to give Sistah what she needed.

Under an old quilt Mrs. Arnold threw out, after the Blue Coats had spent the night in her home, Sistah returned to spinning her web of seduction. "Ooo Pleasant, it's dark under here," she said with a begging desire.

"We's don't need, no light," Pleasant replied, as he squeezed Sistah's nice round ass.

"But what if n you's can't find, what you's looking for?"

Just as Sistah finished her statement, she gasped, which told Pleasant, he didn't have to look any further. And as the old quilt moved with the motion of a caterpillar making its way along a branch, Sistah's nagging itch, was receiving the scratching it so desperately needed. And when Sistah moaned, it told her lover, she was enjoying every slow stroke, he sent deep into her wet pink cave.

As Pleasant and Sistah laid in the loft breathing like a couple of runaway slaves, he stared down at her, as though she were a stranger. And not kowing what to make of the look on her big dick scratcher's face, Sistah closed her eyes, but only for a moment.

"What on earth, are you looking at?" Sistah asked, after opening her eyes.

"I's uh see'd Cowayne do the same thing," Pleasant replied, while believing Sistah had did her best impression of Mrs. Arnold thus far.

"Do what?" she asked.

"Make his eyes do that."

Pleasant was trying to tell Sistah, her and Cowayne had the same type of eyes.

"What I's doing?" Sistah asked, as her eyes shifted from side to side, as if she were her little brother.

"You's moving ya eyes, like he's do, when he's don't know what to say," Pleasant replied, as Sistah sat up.

"I's uh know what to say," Sistah grumbled, as she stood up. "I's uh going, cause you's pose to be talking bout me, not Cowayne," she said sadly.

Pleasant yanked Sistah back down to the floor, which started the female to fighting. And by the time their struggle had came to an end, Sistah was sitting on her friend, like a queen on her thrown. Yet it wasn't a thrown that Sistah was looking for, as she spouted the word, now, while leaning forward. And after placing Pleasant, fresh new erection in her sperm soaked pussy, Sistah let out the most satisfying groan. And the sweet sounding groan pushed all thoughts of Cowayne, to the back of Pleasant's mind. Yet there was one thing Pleasant thought he did know. For Sistah had spent so much time with old Mae's baby, the boy was beginning to act a little lost as well.

Chapter 11

A Perfect Fine

Clora Lee opened her eyes to a plantation in total chaos. The first thing that popped into her head, were the sight of Rebel soldiers, running rough shot over the slaves. And that told the girl, she had to find Matthew, and get him to their hiding place. For in the hiding place, Matthew would be safe, until her and Cowayne put an end to those Rebs once and for all.

IN A SPLIT SECOND, Clora Lee was on her feet and at the door. There she saw old Mae sitting in the usual place, picking at her fingers, while Cowayne sat on the ground looking sad. So the teen quickly left the sanctuary of the doorway, to check on her friend, as she hoped to find out what all the fuss was about. And as she came along side of Cowayne, Clora Lee gave him a gentle bump. But when Cowayne didn't react to her fiscal greeting, she knelt down in front of him, which caused the young male to look away.

"Why theys happy?" Clora Lee asked old Mae, as she picked in Cowayne's hair like a grooming mother.

"Child, a mess of slaves, come through here, and they's said, them Blue Coats done beat them Rebs, and we's free," old Mae replied.

"You's hear that Cowayne, we's free," Clora Lee shouted, as if the boy was a cotton field away.

"I's knows we's free," Cowyane replied sadly.

"Then why you's sad? You's said, them Blue Coats, was gone beat them Rebs."

"I's uh can't be happy, cause you's mad at me," Cowayne mumbled.

"I's uh not mad at ya. I's uh ain't mad uh tall," Clora Lee shouted, as if she were shouting to the Heavens above.

The newly freed slave, threw her arms around Cowayne, and held his head tightly to her breast. And while Clora Lee held Cowayne with more love, than Eve could ever claim, his words played over and over in her head. For Clora Lee had been given something far more valuable then freedom. More powerful, then any army, that could be mustered by man. She had been given conformation of their love. A love, Clora Lee would cherish until she ended up like old Pete, dead in her grave, never to rise again. Yet, her love for Cowayne would still carry on, until the end of time.

When Clora Lee had gotten her fill of holding on to Cowayne, the two newly freed slaves got up and ran across the yard in search of Sistah. Hand and hand, the two ran, as Clora Lee knew there would never be another day, to match the happiest day of her life. She had waited a long time for that day, and with it in her possession, Clora Lee was planning on cherishing it for the rest of her born days. She would be able to tell her children and grandchildren, how their father and grandfather, had professed his love to her, on the day they became free. Be it by the fireplace, or over a tube, washing cloths, Clora Lee could say with pride, how Cowayne said he could never be happy, if she were unhappy with him. Clora Lee will tell them all, how it feels to wake up every day, knowing she was the sole reason for Cowayne's happiness.

While old Mae sat watching the celebration from a far, she never once took her eyes off of Cowayne. And as the old female watched her son with a great deal of concern, she wondered if the boy truly knew what he had said to Clora Lee. For old Mae believed Cowayne didn't bit more know what he said to his friend, no more then she could say what the future held for them that were free. Yet among all of the joy and jubilation over Mr. Lincoln's decision, old Mae knew she would never see freedom beyond the Big A front gate. For the old slave knew there would be no future and no freedom for her, as she feared Mr. Arnold's return.

"Theys ready?" old Mae asked Nelson, as he walked up.

"Pert near," the mysterious one replied, as he sat on the ground, at old Mae's feet.

"Then I's uh gon leave here, when they's go," the old slave said looking sad.

"No," Nelson said softly, yet in a disobedient manner.

With Nelson rejecting her decision, old Mae stared at him with a look that said more then she cared to. For the look of fear, gripped both of their faces, as the two were plotting something, and the often silent slave didn't seem to have what it took, to see their plan through to the end. Yet old Mae was willing to take Nelson down that road, whether he wanted to go or not. And as he turned his head toward the ground, the old slave knew the youngster would follow her any where, just like his father and Jeremiah often did.

As Clora Lee danced about, she noticed Mrs. Arnold and her two slave girls standing in an upstairs bedroom window looking down at the celebration. So Clora Lee took the time to stop dancing, to stare at her former Missis in defiance. For the newly freed slave, was sending a message to the once powerful slave owner. For the teen let her eyes speak to the white woman, as they shouted, Clora Lee is in charge of Clora Lee. And Mrs. Arnold must have gotten the message, seeing that she left the window, taking the girls with her. Yet that didn't stop Cowayne from turning around, to see what Clora Lee was looking at. But all he saw was an empty window. And looking back at his Lee some what confused, Cowayne waited for her to enlighten him, yet she never did.

"Let's get Matthew and find Pleasant," Cowayne shouted over the noisy celebration.

Before Cowayne and Clora Lee could run off, Sistah grabbed the two teens, and held them in a loving embrace. And after kissing Clora Lee on the forehead, Sistah turned and planted a long hard kiss on Cowayne's jaw.

"I's uh love ya, and I's uh never stop loving ya," Sistah said, just before releasing her children to roam freely.

"I's uh was dancing," Matthew cried, after finding himself in Clora Lee and Cowayne grasp.

"Cowayne said we's got work to do," Clora Lee yelled in return.

"But we's ain't slaves no mo," Matthew pouted.

"That's why we's gotta work, na where's Pleasant?" Cowayne asked, as he and Clora Lee shuffled off with the poor boy.

"I's uh don't know," Matthew said, looking back at the other ex-slaves having fun.

After the three checked the blacksmiths shed, and the barn, they found Pleasant sitting on the stool where old Pete use to sit. The slave was crying, and the children couldn't believe their eyes. They were free, which meant their friend should have been celebrating, rather then pawing at his eyes like a cat.

"What's wrong?" Clora Lee asked with a touch of sympathy, only a female could possess.

"I's free, but I's don't know what I's uh gon do," Pleasant said weeping. "Where I's gon go? I's can't go home, and I's ain't got nothing," he continued, while wiping the tears from his eyes.

"Stop it, cause you's strong. And we's all strong," Cowayne shouted with pride.

The young teen, was displaying the very same pride, Pleasant took the time to instill in him. And that was why Cowayne knew Pleasant had to be suffering from what he called a lack of freedom. And the teen had no doubt their friend was still the same person, his mother and Sistah often talked about. But just like many other ex-slaves through out the South, Pleasant found him self trapped in a new situation, not knowing which way to turn. Yet Cowayne knew the only thing his friend needed, was to get away from that old plantation, and he would be back to his old self again. And Pleasant was going to leave the Big A, even if Cowayne had to drag him from the wretched place.

"Come on, we's gotta talk," Clora Lee said to Pleasant.

The four headed for the blacksmith shed, leaving their fellow ex-slaves to celebrate a freedom, that may end up being just as bad, as slavery it self.

"Pleasant, you's get Matthew up fo daylight, so ya'll can ride that horse, so we's can be ready," Cowayne whispered, as if they were hatching some diabolical plan.

"Why we's gotta get up in the dark?" Matthew cried, hoping Cowayne would change his mind about the matter.

But there would be no sympathy, now that the two lovers were ready to put the final pieces of their plan in place.

"You's hush," Clora Lee said, as she pushed Matthew's head with her right index finger.

"Stop, Cowayne, tell her to leave me be."

"Both of ya stop," Cowayne said, as his leadership quality came charging forth.

"We's all can't leave here on that one horse," Pleasant noted.

"Me and Lee, we's gon find some mo. But ya'll gotta be able to ride, when we's ready to leave," Cowayne said firmly, knowing everything depended on the four of them.

"I's uh know'd you's young n was up to something," Pleasant said, looking nervous.

"When we's leaving?" Matthew asked, as if he was ready to go at that very moment.

"When we's ready," Cowayne said, still whispering.

"And don't you's tell no body, not even Sistah," Clora Lee snapped, trying to put a touch of fear in her brother.

"I's uh ain't gon say nothing. Tell her Cowayne, I's uh ain't told nobody, bout our horse."

Cowayne placed a hand on Matthew's shoulder, and looked the little boy straight in the eye, and said, "I's uh need ya to show Pleasant ha to ride that old horse good."

"I's uh show him. I's uh show him better then me."

"I's uh believe ya, na ya'll go find Sistah," Cowayne said, as if he had caught a new idea.

With the final stages of their plan moving forward, Cowayne was off and running again, as Clora Lee stayed on his heels.

"Where we's going?" Clora Lee asked, as they headed toward the fence.

"To check on something."

The two went over the fence, and quickly entered the brush. But for the first time in their young lives, Clora Lee and Cowayne entered the brush as two legally free souls, rather then Mr. Arnold's property.

Yet the two newly freed slaves didn't feel any different, being that the kids had always saw, themselves as free.

While Clora Lee and Cowayne made their way through the thick brush, he was hoping the shooting they heard earlier, would bring them good fortune. Yet he couldn't stop himself from thinking about their encounter with the Rebel soldier. And as he kept his eyes pealed for what ever could bring Clora Lee harm, Cowayne wanted so much to turn around, and go back to the main yard.

"I's don't know, what I's gon do with ya," Cowayne said, as he and Clora Lee walked along a wooded path.

"I's uh know," Clora Lee replied, with a smile.

"Then you's need to tell me, so I's uh know."

"Ain't gonna," Clora Lee said, then shot her friend a big bright smile.

"So you's got secrets."

"I's uh ain't got no secret. I's just ain't ready to show ya," Clora Lee said, as her smile turned in to a very serious stare.

Not knowing what to make of the peculiar look, his friend carried in her eyes, as they spotted three dead Blue Coats and a man in a fancy suit, Cowayne went about the business at hand. And after carefully taking under consideration, the men were lying in the clearance, not to far from a patch of thick brush, the teen quickly took to thinking they were walking into a trap. Yet that didn't stop Cowayne from going over, and picking up one of the dead soldier's rifle.

"Here Lee, if anything move, shoot it," he said, while handing her the rifle, after making sure it was loaded.

"Anything?" Clora Lee asked with a smile.

"Anything, and that ain't no secret," Cowayne replied, while going through the dead soldier's pockets.

"You's moving," Clora Lee said, as she took aim on her friend.

"Then shoot me," Cowayne said, as he pulled a few paper dollars and some coins out of a soldier's shirt pocket.

As Clora Lee looked around, she whispers, "I' uh can't shoot ya yet, cause I's got something for ya to do."

"What?" Cowayne grunted, as he pulled one of the soldier's boots off.

"You's gon know when the time come, Matthew."

"Why you's can't tell me na, old Pete," Cowayne mumbled, as he moved to the second dead Blue Coat.

"Why you's call me old Pete?" Clora Lee cried.

"Cause you's call me Matthew?"

"Cause you's asking too many questions, like Matthew."

"Just be glad, I's uh ain't called ya Pleasant," Cowayne said, as he started to take the boots off of the second dead soldier.

"Whats wrong with Pleasant?"

"Nothing," Cowayne replied, as he moved to the third soldier.

"Cowayne, you's tell me, what's wrong with Pleasant, or I's gon whop you's one," Clora Lee said, as she stood the rifle on its butt.

"When you's was sleeping, he's said I's got eyes like Sistah. Na you's pick that rifle up," Cowayne barked, as he checked the soldier's pockets.

Clora Lee picked the rifle up while laughing, then said, "I' uh guess, you's got legs like her to."

By the time Clora Lee took to prancing around on her toes, as if she were a high society white woman, Cowayne had moved to the well dressed man. And while Cowayne checked the man's coat pockets, Clora Lee continued to prance about, while making fun of her friend's connection to his second mother.

"How de, sir, my name is Cowayne. I's got pretty eyes, and pretty legs," Clora Lee said, while batting her eyes.

But when Cowayne opened the envelope that he retrieved from the dead man's inside coat pocket, Clora Lee's fun and games came to an end. For the envelope held more money, then the kids had ever seen. And seeing that it was new money, the teens didn't know what to make of it.

"Ooo Cowayne, that's shows uh heap uh money," Clora Lee said staring in amazement.

After checking the dead man's pouch, and finding it full of double eagle gold coins, Cowayne was ready to go. Yet before his Lee could take one step, something in the brush caught her eye.

"You's see that over yonder?" she asked.

There was something sparkling in the heavily wooded area across the way. But with Cowayne not having a clue of what it was, and after their run in with the Reb, he wasn't inclined to go and check it out. Yet Clora Lee on the other hand, appeared to be drawn to the glittering light, like a moth to a flaming lantern. And no matter how many times her friend heard the words of Tall Tree in his head, Clora Lee was determine to see what the glittering light had to offer them.

"Come on," Clora Lee said, creeping toward the brush.

"Lee, we's gotta go, fo Sistah start looking for us," Cowayne said nervously, as he could hear the old chief, as plain as day, telling him never to endanger his squaw for any reason.

And Cowayne was looking to follow the chief's advice, as Clora Lee continued to inch toward the sparkling object illuminating from the brush. And seeing that his Lee wasn't going to let it go, the teen sprung in to action.

"You's stay here, and don't you's move," Cowayne said, keeping his eyes on the brush.

As Cowayne slowly moved toward the glittering light, Clora Lee followed him step for step. She was just like a calf following its mother, yet Clora Lee was far too close. And as she placed both her and Cowayne in a dangerous position, Clora Lee did so, without any knowledge of what they were walking into. And if there were to be a need to mount a quick attack, or a hastily retreat, Clora Lee's closeness would surely spoil them both.

When the two came up on the sparkling object, Cowayne noticed a man's boot sticking out of the brush. And as he immediately reversed his footing, Cowayne sent Clora Lee crashing to the ground, thus causing the rifle to fire.

Despite what Clora Lee had told him previously, Cowayne still shouted in no uncertain terms, for her to run. And as he anticipated the man leaping to his feet, Cowayne prepared himself for a different type of fight. Yet as the teen stood with the musket pistol ready to fire, the man never moved.

"He's dead, Lee," Cowayne said, after giving the man's foot, one good hard kick to make sure.

While Clora Lee picked herself up off of the ground, Cowayne peeled back the brush, revealing the sparkling object. It was a gun, clutched in the dead man's hand. A type of gun, the two had seen a long haired man use, to kill another white man, right before their eyes, as they hid in an old great oak tree. Yet the two newly freed slaves had never seen a pistol, to wear the color of a silver coin. And being something new to her, Clora Lee had to have it.

"Can I's uh have it?" Clora Lee asked of the gun, while staring at the bright red gem, mounted in gold, which the man wore on his left ring finger.

Other then fighting Clora Lee the day she stole her first kiss from him, Cowayne didn't know how to tell the pretty brown skin female no. Yet Cowayne also knew they didn't have a moment to lose, as he took to removing the brush, which covered the man's body. And while doing so, the once enslaved teen, thought about how a dead man could never hide himself. Yet Cowayne went right on removing the brush, until he and Clora Lee found that the man was sporting a second silver pistol. And after seeing the second gun resting peacefully in its holster, Cowayne knew his Lee was going to want it as well. But as for the ring, neither teen thought of removing it from the dead man's finger.

With the gun belt unbuckled, and the dead man rolled out of the way, Cowayne gave Clora Lee part of what she wanted. But up on freeing the pistol from the dead man's hand, Cowayne fell back and bumped his head, which brought a hail of bullets storming down on him. And not having a clue of what was happening, Clora Lee, quickly helped Cowayne to his feet. And as the two stood not knowing what to make of the bullets flowing from the brush, the kids also knew it was virtually impossible. So working together, Clora Lee and Cowayne lifted the brush, thus revealing an over turned wagon. And seeing that one of the crates had been busted open, thus giving light to the raining bullets, the children were able to breathe freely again.

"Cowayne, they's got another dead man," Clora Lee utters, as she noticed the large boot sticking out of the brush.

Seeing that Clora Lee was pointing at the ground between his legs, Cowayne couldn't help but to feel, he was becoming too careless with her life. And to Cowayne, that was more then just a bad thing. For the young male, would never be able to forgive himself, if he weren't able to prevent any harm from reaching his Lee. But seeing that they were already there, Cowayne felt they had come too far, to walk away with out checking the men pockets for money.

While looking under the wagon, Cowayne saw that who ever hid the man's body, had laid a saddlebag on his chest. He also noticed that the man was outfitted with two guns, just like his dead friend. And as he reached under the wagon for the bag, Cowayne saw that each holster carried its own belt.

"Here Lee," he said, handing her the saddlebag.

And while Clora Lee proceeded to go through the saddlebag, Cowayne went back under the wagon, to rid the dead man of his guns. But getting the crisscrossing belts wasn't going to be an easy task for the youngster. Yet Cowayne knew he and Clora Lee didn't have a moment to lose, so he fought and struggled with the belts like there was no tomorrow. And when the guns were finally his, along with a knot, that Sistah would definitely notice, Cowayne backed out from under the wagon ready to go.

"What you's doing," Cowayne asked, as Clora Lee was filling the saddlebag with bullets.

"We gon need some bullets to shoot, ain't we?" Clora Lee replied, as she continued to fill one side of the bag.

Seeing that Clora Lee was truly the up to his down, and the in, to his out, Cowayne quickly helped her fill both sides of the saddlebag. And when the two were finally finished, they headed for the main yard, like a couple of bandits, heading for their hide out, leaving the ring, and the dead men to rest in peace.

After going over the fence down by the old barn, Cowayne and Clora Lee carefully hid their stash, where they felt no one would ever find it. Then the two set out to find Sistah, knowing she was going to be looking for them.

When the two young lovers rounded the female shed in the dark, they ran right in to their acting mother. And the children could tell by the way Sistah was standing, she wasn't up for one of their half baked stories.

"I's uh done look high and low for you's two, na where ya'll been?" Sistah asked, while holding the two teens by their shirts.

Like always, Cowayne spoke without thinking. "We's was celebrating," he said.

Then without giving her friend any type of warning, Clora Lee threw her arms around Cowayne, just before laying a great big kiss on his jaw. But before Clora Lee could finish her surprising lip action, Sistah snatched her away.

"I's uh ain't finish," Clora Lee cried, as she acted disappointed.

"You's get in there, missy," Sistah snarled, as she pointed to the female shed.

Clora Lee sashayed pass Sistah, as if she were a bad girl. And as if that wasn't enough, the young female took up a position in the doorway, which sent Sistah's blood to boiling. And as she leaned up against the dying wood, Clora Lee held a look, that was so sexy, Sistah nearly lost her mind.

"We's uh do it again tomorrow, if n you's want," Clora Lee said to Cowayne, knowing she was going to make Sistah hotter then a blacksmith's fire.

"If n I's uh gotta tell ya again, I's uh gon put my hand on yo's bottom," Sistah yelled, as she chased Clora Lee deep into the female shed.

Standing in the very spot where she laid crying, Clora Lee could see her Cowayne walking away with his head hanging low, for the second time in one day. And the young sassy pants, as Sistah some time called her, had no doubt of where her lover was going. Like always, when Sistah was upset with him, Cowayne would seek shelter in the old barn.

But unlike Cowayne, Clora Lee was always left to take Sistah's tongue lashings, which seem to last forever. And no matter how many times, the young female was forced to listen, as Sistah would go on and on, about the pain of having babies, she never got use to it. But there was one thing the teen did know. She wasn't going to be having any babies, until her and Cowayne were far away from the place of their birth.

By the time everyone had closed their eyes for the night, Clora Lee snuck out of the female shed, right on pass Pleasant and Nelson. Then like a runaway slave, Clora Lee darted off, toward the old barn. But the young female didn't stay in the dying structure long. For when Clora Lee came out of the barn, she scampered across the yard like a scared coon. Then moments later, she returned with Cowayne, who was struggling with the boots, pants, and shirts, they took off of the dead white men. And like the good friend that she was, Clora

Lee rushed to open the barn door for her lover. Yet Clora Lee didn't follow Cowayne into the barn, she just closed the door behind him, then made her way back to the female shed.

Upon approaching the shed, Clora Lee slowed her pace, before tipping pass Pleasant and Nelson in the same manner, in which she did leaving. And when she reached the doorway, Clora Lee glared over her shoulder at the barn, as if she was a woman in trouble. But the only trouble, the young female possessed, came from with in herself. For she was wondering what life would be like, if her and Cowayne were living in that old barn together. But Clora Lee knew their day was coming, and she was more then willing to wait on it. And on that day, no one will be able to stop them, not even the one she was curling up next to.

While Clora Lee rested closer to Sistah then old Mae, Pleasant closed his eyes. For the faithful father figure had his eyes on the young female, from the moment she tipped off for her untimely rendezvous with Cowayne. Yet the teen eased her body next to Sistah, believing her skills were some of the best. But Clora Lee had a lot to learn, seeing that she didn't noticed, that Pleasant's eyes were slightly open. And if Cowayne's friend didn't notice Pleasant's eyes, then she had no idea, Nelson was watching Pleasant, as he watched her. For the female's skills were far from being perfect, as she closed her eyes, feeling like those around them, were too old to keep up with her and Cowayne. And Clora Lee would have gone on thinking that way, if it were not for old Mae.

"You's knows, Sistah uh be mighty mad, if n she know'd you's went out uh here," old Mae whispered.

"We's ain't do nothing," Clora Lee mumbled.

"I's uh knows that child, but it don't make no difference, when you's don't mind," old Mae said, before turning her back to the girl.

Staring at the back of old Mae's head, Clroa Lee felt like an unworthy child, as she laid on the floor tangled up in guilt. And when Clora Lee reached out to touch old Mae, it was guilt, which made the teen bring her hand back down to the floor. For Clora Lee was crushed by her own foolish act of defiance, as she promised herself never to do it again.

"I's uh see'd you's young ns take something in that there barn," old Mae said, with her back still to Clora Lee.

"They's just things," Clora Lee replied, as she wiped a tear from her eye.

"I's guess, you's young ns, uh tell me, when you's want me to know."

Old Mae and Clora Lee ended their conversation with a silence, which clung to a touch of uneasiness. And while she wondered about how much old Mae saw, Clora Lee also hoped her life long friend, would not speak a word to Sistah about it come morning. As for Pleasant, he laid on the ground with his eyes closed, wondering why Nelson was watching him so closely. And the newly freed slave, also wanted to know, what Nelson and Effie had going on, being that he had saw the two talking on more then one occasion. But the last time he had seen the two carrying on a conversation, Nelson was pointing in the direction of Clora Lee and Cowayne's entrance into the brush. And not being one to believe in that thing, the white man called coincidence, Pleasant felt Nelson was saying something about his two young friends. So feeling that it was going to be a long night, Pleasant gripped Duval's knife, and hoped old Pete's son wouldn't try anything foolish.

The next morning, Clora Lee rose to the sun shinning on her face. And after sitting up, she took a much need stretch, while listening to old Mae trade words with Isabella.

"What you's gon do na, you's free?" Isabella asked old Mae.

"I's uh gon take care my young ns," old Mae replied, as she watched Sistah pick at her toes.

"Mae, you's ain't got no young ns. All you's got is Cowayne. Ethel knowed she ain't had no call, to leave them young ns on ya like that."

Hearing Isabella's statement, Sistah no longer had a desire to deal with her toes, as she diverted her attention solely toward the talkative female.

"Na Isabella, you's hush, cause I's uh ain't gon have ya talking bout Mae and my babies, and I's mean it," Sistah said, taking her voice above its normal tone.

"All I's said…"

"You's listen to me, Isabella," Sistah shouted, cutting her once picking partner off. "I's uh been Cowayne ma, just as much, as Mae.

And I's been taking care of Clora Lee, from the day she's been born. And if n you's think I's uh was gon let Ethel take that child from here, then wes can go behind this here shed," Sistah shouted, as she stood up.

Sistah knew beating Isabella in front of old Mae, would only upset her friend, and that was one thing the misguided female couldn't bring herself to do. For Sistah would much rather cut off her right hand, then to upset old Mae.

"Na Sistah, you's hush that kid uh talk," old Mae whispered.

"I's uh do no such thing, Mae, cause them young ns is always together, cause they's love one another. And Mae, when we's gone, they's gon take care Matthew," Sistah said, as if the little boy would never grow up, and be able to take care of himself.

Feeling old Mae would stop Sistah, if the two of them got to fighting, Isabella went for broke. "Sistah you's hush, cause you's don't know yo's coming, from yo's going, so ha you's gon know bout love."

"I's knows I's loves Pleasant. And I's knows Pleasant loves me. And that's all I's need to know bout love," Sistah said in a sad, but angry tone.

"Ya'll hush that fuss, cause that child, trying to sleep in there," old Mae whispered strongly.

"I's uh ain't sleep, Mae," Clora Lee said, as she made her way to the door.

"I's uh reckon, you's danced all night," Isabella said, while paying a great deal of attention to the teen.

Stepping out of the shed, Clora Lee slowly walked over to Isabella with an unmistakable swagger. And after showing off the walk of her white blood line, the teen was ready to start her day with a touch of flair. So while leaning over Isabella, and resting her left arm around the talkative female's throat, Clora Lee whispered in her ear.

"I's uh gon be with Cowayne, till I's die. And if n anybody try to come between us, I's uh gon kill um. Na you's member that, or yo's dying, is gon meet yo's living. And if n I's uh hear ya talking down to Sistah again, I's uh gon take a hot knife to ya tongue. Na that's all I's knows about love," Clora Lee said, as her arm nearly crushed Isabella's throat.

Clora Lee had the talkative female hanging out at the gates of Hell. But rather then kick Isabella into eternal darkness, Clora Lee reluctantly gave her the gift of forgiveness. And upon receiving her new lease on life, the talkative female quickly took a much needed breath.

And while Isabella's lungs enjoyed Clora Lee's generosity, the charming teen skipped over to Sistah. Then like the devil in the details, Clora Lee gave Sistah the same delightful hug. Yet it didn't take long for Isabella to notice, the misfortunate female didn't have any trouble breathing with the girl's arm around her throat. And to add insult to injury, Clora Lee gave Isabella a smile, which told old Mae, the young teen had a touch of her grandfather, hidden just beneath the surface.

"I's uh gon wash and plait ya'll hair today," Clora Lee said, as she played in Sistah's head.

"Mine don't need no fussing with," old Mae said with her forever soft voice.

"What Cowayne brought ya'll to eat?" Clora Lee asked, ignoring old Mae's statement.

"Child we's ain't see'd hide or hair of Cowayne. Pleasant brought us a couple of turnips and some berries," old Mae grumbled peacefully.

Clora Lee tilted Sistah's head back, and gave her a kiss just above the right eye. And after giving old Mae a kiss in the same place, the girl headed straight for the old barn.

"Don't you's be giving me no sugar, you's done gave away," old Mae yelled.

"I's uh can give ya my sugar, if n I's want," Clora Lee shouted in return, as she went right on running.

"Ooo Mae, when that child give Cowayne her sugar, he's gon be sweet as pie," Sistah said laughing.

"Na you hush that talk, cause you's knows, yo's boy, is bitter, as cold coffee," old Mae replied with a smile.

"Yea, but her sugar, gon make him sweet. He's gon be so sweet, I's uh gon put him in uh pie," Sistah said, as she stood laughing and dancing, while trying to taunt the old female.

When Clora Lee came up on the barn, she saw Pleasant, Nelson, and Obdi in the doorway. "Morning," the teen said, as she flew by the three males.

Before the trio could utter a word, Clora Lee was in the barn, and on her way to the loft.

"That was the fastest morning, I's ever come uh cross," Obdi noted, after the three males had given Clora Lee their response to her greeting.

"You's hang round here long enough, Clora Lee and Cowayne is gon give ya more then that," Pleasant warned the ex-slave. "Clora Lee, what you's looking for in that there barn?"

"I's got it," Clora Lee shouted, as she made her way up the ladder.

"I's uh ain't ask ya, if n you's got it. I's ask ya, what you's looking for?" Pleasant shouted in return, while watching Nelson, and Obdi smile like a couple of old house cats.

"I's got it," the girl's voice came roaring over the air once again.

"Don't ya'll laugh, cause that child ain't funny," Pleasant said, as he took a quick look in the barn.

But Pleasant didn't see Clora Lee, because the young female had already scampered up the ladder, and was leaning over her friend, who was sleeping peacefully. So with her face glowing like the sun that shined on their first full day of freedom, Clora Lee looked down on Cowayne with the thought of stealing a kiss. Yet the love struck female denied her self of that which she desired deeply, while staring at the boy's thick dark lips.

"Cowayne," Clora Lee whispered.

Cowayne turned over on to his side, leaving Clora Lee no other choice, but to raise her voice a little louder.

"Don't you's turn away from me, you's wake up right na," Clora Lee said, as she shook the love of her life.

"What, Lee?" Cowayne grumbled with a sleepy tone.

"You's get up, cause ya ma, and Sistah ain't had nothing to eat."

After realizing it was well pass daylight, Cowayne leaped over Clora Lee's head, and softly landed on the patch of dirt, the old barn called a floor.

"Don't you's leave me," Clora Lee shouted, as she let her body fall from the ladder, without ever checking to make sure Cowayne was waiting to catch her.

But like the faithful lover that he had always been, Cowayne caught his Lee, and placed her feet safely on the ground. And after taking a quick romantic look in to each other's eyes, the two were ready to face the world once again, as they exploded from the barn like a couple of wild horses. And as the two young lovers flew by Obdi like a strong summer breeze, Pleasant wanted to know when and how, the boy got in to the old barn.

"When you's see Matthew, tell him to stay by the barn," Cowayne shouted, never bothering to answer Pleasant's question.

"You's tell me, when you's come in this here barn!" Pleasant shouted, hoping to get an answer to his question.

But the children were in too much of a rush, to trouble them selves with answering questions. So with her voice ringing in the air, Clora Lee shouted like that white man did many years ago, as he rode his horse through every village and town. Only the girl's words were slightly different, as she shouted, they were going to get old Mae and Sistah something to eat.

"What you and Sistah gon do with them young ns?" Nelson asked.

"First, I's uh gotta find, where theys getting all that there food," Pleasant said, as the three watched Clora Lee stay one step behind Cowayne, as she wore a pair of union britches under her dress.

"All you's gotta do, is follow um," Obdi said, as he stood unaware, of how hard it was to keep up with the two teens.

"And ha he's gon do that, when they's running like deers?" Nelson laughed, as he pointed to the two young lovers going over the fence.

"What na," Pleasant mumbled, after things had calmed down.

It was Dew Dap, and the sight of the teen coming their way, made Nelson put his head down. For the boy's mother, was Nelson's first and only choice, when it came time for pleasure taking. But with Big Willie being Mr. Arnold's prize slave, he often did as he please, ultimately destroying his brother's only dream. And for that, Nelson never touched the boy's mother again, nor did he ever speak another word to his brother. Yet Nelson could never stop fighting the thought, that Dew Dap maybe his son.

"Morning," the three adult males said to Dew Dap in unisons.

"Morning," the boy replied, then held his voice for a moment, while purposely looking across the yard.

And when Dew Dap spoke again, he still had his eyes fixed on something off in the distance, as he asked the adult males about Cowayne, and where the teen could be found.

"You's just missed him," Nelson said, as he found himself staring at the teen, that reminded him so much of his brother.

"You's knows where he's done run off to?" Dew Dap asked, directing his question to Pleasant.

"To get his ma some t'eat," Pleasant replied. "Can we's help ya?"

While leaving Pleasant's question hanging in the atmosphere, Dew Dap turned and headed for the fence. And knowing that the child was troubled over something, Pleasant called out to him, while proceeding to meet the yongster half way.

"Tell me child, what's troubling ya?" Pleasant asked when he reached Dew Dap.

"I's got uh coon, and I's need something to kill it," Dew Dap said sadly.

"Well I's got something for that," Pleasant replied.

As the two made their way, back toward the barn, Dew Dap made a point of keeping his head down, just so he didn't have to look at Nelson. And Nelson did the same, revealing to Pleasant and Obdi, something was hanging in the air between the two of them. And with that in mind, Pleasant tried to make Dew Dap's time around Nelson, as brief as possible, while entering the barn.

After closing the doors behind them, Pleasant went to the very last stall in that old barn, and knelt down. Then like a dog digging for a bone, the thirty one year old male took to the dirt. And the ex-slave didn't stop clawing the ground, until he came up with a nice size knife.

"Here we go," Pleasant mumbled, giving Dew Dap the indication, he was about to receive the knife.

But when Pleasant used the knife to push a spear from behind a support beam, the boy was left speechless.

"Take care of um, and theys uh take care of you," Pleasant said, giving Dew Dap both objects. "Na you's put that there under ya shirt, cause we's don't want nobody knowing you's got it," Pleasant said of the knife.

"I's will," Dew Dap replied, while Pleasant left the barn to rejoin his friends.

"What ailing him?" Obdi asked, as the three watched Dew Dap walk away with the spear.

"Them girls need uh washing, so he's gon go to that old creek, and use that stick, to fetch two pails of water," Pleasant lied, leaving Obdi confused.

Even though he trusted the former house slave, Pleasant didn't see the need, to tell Obdi more then he needed to know. For he knew all too well, how fast, word of a little food could get around. And with the house slaves having less and less to eat every day, Pleasant wasn't about to take any chances.

Chapter 12

New Members

When Clora Lee and Cowayne finally made it back to the main yard, they had five nice size fish, and a bloody sack. And as soon as Matthew saw the happy couple, he got right down to getting the fire started.

"Them some might big fish," Matthew said with a great deal of excitement. "Ha you's catch um?" he asked.

"Lee jumped in the creek and chunk um to me," Cowayne said with a straight face.

"Aw Cowayne, you's joshing me," Matthew squawked.

Clora Lee shook her head with a smile. For the female knew Cowayne was good for her little brother, even though she found their relationship to be a bit odd.

"I's uh see you's young n done made it back. Nelson go out every day, and all he's catch is sketters," Pleasant complained, as he exited the barn, while working on a new spear.

"He's gotta jump in that old creek, and chunk um out?" Cowayne said, some what repeating the statement, he gave Matthew.

"You's ain't jump in no creek, and chunk no fish, nowhere, na you's stop that," Pleasant replied, disputing Cowayne's lie.

"We's did, you's can ask Lee," Cowayne said with a convincing tone.

"I's uh ain't asking that child, no such thing," Pleasant replied, as he went back to making his new spear.

"You's making another spear?" Clora Lee asked, as she saw the two male's relationship, in the same manner, as her little brother and the adventurous teen, yet only in reverse.

"I's uh gave Dew Dap my other one."

Before the fatherly figure could finish his statement, Matthew and Cowayne were opening their mouths at the same time, asking the same question.

"Why," the boys asked.

"Cause he's done trapped uh coon, and he's need something to kill it with," Pleasant replied, as he checked the spear for balance.

"Pleasant, help Lee and Matthew clean them there fish, and get um cooking?" Cowayne said walking off.

"I's uh reckon, I's uh ain't got nothing else to do," Pleasant replied, as he watched Clora Lee's hands immediately go to her hips.

And before the father figure could think it, Clora Lee was giving Cowayne a very large piece of her mind. And when she was finished, Clora Lee immediately lit in on her acting father, and little brother.

"Pleasant, if n you's finish cooking them there fish fo we's get back, you's make sure Matthew take Mae and Sistah theirs. And Matthew, you's wash yo's hands, when you's finish helping Pleasant clean them fish," Clora Lee shouted, as her and Cowayne were walking away.

I's uh tell ya Matthew. Yo's sister is the only female, that can tell ya what to do, while heading off to do something else," Pleasant said, as he scratched his whiskers.

"Na you's tell me, why we's in such uh rush," Clora Lee spat, as she still looked upon Cowayne with anger.

"You's ain't never see'd Dew Dap do no cooking, and you's don't wanna," Cowayne replied looking scared.

"I's uh ain't hardly see'd him, nor them girls, since they's ma died," Clora Lee said, as they both took to running.

"Well if n we's don't hurry up, you's ain't gon see much of that coon, neither," Cowayne assured his friend.

"He's need uh female, for them girls," Clora Lee stated like a woman, who had just about enough of a problem.

As Clora Lee and Cowayne quicken their pace, the boy began to speak like some over the top tattletale.

"I's uh told him, but he's said, he's can't find none."

"Then he's as blind, as old Pete," Clora Lee replied in a tone, Matthew had learned to fear.

When the two came upon a water trough, Clora Lee suggested they wash their hands. But knowing that every minute counted, Cowayne tried to get the girl to bypass her obsession with water, before Dew Dap end up turning that poor coon, in to a chunk of burnt meat. But Clora Lee wasn't having it, as she stood in front of the trough, refusing to move an inch. And seeing that his Lee was adamant about her suggestion, rather then the girls and their stomachs, Cowayne was forced to do as she asked.

"And don't you's dry um on ya breeches," Clora Lee said, as Cowayne went about washing his hands.

When the two was finished washing their hands, they were off and running again. And as Clora Lee's feet carried her across the yard, she couldn't help but to wonder why boys had such a love for staying filthy. And even though the girl didn't know too much about the white man's God, she was willing to wager her life, he was the only clean male in Heaven. And for that reason, and that reason alone, the girl, felt there weren't too many males resting their heels behind the pearly gates.

When Clora Lee and Cowayne came upon Dew Dap and his two sisters, Bessie and Madeline, they were sitting in front of the woodshed. And the sight of the girls, nearly brought Clora Lee to tears. For even by a slave's standard, the girls had a look that was shameful. Their hair was like weeds in a run down cotton field. And the dresses the girls wore, were dirty and raggedy, which made Clora Lee feel a shame, as she mumbled one of Mrs. Arnold's favorite sayings.

By the time, the words, my God had invaded the air, Clora Lee was well on her way to feeling guilty, while Cowayne was having a heartattack. For Dew Dap hadn't remembered a thing he had showed him about skinning animals. And the knife Pleasant gave the boy was as sharp as they come, yet it didn't make up for his lack of skills, as he carved away at the dead coon.

"You's give me that knife, fo you's kill that coon again," Cowayne said, as he and Clora Lee came to a stop.

By the time Dew Dap had given Cowayne the knife, Clora Lee was already telling him, that his fire was too hot. And the way the two young lovers spoke to him, made the boy feel like he was being attacked from two different directions. Yet, Dew Dap had no intentions of curling up like some snake. Nor was the boy, planning on sticking his head in the ground, as if he were some strange bird, from a distant land, he had never heard of. For the teen was determine to make a stand, even if it meant, making it against the wrong member of the double dueling lovers.

"I's uh see'd others, with big fires," Dew Dap explained, as he watched Clora Lee spread out the burning wood.

"And I's uh bet ya, theys had uh pot," Clora Lee said, with more then just a touch of frustration.

Dew Dap scratched his head, which started Clora Lee to thinking. The girl didn't know what she was going to do, but her anger and shamefulness shouted something needed to be done, and done right away.

"I's uh guess, this is one of them time, when Pleasant would tell ya, our best, can't out do a female's worst," Cowayne said, looking at the girls.

"Cowayne, you's stay here with Dew Dap, and don't you's say another word, while I's gone," Clora Lee said, as she walked away.

Even though Cowayne's quoting of Pleasant was harsh, Clora Lee knew he was right. And that was the driving force behind her willingness to storm head first on to dangerous grounds. And if Cowayne had known where she was going, he would have never allowed her to take one step with out him. For Clora Lee was on her way to the mansion. And with a hair brain crazy idea, the girl was determined to solve Dew Dap's problems, even if it were to get her killed.

Finding her self approaching the same backdoor, she learn to hate at a very tender age, Clora Lee found the house slaves sitting around old Pete's spot. The slave, Clora Lee was looking for, was flanked by her mother and Effie, yet the scrappy young female didn't allow Joan's well crafted defense, to detour her from getting the girls some much needed help. For Clora Lee walked right up to Joan, and told the duck high female to come with her. But to her surprise, the little stump didn't move a muscle, as she sat holding the look of a porcupine that was being fucked by a mule.

With the understanding that Joan wasn't going to make her job easy, Clora Lee resorted to a more convincing tone. "I's uh said, come with me," Clora Lee barked, with an extra dish of firmness in her voice.

Knowing that Clora Lee wasn't their fromer master, or the Misses, Joan had no problem with following her first mind. So with out blinking an eye, the girl sat perfectly still, with her eyes on Effie for guidance. Yet Joan, unfortunately found herself gazing up at an empty blank stare, which told the girl, she was on her own. So with no where else to go, Joan looked to her mother. And after receiving a nod of approval, from the female which birth her into the world, Joan took a deep breath, then quickly let it out, as if it were to be her last. Yet before she made an attempt to stand, Joan ran her hands down the medium blue dress that she wore, like some well mannered white girl. Then like a maiden headed for the gallows, Joan rose to her feet, to face Clora Lee's sizeable advantage. An advantage that told Joan, there was no way, she could beat the girl in a scrap, yet the stump high female followed her enemy, not knowing where they were headed.

As the two females departed together, Joan immediately set her back up plan in motion. And as she watched Clora Lee march on ward, Joan kept the same slow pace, thus allowing the distance between the two of them, to grow larger with each passing step. Yet Joan's plan fell far short of success, when Clora Lee stopped and waited for her to catch up.

"You's coming, or not?" Clora Lee growled at the female, who was born one month, three weeks, and six days after Cowayne.

Joan took a few quick steps, and ended up with Clora Lee's right arm around her shoulder. And just as the tiny female thought about turning back, Clora Lee pulled her closer, which sent the poor girl's heart to the brown shoes she was wearing.

And as Joan felt she was about to see her last day among the living, she wondered, what the girl could possibly be holding against her.

"You's hungry?" Clora Lee asked, as the two walked like chums.

"Uh huh," Joan replied.

"You's wanna eat?" Clora Lee continued.

"Uh huh," Joan uttered once again.

"Can you's cook?"

"Uh huh," Joan said, keeping to her enormous vocabulary.

"Can you's say anything else?" Clora Lee growled.

"Uh huh," Joan replied, refusing to start running off at the mouth, with the only person she feared, other then the Arnolds.

When Joan finally got the chance to see what Clora Lee wanted with her, the girl felt like crying. And as she watched Clora Lee go over and kneel down behind the two overly neglected girls, Joan's heart rushed back to its rightful place.

"You's girls, want Joan to stay round here, and help Dew Dap?" Clora Lee asked in her sweetest voice.

Bessie said uh huh, as Madeline just nodded her head. But looking at her brother, Bessie was forced to say he didn't want the girl, because she wasn't family.

"Dew Dap can't take…"

Before Clora Lee could finish her statement, Joan jumped right into the sea of change. "Then we's ain't gon give him none uh our coon," the little stump said, as she touched Madeline on the nose. "I's uh gon need some hot water, if you's don't mind, sir," Joan said to Dew Dap, sending Clora Lee and Cowayne for a whirl, seeing that they had never heard a slave, call another slave, sir before.

After looking at his little sisters, then back at Joan, Dew Dap was left without a word to say. And not knowing what to say, he set out to get the much needed hot water. Yet the teen didn't make his trip alone, being that Clora Lee had given Cowayne a look, which told him, he needed to be helping, his friend.

Finding them selves left with nothing to do, the girls went and found a wash tub, which they lugged back to the woodshed, as if it was their's to keep. Then with the persona of an old friend, Clora Lee joked about checking on Pleasant and his cooking, hoping to get a laugh out of Joan. But the best Clora Lee could get, was a momentary chuckle, which didn't last very long.

"Clora Lee, I's uh gon be all right," Joan said, looking at Bessie and Madeline.

"I's uh know," Clora Lee replied, backing away, feeling she had made the right decision.

And as Clora Lee skipped and danced her way out of sight, Joan knelt down and wrapped her arms around the girls, feeling she had also made the right decision.

"I's uh see you's done made it back. And where's that Cowayne?" Pleasant asked, as Clora Lee appeared to be miles away.

Clora Lee didn't open her mouth, as she stared at the fish being kept warm by the fire, leaving Pleasant to wonder if she was all right. For the ex-slave had never seen the teen look so pixilated before. And he quickly equated the girl's odd stare, to why she wasn't answering his question about their friend.

"What's ailing ya?" Pleasant asked Clora Lee, as he began to look at the fire in fear.

"I's uh all right," Clora Lee replied, still staring at the fire. "Did Mae eat?"

"Just a tad," Pleasant replied. "I's uh don't know what done got into her, na days," he went on to say, while waiting for Clora Lee to stop staring at the fish left by the fire.

"I's uh talk to her," Clora Lee replied, as she had yet to answer Pleasant's first question.

"Child, I's done asked ya bout Cowayne," Pleasant cried.

"He's with Dew Dap," Clora Lee said, as if her words were drunken sailors, staggering down a lonely street.

"Well he's better Dew Dap on back here, fo I's uh give that fish away," Pleasant said, as he headed back to the barn.

Clora Lee went over to the fire, and sat down in front of the fish, yet she appeared to be some what at a lost, when it came down to eating. So she just sat before her morning meal, as if it were a dead body, laid out for the whole world to see. And gripping her stomach, Clora Lee knew full well, she would be faced with another monthly in a few days. And thinking of her last night antics with Cowayne, Clora Lee had to smile, knowing Sistah would be checking for the awful thing. Yet Clora Lee knew her and Cowayne didn't have anything to worry about.

While eating, Clora Lee went straight to thinking about girls. For the girl wanted daughters, just as much, as she planned on giving Cowayne, his share of sons. And the young teen knew in her heart, she would not stop having babies, until Cowayne filled her belly with a girl. But if for some reason, she were to meet an untimely death, Clora Lee knew Sistah would be there to help Cowayne with her babies. A feeling of sadness came over the teen, as she wanted nothing more, then to see her children to adult hood. And on the way, Clora Lee knew she and her girls would enjoy many nights by the fireplace talking, even if it had to be about nothing at all. She could see herself teaching her daughters how to be ladies, and how to cook, as well as clean house. For Clora Lee even saw herself, teaching her girls about their dreaded monthly. And Clora Lee will tell them, how she hated it, just as much as every woman that came after Eve. The young teen laid the fish down and started crying.

When Cowayne finally made it back from helping Dew Dap, Clora Lee was ready to go and check on old Mae. So with no time for sitting and eating, Cowayne was forced to gobble his food on the run. And as Cowayne and Clora Lee came up on old Mae, they saw Nelson sitting on the ground beside her. The old slave was picking in Nelson's hair, as if he were a good child, or a faithful hound, yet the teens were unable to determine, which roll the male was hoping to fill. But what ever the mysterious male was trying to be, Cowayne knew he didn't like it one bit. And if it were not for Pleasant, telling him, Nelson was good for his mother, Cowayne would have confronted the much larger slave a long time ago.

"Ma, you's all right," Cowayne ask, as he stared at Nelson.

"Yo's ma is all right, this fine day," old Mae replied, with a weakness in her voice.

"Pleasant, said you's ain't eat much," Clora Lee cried.

"I's uh eating plenty nough for me," old Mae uttered softly.

"Ma, I's getting that food, for you's to eat," Cowayne said, as his voice took to cracking, like an old man's bones.

Old Mae patted Nelson on the head, and the mysterious one got up to walk away. And walking pass Cowayne, Nelson was mindful not to touch the teen, yet he made a point of making eye contact with the special child.

"Come sit next to ya old ma," old Mae said softly.

Cowayne backed up to his mother, while never losing sight of Nelson, as the two of them went on eye sparring, like a couple of young bulls. But no sooner then Cowayne sat down next to his mother, he found himself at a disadvantage.

"You's look at me," old Mae said firmly, forcing Cowayne to accept an unwanted defeat.

With Cowayne no longer having the opportunity to keep his eyes on Nelson, Clora Lee quickly took up the task. But when old Mae started talking, Clora Lee found it hard to keep her eyes pinned on Nelson.

"I's knows, you's gon leave here, and I's happy. But you's gotta leave, fo masa Arnold get back," old Mae said fearfully.

"We's gon leave, fo he's get back."

"You's just member what I's said. Na you's gon, and let ya old ma rest uh bit."

Old Mae was trying her best, to get the children to accept the fact, she would not, be making the trip with them. But Cowayne and Clora Lee wanted no part in leaving her behind, which placed the two teens and the old slave on the opposite sides of a cruel reality. Yet before Cowayne could come to grips with his mother's words, he heard Sistah's voice.

"I's uh gotta go check my traps," Cowayne said, just loud enough for Sistah to hear him.

Hearing the frustration in the son, she so desperately loved, Sistah quickly pointed to the ground. And seeing that she was pointing to the spot just in front of her feet, Cowayne and Clora Lee reluctantly went to see what his second mother wanted.

"Walk with me," Sistah said, as if she were a highly educated woman.

Unaware that Sistah wanted a one on one talk with her son, Clora Lee quickly followed the mother and child, only to see the misfortunate female come to a complete stop. And understanding the unspoken message for all that it was worth, the young female accepted the fact, she wasn't apart of their little pow wow. And seeing that she was not wanted, Clora Lee felt the conversation had every thing to do with her up coming monthly.

"I want you and Clora Lee to be careful out there, no matter what you do," Sistah said, when they were away from the girl, who couldn't live with out her son.

"We's be careful," Cowayne replied, never noticing the difference in the way his mother spoke.

"And I don't want you eye balling Nelson anymore."

Cowayne looked at his second mother, just as it hit him. The adventurous teen couldn't help but to wonder, what the heck he was hearing. For Sistah was talking far better then Mrs. Arnold, and that was more confusing to the boy, then Pleasant thinking the two of them had the same eyes.

"I know you are in a rush, so you better answer me," Sistah said, patting her right foot, something Clora Lee was beginning to do, when ever Mattthew took to getting on her nerves.

"I's won't," Cowayne said, still trying to figure out who he was really talking to.

"Good. Na I's uh need some sugar," Sistah said in a voice, the teen was accustom to hearing.

Cowayne gave Sistah what she wanted, in the form of a giant size hug, and a large kiss on the jaw. But just as the boy thought he was all done with being the perfect son, Sistah took him in her arms for a little extra hugging. And as Sistah rocked him from side to side, Cowayne felt more comfortable with the mother he knew, rather then the one that had spoken to him just a few seconds earlier.

As she trotted the horse around the field, Clora Lee thought about Joan. The teen wondered if she could ever move pass the point of not liking the little stump. After all, she did catch Joan eyeing her Cowayne, which was an unforgivable sin. But seeing that Joan was willing to take care of the girls, Clora Lee felt they could start a new.

"You's mad at me?" Matthew asked Cowayne.

"Huh," Cowayne replied, as he sat on the ground, next to the boy.

"What you's thinking bout?" Matthew grumbled.

"Nothing, na be quiet," Cowayne said softly.

For Cowayne wasn't mad, he was only thinking of Sistah, and the way she had spoken. The whole thing had Cowayne confused, and he didn't know what to do about it. But what appeared to have bothered Cowayne the most, was how she said be careful out there. For Sistah said it, as if she were trying to warn him about something, which begged the boy to ask, did she know about the Reb? And if so, then how, he thought to himself. And why did she forbid him to look at Nelson? There were so many questions that needed answering, yet the boy didn't have the time to deal with any of them, if they were going to leave the plantation on time. So the teen just sat wondering how he was going to get Clora Lee to leave without Jeremiah.

"Cowayne, look," Clora Lee said, putting an end to the boy's thinking.

Cowayne casted his eyes upon the area just beyond the main yard, and saw two young cows grazing peacefully. And not knowing the first thing about cows, Cowayne yelled come on, as he and Matthew ran toward the animals. But when the cows took off in opposite directions, the kids knew they were in over their heads. Then like a little boy wanting to direct bugs down a perfered path, Matthew told Clora Lee to go after the cow that was headed north.

"Do it," Cowayne said, after seeing Clora Lee, refusing to follow Matthew's suggestion.

"Come on," Matthew said, as he headed for the cow that had abandoned its determination to stay in the South, to obtain a life further West.

But rather then take a straight path to the cow, Matthew skipped and played farther left of the heifer, as if he had no desire to trouble himself with the animal.

"What you's doing," Cowayne whispered.

"You's gotta make um think, you's ain't after um," Matthew said, feeling the trick he often used on scared puppies, was sure to work with the young cow.

And seeing that the cow had stopped running, Cowayne got the feeling Matthew knew what he was doing. But Matthew still had a problem with Clora Lee. For his big sister had driven her cow into the brush, which had the little boy wondering, how to flush the animal back out among the green grass, before its rightful owner came looking for it.

"Cowayne, you's go in over yonder," Matthew said, as he pointed to an area of the brush, just a few feet shy of Clora Lee.

After Cowayne ducked into the brush, Matthew had Clora Lee to chase him with the horse, until he took her far right of the cow. Then like a General commanding his attack force, Matthew sent his sister charging into the brush as well.

By the time Clora Lee and Cowayne had flushed their cow from the brush, Matthew and the other heifer was nowhere in sight. And they needed him more then ever, with nine horses grazing in the brush.

"Don't scare her," Matthew shouted, as he came running from the direction of their make shift corral.

The closer Matthew got, the harder Clora Lee and Cowayne tried to get him to stop running, yet the little scamper kept right on coming with a full head of steam.

"You's stop running," Clora Lee whispered angrily.

"Why?" Matthew asked, as he came to a complete stop.

"Theys got horses in there," Cowayne whispered.

Before Clora Lee or Cowayne could say another word, the little boy was in the brush, as if he were on a treasure hunt. And by the time Cowayne had mounted their horse behind Clora Lee, two of the nine horses came trotting out of the brush, with Matthew close behind them on a mare.

"Here Cowayne, you's take um," Matthew said, while falling off of the horse, that had a buckboard rigging on it.

Fearing there may be white men near by, Clora Lee made a failing attept to tell Matthew not to go back into the brush. But being overly excited, the boy's body was already in motion, as he darted back into the thick foliage, looking to get the other horses.

"Take um Lee, I's uh go get him," Cowayne said, leaving his friend to get the three horses to their corral.

Trusting that Cowayne would bring her little brother out of the brush safe and sound, Clora Lee headed for their hiding place with the horses. And once the animals were put away, Clora Lee went and got her pistols. And as the young female marched across the yard with tears in her eyes, she spotted Cowayne and Matthew with the rest of the horses, and the other cow. But not even the sight of Matthew could stop her heart from beating out of control, as she found herself exhausted.

"I's uh going see bout Joan and them girls," Clora Lee said, as she met Cowayne and Matthew in the woods, behind the hog pen.

"But we's gotta find a way to get them bullets," Cowayne cried, as he watched Clora Lee lay her pistols on the ground.

"You's said, we's got all we's need," Clora Lee barked, feeling the matter wasn't up for debate.

When Clora Lee came up on the woodshed, Joan was attempting to give the girls a bath. The stump size female had acquired a second tub from some where, and wanted to bathe both of the girls at the same time. But just like the heifer Clora Lee had lost in the brush, Madeline had no intentions of cooperating. For the girl, stood screaming and fighting, as she refused to go any where near the tub.

"Joan, what you's done did that poor child?" Clora Lee shouted.

"Clora Lee, don't you's be hollering at me, cause I's uh ain't do Madeline nothing. She's just don't wanna get in no water," Joan shouted, as if she were about to cry.

"Cause you's going bout it all wrong," Clora Lee said, giving Joan the impression, she were an expert at such matters.

"Well if I's doing it wrong, then you's welcome to show me how," Joan yelled, as she placed her hands on her hips.

Frustration had made Joan forget, Clora Lee was the one person she feared the most. And as the little female found herself at wits end, she was in no mood for small talk. For Joan was ready to do battle with the Devil himself. But when Joan saw Clora Lee drop her butt on an old tree stump, as if she didn't have a care in the world, after making such a bold statement, the duck high female was two shakes away from giving the girl a few choice words.

"Come here Madeline, sweetheart," Clora Lee said in a voice so soft, Joan had no other choice, but to roll her eyes.

Madeline walked over to Clora Lee without any knowledge, of what she was about to receive. And when Madeline made it to Clora Lee, the little girl looked at Joan, as if she had did her a great injustice. But when Clora Lee took hold of the bare naked child with one hand,

and gave her two good licks with the other, Madeline found herself crying for all the right reasons.

"Na you's get in that tub, so's Joan can give ya uh washing," Clora Lee said firmly. "And you's hush that fuss, fo Joan give ya some mo," the teen barked.

When Clora Lee released the little girl, she ran straight to the tub, and fell over in the thing. And as Joan grabbed Madeline, to keep her from drowning, she shot Clora Lee a look that wasn't so pleasant.

"I's uh tell ya the truth, Clora Lee, you's bout as sneaky, as that old snake, that got them folks kicked out they's garden," Joan said, trying not to smile.

"Well I's reckon, them folks, might need a hand on they's bottom," Clora Lee said, as she started to help Bessie take her bath.

"I's uh believe, this child, got more dirt on her, then Dew Dap," Joan said of Madeline.

"You's gon wash Dew Dap to?" Clora Lee asked with a sneaky smile.

Having no desire to speak on such an obscene thought, Joan just let her eyes do the talking. Yet the way she rolled them rather overtly, left Clora Lee and the world, clueless to what the little stump was thinking.

"Well I's just asking," Clora Lee said laughing, trying to get an answer out of Joan, one way or the other.

Knowing that Clora Lee could be setting her up, for what may end up being the plantation's newest hot topic, Joan quickly dropped a loaded question of her own. "Ha's it feel?" she asked, thus bringing about a moment of silence.

"What?" Clora Lee asked when she found the nerve to speak.

"To have Cowayne, as yo's own?"

Check, had quickly become checkmate, as Joan left Clora Lee speechless. For the young female never thought of Cowayne as being her very own private possession, as if he were still a slave. And being that it was coming from Joan, the girl didn't know what to make of the question. But before she could come up with a suitable response, or find away out of the situation, Joan attacked her again.

"Na Clora Lee, you's two spend all yo's time together. And we's all know, if n he's leaves here, you's gon go with him," Joan said, as if she were growing impatient with Clora Lee's silence.

"I's uh reckon, the Misses know's it to," Clora Lee barked softly, as she appeared to be preoccupied with Bessie.

"If n she's do, she's ain't let on," Joan replied.

Things got uncomfortably quiet, as Joan searched for the perfect way to lay out her next question, while Clora Lee was left not knowing what to say. And with only the sound of Madeline splashing her water to serenade the air, Clora Lee started humming. And while Clora Lee went on humming, she tried to untangle Bessie's hair, so Joan could wash it. But before Clora Lee could finish her humming, or untangle Bessie's hair, she got hit with a mountain of a question.

Why you's don't like me?" Joan asked, putting an end to Clora Lee's humming.

With the question hanging over her head like hangman's noose, Clora Lee tried to think of some thing quick, even though her brain was reeling from the unexpected frontal attack. Yet the only thing the teen could come up with, to help her derailed brain, was the thought of playing dumb. But it was already clear to Clora Lee, Joan had no intentions of waiting for her passed out brain to get its act together. So with a tangled piece of Bessie's hair in her hand, Clora Lee mumbled the word Cowayne.

"Cowayne," Joan said, releasing the word from her mouth.

Seeing that she wouldn't be able to get away with a one word answer, Clora Lee took a deep breath, and tried it again. "One day, I's uh was hiding from him, and I's uh saw ya looking at him, and I's uh ain't like the way you's was looking," Clora Lee said with a touch of anger.

"When you's was in the loft, or in the pecan tree?" Joan asked, as she rubbed the soap in Madeline's hair.

After hearing Joan say Cowayne's name, Clora Lee felt she was ready to get up on her toes and fight back. But the girl latest question, had Clora Lee back to thinking, she should have allowed Dew Dap to kill that old coon a thousand times. Yet Clora Lee still tried to come up with something quick, as she received a miracle. Before Clora Lee could comment on either spot, Madeline started screaming and rubbing her eyes, giving the teen a chance to think. And while Joan used her dress to wipe the soap from Madeline's eyes, Clora Lee tried to figure a way out of her second uncomfortable situation.

"Aw baby, I's uh done told ya, to keep ya eyes close," Joan said, while bouncing Madeline in her arms. "I's waiting," the tiny teen barked, the moment Madeline stopped crying.

With her feet firmly planted on the down side of fear, Clora Lee was more then willing to call for a truce. And if she couldn't get a truce, then another round of crying from Madeline would do just fine. Yet neither came for Clora Lee, leaving her no other choice, but to answer Joan's question. And just as Clora Lee was about to open her mouth, she heard Dew Dap's voice, which gave the girl one more reason to meet the big man upstairs.

"What you's doing?" Dew Dap squawked, as he stared at Madeline, who was covered from her head to her feet in soap.

"I's uh giving these girls a bath, and don't you's come round here bothering me," Joan stated firmly.

Seeing her opportunity for a quick escape, Clora Lee got up and walked away with Cowayne, leaving Joan to get her make believe house in order. And as Clora Lee rushed off with Cowayne, she prayed for the ex-slave not to call out her name.

With the most work she had ever done in one day behind her, Joan stood in the dark, saying goodbye to Dew Dap and the girls. And as she made the last few steps alone, the kitchen door didn't look the same to the girl any more. For the first time in her life, Joan dreaded the thought of entering the large house, as if it were a prison, rather then a safe haven. And as she took hold of the doorknob, Joan couldn't stop herself from taking one last look at Dew Dap and the girls, as they headed back to the woodshed, to get some sleep.

After quietly closing the door behind her, Joan tipped across the floor, thinking of all the things she was going to need for the girls. Yet before Joan could make it to her room, she was startled by the sound of Effie's voice.

"I guess, you have forgotten, your role as a house slave?" Effie whispered, just before striking a match, and placing it to a candle.

"I's uh was just trying to help them girls," Joan replied.

"Go to bed," Effie said, after opening the door to the room, Joan shared with her mother, and two other females.

"But I's…"

With Joan's words cut short, by the fingers to Effie's right hand around her throat, she was forced into a state of silence.

"Go, to, bed, and I won't tell you again," Effie whispered firmly, as she stood with her hand tightening its grip against the tiny teen's throat.

Effie gave Joan a slight shove, which landed the girl in her room. And after closing the door to the cramped little room, Effie quickly blew the candle out, as if she were some conspirator, looking to hatch a well laid plan. And as she sashayed through the dark without bumping into a single object, Effie once again, disappears into thin air.

The next morning when Clora Lee and Cowayne were done eating, they set out for Dew Dap and the girls. The two had seen the boy earlier, as he was headed toward the woodshed, with two rabbits and a possum. And Clora Lee was hoping Joan had taught the boy a thing or two, before rushing back to the mansion. But what Clora Lee dreaded most of all, was having to face Joan for a second day, seeing that she had never answered the girl's questions. And the very thought of Joan's questions, made Clora Lee grab Cowayne's hand, as if it were her wall of protection. But the invisible wall came crumbling down, when she saw the bristles of a broom, kicking dirt out of the woodshed.

"Dew Dap, what you's doing?" Cowayne asked, nearly sending Clora Lee in to a state of panic.

Clora Lee wondered if her friend had lost his brain, some where along the way. For if it were obvious to her, the teen was practicing his spearing techniques, then it should have been common knowledge to Cowayne. Yet he had to toot his bugle like some rooster, signaling Joan that they were there. But Clora Lee was armed with a backup plan, as she set Cowayne's hand free.

"Goodmorning," Joan said, as she stuck her head out of the shed.

While Cowayne gave Joan a hardy good morning, Clora Lee reluctantly mumbled the words, giving everyone the impression, she were a bit under the weather. And being that Joan was staring directly at her, Clora Lee felt they needed a touch of bad weather, just so she could avoid those stupid questions.

"Dew Dap, I's uh done told ya, I's need some hot water," Joan said, as she appeared to be a little testy.

"What you's gon do with it?" Dew Dap asked.

"If n you's don't go get that water, I's gon take that stick to yo's bottom," Joan yelled, which started Bessie and Madeline to laughing.

"It's uh spear," Dew Dap said, correcting Joan.

"I's uh don't care, if n its Mr. Lincoln's walking stick, you's go get that water, and I's mean it. And don't you's forget my cotton sack," Joan spat, as the boy headed out to get the water, with a couple of old pails.

"What you's need uh cotton sack for any huh?" Dew Dap asked, while coming to a stop.

"Dew Dap, I's uh don't believe, you's ever listen to me," Joan said, as she stepped out of the shed. "I's need to make them girls some undergarments, na you's get," Joan said softly, as she tapped Dew Dap on the leg with the broom.

"I's uh got it, Lee," Cowayne said with a great deal of excitement in his voice.

"What?" Clora Lee asked, as she stood confused.

"We's need uh cotton sack."

After giving Clora Lee a big hug, Cowayne ran in the direction of the large storage house, shouting, "Come on Dew Dap, I's uh know where them old sacks is."

Like two little boys chasing dragonflies, Cowayne and Dew Dap darted off, leaving the girls and the pails in a cloud of dust. And just like that, Clora Lee found her self alone, to face Joan and her ridiculous questions. Yet before Clora Lee could think about Joan and her dreaded questions, she noticed the two rabbits tied to the woodshed. They were held captive by the string tied to their right hind legs. And the teen couldn't help but to feel their pain, as she thought of those on the plantation, who was forced to wear Mr. Arnold's idea, of an insurance policy. And to the young teen, as long as the newly freed slaves wore their rings, they were still tied to slavery, even though Mr. Lincoln had set them free.

"Clora Lee," Joan said, cutting into the girl's thought.

Clora Lee raised her head, giving sight to the most bewildered look, she had ever displayed.

"You's all right," Joan asked, as she thought the girl was pregnant.

"Uh huh," Clora Lee replied, as if she wasn't really sure.

"Did you's hear what I's said?" Joan asked, but not getting a response. "You's wanna go with me, to get some water to wet the girl's hair?" Joan said, reiterated her question for the second time.

When Clora Lee stood up, her eyes went straight to Joan's right leg. Just like her, Cowayne, and the other young ones, Mr. Arnold had left for the war, before branding them with their rings. Yet Clora Lee knew, in order for the older slave to truly be free, they must rid themselves of their link to capivity.

"Clora Lee," Joan said firmly, but with concern.

"I's ready," Clora Lee replied, as she went and grabbed a pail.

On their way to get the water, Clora Lee didn't say a word, as Joan played with the girls, while complainting about Dew Dap and his spear. And ever so often, Joan would say how much she hated, that Pleasant had given Dew Dap the wretched stick. But unlike Dew Dap, Clora Lee had no intentions of correcting the girl, about the well crafted spear. For the teen just kept her mouth shut, as she hoped Joan had forgotten about those stupid questions.

"You's knows, you's ain't answer me," Joan said, the moment they made it back to the woodshed with the water.

"Bout what?" Clora Lee mumbled, while hoping Dew Dap would show up, giving her another chance, to disappear for a second time.

"The loft, or the tree?" Joan asked, as if she was demanding an answer.

"When you's see'd me in that old loft?"

"All the time, just like I's see'd ya in that tree, all the time. But I's knows you's talking bout that tree," Joan said. "And I's knows what day, you's talking bout."

"Then why's you's was looking at him?"

Right away, Joan knew why Clora Lee had been mad at her for the last three years. And the girl didn't know whether to breathe a sigh of relief, or laugh herself to death. "Why Clora Lee, I's think you's jealous," Joan said, knowing the girl had nothing to worry about.

"I's uh ain't jealous, cause I's knows he's mine," Clora Lee stated with a confidence, Joan clearly understood.

"Then you's knows, I's uh don't want him. I's was just thinking ha good it would be, if n I's had some body to take my beatings, when I's make the Misses mad," Joan said.

"Ha you's knows bout that?"

"Cause I's saw ya," Joan said, then made a face, just like the one Clora Lee shot Cowayne, on the day she spilled the pail of milk.

"I's uh reckon, you's told the Misses," Clora Lee said, as Joan began to wet Bessie's hair.

"If n I's had, she's would uh beat ya," Joan said, right before asking Clora Lee, how did it feel to have found love?

"I's uh don't know," Clora Lee replied, right before lowering her head.

"Why Clora Lee, I's done see'd ya face too many times, na you's Tell me ha it feel," Joan said once more, as if she was ready to put her hand down the girl's throat, to bring forth the answer.

With Joan talking as loud as she was, Clora Lee felt everyone on the plantation heard the big mouth girl. And to say that Joan weren't much bigger then Bessie, her mouth appeared to be larger then the very plantation they were born to serve.

"That was a good hiding place, wasn't it?" Clora Lee said, as she tried to change the conversation.

"But it ain't hid that look on ya face, na you's tell me ha it feel."

After noticing how Bessie and Madeline had taken to Joan, Clora Lee brought herself to speak. "It's uh lot like them girls taking to ya. You's feel safe when theys with ya, and you's don't care what others think about ya," Clora Lee said, as if she was drifting into a trance. "And if n you's stick with um, theys uh stick with ya, no matter who's ya find to love ya."

Before Joan could comment on Clora Lee's words of wisdom, Cowayne and Dew Dap came charging up like a couple of playful pups. And Dew Dap, who was holding a sack in one hand, and his spear in the other, held the look of someone lost between being a slave, and a warrior tracking through the darkest jungles of Africa.

"Where you's want it," Dew Dap asked, while holding the sack up, as if it were a fresh kill.

With Dew Dap holding the sack, Joan cut two chunks out of the thing, and placed them in the pot of boiling water.

"Why you's do that?" Clora Lee asked, of Joan placing the two cuts into the boiling water.

"I's got uh wash it, or my girls, gon be scratching like one of masa Arnold's hounds," Joan replied.

"We's ain't got no masa," Clora Lee said boldly.

With everyone looking at her, as if she were old Pete's ghost, Clora Lee felt a chill come over her. For their silence, told the girl, her friends had yet to understand the true meaning of freedom.

"Well I's uh reckon, them Blue Coat ain't beat them Rebs after all," Clora Lee said sadly.

"Na Clora Lee, you's hush that kind uh talk," Joan said, as she took the spear out of Dew Dap's hand.

"I's uh got uh go check my traps," Dew Dap said, reaching for the spear.

"Did you's get my water?" Joan asked, as she struck Dew Dap with the spear, causing everyone to laugh.

As Dew Dap grabbed a pail, and set out to get Joan, her water, Clora Lee took Cowayne by the arm and led him away. Yet their walk wasn't a quiet one, as Clora Lee told Cowayne to get her as many rabbits as he could find. And along with the rabbits, she wanted some potatoes and carrots. And as Cowayne ran off to make Clora Lee wish come true, she headed back to Joan, to inform the female of their plan. Then like before, Clora Lee set out for the barn. But on her way to the once bustling building, Clora Lee stopped to tell old Mae and Sistah of what she and Joan were planning to do. And if old Mae and Sistah said it wasn't a good idea, then the other slaves would have to find a way to feed themselves.

Chapter 13

Kicked Out

When Cowayne had finished checking their traps, he held five rabbits, and two of the critters weren't all that big. And having a feeling that five rabbits weren't going to be enough for his Lee, Cowayne went in the direction of the blacksmith shed, hoping to find her there.

"This all we's got," Cowayne said, as he stood in front of Clora Lee, holding the five rabbits.

"Theys fine, cause I's uh gone put um with Joan's two. Na you's go get them tators and carrots."

"I's uh try," Cowayne said, as he headed for the front gate.

"Come here," Clora Lee said, as she took hold of Cowayne's shirt. "I's uh know it's hard to get everything I's want, but they got some, who ain't eat in uh day or two. Na ha you's think we's uh feel, if n we's ain't eat everyday?" Clora Lee asked, with a deep sense of emotional pain.

"I's gon get it, Lee."

With her ability to read Cowayne like she could read her name, Clora Lee stepped in front of him, thus preventing the boy from walking away. And after Clora Lee placed her face to his, she spoke softly. "I's uh know you's gon do ya best, but I's uh need ya to know why I's doing it. Everybody ain't gotta Cowayne," Clora Lee said, right before kissing his ear.

"And I's uh don't want everybody," Cowayne said, assuring Clora Lee that she stood alone in his heart.

I's uh know you's want yo's Lee. And I's uh gon always be yo's Lee, till I's die."

With her trembling lips only a hair away from Cowayne's ear, Clora Lee was ready to give up the fight, and defy Sistah in the worst way. Yet she never got the chance.

"I's uh gotta go, Lee, if n I's uh gon get them tators," Cowayne said, as he ran for the barn, with Clora Lee on his tail.

Not wanting to use any of their horses, Cowayne took the Arnold's old mule, and rode the animal toward the north fields. For that was the only way, the teen could get the mule off of the plantation, without his mother or Sistah seeing him. And once he reached the other side of the brush, Cowayne headed straight for the creek. The teen was going to check their fishing lines, hoping to have nabbed a few fish, to pay for the deed he was about to do.

After pulling up two nice size catfish, Cowayne remounted the mule, and rode in the direction of the Bray plantation. There he sat in the brush, looking for the perfect way to reach the storage house without being seen. Then like a thieving fox, Cowayne left the brush, and worked his way from one hiding place to the next, until he reached the unprotected storage shed. And while keeping his eyes pealed for trouble, Cowayne eased into the building, and closed the door.

But when Cowayne emerged from the nearly empty shed, he was deeply disappointed. For his little rummaging expedition, wasn't as fruitful, as his fishing trip. Yet a promise was a promise, even if he was giving up two large catfish, for five medium size carrots, and a hand full of green beans. And after all, it wasn't like the people of the Bray plantation was being given a choice in the matter, the boy thought to himself. So with the confiscated goods in his possession, Cowayne took his catch of the day, to the front door of the mansion. And after hanging the fish on the doorknob, Cowayne took hold of the door knocker, and gave it three hard thumps, right before disappearing.

When Cowayne had safely returned to the Big A plantation with his best efforts, he once again went in search of Clora Lee. And he found his Lee in the most unlikely place of all. For Clora Lee stood in the middle of the yard with his mother, Sistah, and Isabella. And as Clora Lee appeared to be directing her own little army, Cowayne noticed Mrs. Arnold looking down from an upstairs bedroom window. Yet the teen didn't let that deter him from giving Clora Lee the much needed package.

"Here Lee," Cowayne said, as he approached her with the bundle. "Theys ain't had no tators."

"I's uh speck, theys won't mind, if n it's tators or beans," Clora Lee said, while expecting the bundle. "Na you's go get some sleep," she said, while gently touching his hand.

Before Cowayne could make his departure, Joan and the girls came strolling by him. And the teen couldn't believe his eyes, as he took notice of how clean Bessie and Madeline were. And each of the girls had on a pretty little dress, which the Misses daughters could no longer stuff their bodies into. And Bessie's hair was neatly braided, while Madeline held the look of a deranged Mohican.

"Ha I's uh gon get some sleep, when I's uh don't know who them pretty little girls is," Cowayne said, smiling.

"Na you's knows, them is Bessie and Madeline, so you's leave them girls be," Clora Lee said, as she pinched Cowayne.

"That's who theys is?"

"I's uh don told ya, to get," Clora Lee said, as she laid the back part of her hand to Cowayne's hip.

"I's going, but I's uh waiting to see Joan do the same for Dew Dap," Cowayne said, walking away laughing.

"If n you's don't hush, I's uh gon plait yo's hair like Sistah," Clora Lee said, then pranced around on her toes.

"But what about our sacks?"

"I's uh got it," Clora Lee replied with a great deal of confidence.

Hearing Clora Lee say she had everything under control, Cowayne headed for the barn, knowing the sacks were already being made.

Looking as tired, as a slave who had been toiling in the field all day and half of the night, Joan told Clora Lee, her and the girls were taking a walk, so she could give her fingers a bit of rest.

"Come on child, and find you's some where to sit, cause we ain't doing nothing, but trying to see if n Clora Lee and Sistah knows ha to cook," old Mae said smiling.

"So you's old Mae," Joan appeared to be saying, rather then asking the old slave a question.

"Mae," Clora Lee said firmly, while looking a little angry.

"Child, don't you's pay Clora Lee no mind, cause I's was old when she's come here, and I's plenty old na," the old female confessed.

"I's heard uh lot about ya," Joan said, as her and the girls took a seat on a bench across from the old slave.

But from the moment Joan and the girls walked up, the half size female appeared to be preoccupied with Sistah. And with Sistah cooking, Joan got the perfect opportunity to watch the female, without anyone accusing her of staring.

"Child, it ain't much, you's can hear bout an old slave, who ain't got much time left," old Mae said softly.

"Na Mae, I's uh done told ya, I's uh ain't gon be hearing that kind uh talk," Clora Lee grumbled.

"Clora Lee, I's uh ain't doing nothing, but saying, what God love. And you and Cowayne ain't gon stop him, when he's come for me," old Mae said, looking at her feet.

"What you's heard?" Clora Lee asked Joan, as she tried her best to change the conversation.

"Theys said, the plantation, ain't gon be nothing with out her."

"Child, this old plantation was here when I's come, and its gon be here when I's gone," old Mae uttered.

"But when the Misses wrote and told masa Arnold, the soldiers took everything, he's said, as long he's got old Mae, he's uh be alright."

"She's free, so he's gotta get some of them in that house, to do his picking," Clora Lee snarled, while dumping the carrots in the pot.

"Na Clora Lee, I's uh can talk for myself," old Mae said, as she tried to protect Ethel's first born.

Clora Lee dropped her spoon in the pot, and angrily walked away. And as her body movement shouted for everyone to keep their distance, Joan bravely ignored the fiscal warning.

"Ya'll sit here with Mae and Sistah," Joan said to the girls, in a soft and sweet voice.

"Yes um," Bessie replied, giving the females cause to smile.

But before Joan could walk away, the females got a hot new topic to talk about. For Madeline leaped to her feet, and ran behind Joan, while screaming, as if some one had struck her with a nice little switch. But the little girl didn't have to cry long. For Joan scooped Madeline up, and went back to walking without saying a word.

"Whats wrong?" Joan asked, as she came up behind Clora Lee.

"I's uh hate it, when she's talk like that," Clora Lee said, crying.

"Mae is only trying to tell ya, she's old," Joan said, as she placed her free arm around Clora Lee.

"I's uh know, but if n anything happen to her, it uh kill Cowayne."

"Na you's listen to me, Clora Lee. You's hush that crying, cause Cowayne loves ya, just as much as he's loves his ma. And if n anything happen to her, you's gon help him through it. I's uh done see'd you's two together, and you's make him happy. Na you's come on back, fo you's get Mae to crying," Joan said, hoping Clora Lee would see the logic in her words.

Joan and Clora Lee headed back to the pot, as if they had been friends all of their born days. And once she gave old Mae a hug, accompanied by a kiss on the forehead, Clora Lee quickly went back to helping Sistah with what ever it was they call themselves cooking. Yet Sistah wasn't about to let Clora Lee off so easy. The unfortunate female asked Joan, what else did she hear about the old slave?

"Nothing," Clora Lee said, as she gave Sistah a playful bump.

"Ooo Mae, you's see'd what that child done did me," Sistah cried, as she gave Clora Lee a hug.

Joan didn't make an attempt to answer Sistah, knowing the female was up to another one of her playful tricks. So rather then keeping a bad conversation going, the tiny female went back to braiding Madeline's hair. But with Sistah having years of experience in instigating, she was determined to keep the new comer talking.

"What you's heard bout me," Sistah asked, looking at Clora Lee.

From the moment Joan started talking, she couldn't take her eyes off of Sistah. But after many words said, the young female took that time, to look sadly at old Mae. And Joan kept right on looking at the old female, as she didn't say a word, while still braiding Madeline's hair to perfection. But Joan's perfection didn't stop the little girl from crying, when the comb ran upon a nap it didn't like, thus putting an end to Sistah's hopes, of getting an answer to her question.

"I's uh sorry," Joan said, as if she were about to cry.

"Child, you's hurting," old Mae asked.

"You's alright, dumpling?" Joan asked, while leaning over to check on Madeline.

"Child, I's talking bout you," old Mae said to Joan.

"No ma'am, I's uh ain't doing no hurting."

"Mae, she's looking like that, cause them girls ain't got nobody to care for um," Clora Lee said, as she added the green beans to her and Sistah's brew.

"Child, Dew Dap don't know nothing bout bringing up no girls," old Mae cried.

"I's uh know that, and I's uh ain't blaming him, cause he's done the best he's could. But theys got enough females round here, for them not to be looking like theys was," Joan said, as the tears ran from her eyes. "I's uh was up in that there house, just looking out them windows, too afraid to come round here," she went on, while using her shoulders, to remove the tears that wouldn't stop falling.

When Joan had finally laid her words to rest, it was obvious to the females, including old Mae, how the girl felt about them. Yet no one said a word, to the girl who lived her entire life, in that big beautiful house, not knowing the true meaning of hard work. And Joan knew that, as she waited for one of the females to lash out at her. For the teen had often heard about how the field slaves suffered under the burning sun, and the pouring rain, while trying to satisfy their master's selfish desire for an even greater amount of wealth. Yet the girl felt that was no excuse for any of them, not to help Dew Dap with his sisters. Nor did the privilege house slave feel, she or any of them in that old house, including Mrs. Arnold, would be given a pass, when God ask, why did his young ones go unattended.

"I's uh done comb theys hair uh time or two, but I's uh had to put my hand on theys bottom," Clora Lee said, breaking the silence.

"And we's all knows, Dew Dap don't take kindly, bout folks touching his sisters up uh bit," Isabella said, as the other females nodded their heads in approval.

If she could have been God for one day, Joan would have rose up and struck them all down, even Clora Lee. For the girl, saw through their worthless lies, as they tried to disguise them as excuses. Yet their words made them sound like poor souls, begging to be burned in the dark firy pits of Hell. And the thought of the females, trying to lay the blame on Dew Dap, made Joan madder then the master, that was born to abuse them.

"You's can't blame him, cause he's done lost his ma, and theys, all he's got left of her," Joan said, as her tears fell like raindrops in a storm. "I's uh might be the same way, if n I's uh had young ns to see after," she went on.

Seeing that Joan was looking at her, Clora Lee couldn't help but to feel a sense of guilt. And recalling the look on Joan's face, from her last encounter with the little girl, Clora Lee knew exactly why the female was looking like a mad mother wolf. Yet the crafty teen, had already came up with a way to make things right between the two of them, as well as Madeline. For if Joan was willing to turn her back on the Misses, Clora Lee had already made up her mind, to ask the little female, to go with them, when it came time to leave that old plantation.

"What if n Dew Dap, take them girls and leave with um?" Clora Lee asked, as she sought to test the waters, which ran deep through Joan's river of dedication.

"Ha he's gon take care of um out among them white folks, when he's can't take care of um here? But if n he's take um, I's uh do my best to stop him," Joan said, as she wrapped her arms around the girls. "And if n I's uh can't stop him, I's uh be praying for him to find some female to help him take care of um. But until he's take um from me, I's uh gon be here every morning, to do for um. And if n he's don't find nothing with that old stick, we's uh graze like cows," Joan said with a deep sense of devotion.

"Na child, Cowayne and Clora Lee always find more then we's can eat," old Mae said, while Sistah backed her up.

"Cowayne gotta do for his own, and Dew Dap, is gon do what he's can for us. We's can't look to take from others, cause times is hard, and food ain't much these days," Joan said, as she put the finishing touches to Madeline's hair.

But Joan's work was far from finished, as she took one of the cuts from that old cotton sack, and the cigar box of sewing things from Bessie. And when Joan came out of the box with a threaded needle and a pair of scissors, the females couldn't believe their eyes. Without missing a beat, Joan got right down to sewing the girls some undergarments.

"Pull ya dress up, dumpling, theys ain't got nothing but females round here," Joan said to Bessie.

Trusting Joan to no end, Bessie did as she was asked. And after Joan had measured the cloth against Bessie's body, she went straight to cutting it, without any doubt of her measurements. Yet the females couldn't believe their eyes, as they all waited for the girl to take at least one more stab at it. But Joan just went right on cutting the old cotton sack, as if it had some sort of markings to guide her. And when she finished cutting, Joan didn't think twice, as the little seamstress put her needle and thread to work.

"Joan, don't you's speck, you's need to get some rest?" Sistah asked.

"I's uh don't speck rest, is gon sew my girls, theys undergarments," Joan replied respectfully.

Clora Lee gave Joan a gentle pat on the shoulder, just before walking off to go find Matthew. For if her plan was going to work perfectly, Clora Lee needed Matthew to dabble in his specialty. But first, she had to find the little wild spirit.

When Clora Lee found Matthew, he was with Pleasant, on the far side of the corral. The two were going at it with a couple of short sticks.

"Why yous two, playing with them stick?" Clora Lee asked.

"Cause we's knife fighting," Matthew shouted, as Pleasant killed him for the tenth straight time. "Aw Clora Lee, you's got me killed," Matthew cried.

"Good, na you's can stop playing," Clora Lee said with a smile.

"We's aint playing, we's knife fighting," Matthew shouted in frustration.

"You's ain't got no knife, so you's stick fighting. Na you's come on, cause I's got something for ya to do."

"We's knife fighting, ain't we Pleasant?"

"And we's aiming to knife uh female, if n she's come round here sassing us," Pleasant said, giving Clora Lee fair warning.

"Well fo ya'll kill me, I's uh need ya to tell everybody, we's gon be eating in front of the main house," Clora Lee said, as her left arm rested on Matthew's shoulder.

"Everybody?" the little fellow asked, to make sure he heard his sister right.

"Ain't that what I's said? Na you's go tell um up in that there house to."

"Even the Misses, and her own?"

"Even the Misses, and her own, and make sure you's wake Cowayne," Clora Lee replied, which sent Matthew running.

"If n ya'll ma was here, she uh be mighty proud of ya," Pleasant said, as he and Clora Lee headed for the pot.

"Well she's ain't here, and I's uh speck, Mae and Sistah is pretty nough proud," Clora Lee grumbled.

The teen held a strange look on her face, which left Pleasant a little worried. For he didn't know if it was a look of sadness, spawn by anger, or anger born out of sadness. Yet there was one thing Pleasant did know, as he put his arm around Clora Lee. He was proud of the girl, and there was nothing she could do, to make him feel any different.

"Well I's mighty proud of ya to," Pleasant said, as they walked together, like father and daughter.

As everyone gathered to be fed, Sally, Joan's mother, walked up, and gave old Mae a warm hug.

"Mae I's uh tell ya the truth. I's speck that old stump, follow ya in them fields," Sally said, as she started her conversation off with the five words, the slaves appeared to love so much.

"Child, I's uh got two stumps, na days. This here is my traveling stump," old Mae said, as Sally gave her a kiss.

With the help of Pleasant, Clora Lee made her way on top of a bench. There she began to beat on a pan with a cooking spoon, until the ex-slaves gave her, their undivided attention. But the ex-slaves found themselves at a lost, when the young teen couldn't bring her self to speak. For Clora Lee's mind fell on Ethel, and her baby sister. Yet the thought only lasted for a brief moment, as the teen got back to the task at hand.

"I's knows ya'll ready to eat," Clora Lee said, as she eyed Sally whispering to old Mae. "We's gon feed them young ns first, then the females. And after the females, you's males gon eat. Na there ain't no call, for none uh ya to be worrying, cause we's got plenty nough for all of us."

Clora Lee's much anticipated speech ended rather abruptly, when she caught sight of a familiar face working its way through the crowd. And after placing a hand on Pleasant's shoulder, the teen sought to place her feet back on solid ground. And with the luck of the draw, Clora Lee completed her task at the most opportune moment. For the teen found herself standing face to face with Effie once again. And as she stared at the four fine plates in the preferred slave's hands, the poor girl caught a chill, just like all of the other times, when she found herself, in the company of her grandmother. But Clora Lee wasn't alone, and she was planning on taking full advantage of having Pleasant and Sistah at her side. So with no intentions of passing up a perfect opportunity to make her self heard, the teen took a deep breath. But just as Clora Lee was about to cut loose, Matthew came charging up.

"Clora Lee I's uh forgot to…."

"Not na, Matthew," Clora Lee said, cutting the boy off.

But feeling what he had to say, was of great importance, Matthew didn't give up on his quest. "I's uh ain't…."

"I's uh said, not na," Clora Lee said, as she put her hand over Matthew's mouth. "I's uh see, you's come to serve ya Misses," Clora Lee said, while stepping in front of Matthew, preventing Effie from getting a good look at the boy. "You's go back and tell her in that house, the war is over, and we's free. So if n she's want her young ns to eat, theys gotta be out here, fo I's uh feed the last young n. And if n she's wanna eat, then I's uh better see her, fo I's feed the last female. And that go's for you too," Clora Lee said, as she no longer feared Effie's blank stare.

"Clora Lee," old Mae called out to the girl.

"I's uh all right, Mae," Clora Lee said, as she started serving the make shift soup.

Seeing his chance, Matthew told Clora Lee, he had forgotten to go and wake Cowayne, like she had told him to. But Clora Lee wasn't worried about the mistake, as she assured her brother, everything was well in hand. So after giving a little girl a cup of the rabbit soup, she gave Matthew his portion, and told him to run along.

The very next little girl in line was Madeline, with Joan faithfully at her side. In her attempt to kill two birds with one serving stone, Clora Lee tried to give Joan her soup, after handing the teen a cup for Madeline. But Joan politely refused, reminding Clora Lee that it is for the children to eat first. So being forced to hold true to her statement, Clora Lee set the pan down, and gave Bessie a cup of the hot soup, allowing Joan to escort the girls back to their seat.

When Joan made it back to the bench with the girls, old Mae and Sally were talking joyfully. And Joan didn't say a word to her mother, as she sat holding Madeline, while feeding the little girl the hot soup.

"I's uh tell ya, Sally," old Mae said looking at Joan. "Yo's child, show nough can work."

"Mae, you's ain't telling me nothing, I's don't know," Sally said, with a fearful look on her face.

"That there is some of her work," old Mae said, referring to Bessie's hair.

"I's uh reckon, I's knows my child plaiting, like I's knows her stitching."

"Na that child, show nough can do that," a female said.

"Who you's telling. I's uh be in them fields, if n the Misses know'd what she's can do," Sally boasted, as she touched the collar to the dress Bessie was wearing.

Joan didn't say a word, as old Mae and Sally went on talking about her abilities. For the teen just went on focusing her attention on Bessie and Madeline, as if she and the little girls were the only ones left on that old plantation. And the way Joan blew the watery soup between sips, told the two older females, the girls were going to be all right, with Joan by their side.

When Mrs. Arnold's children made it up to the pot, Chirstine stood in front of her younger brother and sister. And Clora Lee knew the three had to have jumped the line, yet she wasn't going to argue the fact. Instead, the fiery young teen, just lowered the hammer on Christine.

"You's come here fo I's did, so you's gotta eat with the females," Clora Lee said, with her arms fold.

At that very moment, old Mae couldn't bring herself to fear Mrs. Arnold, or the man she married. For the old slave looked upon Ethel's first born child, with a great deal of pride. And when she saw Christine step out of the line, it made old Mae feel some what vindicated. But the old slave knew as long as Clora Lee and Cowayne stayed on the Big A plantation, they would forever be in danger. Yet the old female had no doubt in her mind, the children would soon be leaving the land of their birth.

Dew Dap brought Joan her food, along with a spoon, Clora Lee and Cowayne got off of a dead soldier. Yet as he tried to trade Joan the pan for Madeline's cup of soup, the teen ran in to a bit of resistance. And no matter how hard he tried, Dew Dap couldn't get Joan to give up the cup, or his sister.

"I's uh can't eat, and feed Madeline to," Joan said, looking up at Dew Dap.

"I's uh can feed her," Dew Dap replied, while feeling he was losing his sisters.

But Joan wasn't buying it, as she went right on feeding their little dumpling, leaving the boy to stick out like a sore thumb. But when Dew Dap resorted to a much firmer tactic, brows quickly rose.

"Here," the young well built male said, as he found himself on one knee, holding the spoon filled with soup to Joan's mouth.

With her heart on the other side of the stars, Joan stared deep into Dew Dap eyes. And he didn't have to ask the little stump twice, as she opened her mouth, allowing the spoon safe passage. And when the spoon was in position, Joan closed her mouth, as well as her eyes, leaving Dew Dap to slowly remove the empty eating utensil. Yet Joan knew that she was in no position to counter Dew Dap's bold act, so the small female quickly surrendered Madeline over to her big brother.

"You's see that boy foots?" Sally asked old Mae, shaking her head.

"Foots, child I's looking at them hands," old Mae replied softly. "Them fingers, mighty big," old Mae cried. "I's uh hope you's done told that child, bout them big foots and big hands, cause she's gon be in trouble," the old female said, after pausing for a moment to shake her head.

"You's gotta blow it," Joan said, as Dew Dap sat down, and placed Madeline on his knee.

"Child, the way he's feed you, I's uh reckon, he's knows what to do," a female said, bringing about a mountain of laughter.

Looking at Dew Dap, Joan wondered if he would eat from her, as freely, as she had eaten for him. But something told Joan it was neither the time, nor the place, for her to search the boy's heart. But when the time was right, Joan felt she would know it, just as she knew how to sew a rip in an old shirt. So the teen just ignored all of the talk which fluttered around them, and ate her soup, while giving Bessie a helping hand.

As Clora Lee gave Sally her soup, she told the female they needed to talk. And even though Sally didn't have a clue of what the girl could want with her, she was more then willing to listen. For Clora Lee and those around her, were eating everyday, a luxury Sally surely didn't have. So what ever the teen wanted to talk about, Sally was hoping it had everything to do with food.

Isabella came after Sally, and right away, she tried to apologize for speaking ill of the girl's mother, as well as talking down to Sistah. But Clora Lee quickly cut the female off.

"You's told the truth, and I's told the truth, na we's gon eat," Clora Lee said, as she gave Isabella an extra spoon full of soup.

With the past officially behind them, the problem between the two females was no more. And Clora Lee would have been the first person to pat Isabella on the back for speaking her mind. Yet it wasn't what the female said, that made the teen mad. For it was whom she said it to, and how she spoke of Sistah's problem. But all was forgiven, and everyone was ready to move on, just like the North and South were hoping to do.

When everyone had received something to eat, Clora Lee poured the last of the soup in a small pot, and gave it to Dew Dap for Joan and the girls. Then without saying a word, she set out for the old barn, with enough food for her and Cowayne. And as she strolled across the yard, Clora Lee thought about Isabella's statement. Ethel was wrong for leaving her and Matthew behind. Yet Clora Lee felt they had gotten the better end of the deal. For her and Matthew didn't have to wake up to Big Willie every day, which was a blessing in it self. And Clora Lee was glad to hear Sistah say, she would not have allowed Ethel to take her and Matthew away. Yet the words weren't enough to stop the teen from hating the two individuals, who were responsible for her very existence. For the hate, would forever live inside of Clora Lee like a never ending storm.

Clora Lee entered the barn, leaving her hate for Ethel and Big Willie at the door. And with her one free hand, she carefully made her way up the ladder, to find Cowayne still sleeping peacefully. And after sitting their food down, Clora Lee decided to take another piece of that, which was her's for the taking. So she placed her nose to Cowayne's, and waited for him to breathe out. And when he did so, Clora Lee pulled into her nostril, every ounce of air that Cowayne had released, as if it were he himself, she was inhaling. And when Cowayne softly drew in a breath, Clora Lee released every bit of the air in her lungs. For the young female was telling the boy, she was willing to give him, the very life that was her's to lay down in his name.

With Cowayne helplessly asleep, Clora Lee felt it was a good time, to steal a touch of his sweetness. So while keeping her face close to his, Clora Lee raised the cotton sack dress she was wearing over her pants, high above her knees, just before straddling him. And being in the most perfect position, Clora Lee moved her lips forward to steal a gentle kiss. But what was supposed to be an innocent peck, ended up with the teen sucking the boy's bottom lip into her mouth. And as she held the unresisting flesh captive, her body, sinfully cried out for more. But Clora Lee was too afraid to give herself more, as she yearned to ease the pounding that rested safely behind her fat furry lips.

"I's uh love ya, Cowayne. I's uh love ya, more then Sistah loves ya. So don't you's go get ya self killed, cause I's gon die to. You's hear me

Cowayne. I's uh gon die, cause I's uh can't live without ya," Clora Lee whispered. "Na you's wake up," she said, a tad bit louder.

When Cowayne didn't wake up as she commanded him to, Clora Lee squeezed his nose, knowing it would do the trick.

"What you's doing, Lee?" the boy grumbled.

"You's wanna eat, don't ya?" Clora Lee asked, while trying to look innocent.

Feeling that Clora Lee was asking him another one of those crazy questions, Cowayne ignored her, as he tried to sit up. But no sooner then the teen tried, he found himself fighting a losing battle.

"Well let's eat," Clora Lee said smiling, as she dismounted her human horse.

"You's had enough?" Cowayne asked, as they both ate from the same small pot.

"We's had more then enough," Clora Lee said, before kissing Cowayne on the jaw. "You's ever been wrong?"

"Lee, you's knows, I's been wrong," Cowayne replied, while studying the sad look, his friend held on her face.

"I's talking bout, wrong, wrong," Clora Lee said, as if there were more then one type of wrong.

"What other kind uh wrong, they's got?" Cowayne asked, as he sat confused.

"I's uh don't know, but I's been wrong bout Joan. She's good to them girls, and she's good to everybody," Clora Lee said trembling.

"So what you's gon do?" Cowayne asked through his chewing.

"We's gon take her and them girls with us. And you's stop talking, with food in yo's mouth," Clora Lee replied, with her head on his shoulder.

"Lee, ha we's gone keep up with them girls, and my ma to?"

"You's uh think uh something," Clora Lee said, knowing that Cowayne would never let her down.

Like so many times before, the teen knew better then to continue their conversation, being that Clora Lee had already made up her mind about the matter. So with no intention of saying another word, Cowayne went on eating their naked soup.

After Joan finished sewing Madeline and Bessie's undergarments, she had Dew Dap to put a pot of water over the fire. Then the nearly exhausted female, sent Dew Dap to get a cotton sack of soft grass. And like Cowayne, Dew Dap went about getting Joan what she wanted without saying a word, or taking his spear with him. The boy was trying to take Cowayne's advice, and stop asking Joan what for, every time she needed him to do something. But it didn't take Dew Dap long to find out, the only thing the advice got him, was more work. And that made the boy feel he couldn't win for losing. Yet Dew Dap found Joan to be a breath of fresh air, in his seriously stale world.

"What we's gon do with this," Dew Dap asked, as he came up behind Joan with the sack of soft grass.

"We gon put it on the floor, so our girls can sleep on it," Joan replied.

After helping Dew Dap lay the grass field sack in the shed, Joan once again found herself a few yards from the backdoor, she was beginning to hate, just as much as Clora Lee. And seeing that she had given the girls their kiss goodbye, Joan backed away smiling, while her eyes said goodnight to Dew Dap.

"The Misses would like to see you," Effie said from the shadows, as Joan peered out the window at a job well done.

After feeling her way through the dark, Joan laid the cigar box on the kitchen table in front of Effie. And even though Joan couldn't see the lead house slave, she knew the female was still there. So Joan just calmed herself, and headed for the light at the top of the staircase. And knowing that Mrs. Arnold would be in her bedroom, Joan grudgingly climbed the stairs in fear. But by the time she was near the end of her climb, Mrs. Arnold appeared from out of no where, nearly giving the poor girl a heartattack.

"Effie said you's wanted to see me, ma'am," Joan mumbled, as she stared up at the vile white face, that hung over her with the look of an angry moon.

Like the sound of lightning striking an unsuspecting cloud, Mrs. Arnold's hand crashed against Joan's face. And as the stinging burned them both, neither cried out in pain. Nor did a tear fall from Joan's eyes, as Mrs. Arnold's thunderous slap, landed her on the opposite side of the stairs.

"I don't know what possessed you to take my children fine dresses, and put them on those filthy animals, but you will be sorry," Mrs. Arnold spat, with a great deal of hate.

"I's uh go get um, ma'am," Joan said as she could still feel the stinging blow, which continued to burn the left side her face.

"Do you think I would want anything, those filthy pigs touched? Do you?" Mrs. Arnold shouted, as she gave Joan another painful slap.

Just as Joan was about to give her reply, Mrs. Arnold took hold of the little stump's throat with both hands. And while she did her best to choke the life out of the girl, Mrs. Arnold spoke in a tone so vile, the stench from her breath, nearly turned Joan white.

"Don't you ever, open your mouth to me again, do you hear me? And don't you ever set foot in this house, or I will kill you myself," Mrs. Arnold growled, as she pushed Joan away, nearly sending the girl tumbling down the spiral staircase.

Clinging to the wall like some dying faded portrait, Joan stood too afraid to move, as she fought to catch her breath. And as the girl appeared to be unable to take her eyes off of the descending stairs, Joan could see her body rolling down each and everyone, of the cold hard steps. But when the words, get out, exploded in her ear, while feeling another burning slap against her face, Joan quickly put her feet in motion.

With her face feeling like it had been hit with a hot branding iron, Joan ran down the staircase and across the floor. And the girl went right on running in the direction of the kitchen, where she grabbed her sewing box from the table, right before bolting out of the house.

Seeing Mrs. Arnold's mistake, Effie felt she had no other choice, but to confront the woman. "Do you have any idea, of what you just did?" Effie shouted, from the foot of the staircase.

"Don't you use that tone of voice with me, you ungrateful bed pan."

"And what are you going to tell Master Arnold, when he find, his young ones has starved to death, for two old dresses?" Effie snapped. "Because I assure you, when that child, tell Clora Lee of this, she will never feed you, or those children again," the preferred slave said firmly.

"This is my home, and if I say there will be no cooking, then they will starve right along with us," Mrs. Arnold shouted, as if Mr. Lincoln never issued an order of emancipation.

"I'm going to bed," Effie said, as she walked away from the stairs.

"You tell them. You tell them all. There will be no cooking on this plantation, unless I give them permission to do so," the angry white woman yelled, as if she was still in charge of what took place on her land. "You tell them what I said," Mrs. Arnold shouted once again, to an empty room.

Walking across the yard, thinking of the girls, Joan gently touched her burning face. And while doing so, the girl didn't know whether to go to the female sleeping quarters, or head for the woodshed. But after giving it some thought, Joan made a sharp turn toward the woodshed. And as her pace slowed to a near halt, she wondered what Dew Dap was going to say. But as she hoped he would not send her away, Joan swore to herself and the almighty, she would take her own life, before returning to that house.

Finding herself in front of the woodshed, Joan laid one light tap on the door. And when Dew Dap emerged with the knife Pleasant had given him, the poor girl was more then ready to head for the female shed.

"Why you's not sleep?" Dew Dap whispered.

Staring at the knife, Joan forced herself to speak. "Cause I's uh ain't got no where to sleep."

"Why you's ain't got no where to sleep?" Dew Dap whispered once more.

"Dew Dap, you's let me in this woodshed, or I's uh gon sleep out here on this here ground," Joan whispered angrily.

With the door open wide, Joan entered the tiny structure, and took a spot next to Bessie. And after placing the knife under the grass field sack, Dew Dap slid Madeline over toward her big sister. Then like one little happy family, Dew Dap laid down with out ever asking Joan a single question.

"Joan," Bessie grumbled.

"I's uh here, sweetheart."

"Dew Dap smell," Bessie mumbled in her sleep.

"Well?" Joan whispered.

"Well what?" Dew Dap asked, as he sat up in the dark.

"You's can't sleep in here with us, smelling like you's been wallowing with hogs," Joan said firmly.

"What you's want me to do?"

"Dew Dap, you's gotta sleep outside, till you's take a bath," Joan said with a bit of reluctance in her voice.

"I's uh sleeping, where I's always sleep."

Joan could tell by the firmness in his voice, Dew Dap was making a stand. But his stand was going to be another defeat for the South, seeing that Joan had the upper hand. And being a female, the girl was born knowing how to handle such a delicate situation. So without giving Dew Dap a chance to raise the stakes, the young female threw down her next card, which had to be a club, being that it hit the boy hard.

"Then me and the girls, uh sleep under the stars," Joan whispered, as the door flew open.

"Ain't nobody told ya, to wash them girls no huh," Dew Dap whispered, as he scooted out of the woodshed with his spear.

With Dew Dap gone, Joan quickly took up a new position. The acting mother had Madeline cradled in her right arm, while Bessie rested peacefully on her left shoulder, as she gave the darkness a good yawn, before falling off into a deep sleep.

"Dew Dap. Dew Dap," Joan said, as she shook the boy under the dark sky.

Dew Dap jumped up, and nearly scared the life out of Joan, as he frantically moved about with the spear, as if he was ready for battle.

"You's gon kill me, if n you's don't get rid of that stick," Joan cried, as she found herself on the ground.

"What you's wake me for?" Dew Dap asked, while standing over the girl.

"We's gotta get the girls up, so theys can tee tee," Joan said, as Dew Dap helped her up off of the ground.

After Dew Dap had Bessie safely in his right arm, Joan gave him a hand with getting Madeline up on his left shoulder. And while the girls went on sleeping, Dew Dap carried them out into the night air. And when the two little angels were finished, Joan held the door once more, as Dew Dap returned his sisters to their spot on the cotton sack.

When Pleasant found him self rudely awaken by the sound of Dew Dap jabbing his spear in the ground, he became more then a little edgy. "Boy what you's doing there?" Pleasant asked, as he sat up.

"He's been sitting there for uh spell," old Mae's said, as her soft voice came easing out of the female shed.

"Morning Mae," Dew Dap said, as he continued to poke his spear in the ground.

"Morning, child, is there something wrong?" old Mae asked.

"Yes um, Joan took my sisters," Dew Dap replied.

"Na boy, I's uh don't believe that child uh do such uh thing," Pleasant said, as he noticed, Cowayne playing possum.

"I's uh telling the truth, Mae. She's done put me out the woodshed, and I's can't go back," the boy cried honestly.

"What you's do her?" Cowayne asked, as he no longer acted as if he were asleep.

"I's uh ain't do her nothing."

"Na Dew Dap, you's tell me what that child done told ya, so I's can help ya," old Mae said, while still lying on the floor.

"Bessie said I's smell, then Joan said, I's uh can't stay in there with them, till I's uh take uh washing," the boy mumbled painfully.

"You's do smell," Pleasant said, nearly shouting.

"Na Pleasant, you's hush that fuss, and leave that child be," old Mae said, as she fought to keep from laughing.

"Mae, that child, smell worst then them hogs, theys had round here. And I's uh reckon, these two hogs we's got, gon be smelling like him, if n Clora Lee don't run um down to that there creek," Pleasant said, as he stood over Matthew and Cowayne.

"I's uh don't need, no washing," Matthew said, rushing to his own defense.

"You's do, na hush, fo I's dash some water on ya right na," Pleasant barked.

"Aw Dew Dap, why you's come round here?" Matthew cried, as he could see his life passing before his eyes.

"Matthew," Cowayne said firmly.

"But he's...."

"Matthew," Cowayne called out to the little boy once more. "Come on Dew Dap, we's gotta go check our traps," Cowayne said, as he tried to keep things from getting out of hand.

When Dew Dap and Cowayne were gone, the female shed burst in to laughter. And Sistah being the worst, of the worst, fell out of the shed, grunting like a hog, as she headed straight for Matthew. But the little boy didn't see anything amusing, being that a bath would put an end to his reign, as the king of dirt. And that was a title Matthew wanted to keep, until the day he died. But thanks to Dew Dap, come daylight, the king was going to shamefully lose his crown, as well as his dirty cloths.

Chapter 14

A New Life

Shortly after breakfast, Clora Lee, Joan, and her girls, found themselves walking the main yard in search of Matthew, Dew Dap, and Cowayne. The boys had some how given the girls the slip, after gobbling down their food, giving light to Joan's statement about hogs. And it was obvious to the girls, the boys, didn't want to take their much needed bath, which angered both Clora Lee and Joan to no end.

"I's uh tell ya the truth, Joan. You's uh work in ya sleep, if n the good Lord let ya," Clora Lee said, as they came up on the old barn.

"I's uh reckon, when you's behind, you's gotta work to catch up," Joan said, pulling the girls close to her.

"You's reckon Dew Dap is still mad?"

"If n he's gon sleep in that woodshed, with me and my girls, he's gon take uh washing everyday," Joan said, revealing to Clora Lee, who was truly in charge.

"You's ain't scared to be sleeping in there with him?"

"Scared of what?" Joan asked, hoping Clora Lee would take the hint, and let the conversation die.

Clora Lee whispered in Joan's ear, and waited for the girl to answer her. But all the stump high female did, was to look at Clora Lee, as if she couldn't believe her ears. And when the shorter then short female took her eyes off of Clora Lee, she laid them on Bessie and Madeline.

"I's uh ain't gave it much thought," Joan said, cleaning a spot of cold from Bessie's eye.

"What if n he's ask ya to be his?"

Looking at Clora Lee, as if she were being intrusive, Joan gave an answer that was just as shocking, as the disturbing question. "Well I's guess, I's uh be, if n that's what he's want," Joan said, as they entered the old barn.

With her virgin brain working over time, Clora Lee quickly stepped in front of Joan, cutting the girl off. And with Joan and her girls wanting so much to continue their search, Clora Lee asked the pivotal question.

"What about his foots?"

"What about um?" Joan asked, as she stood just as naïve, as her friend.

"Yo's ma, said he's got uh might too much foots for her," Clora Lee said, with a touch of fear in her voice.

"I's heard her," Joan replied, noticing Pleasant and Sistah staring at them.

"What she's mean?" Clora Lee asked.

"I's uh reckon, she's talking bout him not wearing no shoes," Joan replied, while studing Sistah's face.

Sistah started laughing, revealing to Clora Lee, she was in the barn. And seeing the misfortunate female, Clora Lee felt if anyone would know what Sally meant by her statement, then it had to be Sistah.

"Sistah, can we's ask ya something?" Clora Lee asked.

"I's uh ain't gon do no cooking today," Sistah blurted out. "Na you's girls, gone wash them boys, fo they's foots grow long as ya'll arms," she said, while leaving the girls with nothing but the sound of her laughter, for comfort.

Being that he was the only one left in the barn with the girls, Pleasant quickly pointed to the loft. And when Clora Lee started for the ladder, Pleasant felt relieved. That is, until Joan stopped her. But when Joan asked the helpful male if he had any pants, or shirts that would fit Dew Dap, Pleasant knew he was off the hook. And knowing that Clora Lee and Cowayne were using the place for their own private storage shed, Pleasant immediately told the girl to go check the loft. Then just like a good slave, who was looking to keep his master happy, Pleasant went back to his tinkering.

"You's told um," Matthew shouted, as he leaped to his feet.

Turning around with a surprise look on his face, Pleasant spoke without cracking a smile. "I's uh thought you boys, done left that old loft," he said, looking at the girls.

"Dew Dap, you's find ya something to put on, while you's up there," Joan yelled, as if she were the boy's mother.

"Ha you's knows I's up here?" Dew Dap shouted, even though Joan had yet to see him.

Pleasant dropped his head in shame. The helpful ex-slave couldn't believe the boy would surrender himself, like a biddy walking into the mouth of a fox, assuming it were a perfect place to hide.

"If n you's don't hurry up, I's uh gon come up there, and drag ya down to that there creek, and wash ya myself," Joan yelled, with her arms fold.

Clora Lee looked at Pleasant, and he at her, as they both tried to deal with Joan's bold statement. Yet from the look on the little female's face, the girl was more then willing to do just as she stated. And as Clora Lee scratched the back of her neck, she was forced to think about Dew Dap's feet. Would Joan, wash them as well, the teen asked herself, as she watched Dew Dap's head slowly emerged out over the edge of the loft. And from the look on the boy's face, Clora Lee knew the teen felt Joan would take him to task.

"I's waiting," Joan said softly.

"And Cowayne, you's stop that laughing, and get yall something to put on," Clora Lee growled.

Seeing that the girls were hotter then last summer's heat wave, the boys reluctantly gave in, and did as they were told. And no one could have been happier then Pleasant, being that he saw the girls's power over the boys as a good thing. Yet anyone with a nose, and a touch of good sense, knew better then to get caught down wind of the trio.

With one of Clora Lee's pistols wrapped in an old shirt, Cowayne led Matthew, Dew Dap, Clora Lee, and Joan to the creek. And while the girls walked along the path without saying a word, the boys stayed on their heels. And Cowayne kept a constant eye out for anything that would come close, to looking like a white person. For the last thing the teen needed, was to have another incident, like the one he and Clora Lee had with that big Reb. And with his hand on the pistol, Cowayne had no intentions of hesitating, if they were to be confronted by another Reb, or any other white person.

When the five came up on a fork in the path, Matthew, Cowayne, and Clora Lee stopped. Already nervous from being out side of the main yard, Joan quickly beckoned everyone to continue on. But Clora Lee assured Joan, everything would be all right, just before promising to meet her back at the female shed. But still driven by her fear, Joan watched, as their friends continued down a much narrower path.

"I's uh reckon, we's can go back na," Dew Dap said, hoping that Joan would agree.

"If n you's don't come on here, I's uh gon drag ya to that there creek, and I's uh mean it," Joan snapped.

After already being convinced of her intentions back at the barn, Dew Dap was not about to test Joan without anyone around to save him. So like a good soldier, the boy marched on, as if he was going in to battle. And with every nervous step Dew Dap took, drew the teen closer, to an enemy which he dreaded.

When the two ex-slaves reached their destination, Joan couldn't believe her eyes. The short young female stared out across the crystal clear water, as if it was the very freedom, everyone had been hoping for.

"You's been here before?" Joan asked, as she stood in a state of euphoria.

"Yea," Dew Dap replied.

"It's so pretty," Joan uttered, as she stood speechless.

After a moment of silence, Joan found the strength to speak again. The words, I's waiting, stumbled out in to the air. Yet Dew Dap looked at Joan, as if he had no problem with sleeping on the ground another night. But just like every problem that blew her way, the little female was prepared to handle Dew Dap, and his determination to stay filthy, as she picked up a rock.

"If n you's don't get in that water, you's gon be sorry," the girl said, as she held the stone in a threaten manner.

"Na Joan, you's put that rock down," Dew Dap squawked.

Joan threw the rock, hitting Dew Dap on the shoulder, as he tried his best to turn away. And before the boy could cry out in pain, Joan had reached down and rearmed herself.

"If n you's don't get in that there water, I's uh gon hit ya again. Na you's get," Joan yelled, forgetting they were a long way from the main yard.

Dew Dap slowly backed up, until he felt the cold water hit his right foot. And like a cat responding to a sudden loud noise, the boy darted forward, bringing about a quick reaction from Joan, as she sent the rock zooming his way.

"You's nearly hit me in my head," Dew Dap cried.

But Joan saw her throw to be perfect, seeing that Dew Dap had retreated backward, which landed him ankle deep in the water.

"This water, cold" the boy complained, as he danced about.

"I's uh don't care. And you's stop that yelling, fo somebody hears ya," Joan shouted, as she held another stone with Dew Dap's name on it.

With his body already shivering from the chilly water, Dew Dap backed up, until he found himself knee deep, in the brutal enemy. But before the teen could bring his feet to a stop, Joan spoke up. And with the words, gone back, being escorted by another rock, Dew Dap had no other choice but to keep his feet moving. But if Dew Dap only knew Joan had no intentions of hurting him, he would have saved himself from another surprising introduction to the creek. But being that males were born in the dark, Dew Dap went right on moving, as he made every effort to fulfill Joan's demand, while forgetting about his all important first encounter with the plantation's biggest and best creek. And just like on that day, the boy took one too many steps, as he slowly moved backward. And by the time he realized it, the poor teen had once again, found the creek's drop off. And in doing so, the boy went down faster then a rock, which made Joan laugh. And the girl continued to laugh, as Dew Dap fought to regain his footing.

"Why you's laughing?" Dew Dap shouted, as he slapped the water from his face.

"You's hush, and take them cloths off," Joan said, through her laughter.

"I's uh do no such thing."

"Dew Dap, you's can't take no bath, with yo's cloths on, na you's take um off," Joan said, as if she meant business.

"I's uh done told ya, I's uh ain't gon do it," Dew Dap said angrily.

"If n you's don't take um off, I's uh gon come in that there water, and take um off ya myself," Joan said, as she started for the creek.

"Joan, don't you's come in this here water."

"Then you's take um off."

Seeing Joan standing with her hands propped up on her hips, like his mother often did, when he had done something wrong, told the teen, he was in trouble. And if the girl was anything like his mother, then Dew Dap wanted no part of the kind of trouble she would be bringing his way, so he asked her to turn around. And with her turn to be obedient, Joan turned around and waited, as Dew Dap came out of the creek, while taking his shirt off. And no sooner then the boy laid the shirt on the log that sat a few feet from the water's edge, he was off and running. But in his hastily retreat, Dew Dap had once again, forgot about the hidden drop off, that had victimized him a moment earlier. But he was soon reminded of the menacing step, when it reintroduced him to the creek for the second time in one day. And the sound of Dew Dap going under the water once more, had Joan turning around in fear. But when she didn't see as much as a hair on the boy's head, Joan started for the water, only to be scared pert near out of her undergarments.

"Joan!" Dew Dap shouted, when he regained his balance.

"What?" Joan asked, as her fear gave way, to a little thing known as female desire.

"What you's holler for?" Dew Dap asked nervously.

"You's scared me," Joan said, as she appeared to be falling under some kind of spell.

Dew Dap's wet dark skin glistening under the late morning sun, took full control over Joan's body and mind. And as she stood prisoner to a complete state of uncontrollable desire, the rock unconsciously fell from her hand. For Joan was getting a chance to see the boy from the well, the way she always dreamed of him. But unlike her dreams, Joan real life experience was short lived, as Dew Dap began to clear the water from his eyes, which sent her spinning around.

The up heaving of Joan's breast, told her, she was no longer a little girl. And as often, as Joan stared out of the window at Dew Dap, she never thought in her wildest dream, a close encounter with the teen would be so wonderful.

"I's uh need the soap," Dew Dap yelled, dragging Joan from her sweet day dream.

"You's gotta, take yo's breeches off."

"Joan, I's uh can't take my breeches off."

Hearing the firmness in Dew Dap's voice, Joan started to turn around, but quickly caught her self before doing so. "If n you's don't take them breeches off, and put um on that there log, so I's can wash um," Joan said, pointing behind her. "I's uh gon come out there, and I's uh promise ya, Dew Dap, I's uh gon take um off of ya, if n I's gotta fight ya."

Joan spoke as if she was hoping the boy would refuse to carry out her demand. And seeing that he was wasting their precious time, by not answering her, Joan was ready to take a much firmer approach. But by the time she had turned around, Dew Dap was dipping his body in the creek faster then a beaver.

"I's uh gon do it," he said, causing Joan to turn her back to the water, while repeating one of Duval's favorite statements.

"Then I's reckon, we's understand each other," she said, with a self pleasing smile.

Armed with her victorious smile, Joan backed up and placed the soap and a washrag on the log. And the sound of Dew Dap shivering, told Joan, he would soon be naked, so she closed her eyes and prayed. For Joan prayed with hopes of not giving into the temptation, that ultimately gotten the first two humans thrown out of their garden. But no amount of praying was going to help the girl, as she could feel herself slipping fast.

"You's hurry up, cause we's ain't got all day," Joan said, as her unspoiled purse, begged to be touched.

But Dew Dap wasn't in the mood for talking, as he silently went about removing the wet pants from his body. And when he had finished coming out of the wet breeches, the teen tossed them on the log, and started back for the water. But seeing that he had forgotten the soap and the makeshift washrag, Dew Dap quickly went back and grabbed the much needed items, and hurried off, as if the creek wasn't going to wait for him. And once his feet hit the water, Dew Dap quickly slowed down, trying not to make the same mistake for a third time. But even with all of his carefulness, Dew Dap still found himself to be a sunken ship, as he went down in frustration. Yet that wasn't the thing that bothered him the most. For Joan was yapping at the boy so fast, it had him ready to walk home butt naked, allowing the whole world to see his toy.

"You's wash yo's head, first," Joan said, while taking advantage of a perfect situation.

For the girl was already facing the water, waiting for her human portrait to keep still. And when Dew Dap finally did calm down, Joan took in the sight, as if she was Mrs. Arnold, on her first visit to Paris. Yet while Joan stood laughing, she was still able to keep her eyes pinned to the two large mounds of muscle and dark flesh that made up Dew Dap's chest.

"All you's do is laugh," Dew Dap said, after he finished clearing the water from his throat.

"Cause you's make me laugh. Na you's hush, and wash yo's head."

Joan may have been green as mid summer's grass, yet she knew enough to take full advantage of the opportunity that had been laid at her feet. And while she stood looking at Dew Dap, one of the deadliest instincts, that all females will forever carry deep with in their souls, took over the girl's mind.

"Are you's washing it?" she asked, keeping the boy off balance.

Dew Dap didn't utter a word, as he went right on rubbing the soap over his thick woolly hair. And with his eyes shut tighter then a fat lady's corset, he had no idea of what Joan was doing.

But Joan had problems of her own. After finding herself trapped by the sight of Dew Dap's body, as well as her womanly desires, the little stump was beginning to move closer to the water's edge. Yet, Joan's ability to walk wasn't all that easy, being that her feet, felt like led, as she basked in the delight of Dew Dap's flesh. And right then and there, the former house slave staked her claim on the well built teen. For Dew Dap was her's, and her's alone, as she planned on being the only female to touch his body.

"Do I's got enough soap in my head?" Dew Dap asked, as he stood with his eyes shut.

"You's got plenty," Joan said so soft, she could barely hear herself.

"Joan," Dew Dap called out.

"I's uh here, Dew Dap," Joan said, not knowing she was still speaking too soft, for the poor boy to hear her.

"Joan," Dew Dap said nearly shouting.

"I's uh told ya, I's right here," Joan said, a tad bit louder.

"What you's doing?"

"I's uh ain't doing nothing, na you's scratch that soap in ya head," Joan said some what seductively.

"You's doing something," the teen argued.

"I's uh ain't doing nothing, na you's do as I's told ya."

Even though Joan's voice held a strange tone, Dew Dap didn't bother to question the girl any further. For he just went about doing as Joan asked, leaving her with a front row seat to ecstasy. And in no time at all, Joan started thinking about a dream she had one night. It was a night, after seeing him at the well earlier that day. And the dream was far better then their time at the well, as they did everything she saw Mrs. Arnold and Jonathan do one late night, on the parlor floor in front of the fireplace. And Joan remembered how she woke up with her gown soaking wet from sweat, while her tender spot held a wetness of its own.

With Dew Dap about to reopen his eyes, Joan quickly retreated back to the log and took a seat.

"I's uh finish," Dew Dap said, after washing his body, and starting for dry land.

"You's wet that towel, and bring it to me."

Joan request was met with another round of resistance, as Dew Dap tried once more to make a stand. And by the time the girl had made it to her feet, he was up in arms about the matter.

"What you's doing?" Dew Dap asked, as he immediately took his body back down into the water.

"Who's gon wash, yo's back?" Joan asked, as she waited for Dew Dap with her back to him.

"You's ain't gon do no such thing. And I's uh ain't coming out, till you's sit down," Dew Dap argued.

"Then I's reckon, I's uh gotta take my cloths off, and come in there and get ya," Joan yelled, as she made an attempt to raise her dress.

With the voice of a nervous child, Dew Dap didn't waste any time, telling Joan he was coming out. But like a little boy not wanting anyone to see his very first toy, Dew Dap warned Joan not to look, as he placed his feet on dry land.

"Give me that soap and rag," Joan said, when she heard Dew Dap come up behind her.

When Dew Dap placed the soap, and dripping wet rag in her hand, Joan told him to turn around. But knowing that he was still naked, the teen firmly refuses to do such a thing. Yet Joan acted as if she had planned for such a refusal. While making sure she kept her eyes up when facing him, Joan's free hand mysteriously found its way to Dew Dap's chest, as she spoke.

"I's uh knows you's worried bout me, but we's need ya in that shade with us," Joan said, while she unconsciously stroked Dew Dap chest with her nails.

Joan may never know if it was what she said, or her stroking of his chest, that made Dew Dap give in to her demand. And if the girl had to tell the truth, she would gladly say, it didn't matter to her, one way or the other. The boy had given in to her, and that was all that mattered to Joan.

"Joan," Dew Dap said softly, as he stood with his back to her.

"Huh," Joan replied, as her voice clung to a sweetness born of love.

"Close ya eyes."

"They's close," Joan replied, as she stared at Dew Dap's ass.

And when Joan washed his ass, the young male got an erection like never before.

"Na you's go wash ya self off," Joan said, after placing the rag in his hand, before giving him a backhand on the butt, like Sally often did her.

"Don't you's look," Dew Dap said, as he took off running, while looking back until he reached the water.

When Dew Dap came out of the water for the last time, Joan scrubbed his neck and back to perfection. She then cleaned his ears, the way a mother would do her child. And as Joan did so, the little teen saw in Dew Dap, that special something, which every female see in a male, who she would unselfishly lay down her life for. And that told the girl, she was truly in love.

No sooner then the two made it back to the main yard, Dew Dap and Joan headed straight for the woodshed, where the girls were sitting with Sally. And as Madeline ran to the safety of Joan's warm embrace, Dew Dap took a seat on the old milking stool next to Bessie.

"What?" Joan asked, as she caught sight of her mother's auspicious smile.

"Child, I's uh ain't said uh word," Sally replied, as she watched Joan balance Madeline on her hip, while picking in Dew Dap's hair. "I's uh done told Mae, I's uh was gon see her today," Sally said, just before walking away, while still holding to her favorable smile.

"Thanks ma," Joan said, as she sat Madeline next to Bessie, while hearing Sally uttering the words, any time.

Then like a woman, who was unable to get out infront of her work, Joan put the comb to Dew Dap's hair. And with her left hand clinging to a fist full of the black wool, she tilted his head back. And as Joan's right hand rested on her hip, she gave Dew Dap a firm, but joyful stare.

"I's uh ain't do nothing," Dew Dap confessed.

"Then I's reckon, that's why you's still got soap in ya head," Joan said firmly, before giving Dew Dap a tap on the nose.

"You's told me to wash it."

"Na I's uh telling ya, to go get me some water, so I's uh can get this her soap, out of ya head."

After turning around to face Joan, Dew Dap wrapped his arms around here legs, right before standing up with the little angel. Yet the boy's lack of knowledge, didn't allow him to realize, his face was less then an inch, from Joan's tingling purse. And while he went on looking up at her with a smile, as if she were Heaven's glory shining down on him, the smile told Joan, more then Samson ever revealed to the female, which brought about his down fall. Yet if it weren't for Bessie and Madeline's laughing, Joan would have been more then happy, to stay wrapped in the boy's arms for all eternity.

"Dew Dap, you's put me down, and I's mean it," Joan said, as she did a poor job of hiding her smile.

Dew Dap didn't give Joan a reply. For he just stared up at her, as they both realized, something was happening between the two of them. And as Mother Nature's plan took off, no one knew better then Joan, how it was going to end. For the little spider, had finally gotten hold of the boy from the well, and she wasn't about to let him wiggle free.

"Na Dew Dap, you's can't be carrying on, in front of our girls," Joan said softly, as she held his face in her hands.

"Them girls, knows I's ain't gon hurt ya."

"I's uh don't care, you's put me down, fo I's bite yo's nose," Joan said, as she gently bit her bottom lip.

"I's uh the strong one here."

"But you's strong, for me and our girls," Joan said, as she folded her arms, while shooting Dew Dap a smirk.

When Dew Dap was done showing off, he grabbed the bucket, and went got Joan her water. And upon his return, the teen found Joan and his sisters laughing and playing up a storm. And for the first time, the boy saw the much needed change in his life, as the look on Madeline's face, told him, Joan was there to stay. But before the thought of Joan being apart of his family sunk in, Dew Dap heard Bessie asked the girl, if they were going to leave them again, which made him feel like he wasn't being a good big brother. But when he heard Joan answer his sister, Dew Dap knew he was more then just a good brother. For Joan's vowing, that they would never leave the girls again, even if it meant lugging them on their backs, told Dew Dap, he was one half of something better. But the boy also knew he had to go out, in order for his family to go on eating.

"Joan, I's uh gotta go out, so we's can eat," he said rather nervously.

"And when you's do, I's uh gon be here with our girls," Joan said, as she held Bessie and Madeline to her body.

After a long hard day of taking care of her family, Joan sat in a tub of warm water. And while she rested her small body in the old tub, which Dew Dap lugged from the other side of the yard, Joan smiled. For the little stump knew, she no longer had to ask Clora Lee how it felt. For Joan had her own, and she knew Dew Dap and the girls were hers to keep, provided, they find a way off of that old plantation.

As Joan began to think of how hard it would be for them to leave that old plantation, she burst in to laughter. For her mind, fell on the day's events. She could see the girls taunting Dew Dap, as he squirmed, while she cleaned his teeth. And the look on Dew Dap's face, when she placed his hands on her hip, to help him with the uncontrolable squirming, was the highlight of the girl's day. She could see it all, as if life was being relived right before her eyes, as she began to wash her body, knowing they were ready to cross that final hurdle, which would make their relationship complete.

With a fresh new feeling, Joan took her family over to the female shed, hoping the girls would get a chance to hear Sistah sing. But what the ex-house slave found instead, were Clora Lee and the rest of the field slaves sitting around talking, as they waited for the sun to go down.

"Ooo Mae, you's see, what them girls, done did them boys," Sistah said, teasing Dew Dap and Cowayne.

"Na Sistah, you's leave them young ns be," old Mae said, looking at Dew Dap.

"I's uh reckon, them breeches fit mighty fine," Pleasant joked, as Dew Dap stood looking like a shiny new coin.

"We's uh be owing to ya, for um," Dew Dap replied, as he shook Pleasant's hand.

"Na don't you's worrying bout that, cause we's got plenty of them old breeches," Cowayne noted.

"Why we's talking bout breeches, when Sistah can be singing," Clora Lee said, as she sat next to her friend.

With the call for her to take center stage, Sistah politely released her voice. Slaves that once worked the fields were emerging from every nook and cranny, to hear the heavenly sound. And for the first time in her life, Joan was getting the chance to hear, what everyone had been talking about for years. But for the field slaves, it was like old times again, as Sistah gave her best performance by far.

Sistah sung fast, as well as slow, and a few tones in between. Sistah sung a song that was soft as a baby's kiss, as she placed Joan and Dew Dap's hands together. Then the plantation's songbird directed her attention to Bessie and Madeline, as she stroked their little faces. And after ending her song on that note, Sistah then gave her audience a song with a bit of rhythm, which made the ex-slaves clap and dance. It was safe to say, Sistah was in a rare form, and she knew it, as her voice touched each and every ear. Then the beautiful dark skin female with a voice to match, gave the former slaves a song so sad, it brought many of them to tears. And when Sistah was ready to call it a night, she sat on the ground at old Mae's feet, and serenaded the slaves with an old Cajun song, Duval had taught her. And the song made old Mae weep to no end, as she thought of the white man, who had given her more then any slave could ever ask for.

Seeing that Sistah had given her last performance, Joan and Dew Dap gathered up their girls, and said goodnight.

By the time Dew Dap and his newly formed family was halfway to the woodshed, Madeline released Joan's hand, and gave her big brother the signal. And upon feeling Madeline tugging on his pants leg, Dew Dap got down in a squatting position, making it easy for Bessie to climb on his back.

"You's holding on tight?" Dew Dap asked Bessie, when she was safely aboard.

And when Bessie had given her reply, he swept Madeline up in his arms, and continued on with their evening stroll back to the woodshed. But the walk home took a strange twist, when Joan stepped out in front of Dew Dap. Then like a good motherly figure, Joan asked Madeline for a kiss. And when the little angel puckered up, Joan moved in for more then just a spot of sugar, as she also gently squeezed Dew Dap's dick, right before spinning away like a tiny ballerina.

When they finally reached the woodshed, Joan lit the torch Pleasant showed Dew Dap how to make. And with the torch burning well, Joan entered the woodshed, leaving Dew Dap and her dumpling out in the night air. For the overly protective motherly figure, was checking to make sure there weren't any bugs crawling around the crumbling structure. And when Joan didn't see a single bug, a smile came to her lips, for Sistah's perfect little trick.

"You's can bring um in, na," Joan said, as she stood back out of the doorway.

After Dew Dap sat the girls down, Joan asked him to step outside, which brought about a sad look to the boy's face. For the teen felt he was about to spend another night under the stars, which made him somewhat disappointed.

"Joan, I's uh done had my washing," Dew Dap said, ready to argue his point.

"I's know that, but we's girls, gotta get ready for bed," Joan replied softly, as she held his hands.

Hearing Joan's words, Dew Dap felt a little shame, as he made his way out of the door. But before his feet could hit the ground good, he heard Joan say something about not getting a speck of dirt on him. Yet as he watched Joan close the door, the big foot teen, tried to think of what he could do with his free time. But before his mind could start turning out thoughts, he heard his sisters giggling. And as long as they were giggling, the boy knew they were happy, which meant he was happy as well.

"You's can come in na," Joan said, standing in the doorway, wearing a union shirt for a nightgown.

But how could the boy enter the woodshed, being that he stood in a state, of complete and utter bliss.

"You's gon come to bed, or you's gon stand there looking at me?" Joan asked, as her smile said, she was pleased with Dew Dap's sudden case of fascination, over the sight of her legs.

Taking hold of Joan's out stretched hand, Dew Dap entered the woodshed and closed the door behind him. But for some reason, other then not knowing where to lay his head, the boy stood with his back against the door looking down on Joan. For he was a bit confused, seeing that Bessie was lying on the far left end of the cotton sack, with Madeline next to her. And next to Madeline was Joan, which started the teen to wondering, where was he to lay in the equation.

"You's can blow the candle out," Joan said of the little burning stick, which sat on Dew Dap side of the cotton sack.

Dew Dap put his head down in shame, while moving to do as Joan asked. And as he laid down in the dark next to the girl, the teen could hear his little sisters laughing. But unlike so many times before, the boy didn't ask the girls what they were laughing at, as he laid with his back to Joan, feeling the girls were lost for ever. But when Dew

Dap heard Joan tell him to give his girls a kiss goodnight, he became as happy, as a dog chasing its tail.

"I's uh can't see um," he said, as Bessie and Madeline went on serenading the darkness, with their laughter.

"I's uh gon help ya," Joan said giggling. "You's feel my hand?"

"Uh huh," Dew Dap said of Joan's hand on his face.

"Na this Madeline, ya night sunshine," Joan said, as she guided his lips to the little girl's forehead. This Bessie, ya sunshine," Joan said, as she did the same, for the larger of their two girls, after the boy had kissed Madeline. And before letting Dew Dap go, Joan said, "This is me, ya star that twinkles in the night."

And hearing his sisters laughing, Dew Dap was more then sure, they knew Joan was kissing him. Yet, the boy hoped, his sisters didn't know that Joan was kissing him on the lips. But more then anything, Dew Dap didn't want his sisters, or anyone else to know what his body was doing, as he and Joan laid wrapped in each others arms.

"Na we can go to sleep," Joan said, turning her back to Dew Dap, yet never letting his arm leave her waist.

When the sound of the girl's breathing, told Joan they were asleep, the teen made her move.

"You's sleep?" the little stump whispered, while rolling over, and placing her hand on Dew Dap's chest.

"No," Dew Dap whispered in return, as Joan was already making her move.

The young female was undoing the buttons to the boy's shirt, which prompt him to ask her, what was she doing? But rather then verbally answer the question, Joan gave Dew Dap a kiss, while placing his hand on her breast. And as her breathing went from calm to climatic, Joan ripped his shirt open, leaving the poor tattered garment without a button to call its own.

"What ya do that for?" Dew Dap whispered nervously.

While kissing his chest, Joan whispered, "I's uh ain't gon let no female give ya, what you's need."

With Joan's bold statement clinging to the darkness, Dew Dap took his pants off. And no sooner than he laid the garment down, Joan was on top of him, taking his erected cock, in her hand. But rather then rush to wrap her pussy around the throbbing dick, Joan tried a little something she saw Mrs. Arnold do with Jonathan. With the head of Dew Dap's dick against her fury wet purse, Joan rotated the swollen muscle at Heaven's doorway, until it gently worked its way deep into her fur covered cave. And no sooner then her walls exploded, Joan surrendered herself to Dew Dap for his pleasure.

With his innocence ready to abandon him, Dew Dap kissed Joan, as she sought to lie on her back. And before he knew it, Dew Dap found himself on top of the tiny female, too afraid to move. For the boy didn't want to crush Joan with his large body, for what he took to be a selfish male act. But Joan had other plans, as she guided his head down to her breast. And better then any baby could have ever done, Dew Dap proceeded to suck Joan's tits, as if he had been doing such a thing all his life. And the boy had to be doing his job well, seeing that Joan's breathing had become that of a well satisfied woman.

When Dew Dap came up from sucking on Joan's tits, his dick followed him. Yet the teen didn't make an attempt to insert himself in her warm tight pussy, as the two of them went back to kissing. But as they kissed, Dew Dap could feel Joan sucking his tongue deep into her mouth, while his throbbing erection found its own way to a place, where no male had ever been before.

"I's hurting, ya'?" Dew Dap asked, after hearing Joan grunting, just before gasping.

"I's uh trying not to wake our girls".

The way Joan wrapped her arms around his neck, and squeezed him with all of her might, along with her painful reply, told the boy, his friend wasn't telling the truth. And not wanting any part in causing Joan any pain, Dew Dap attempted to do that, which every female was born to hate.

"I's uh stop, if n you's want me to," Dew Dap whispered softly, as he attempted to roll off of Joan.

But the boy was unaware of the female's ability to predict a males every move, when it came down to seeking satisfaction. And being armed with such a gift, Joan closed her eyes, and wrapped her legs around his waist, knowing she had set herself up for a greater level of pain. Yet Joan knew she would do it a thousand times over, to give Dew Dap what he needed to be satisfied. For the teen knew there were females, who would be with Dew Dap for food, while never even trying to take care of their girls. And that was why the twinkling star, bit her bottom lip, while clawing Dew Dap's back like a mad cat, as he dug his dick deep into her warm wet cherry. But no amount of clawing was going to detour the boy from plowing through her luscious virgin field, as he rushed, to release his little life seeking critters.

When Dew Dap was all but finished with his rampaging climax, Joan kissed him, then swore she would always be his.

"Can I's uh sleep close to ya, tonight?" Joan asked, as she did the last button to her Union shirt nightgown.

"You's can always sleep next me," Dew Dap replied, as Joan was already snuggling up next to him.

With her body wrapped in Dew Dap's arms, Joan eased in to a peaceful sleep, while promising herself to thank Clora Lee for such a wonderful gift.

Like the night before, Joan woke Dew Dap, so they could take the girls out. But unlike the previous night, Dew Dap had an old pail waiting for Joan and his sisters. Yet the pail wasn't to be the only surprise of the night. For when everyone was back in the shed, and lying on the cotton sack, Bessie spoke through her sleep, asking Joan, was she going to be their mother.

"No, but I's uh gon be ya'll sister, if n Dew Dap will have me," Joan said, as she reached over and stroked Bessie's face in the same manner, in which a mother would do a child from her own womb.

"We's ain't got, no bugs," Bessie said, as she fell back into a deep sleep.

After kissing Dew Dap, Joan laid her head on his shoulder, and tried to catch up with Bessie and Madeline. But the little female wasn't about to get any sleep, until Dew Dap got the chance to ask his question.

"Ha long you's gon stay here?" he asked, while caressing Joan's ass.

Knowing that she had just as many weapons, as any white woman or a whore, Joan stayed with the ones that served her the best. "You's want me to leave?" she whispered, after resting her face in his chest.

"I's uh don't want ya ma, to be worrying bout ya".

"My ma ain't worried bout me," Joan replied. "Na ha long you's want me to stay?" the little stump asked, knowing full well, no male had ever beaten a lady in a battle of wits.

"You's can stay, till the Misses tell ya, you's can't stay no mo," Dew Dap replied in a voice that told Joan, she didn't have to worry about leaving the woodshed, until they found away off of that wretched plantation, to make it in the white man's world on their own.

The next morning when Dew Dap returned from resetting his traps, he found Clora Lee, Sally, and Cowayne with Joan and the girls. And the sight of Joan sewing as Bessie and Madeline sat directly up under her, made the boy feel more like a father, then a brother. Yet Dew Dap knew he would always be just a big brother, who had the job of being a father. But the young male was hoping his time with the girls, would help him to become a pretty good father, to the children he hoped to have someday.

"What you's eating," Dew Dap asked Madeline, after he said his good mornings.

"You's ready to eat," Joan asked, as she took a quick look, at the boy, who laid claim to her virginity.

"Dew Dap, you's better eat, while you's got Joan to cook for ya," Cowayne said jokingly.

"Sure as I's tell ya, cause you's don't know, when Clora Lee and Joan gon find another female to help ya," Sally said, as she went about her sewing.

"I's don't need no female, cause we's got Joan," the boy replied.

"Well if n you's wanna keep her, you's better take her from here, fo Mr. Arnold get back," Clora Lee said, causing Sally to wonder, why she didn't call the man master.

But rather then think about what his Lee called her grandfather, Cowayne thought about what she was up to, which gave him cause to act. "You's wanna come with me, to check my traps?" Cowayne asked the boy, as he stood up.

Dew Dap glared at Cowayne briefly, before turning his eyes back to Joan. And seeing that he was confused, Joan told her lover, it was alright for him to leave them for a while, but not to forget about their trip to the creek. Then like a good father figure, Dew Dap gave his two sisters a kiss on the jaw. Yet before he could walk away, Joan called him back.

"You's ain't kiss me," the girl said, when Dew Dap reached her.

As Bessie and Madeline started their laughing, Dew Dap went to give Joan a peck on the forehead, but she quickly took control of the situation, and gave him a big wet kiss on the lips.

"Na you's hurry back," the girl said, as she went back to sewing.

After washing his hands, Dew Dap grabbed his portion of the coon that was resting over the simmering ashes, and headed off with Cowayne. And while the boys left the females alone to do their talking, Cowayne couldn't help but to notice, that Dew Dap had a different flair about him.

"You's alright?" Cowayne asked.

"Uh huh," Dew Dap hummed, while chewing with his mouth closed.

"You's ain't scared to kiss her, in front of her ma?"

"I's reckon, her ma don't mind."

Cowayne was left speechless, as he and Dew Dap went over the fence. And Cowayne couldn't help but to notice, Dew Dap had swallowed his food before speaking, which made the boy feel bad for his friend, as he felt Joan was changing the large teen into something strange.

Chapter 15

A Invitation

After being knocked flat by Joan's jaw dropping kiss with Dew Dap, Clora Lee and Sally sat looking at each other. The two females were eyeing one another, trying to influence a comment on the surprising show of affection. But when Sally shook her head no, to Clora Lee's shifting eyes, the stump high female, felt she should also join the conversation.

"I's uh reckon, ya'll ain't see'd folks kiss before," Joan said, sending her girls in to another round of laughter.

"Na Joan, you's can't blame us for wondering," Clora Lee said, as she was still finding it hard to deal with the sight of the two teens kissing.

"I's uh ain't blaming ya, cause I's thankful, for what you's done gave me," Joan said, as she kissed Madeline.

"Well I's uh hope, you's can get pass them foots, cause he's uh be good for ya," Sally noted, while sewing a pouch for Cowayne.

Before Clora Lee could ask Sally what was wrong with the boy's feet, she was nearly knocked out of her undergarment.

"I's uh reckon, his foots can't do no worst, then what he hurt me with last night," Joan said, as she ran the needle through Bessie's dress.

Clora Lee stared at Joan with her mouth open, waiting for the girl to explain herself. And Sally, who hadn't stop sewing all morning long, found her fingers frozen stiff, while Joan went on stitching, as if she hadn't spoken at all. But seeing that her mother and Clora Lee were still in a state of shock, the girl felt it would be better if she spoke on the matter at hand, before a flock of crows, came and nested on their heads.

"Well they's can't," she said with a painful look on her face.

"Child, I's wondering, ha you's can sit down," Sally said, as she went back to sewing.

"Well I's uh reckon, if I's uh gon give him one of his own, I's uh gotta hurt, uh might worst then that," Joan said, dropping another cannon ball on Clora Lee and Sally.

"I's uh reckon, them girls was good and sleep, while ya'll was carrying on," Sally said, looking under eyed at her daughter.

"Na ma, you's knows, my girls was sleep," Joan replied.

"Well I's speck, you's had to do a heap uh hollering," Sally continued, with a half hearted smile, which soon turned into a knee slapping laugh.

"Na ma, you's knows that ain't funny."

Clora Lee could tell by the look on Joan's face, the teen had suffered an enormous amount of pain. The kind of pain, Clora Lee knew Cowayne would never put her through. But as Clora Lee sat listening to Joan and Sally, the teen knew she had to change the conversation, before one of them popped a question about her and Cowayne.

"If n Dew Dap take Joan from here, you's gon go with um?" Clora Lee asked, hoping the question would do the trick.

Sally hesitated before responding, as she tried to figure out why the teen would be asking her such a question. And after giving it some thought, Sally rested her needle and said, "I's had wanted to go with ya ma and pa, but I's uh was scared to bring my child out among them white folks."

"I's uh speck, Dew Dap ain't gon take her round no white folks."

"Child, I's hope to God, he's don't do such a thing," Sally replied with fear in her eyes.

"Well I's uh don't reckon, we's uh be going nowhere," Joan said, as she bit the thread, which stated the little sewing wizard, was finished stitching another cotton sack dress.

Clora Lee didn't think it was the right time to tell her friend, why she was asking so many questions. Nor did the plotting, and planning female wanted to over play her hand, until she found out exactly where Sally stood, when it came down to Mrs. Arnold. For if Sally were to run back to that house, and spill her guts with a bit of valuable information, it would spoil everything, and that was a chance Clora Lee couldn't afford to take, with their day of departing being just over the horizon.

"I's uh hope Joan made you's wash good," Cowayne joked.

I's reckon, Clora Lee ain't let ya miss uh spot," Dew Dap laughed, as they said goodbye to another trap.

The two young males laughed and joked all the way to the next trap. But by the time they reached the trap, Cowayne hit the teen with a serious question.

"What you and Joan doing?" Cowayne asked, as he checked his trap.

"We's ain't doing nothing," Dew Dap said, as he had no plans of being a kiss and tell male.

For Dew Dap had often heard those type of males talking about his mother, as well as the other females they had laid with. And after crying, far too many tears, over the things, that was said about his mother, the boy vowed, never to be like those who kissed, and stood around talking about it. So as he and Cowayne went back to walking, Dew Dap mind fell on Nelson, the only male that the boy had never heard speak ill of his mother, or any other female. Yet the teen knew Nelson was still taking pleasure, because he had seen him going in the new barn with a couple of females a few times.

"Well I's mighty glad, she's got ya to take a washing," Cowayne said as he laughed.

"I's knows, ha to take a washing, just like you's do."

"Well why's, you's ain't been taking none?"

"What we's was gon put on, after we's take one?"

"Pleasant told ya, we's had clean cloths."

"Did he have dresses for my sisters?" Dew Dap asked with a look of sadness about him.

Cowayne didn't know what to say, as Dew Dap's question told him why, Clora Lee wanted to take the boy and his family with them.

But Cowayne had yet to come up with a way to transport the girls, on what would be a long hard trip.

"I's uh think, we's can catch some turtles here," Cowayne said, breaking the silence, as they came upon a narrow shallow body of water. "I's uh don't know, why Lee want turtles, cause they's ain't got no turtles out here."

"Turtles, why you's ain't tell me, you's want turtles? Give me ya sack," Dew Dap said, as if he had a plan.

With the cotton sack in his hands, Dew Dap quickly put the knife to the tattered cloth, as if he were a larger version of Joan. And when he was finished cutting two large chunks out of the sack, Dew Dap finally noticed the look on Cowayne's face. The poor boy carried a look, which mirrored the one Mrs. Arnold wore, the day Biscuit and his family went rolling out the front gate. But how was Dew Dap to know, Cowayne needed the sack to get his bullets out of the brush. For when Cowayne said he was looking for turtles, the boy quickly equated the sack with their quest.

"What's ailing ya?" Dew Dap asked, looking up at Cowayne.

"Nothing," Cowayne said, realizing why he always preferred to work alone.

"Then we's gon need some vines," Dew Dap said, as he stood up.

When the two had gathered three long vines, Dew Dap took to twisting Mother Nature's rope, while Cowayne went right on cutting.

"Ain't you's glad, you's ain't gotta do that no mo?" Cowayne asked, as he stood holding an arm full of vines.

"Do what?"

"That," Cowayne said, pointing at the vines, as Dew Dap went about plaiting, the main part of their traps.

"I's uh ain't got no quarrel, with doing for my sisters."

"Yea, but I's uh reckon, them girls mighty glad, theys ain't got you's doing it no mo."

"I's uh done the best I's can, and I's uh don't speck my ma, is any kind uh mad at me, for not doing better," Dew Dap uttered rather sadly.

Dew Dap appeared to be deeply disturbed by their conversation, as he went about trying to complete the trap. And as he kept his head down, Cowayne felt it was a good time for him to take a walk.

"You's need something else?" Cowayne asked.

"You's can go get some mo vines," Dew Dap said, without raising his head.

Feeling he had treated his friend badly, Cowayne didn't know what to think of him self, as he violently hacked away at the vines. And maybe Sistah was right. Maybe he didn't take time to think about anything. And maybe that was why he went on chopping at the vines, like a mad man looking to kill something. But killing the vines wasn't going to bring Dew Dap's mother back, nor was it going to take away the things that were said about her. Yet, Cowayne went right on hacking the vines just the same, as he promised to be more careful with his mouth in the future.

When Cowayne returned with the second load of vines, he made a point, of not returning to their previous conversation. And after dropping the vines on the ground, the teen asked Dew Dap what he had to do next.

"You's can pull the leaves off um, so they can be more like rope," the teen said, sending Cowayne straight to work.

After removing the leaves from a few of the vines, Cowayne spoke. "Ha these vines, gon help us catch Lee some turtles?"

"You's uh see," Dew Dap replied, while still keeping his head down.

With the two boys returning to their state of silence, they had no other choice, but to push onward with the odd looking trap. And no sooner then Dew Dap finished with the hardest part of their trapping system, he broke his silence. For walking along side the creek, the boy started to laughing, which prompt Cowayne to speak.

"What you's laughing bout?" he asked, while looking at Dew Dap, as if the teen had lost his mind.

"I's, uh just thinking. When them girls get up in age, they's gon try to follow me, and Joan ain't gon let um."

"Why you's laughing bout that?"

"Cause theys gon come crying to me, and I's uh gon laugh at um, the way theys laughed at me," he replied with a smile.

Feeling that Dew Dap knew something he didn't, Cowayne wondered what he was missing. And how could his friend be so sure, Joan would be around long enough to see the girls grow up?

There had to be more to the statement, than Dew Dap was letting on. But the adventurous one had vowed to watch his mouth, so he just ignored the statement, as they went about completing their traps.

Standing at the highest point of the narrow waterway, Dew Dap was ready to show Cowayne a little turtle catching magic. So he grabbed a group of the plaited vines, and started for the falling tree, which acted as a bridge across the water. But just as the teen straddled the fallen tree, Cowayne threw him another question.

"Ha you's know, Joan gon be with um, when theys get some size on um?"

"Cause my ma told me," Dew Dap replied, then asked Cowayne to find some nice size rocks.

Cowayne gathered up as many plum size rocks as he could find, while wondering how the boy's mother could tell him something about Joan, when she was dead. Yet the teen didn't say anything, as he brought the rocks over to Dew Dap. And one by one, he silently tossed the stones to his friend, who was sitting dead center of the fallen tree.

"You's trust Joan," Cowayne asked, after Dew Dap caught the last rock.

"I's uh reckon, I's uh trust her, like you's trust Clora Lee."

Dew Dap's statement caught Cowayne by surprise. And as he stood scratching his head, while watching Dew Dap secure the rocks to the four corners of the cloth, Cowayne couldn't think of anything to say. But when he saw the teen kill one of the two frogs they caught earlier, Cowayne was ready to speak.

"Why you's kill um?" Cowayne asked, as Dew Dap tied one of the frogs to the first trap.

"So they's won't mess up the trap."

With the traps set, the boys made their way off of the fallen tree. And while Dew Dap was sure the traps would work, Cowayne wondered who would come along and see the vines tied to the fallen tree. Yet he didn't say a word, while the two of them made their way off of the bridge, Mother Nature built with strong winds and powerful tears.

"Ha long you's had that notion?" Cowayne asked no sooner then his feet touched solid ground.

"I's uh got it a while back, but I's uh ain't had no cloth to make it," Dew Dap said of the traps.

"No, bout me trusting Lee," Cowayne said, leaving no doubt, to what he was asking.

"Ain't nothing wrong with trusting ya female," the large teen replied.

Hearing Dew Dap call Clora Lee his female, had Cowayne adding one more label to the girl, who swore to kill anyone that would attempt to hurt him. For Clora Lee had became his Lee, his squaw, his girl, and with Dew Dap's label, she was his female as well. Yet Cowayne stood wondering why their lips had never touched. How could Dew Dap get a kiss, when he barely knew Joan? Was Joan, his female? And what else, were they doing, Cowayne thought to himself, as he and his friend headed for the next trap.

"You's wanna know, when my ma told me, Joan, was right for them girls?" Dew Dap asked, as they came up on a trap that had been sprung, but didn't catch anything.

"I's uh reckon," Cowayne replied, while kneeling down to reset the trap.

"It was when ya ma, told me to go and sit with her. When I sat on the floor, my ma told me to take care of her girls, till a good female come along and help me," Dew Dap said, as his voice began to drag. And while acting as though something was in his eyes, the boy continued. "She said, I's uh know when it's the right one, cause them girls uh take to her, as if she was mother's milk. And I's reckon, them girls done taken to her all right," the teen said of Joan, while looking away.

"I's reckon, you's gon keep her," Cowayne said smiling.

"Na Cowayne, you's knows, if n you's had the prettiest female, you's uh keep her."

Being that the teen had already done more harm then good, Cowayne didn't have the heart to tell his friend, he did have the prettiest female. And the way Cowayne saw it, his Lee wasn't just pretty. For the boy, felt his Lee, was the prettiest female to ever live. But rather then crush Dew Dap's feelings for a second time, Cowayne just made sure his trap would work, when the next critter decided to use it for a hiding place.

"Then why's you's ain't say nothing to her at the well?"

"Cause I's was dirty," the teen admitted shamefully.

Dew Dap stopped walking, as if he had suddenly decided to play like a tree, for his little sisters amusement. And knowing Cowayne was about to speak, he quickly signaled the teen to be quiet. Then with the shrewdness of a fox, Dew Dap pointed to a deer standing at the edge of the brush, on the opposite side of the waterway.

Seeing the animal cautiously looking about, Cowayne slowly went under his Union shirt, and came up with one of Clora Lee's pistols. And while Dew Dap gazed at the weapon with amazement, Cowayne quickly took aim. And after slowly cocking the pistol without making a sound, Dew Dap heard it. Cowayne had squeezed the trigger, thus sending the bullet roaring from the sparkling barrel. And when the deer staggered, it told the boy, Cowayne knew a little something about shooting. But when the medium size doe darted into the brush, rather then fall helplessly to the ground, both he and Cowayne were at a lost.

With what would be their biggest catch ever, trying to become scavenger's food, the teens had no other choice, but to go down into the narrow body of water. And as the two dashed across the turtles foul smelling home, with a great deal of urgency, neither thought of the consequences that would follow their actions.

"We's gotta hurry," Dew Dap said, as they crawled up the muddy wall, that dwelt on the shady side of the waterway.

As the two made it to their feet, looking like a couple of giant mud bugs, from some lost Bayou, they darted into the brush, without giving it a second thought. And while Dew Dap ran recklessly through the thick green foliage, Cowayne tried to make use of Pleasant and the Indians teachings. For he was doing his best to catch sight of the blood dropping that would have been left by the young doe.

After a two hundred yard chase, and a large number of scratches administered to them by nearly every branch and twig they passed, the boys came to a stop. And standing as if they were afraid to move, the boys found the doe struggling to stay on her feet, as it fought to keep moving. But the dying animal had lost far too much of the precious liquid, that all creatures need to live. And as her legs gave in to the call of death, the doe collapsed, still clinging to what little life she had left.

With both Dew Dap and Cowayne feeling their victory was a thing of shame, neither boy felt like smiling. For the two, just sat with their backs to each other, clinging to a sadness neither could explain. Nor could the boys say why they refuse to look at the doe, until she was long dead, which said something about the two newly freed slaves.

The journey home wasn't a pleasant one, seeing that the boys were thinking of death. For the doe's dying, made Dew Dap, think about his mother. Cowayne on the other hand, thought of the day, when his mother would be clinging to her life, fighting death, like some poor helpless deer. And he wondered how Sistah's God would see him then. For would he be just another ex-slave, or the boy, that foolishly killed one of God's creatures. And the thought of the unseen God, looking down on him, made Cowayne see Clora Lee's pistol for what it was truly worth. For it was death, and the boy desperately wanted to rid himself of the powerful killing tool.

By the time Dew Dap and Cowayne reached the main yard with the gutted deer, they had attracted a dozen or so followers. And as the two teens proudly marched right up to the female shed, with the deer resting on Dew Dap's shoulders, the girls couldn't believe their eyes.

"Dew Dap!" Joan screamed. "What you's do?" the little stump shouted, as she sprung to her feet.

"I's ain't do nothing," the boy replied, as he dropped the deer on the ground.

"I's uh ain't wash yo's dirty cloths, yet," Joan cried, as the boy stood covered with mud and blood.

Seeing the dead deer, Madeline immediately took to screaming as she did her best to climb up Joan's leg to safety. But the little night sunshine didn't have to try long, being that Joan took hold of the girl, and lifted her up without ever taking her eyes off of Dew Dap. And while in her state of silence, Bessie's actions spoke loud and clear, as she leaned against Joan in fear.

"Clora Lee, I's uh thought ya'll gave them boys a good washing," Sistah said laughing.

"Na Sistah, you's leave them girls be," old Mae cried, as she also laughed.

"Mae, I's uh thought the same thing," Sally said, as she laughed right along with the two females.

Sparked by Sistah's agitation, Clora Lee snapped. "Cowayne, if n you's don't get down to that there creek, I's gon put uh stick to ya," she yelled in frustration.

Cowayne eyes went to Sistah, wondering why she picked that time, of all times to speak. For the last thing old Mae's child wanted, was to march back to the creek for another bath. But with Sistah's statement having Clora Lee mader then a mess of hornet, Cowayne knew he no longer had a voice in the matter.

"Don't you's be looking at Sistah, cause she ain't gon help ya none. Na you's get to that there barn," Clora Lee said angrily. "And you's go with him, Matthew."

Being that he was quieter then a church mouse on a Sunday, the little boy didn't understand why he had to take another washing, when he wasn't even dirty yet. And knowing that another bath would earn him, a new unwanted name from his friends, the poor boy felt like running away, before his world came to a disturbing end.

"Me and my girls, ain't gon have ya walking round here like you's some seasoned hog, when we's presentable," Joan said, as she bounced Madeline on her hip. "Na you's gone with Cowayne, so we's can get ya cleaned up," the little female barked.

"I's uh reckon, yous boys ain't gon be running round here dirty no mo," Pleasant said with a smile.

But as Matthew stood helpless, old Mae tried her best to help the little dirt hugger, by telling Clora Lee, she didn't need to take him to the creek. But when the cheerful dirt hustler heard old Mae say that he was still small enough to fit in that old tub, the child nearly fell out. And as the poor boy was left wondering, what could he have possibly done, to deserve such a wonderful friend, his sister quickly agreed with the old female.

With the boys on their way to the barn, Clora Lee began to dish out her orders, as if the Misses's word wasn't worth spit. For she sent three females to go and clean the roasting irons, while telling her uncle Nelson to help Pleasant skin the deer. Then without giving it a second thought, Clora Lee shot her eyes toward Joan, who had already asked Sally to watch the girls, and was waiting on her. So with the extending of her hand, Joan gave the signal for the two of them to head for the barn, while everyone else sat in silence. But no sooner then the girls were well out of sight, the ex-slave went to laughing and talking up a storm.

"Mae, I's uh never thought, I's uh see the day, when I's could laugh as a slave," Sally laughed, while slapping her leg.

"Them young ns is something, I's tell ya," old Mae laughed.

"I's tell ya, Mae, them girls got them boys wrapped around theys fingers" Sally laughed.

"I's uh reckon, Sistah ain't his ma no mo," old Mae said, right before she poked her tongue at the misfortunate female.

"He's gon always be my baby, Mae, na you's stop," Sistah cried, while everyone laughed at her.

"Na Sistah, I's uh ain't make him go down to that old creek, and take uh washing," old Mae said, as she clapped with joy.

With her demeanor saying she was ready to do some serious pouting, Sistah went and sat in the doorway of the female shed. But being that she was in striking distance of old Mae, Sistah soon found herself at a disadvantage. For the large female took hold of Sistah's head, and moved it around at will.

"Mae I's ain't bothering you," Sistah pouted.

Yet no amount of pouting was going to stop old Mae from having a little fun. So with her gentle touch, old Mae went to tugging on the long black plaits that Sistah wore with pride. But the misfortunate female wasn't in the mood for playing, as she secured all four of the long hanging ropes. And after seeing the counter move, old Mae went straight for her most favorite spot of all. And as old Mae squeezed Sistah's nose, the half wit female walked right into the well laid, trap.

"Leave me lone, Mae," Sistah cried, with her voice echoing, as if she were talking into a bucket, which caused the little children to laugh. "Them young ns, laughing at me," she said, as old Mae went right on holding her nose.

Seeing that there was only one way out of her dilemma, Sistah got up and went in the female shed. There Sistah stood against the wall, which allowed her to touch old Mae on the head, when ever she felt the old female was ignoring her.

Watching Sistah meddle old Mae, Sally couldn't help but to think of what she over heard Mr. Arnold tell Duval, the night she found herself cleaning up Jeremiah's coffee. "Mae you's see Sistah meddling ya," Sally said, as she stared at the misfortunate female.

Yet while Sally stared at Sistah, Pleasant kept a close eye on her, which made the female very uncomfortable. For the house resident, knew that the misfortunate female had already laid claim to Pleasant. And like Clora Lee, Sistah didn't play, when it came down to what she deemed to be her own. Yet Pleasant was eyeing her, which made Sally wonder, what he was going to tell Sistah, when she asked him about doing such a thing.

For the second time in two days, Clora Lee and Joan found themselves marching the boys to the creek for a bath. And even though Joan still had reservation about leaving the guaranteed protection of the main yard, she was dead set on keeping Dew Dap clean. But unlike Clora Lee, Joan had no idea, of how hard it was to keep a male away from filth.

As they walked along the dirt path, holding their lovers clean cloths and towels, Clora Lee and Joan talked about what ever came to mind. But Cowayne and Dew Dap on the other hand, talked about the gun, which lead to the two of them discussing leaving the plantation.

"Where you's get that kind uh gun?" Dew Dap asked.

"I's found it," Cowayne replied. "But you's can't tell none uh them others bout it, not even Joan."

"It sure, make uh heap, uh noise."

"Yea, but with this, them white folks ain't gon mess with us, when we's leave here," Cowayne stated with confidence.

"What us?" Dew Dap whispered.

"Me and Lee, and who ever wanna come."

"Where you's, gon go?"

"I's gon follow the sun," Cowayne said, even though he knew where they were going to ultimately end up.

Cowayne didn't want to tell Dew Dap too much, too soon, with out knowing if he were going to make the trip with them. And even though they were friends, Cowayne knew the white man had ways, to make people talk.

"I's uh reckon, I's uh gotta start thinking bout me and them girls leaving," Dew Dap said with a certain kind of sadness.

"You's think, Joan uh leave, beings that her ma, might not wanna go?" Cowayne asked.

"I's uh reckon, I's uh ask her bout it tonight. But I's uh gotta find out, ha to get my way North."

"I's uh reckon, ya'll uh do better going with us."

"You's taking ya ma and Matthew with ya?"

"Na you's knows, I's uh ain't gonna leave my ma and Matthew," Cowayne said, as if he took an offense to the question.

All at once, things became quiet, as the boys continued to walk grudgingly behind the girls. Yet both Dew Dap and Cowayne knew how lucky they were, to have such good females in their lives. And with only a few days between the two of them, Dew Dap would much rather give up eating, before entertaining the thought of losing Joan. For with the tiny female at his side, the teen felt he could accomplish just about anything, including, finding his way north.

Once again, when they reached the fork in the path, the two couples went their separate ways. And with the two life long friends walking side by side, like they had done so many times before, Clora Lee gave Cowayne one of her gentle bumps. A bump that told him, things were back to the way they should be. Yet Cowayne wasn't worried, because he knew Clora Lee was his squaw, his female, his woman, and his lady. And the adventurous teen, didn't need a kiss to tell him that. All Cowayne needed, was for Clora Lee to keep being Clora Lee, and his life would be just fine, even though they were still a couple of virgins.

"I's uh tell ya Dew Dap. I's uh mighty happy you's got dirty," Joan said, looking out across the creek with amazement.

Then with a certain type of boldness, Joan took a ring side seat on the log, and waited for her big foot lover to get undress. But the teen didn't move a muscle, as he waited for her to turn around. Yet Joan just sat with her arms resting on her knees, as she held the soap in one hand, and a wash rag in the other. And the way Joan flipped the rag back and forth, while staring at the creek, told the boy, they were at an impasse.

"What you's waiting for?" Joan asked, after waiting for the boy to take his clothes off.

"You's got uh turn around," Dew Dap replied rather nervously.

"I's uh do no such thing."

"Joan, you's can't be watching me," Dew Dap said shamefuly.

"You's take them cloths off, and get in that there water, cause you's mine, and I's don't care what folks think," Joan said, putting an end to their little debate.

And while Dew Dap reluctantly gave in to another one of Joan's demands, she knew he was only thinking of her reputation. But from where the duck high female stood, Dew Dap meant more to her, then some silly non existing reputation. For they were all once slaves, and did just as their master told them to. So if those newly freed slaves had an unkind word for what she and Dew Dap were doing, then they only needed to take a good look at their yesterdays. The days when their master told them to lay down, and the hypocrites did so without shame. But being that Mr. Lincoln had given Joan control over her own life, she had no intentions on surrendering it to those who would surely bow down, if their master were to return at that very moment. So Joan stood up and took hold of Dew Dap's shirt, while thinking of Clora Lee and Madeline. And with one quick move, Joan snatched the shirt open, thus sending its buttons scattering in the wind.

"Joan, what I's gon do na," Dew Dap cried.

"Dew Dap, if n you's don't hush that fuss, and take them breeches off, you's ain't gon be in that shed, with me and our girls," Joan growled.

"Na Joan, you's knows, I's uh gon be in that shed," Dew Dap said, as he started to unbutton his pants.

Finding herself off balance for the first time in three days, Joan didn't know what to say. And even though she would never admit it, Joan knew every word the boy said was true. Yet the little stump also noticed the boy was beginning to figure her out. But Joan didn't feel she was losing any of her leverage over Dew Dap, being that he was taking his pants off, without any more back talk. And when Dew Dap finished getting undress, Joan found herself staring at a stiff erection.

"You's can't wait till tonight?" she asked.

"I's uh can wait," Dew Dap replied, before heading for the water.

By the time Dew Dap got around to washing his head, Joan slipped out of her cloths, and joined him in the creek.

"Joan, theys got something in this here water," Dew Dap shouted, with his eyes still closed.

"I's uh know," Joan said softly, as she bounced around, hoping to kill the water's chilling affect on her body.

Hearing Joan's voice so close to him, Dew Dap immediately sought to remove the water from his eyes. But before he could wring the rag out, Joan scooped up some water, and tossed it in his face.

"Joan," Dew Dap shouted, as the girl laughed. "That ain't funny," he said, rushing to dry his eyes.

"You's lean over," Joan said, reinserting her control in their relationship.

But Joan's control came with a price, she was more then happy to pay. For Dew Dap's hands went straight to her ass, which she saw as a good thing. Yet Joan wasn't about to let the boy view her body as a one dimensional treat.

"Dew Dap, theys got more of me, then my bottom," Joan cried with a smile.

"I's knows that."

"You's do?" Joan asked, as she rubbed his face against her breast.

When Joan had finish washing Dew Dap's hair, he was ready to move out to the deeper part of the creek. But with the duck high female not knowing how to swim, she was reluctant to follow him. And while Joan stood watching the distance between the two of them, as it grew larger with every step the boy took, a look of fear, covered her face.

"What's wrong?" Dew Dap asked.

"I's uh scared," Joan said with her arms stretched out.

After Dew Dap went back, and gathered her up in his arms, she wrapped her legs around his muscular body. And when it came time to set Joan down, Dew Dap let her slide down his massive body.

"You's want me?" Joan asked, after rinsing the soap out of his head.

"Yea I's want ya, you's good for me, and them girls," Dew Dap admitted, as Joan checked to make sure all of the soap was out of his hair.

"Do you's want me out here?" Joan asked, while holding his stiff hard erection in her hand.

As Dew Dap's body told Joan what she already knew, the young female went about scrubbing the dirt from his body. And in doing so, Joan's breast bounced like crazy, which made the boy want her even more, as he stared at the two luscious melons.

"What you's doing," Joan asked, after Dew Dap had pulled her to him.

While attempting to kiss Joan, and talk at the same time, Dew Dap spoke with a passion so strong, it started a pounding in the girl's purse.

"I's uh want ya bad," he whispered.

"You's gotta wait, till I's uh get this here dirt off ya," Joan replied seductively.

But Dew Dap couldn't wait, as his mouth went from Joan's lips, to her luscious ripe melons. And his squeezing of the meaty breast, while nibbling on its hard dark nipple, sent Joan burning out of control.

By the time Joan had washed Dew Dap's family jewels, she was ready to take their bath in a more satisfying direction. So Joan placed the soap in his hand, and told him, she needed a washing as well. And when Dew Dap went straight to washing her breast, Joan knew her lover had found himself a couple of new favorite toys. Toys, that would undoubtly, bring him many years of joy, and satisfaction.

With Dew Dap's large hands, tenderly touching her body, Joan smiled with a bit of peacefulness, as she took to guiding them all over her body. And Joan gave the teen's right hand, the pleasure of washing her hairy fat pussy, while the left, enjoyed putting the rag to every inch of that thing, Joan called an ass. And Dew Dap washed Joan's ass, the same way she did his. Yet Joan enjoyed the ass washing, far more then her lover, being that she rode the middle finger of his right hand, to a most satisfying climax.

"Pick me up," Joan said, after the two had finished removing the soap from their bodies.

With her tiny body, in the arms of her lover, Joan quickly became an acrobat. For, she wrapped her arms around his neck, leaving her legs, to take the boy's waist hostage. Yet Joan didn't have to tell her lover what to do, as he wisely placed his throbbing club between her two wet lips.

"Hold me," Joan said, as she felt herself slipping.

With Joan's ass already in his hands, Dew Dap tried to pull her lower body closer to his. But when Joan tried to raise her legs higher, the boy quickly realized, he had to change his grip. And as he went to get his arms under her legs, Dew Dap made it just in time.

"Hold me Dew Dap, hold me," Joan cried, as her walls gave way for the second time, in a matter of minutes.

And while Dew Dap tried to maintain his grip, the poor boy's movement began to mirror that of a violent massacre, which told Joan, he was about to give her more then she could handle. So like a cannibal feasting on human flesh, Joan ate at his bottom lip, as she unselfishly surrendered her tiny pussy to him with a firy burning love. And as the pain ran through her body like a bolt of lightning, Joan could tell by Dew Dap's reaction, he would never betray their love for another.

"You's give it to me, Dew Dap, you's give it to me, cause I's uh ain't gon never leave that woodshed," Joan whispered. I's uh swear, I's uh ain't gon never leave ya. For as long as I's live, I's uh gon be yo's," Joan said, as her pussy released its juices, like an over flowing river.

With the two newly freed slaves, love making being just as much of a success, as their bath, Dew Dap watched Joan, as she dried herself off. And when Joan gave him the towel she cut from a wool blanket, Dew Dap got more then just an opportunity to dry his dripping wet body.

"Come here," Joan said, after sitting on the log, with nothing on, but her undergarments.

Dew Dap walked over to Joan, looking to get his fresh pair of pants. But when the boy found himself standing before the girl who would always be his, he got a startling surprise. For Joan took his sagging penis in her hand, and looked upon the thing, as if it were an object of great wealth. And after pushing the skin back, she gently went about cleaning the precious chunk of muscle and flesh, while Dew Dap held a look on his face, which begged Joan to speak.

"I's hurting ya?" she asked.

The mild shaking of his head, told Joan, Dew Dap was standing closer to pleasure, then any amout of pain. But if Dew Dap thought he was some where near Heaven, the girl's next act, placed him smack dab in the middle of Glory Town. For the tiny female, gently wrapped her mouth around the exposed head of the uncircumcise dick, and closed her eyes. And with nothing but love for experience, the little stump softly gave Dew Dap a sample, of what he would be receiving, for many years to come.

Chapter 16

New Rules

No sooner then the teens made it back to the main yard, Sistah started in on them, which prompted old Mae to act.

"Ooo Mae, them boys, show nough clean," Sistah said, as she clapped her hands and laughed.

"Na Sistah, I's uh done told ya, bout meddling them young ns. Na if n you's don't stop, I's uh gon take uh switch to ya," old Mae said, hoping her threat, would shut the female up.

"Mae, I's uh ain't do them young ns nothing. I's uh just saying, ha Clora Lee and Joan got them boys cleaner then the Misses table," Sistah said, as if she were about to cry.

"Na Sistah, them girls gotta right, to clean up theys boys, if n theys want."

"Mae, I's uh thought Cowayne was my boy," Sistah cried.

"Well if n he's yo's boy, then why you's ain't take him down to that there creek, and give him uh washing?" Isabella said, starting the other females to laughing.

"Mae, she's knows, Cowayne foots, done got too big, for me to be giving him uh washing."

"Na Sistah, you's hush that kind uh talk, in front them young ns, and I's mean it," the old female said firmly.

287

"Mae I's uh was just saying…"

"Na Sistah I's uh done told ya to hush, na, and I's mean it," old Mae said, nearly taking her soft voice to a shout.

"You's don't never let me talk, so I's uh ain't gon say nothing no mo," Sistah grumbled, as she cut her eyes at Clora Lee.

"Come here Sistah," old Mae said softly.

Even though she stared at the two large out stretch arms, that often brought her comfort, Sistah didn't move an inch. For the misfortunate female just stood pouting like a little child. And like a little child, Sistah wanted old Mae to make her pain go away. Yet there was nothing the old female could do, seeing that Cowayne was going to leave the nest, whether his mother wanted him to or not.

"Na you's come on to me, Sistah, like I's uh done told ya."

Seeing how old Mae was calling out to Sistah, started Joan to thinking. For the girl was thinking their former master, top picker, had a right to know, what every mother should know, even if it were to cost her, that precious little thing called life. And as Joan watched Sistah slowly make her way over to old Mae, still sporting her sad face, she felt sorry for the mother and daughter combination. But when old Mae put her arm around Sistah, just as she did Clora Lee, the day love and Cowayne drove the girl home crying, Joan was ready to speak up, despite logic and fear telling her other wise.

"Na you's hush that fuss, just uh buzzing round here, keeping up all that racket," old Mae said, speaking as if she was talking to a baby.

"Mae I's ain't no baby," Sistah said with a tone of a little girl.

"Na that Clora Lee done up and took Cowayne, you's gotta be my baby," old Mae said, as she squeezed Sistah's nose.

Sistah gently pulled her head back, thus freeing her nose from the old female's grip. She then laid her face on old Mae's head, and stared at Clora Lee. Yet it wasn't an evil stare, nor did it carry a hint of spitefulness. For Sistah was staring with a touch of pain, and a dash of peacefulness. It was as if Sistah were reluctantly accepting the lost, that she knew one day would come. But like all mothers, the misfortunate female didn't believe in her wildest dream, the day would come so soon. And with her young son being just an eye wink away from starting a life of his own, Sistah had only old Mae to cling to.

"I's uh reckon, them boys uh stay clean, if n they's knows what's good for um," Sally said, while watching over Bessie.

Sally was trying to help old Mae calm the waters, while keeping an eye on Bessie, who was trying her best to thread another needle. To Sally, that was the first step to becoming a good seamstress. For that was how she started Joan on her way, to becoming the best, anyone had ever seen. And the young female didn't see anything wrong with introducing Bessie to the craft, in the same manner.

Seeing his little sister staying with her struggle, Dew Dap went over and knelt down next to the little Miss. Sunshine. Then like the days before Joan, Madeline crawled up on his knee, right before glaring up at her acting mother. And hearing their little Night Sunshine call for her to join them, Joan went over and watched right alone with Dew Dap, as Bessie took her time, and got the thread through the eye of the needle.

"What you's doing?" Dew Dap asked Bessie, after she had completed her task.

"I's sewing," the little girl replied joyfully.

"Na if n you's mind Sally, you's uh be the best little sewer in the whole world," Dew Dap assured his sister.

"I's is," Bessie said, while holding the threaded needle, as she waited for Sally to take it, and give her another one.

Dew Dap gave each of his sisters a kiss on the forehead, then like the day before, he and Joan shocked everyone, with their show of affection. And after Joan received her kiss on the jaw, there wasn't a sound to be heard, other then Dew Dap telling Cowayne to come on, and leave the females to themselves. Yet the talkative females had appeared to have lost their will to speak, as they watched the boys head for the old barn.

"I guess the Misses changed her mind," Effie said, in her forever sarcastic tone.

The females turned around to find Effie standing with her hands together, resting against the clean white apron that she was rarely seen without wearing. Her cat like eyes, quickly sought out Clora Lee, as if she were trying to strike fear in the young teen, for being the ring leader of the bunch. But the only one she succeeded in scaring was Bessie, as the little girl quickly ran to Joan, while Madeline stayed seated. For Madeline was the only one to see Effie, as she appeared from behind the female shed, and took up a position against the building. And the sweet little night sunshine, smiled and waved, when Effie made a funny face that was strickly a thing of beauty.

"We's ain't mean, the Misses no harm," old Mae cried, when she saw Effie's eye leave Clora Lee to follow Bessie.

"You's ain't gotta beg her, Mae," Clora Lee said, staring at her grandmother.

The words brought the sharp cat like eyes back to her, just as Clora Lee hoped they would. The young teen was not about to let Effie harm Joan, or the girls, as she stood ready to fight. And with both of old Mae's arms wrapped around Sistah, Clora Lee knew her old friend was at a disadvantage, if she and Effie were to have at it. But what Clora Lee didn't see, was Nelson standing behind the female shed, as if he was waiting for such a thing.

"This is still the Misses land, and there is still a big A on the front gate," Effie said firmly.

"But we's ain't no slaves, no mo," Clora Lee snapped.

"Then I suggest, you move on," Effie said, as if she was sending her granddaughter a strong message. And before Clora Lee could utter a word in response to the statement, Effie spoke again. "But until you do, the owner of this plantation, and her children will be in your line," the preferred house girl said, right before disappearing, just as fast as she appeared.

Feeling that Effie was on her way to tell Mrs. Arnold about Clora Lee and the deer, a few of the females quickly did like the favorite house girl, and disappeared as well. But knowing that she was free, Clora Lee had no intentions of running, or hiding, like some scared animal. For the fiery young female, was ready for the long awaited show down with her grandmother and Mrs. Arnold. And the way Clora Lee saw it, for there was no better time then the present.

"Na we's got more then enough for the Misses and her young ns," old Mae said, as she still held on to Sistah.

"I's uh throw it away, fo I's give um some," Clora Lee snarled.

"You's uh do no such thing," Sistah said, before old Mae could start pleading her case. "Them white folks, could uh caught them boys out yonder, and we's uh never see um, no mo. Then what ya'll gon do?" Sistah asked, pointing at Joan. "Na you's gone feed the Misses and her young ns, cause we's got young ns running round here hungry, just like she do."

With her head down in shame, Clora Lee refused to allow a single tear to fall from her eyes. But the young female knew in her heart, every word Sistah said was true, yet she still found herself angry just the same. For Clora Lee's anger was that of Effie and Ethel doing. And if there was one thing Clora Lee did know, she didn't have to look far, to find out where their mother had gotten her empty motherly skills. Skills, Effie had taught their mother well. And that was why Clora Lee hated them both. And the mere thought of Effie, brought hate and anger spewing out of Clora Lee like an erupting volcano.

"Come here," Sistah said, with her arms reaching out to Clora Lee.

When Clora Lee made it to Sistah, she received a great big hug, filled with love. But not even Sistah's loving arms could make Clora Lee feel better. And as for the song bird's humming, it wrapped around Clora Lee like a warm blanket, yet the sweet sounding melody couldn't ease the girl's pain. For the vile Arnold's venom was spewing through Clora Lee so fast, the poor girl didn't believe, Cowayne could fix what was ailing her. For she just stood listening to the soft sound of Sistah's voice, as if it were a dead soldier's call to rise again.

The morning after what Clora Lee considered to be a miserable day, she found herself still fuming with anger. And as Clora Lee stared out at the darkness, she revisited the image of Mrs. Arnold and her children walking away with far more meat, then she or Joan cared for them to have. But Clora Lee knew that was yesterday, and unlike the darkness, it would never change. And while facing the fact, she had no other choice, but to live with the unstomaching dilemma, Clora Lee was ready to start a new day. So after giving Sistah her kiss first, Clora Lee then kissed old Mae, which told the two females, the teen was heading out to find their son.

No sooner then Clora Lee was good and gone, old Mae spoke softly. "I's uh reckon, she's ain't mad at ya no mo," the old female said to Sistah.

There was no reply to old Mae's statement, as all of the females appeared to be sleeping peacefully. But old Mae knew Sistah was no more asleep, then she was white, yet the large old female was willing to play along, as it appeared, she had turned over to catch a few more winks. But when the darkness was captured by the most horrible sound anyone had ever heard, the shed nearly came crumbling down. For the old female was making a horrible attempt at singing, as her voice could have made a deaf mute cry.

"Mae, what you's doing?" Sistah cried.

"I's uh reckon, you's was sleep," old Mae said laughing.

"Na Mae, you's knows, nobody can't sleep, why you's doing that," Sistah replied, which gave everyone cause to laugh.

"Well you's aught uh been up, then," old Mae said.

"You's weren't sleep no ha," Isabella grumbled, as her voice crawled across the darkness.

"I's was to," Sistah said, as her little white lie, had no way of convincing the toddler that was crawling on its mother.

"Na Sistah, you's need uh good taste of that old whip," a female said, causing another round of laughter.

When Clora Lee found Cowayne, he was with Dew Dap, Pleasant, Nelson, and Obdi. The five males were watching over the smoke house, in case someone got the notion to commandeer the remaining deer meat.

"Ya'll been up all night?" Clora Lee asked, looking at Cowayne sitting on the ground.

"I's uh reckon, we's took turns sleeping," Pleasant replied.

The five males, stared at Clora Lee without saying another word. And the way they were looking, made the girl wonder what the five of them was thinking. But after hearing the other females talk about God's first created human, Clora Lee felt the five could have been lost in their own mind, and wouldn't even know it.

"What?" Clora Lee asked, looking down at herself.

"They's ain't looking at nothing," Cowayne said, as he stood up.

For some reason, Clora Lee didn't believe the boy was telling the truth. The young female had heard enough about males, to know the five of them wouldn't be staring at her, just for the sake of looking. Yet Clora Lee had no intentions of pressing Cowayne in front of a group of males, when she knew their feelings were that of an old cat. And that was about the only thing Clora Lee could say, she learned from

Big Willie. For the large male was more fragile, then any female she had ever known, Mrs. Arnold included. So with that in mind, Clora Lee put her hand on the bridge of Cowayne's shoulder, as the two of them set out to go have an early morning chat.

Looking at Clora Lee and Cowayne walking away, Nelson said, "I's uh still say that boy is caught, better then a fish frying in uh pan."

Then like Clora Lee, Nelson found everyone looking at him, as the three pair of remaining eyes held different looks.

As Clora Lee and Cowayne faded into the darkness, the once angry female thought less about the Arnold's, and focused more on her self. For there was something the teen felt inadequate about, and she needed a bit reassuring.

With her arm around Cowayne, Clora Lee spoke softly. "You's think, I's uh got enough bosom?"

"I's uh don't know," Cowayne replied, not knowing what constituted a legitimated amount of breast.

"You's answer me," Clora Lee said, while peeping inside her dress.

Not knowing what to say, Cowayne said the first things that popped in to his head. "I's uh reckon, they uh do," he mumbled.

Still young and naive, Cowayne didn't have a clue of what he was doing to him self. Nor did the boy know the consequences of such a statement. But it didn't take the poor fellow long to find out, there are some things a male should never take lightly, when it came down to females. For Clora Lee took her arm from around Cowayne's neck, and quickly distance her self from him. And when it appeared as if he didn't care that she no longer wanted to be as one, Clora Lee gave him a firm shove.

"What you's do that for?" Cowayne asked, as he stood totally oblivious, to the female's strange and often changing disposition.

"Cause you's ain't look," Clora Lee replied angrily.

Cowayne took Clora Lee by the hand, and led her in to the red barn. There he lit a lantern, and proceeded to hang it on a beam over her head. And as he stretched to reach the nail that was driven part ways into the beam, Clora Lee looked up at him, as she could feel his body pressing against her. And the force from his body, made Clora Lee slowly close her eyes, as her hands mysteriously found their way to his waist. And when the lantern was hung, the two were left staring into each other's eyes. And the way they stared, left Clora Lee hungering for a kiss, yet the girl knew if that were to happen, there would be no stopping their uncontrollable passion. So like a good little angel, Clora Lee held the neck of her dress out, allowing Cowayne the chance to take a good look at the two tits, that couldn't have been no more then a handful of light brown flesh.

They weren't as big as Joan's, but they were all right with him, Cowayne thought to himself. They weren't hanging either, like his mother's and a lot of the older females, and that made him feel good, even though he didn't know why. But deep down inside, Cowayne knew if Clora Lee's breast got as big as the moon, he would still love them just the same. And if they were to end up hanging like a broke neck chicken, the boy wouldn't have a problem with that either. For the way Cowayne saw it, he were happy with his Lee as she were, and how she may ultimately end up.

"What you's looking at?" Clora Lee asked softly.

"I's uh was just thinking," Cowayne replied.

"Bout what?" Clora Lee asked, as her hands softly went up and down his side.

"Ha it feels to suck um."

Clora Lee quickly snatched Cowayne's hand from her dress. "You's uh do no such thing," she said firmly.

"Then why you's want me to look at um?"

"Cause if n I's had mo, then I's uh might be good with babies."

"Lee, you's gon be good with babies, and freedom to," Cowayne said, having no doubt in the girl's ability.

"You's think so?"

"You's good na, Lee. Look ha you's handle Matthew."

"So you's won't mind, if n I's uh have babies?"

"You's can have anything you's want," Cowayne replied.

Once again, Cowayne had given his word, without knowing what he was committing himself to. For the teen had given Clora Lee the freedom, to always do, what ever her heart desired.

With her arms around Cowayne's neck, Clora Lee whispered, "I's uh love ya, and don't you's ever forget it."

Then like a lady trying to satisfy a burning need, Clora Lee took to sucking on Cowayne's neck. And by the time she started breathing some what heavily, Clora Lee could feel her left leg taking a small step outward. And the girl could feel her lover's club, knocking at Heaven's door, shouting its time to take that extra step. And when the teen heard Cowayne say he would never forget she loved him, her legs unconsciously parted a little more. And if it were not for the long brown dress that she was wearing, Cowayne's dick would have already found its way through her virgin walls. But the dress was far from being a suitable defense, when it came down to Cowayne's hard driving movement against her body. And by the time their breathing became that of two raging animals, Clora Lee's body and mind were at war. And while her body cried out for its virgin walls, to be torn down, her brain shouted, run. Run, it shouted. Run with all of your might, if you ever want to leave this wretched plantation, the little voice cried out in fear.

After pushing Cowayne away, Clora Lee took the little voice advice, and ran from the barn as if it were on fire. And she ran toward Pleasant, just a laughing and looking over her shoulder all the way there.

"Don't let him get me, he's gon make me eat worms," Clora Lee yelled, as she stood behind Pleasant.

It wasn't the girl's laughing, that told Pleasant she was telling another tall one. For the fatherly figure knew Clora Lee well enough to know, if Cowayne wanted her to eat worms, she would be chewing like a cow grazing in a field, and liking it.

"You's young n hush that racket, fo you's wake the whole plantation," Pleasant said softly.

"But he's gon get me…"

"Na I's uh ain't gon tell ya no mo, you's hush that racket," Pleasant said a second time.

Like a good little girl, Clora Lee did as Pleasant asked, without saying another word. Yet she was still able to send a message to Cowayne. For with her head on Pleasant's shoulder, as her sparkling eyes enhanced the victory smile she wore out of regret, spoke to the boy loud and clear. Yet it was Clora Lee's look of regret that stayed with Cowayne, as his eyes said, he had grown tired of their little game. But Clora Lee knew there was more riding on her, than the virginity she would surely give to Cowayne, when the time was right. Yet she still hated to see her friend suffer, for what was rightfully his.

By the time Clora Lee was done with eating breakfast, she had reached the conclusion, that Sistah was the answer to her problem. There she would be protected from her own lustful desires, as well as Cowayne's hard burning need. Yet Clora Lee wasn't going to fool herself in believing, she would be all right after a day or two. For the young female knew their problem wasn't going to go away, until they truly address the matter. So until the two of them say goodbye to the Big A plantation, the young female knew she had to watch her every step, as if they were walking along a steep cliff.

As Clora Lee stood combing old Mae's hair, while laughing at Sistah's sad attempt at sewing, Dew Dap and Cowayne came walking toward them. And like always, Clora Lee's eyes instantly collided with Cowayne's, revealing the fact, that the two of them were still yearning to try their hand at love making.

"You's got any more of them sacks?" Cowayne asked Sally, after pulling his eyes away from Clora Lee.

"Some is uh might bigger then them others," Sally said, as she gave Cowayne the newly sewn sacks.

As Cowayne took the sacks from Sally's hands, Sistah noticed the tension between her stolen son and Clora Lee. Yet Sistah weren't the only one to notice, the ripple in Clora Lee and Cowayne's waters. For Cowayne to walk up and not say a word to Clora Lee, or she to him, was more shocking to the females, then hearing that the war was over. And when Cowayne turned to walk away with the sacks, the females took to holding their breath, as if they were being thrown off of a slave ship, into some deep black sea.

It didn't take Joan long to see that Clora Lee needed her help. So the duck high female quickly used Dew Dap's playing with Madeline, to sew Clora Lee out of her bad situation.

"Dew Dap, what you's hanging round us females for?" Joan asked.

"Cause I's playing with Madeline," the teen replied.

"Na Dew Dap, you's can play with us, when we's get home," Joan said, as if they had a place of their own.

Knowing that his life was far better than it had ever been, Dew Dap left without saying a word. And seeing the boy leave in such an orderly fashion, the females didn't waste any time getting on Joan's case. Yet Joan didn't mind the females yapping, being that they were no longer looking at her friend.

When Dew Dap caught up with Cowayne, he walked in silence, as if it would hurt him to speak. The young teen was so drawn in to his thoughts of Joan, he couldn't see that something was troubling Cowayne. Nor did Dew Dap know where they were going, as he just went on thinking about the creek, and all that happened there.

"Where we's going?" Dew Dap asked, after waking up from his daydream, to find himself in unfamiliar territory.

Cowayne was so torn with frustration, he never thought about Dew Dap or the bullets. But Dew Dap's question was more then enough to put the quick thinking teen back on the right track. With his thinking ability reinforced, Cowayne found himself faced with a dilemma. If he were to turn around and take Dew Dap back to the main yard, it would cost him that all important second load. So the boy stopped and thought for a moment. And after thinking clearly, Cowayne sought to find out where the teen stood, as for as leaving the plantation.

"You's can't tell uh soul, bout where we's going," Cowayne said, as he looked his friend in the eye.

"Where we's going?" Dew Dap asked.

"You's can't even tell Joan bout this, just like you's can't tell her bout that gun," Cowayne said.

"I's ain't, na where we's going?"

"You's uh see, when we's get there," Cowayne said, still looking his friend in the eye.

When the boys came to a stop, all Dew Dap saw was a whole lot of brush, supported by a foul smell. But no sooner then he and Cowayne got to feeling comfortable, a small group of coyotes scrambled out of the brush. And as the four legged scavengers sought to defend their bounty, Cowayne pulled his pistol and fired, dropping one of the coyotes instantly. But unlike the doe, Cowayne didn't have any remorse for killing the animal, or for breaking his vow. For like the white man, the coyote was a threat, and Cowayne didn't make a vow, never to kill a threat.

"Theys got uh dead animal in there," Dew Dap said, as he watched the coyotes retreat in fear.

"Theys, men in there," Cowayne replied.

Dew Dap looked at Cowayne, as if he were the one who had killed the men. And Cowayne didn't make things any better, when he didn't respond to his friend's stare. Instead, Cowayne went right to removing the brush, which hid the massive treasure of bullets. But when the two boys saw how nature's creatures had done the foul smelling bodies, they wanted to puke. And Cowayne would have, if he had not caught sight of the ring. The ring, Clora Lee wanted him to take, long before the coyotes, took to chewing half of the man's finger off.

"What you's doing?" Dew Dap asked, as Cowayne started to dig a hole, after collecting the ring.

"I's uh gon burry it, so nobody can get it."

"You's don't want it?" Dew Dap asked, with a gleam in his eye.

"We's don't take theys rings," Cowayne said, as if he and Clora Lee, had ran across many dead white men, who had rings on their fingers.

Like Clora Lee, Dew Dap didn't understand Cowayne's logic. Yet the teen didn't see any reason to argue, over something that wasn't his in the first place. So Dew Dap just stood looking over his shoulder, as if he was expecting some one to walk up, and take them away in chains.

After Cowayne had laid the ring to rest, he and Dew Dap went about filling the sacks. But while he held a sack for Cowayne, the teen got an idea.

"Hold up," Dew Dap said, as Cowayne picked up another hand full of bullets.

While holding the sack open under the wagon, Dew Dap told Cowayne to hit the crate. And when Cowayne did as the boy asked, the sack was filled so fast, some of its bullets had to be poured out.

"You's got it," Cowayne said to his fast thinking friend.

When Cowayne had finished filling four of his ten sacks, he was ready to go, but Dew Dap stopped him. The taller and more muscular teen convinced Cowayne to fill four more sacks, even though he didn't want to. And when the four extra sacks were filled, the boys were faced with a test of endurance. Dew Dap showed Cowayne how to carry two of the sacks around his neck, while lugging the other two in his hands. And it didn't take the boys long to find out, they had set themselves up for a whale of a task. But the boys had made a commitment, and they were determined to see it through to the end, knowing it would only make them stronger.

While Cowayne and Dew Dap were off gathering bullets, Clora Lee had a full morning of her own. After plaiting old Mae and Sistah's hair, Clora Lee helped the old female with washing up. She then sat down in the doorway of the female shed, and without saying a word to anyone, Clora Lee took to plaiting her own hair. And as Clora Lee went about the chore of dealing with her long brownish black hair, she never noticed the other females. One by one, or some times all together, the females looked at her with an enormous amount of concern. It was as if the females could feel Clora Lee's pain. There was no mistaking it. The females had a strange connection, which seem to come from all of their talking and touching. And that bond would always tighten, when ever one of them had a problem. And if by some chance, the white females would join forces with the once enslaved females, and together, they united the females through out the world, the white man, along with all the other male species would be in serious trouble.

With her hair in four long plaits, Clora Lee sat laughing and talking with the other females, as they patiently waited for the day to pass them by. But as she enjoyed herself, while learning a few more things about males, a feeling came over Clora Lee like a rushing wind. And from the moment the feeling hit her, Clora Lee knew Cowayne was back under the protection of the main grounds. For Clora Lee had it like that. She could feel Cowayne's presence in an army of slaves, and would have no problem in seeking him out. And if Cowayne didn't think Clora Lee could feel his pain, then the boy was wrong. For Clora Lee couldn't stop thinking about what their earlier encounter in the barn was doing to him, as she believed ripping her heart out, would be less painfull, then worrying about Sistah's son.

Clora Lee stood up and took a long stretch, as if it had been an extreamly hard day. But Clora Lee wasn't tired, she was looking to have a talk with her friend, while pretending to be bored with the females and their conversations.

"You's can't go crawling back to him," Sistah said, as she still fought the same piece of cloth, with the same needle and thread.

Clora Lee stopped walking, but for some reason, the young female couldn't bring herself to turn around. Then like a bolt, of lightning, Clora Lee heard a voice come to her rescue.

"Na Sistah, you's can't say that child, is running back to ya boy," old Mae said.

"Mae she's ain't gon never whip him, if n she's don't stop running behind him, like she's some puppy," Sistah complained with a touch of frustration.

"Na Sistah, you's can't say that child is uh puppy," old Mae barked, even though she knew Sistah was telling the truth.

But after hearing Sistah speak of Cowayne being whipped, Clora Lee felt she didn't need old Mae to back her up. And not knowing what Sistah meant by the word whip, Clora Lee spun around with bad intentions, as she stood two shakes from exploding. But when the teen saw the fearful look in Sistah's eyes, she quickly jumped to the wrong conclusion.

"I's uh ain't gon never hit Cowayne," Clora Lee said strongly. "And I's uh ain't going looking for him, neither," she lied.

The females started laughing, as if Clora Lee had told a good joke. For the females had accepted the first part of Clora Lee's statement with all honesty. But as for the second half of the girl's rushing words, the females weren't buying it. For Clora Lee couldn't sell that lie to Madeline on a rainy day.

"Then you's come back here, so you's can learn how to sew," Sistah said, as she stuck herself again.

"Sistah you's can't watch that there needle, and Clora Lee to," Sally said laughing.

"It serves her right, she's always meddling," old Mae said, while enjoying another laugh at Sistah's expense.

"You's ain't sewing," Sistah said to the old female, as Clora Lee took a seat next to her.

"You just hush, and teach that child bout that whip, cause she's gotta put on yo's boy," old Mae said, while the other females took to laughing again.

And as the young teen began to understand the nature of their conversation, she wondered why the females had to make everything so complicated. For Clora Lee realized, the whip had nothing to do, with striking Cowayne at all. The females were talking about one thing, while meaning something totally different. But what was the whip, and how was it used? The teen was at a lost, as she waited for the conversation to continue.

"Look at me," Sistah said to Clora Lee.

"Sistah, that child ain't bit mo been touched, then Madeline," Isabella said with confidence.

Clora Lee clearly understood Isabella's statement, yet she wondered why the nosey female was sniffing up behind her. But the teen didn't have the time to jump Isabella, being that she was too busy trying to figure Sistah out. For Sistah was getting stranger with each passing day, and just like Duval, the girl couldn't seem to make sense of it. Yet she wasn't about to give up, on trying to figure out the not so misguided female.

"Here come them boys," a female said, putting an end to Clora Lee and Sistah's mental examination of each other.

The sight of Cowayne didn't make things any better for the girl, as she tried to figure out what was going on with his mother. Nor did his tapping Sistah on the head, while on the way to take a seat next to his birth mother, help Clora Lee any. It appeared to Clora Lee, the boy was doing everything in his power, to make her suffer for their early morning fiasco. But the broken hearted teen was not about to give up on the only person she would gladly follow to Hell and back. For Clora Lee knew in her heart, Cowayne was suffering just as much as she was.

"Sally, you's want me to take some mo of them sacks," Cowayne asked, as he noticed Nelson lingering around the large magnolia tree.

"Theys ready, when you's ready for um," Sally said, while looking at Clora Lee.

Cowayne didn't move an inch, as he tried to out fox Nelson, without giving Sistah cause, to think he was disobeying her.

"I's uh reckon, you's got something to do with them there sacks," old Mae mumbled.

Looking at his mother, Cowayne told her, he wasn't doing anyhing. Yet the old female knew Sistah's boy well enough to know, he wasn't being entirely honest with her. So with out ruffling any feathers, old Mae decided to dabble in some finagling of her own.

"Na child, I's uh ain't said you's done uh thing," the old female said, as she picked a twig out of her son's hair. "But I's uh reckon, you's need to talk to ya ma, cause she's been worrying uh heap," old Mae went on, as she tried to get Cowayne to go sit with Sistah.

Being that Clora Lee was sitting next to Sistah, Cowayne wanted no part of his mother's suggestion. But still wanting to be the perfect son, Cowayne didn't have the heart, to hurt his loving mother for Clora Lee, or any one else. So with his eyes on Sistah, the teen could see Clora Lee with her head down, picking at her right foot. And everything about his Lee, told Cowayne, she wasn't handling things well. But he felt it was all her fault, seeing that she started the whole thing, with that crazy question about her breast. Yet being at odds with Clora Lee, left the boy feeling like life, was no more then just another stinging blow from Mrs. Arnold's riding crop.

"I's uh can take them sacks na, if n you's want me to," Cowayne said to Sally, as he tried to find a way out of the trap, his birth mother had laid for him.

By the time Cowayne gathered up the sacks and headed for the old barn, Clora Lee's eyes were locked on him. And as she waited for him to say, come on Lee, he went right on torturing her with his silence.

"You's wait," Clora Lee said, forgetting what she had stated just a few minutes earlier.

Cowayne came to a halt, as if he were a soldier in the white man's army.

"Come on," Clora Lee said, as she came along side of him. "You don't want me with ya no mo?" she asked, as they headed in the direction of the old barn.

"Lee, you's know I's want ya to come," Cowayne replied, even though he had yet to look at her.

"Then why you's ain't ask me?"

"Cause I's uh thought, you's wanted be round them females."

"I's uh wanna be with you to, but you's acting like that old dog, that up and died last year," Clora Lee said rather sadly.

With nothing left to do but shake her head, Sistah nor the other females could believe their eyes. And no sooner then the females started their laughing, as if they were a bunch of cackling hens, Sistah cut her eyes at old Mae. For the old female was laughing the loudest.

"Sistah, you's can't blame Mae for that," Isabella said, while laughing as well.

"I's uh gon skin that boy of yo's, and you's gon be crying," Sistah said, trying to fight off old Mae's antics.

"Na Sistah, what I's do?" old Mae laughed.

And as the old female held the look of an innocent angel, Sistah knew she was as guilty, as Clora Lee's lie. And that was why Sistah sat sulking, as old Mae had the other females laughing so hard, many of them ended up in tears.

"You's mad at me?" Clora Lee asked Cowayne, as they took the horses out to graze.

"No, I's uh ain't mad at ya."

"I's sorry, for this morning," Clora Lee said sadly.

"And I's sorry, for trying to make ya eat worms," Cowayne replied with a smile.

Clora Lee couldn't help but to embrace Cowayne's joke. For the teen knew she was truly blessed, to have such a boy to care for her. And as she stood behind him, with her arms wrapped around his waist, Clora Lee softly asked Cowayne about his day.

"We's ain't do nothing, but go get some of them bullets, and put um behind the barn," Cowayne said, causing Clora Lee to turn him loose.

"You's ain't scared, he's gon talk?" Clora Lee asked, while taking hold of the tie down straps, to the four horses that she was walking.

"Lee, he's gotta know, if n we's gon take um with us," Cowayne said, as he rubbed the face of a brown mare.

After releasing the tie down straps just as fast as she gathered them up, Clora Lee stepped in front of Cowayne with a smile on her face. And as she placed her arms around his waist for the second time, the teen said, "I's uh love's ya. I's uh love ya with all my heart."

"I's uh know," Cowayne replied, spinning out of her grasp.

To see Cowayne, remove himself from her arms, made Clora Lee feel a touch of emptiness in her soul. Yet some how, she knew Cowayne would not seek another to end his suffering, as the other females suggested he would. For they didn't know Cowayne the way she and Sistah knew him. And they weren't there to see his face, when he told her to run from that stinking Reb. How the fear in his eyes told Clora Lee, he would much rather die, then to see any harm come her way. Oh no, her Cowayne would never seek another, and Clora Lee would stake their lives on it. And that she would, do with out an ounce of fear, or regret. For Clora Lee knew, she had what most females would gladly trade their souls for. She had someone to love her, far more then he could ever fear, that ugly thing call death.

Chapter 17

Twinkle's

One day when Clora Lee was looking for Cowayne and Matthew, she spotted Effie clutching a bundle, while approaching Joan, who was sitting in front of the woodshed. And the little work a lot, was sitting on the poorly built stool, which Dew Dap had made for her. Yet Joan appeared to love the thing, more then Mrs. Arnold cared for all of her fancy furniture, which once crowded the large mansion. And for all the work Dew Dap put in to making the dang blasted thing, Clora Lee couldn't figure out how it ended up so ugly. She could see the teen in her mind. Day in, and day out, for over a week, the boy worked tirelessly, cutting, chipping and scrapping the wood, he had taken from an old fallen tree. And if Dew Dap didn't worry Pleasant darn near to death over that unsightly thing, he didn't do anything at all.

FEELING THAT HER GRANDMOTHER was up to no good, Clora Lee sought to do a little investigating. So with the cunningness of an old wood rat, Clora Lee made her way around the yard, hoping to catch Effie off guard. And as she ducked behind the smokehouse, Clora Lee could see Joan rising to her feet, as if she was expecting trouble out of the executrixes. And when Clora Lee saw the little stump move her lips, she knew time was running out for her to help Joan.

"I can see, you are dead set on staying out here," Effie said to Joan.

"Hear I's is, and here I's gon stay," the girl replied.

"I figured as much, so I brought you a few things," Effie said, holding out the bundle, she held in her hand.

"I's uh don't need, nothing from that house," Joan snarled, as she refused to take the bundle.

"I never picked you for being a fool," Effie said, as she stared down on the girl, with her forever blank stare.

"I's uh don't need ya Misses, coming out here taking nothing, from me and my girls," Joan said, standing her ground.

"And if you don't take this, then what are you going to have? Nothing! Nothing but two needy girls, and a struggling slave," Effie said harshly.

Before Joan knew it, she was up in arms over Effie's statement. With fire in her eyes, and Hell in her heart, Joan sought to tell the preferred house girl a thing or two. "Ya Misses things, ain't no mo mine, then them dresses my girls got on. But as long as I's got breath in me, theys ain't gon go dirty or naked, cause I's uh could drop a stitch, better then many. And as for as my struggling slave, all he's knows ha to do, is keep us eating. And when night come, I's uh ain't gotta be in no rotation, cause he's makes me whole," Joan said, as she stood with a great deal of pride. "And if n I's uh hear you's said any thing bout him, so help me Effie. I's uh, I's uh," Joan shouted with her fist raised, as if she were about to strike the favorite house girl.

"Now you listen to me. You take this, because you will need it, when the time comes. And don't you use it, a day before it's time," Effie said, holding the bundle out, as if she were offering a gift to a queen.

"I's uh done…"

Before Joan could finish her statement, Effie had stuffed the bundle in her gut. And as Joan grunted while bending over, hoping to cushion the thrusting impact, she was a little too late. For Effie was far too quick. And as the bundle took the air from Joan's lungs, Effie placed a hand on the tiny teen's shoulder, and guided her down to the stool that was born out of love, as well as hard work.

"Well I's uh reckon, I's uh be going, na," Effie said, in her best slave voice.

Like every one else, Joan knew Effie only spoke in that manner around whites. But Joan didn't see any white folks, which started her to wondering. What was Effie trying to prove, by using such a tone with her? Joan smelled a rat, and it wasn't under the woodshed.

"I's uh reckon, she's want you to go back to that house," Clora Lee said, stepping from behind the woodshed.

Seeing Clora Lee, explained everything. Right away, Joan knew Effie wasn't talking like a slave for her benefit. For Effie was sending a message to Clora Lee, telling her grand-daughter, she had a lot to learn, before mastering the craft of their ancestors. And who was better to send such a message to the girl then her grandmother, seeing that she could appear, and disappear just as good as Nelson, a art, Clora Lee had yet to learn, let alone master.

"What ya'll was talking bout?" Clora Lee asked.

"We's wasn't talking," Joan snarled, while walking over to check on the girls.

Hearing Joan's reply, Clora Lee quickly regretted not being able to get behind the woodshed in time. For the teen desperately wanted to hear what Effie had to say. Yet something told the girl, what ever her grandmother said, it wasn't good. For Clora Lee believed Effie only had kind words for whites. And the way the girl saw it, a blind man could see, Joan had no chance of being white, or pert near white.

"I's uh don't want you's girls, to ever let folks say bad things bout Dew Dap, you's hear me? Cause he's do too much for us. And we's knows what we's is to him, don't we?" Joan asked the little girls.

Bessie and Madeline quickly gave Joan their typical response, which brought Clora Lee back to that uh huh day. Then Clora Lee heard the sweetest thing anyone could ever hear, when Bessie gave her reply to Joan's question, asking the little girl, what was she to Dew Dap?

"I's uh his sunshine," Bessie replied.

"And what you's is?" Joan asked Madeline.

"Night, sunshine," the little dumpling said with a great deal of excitement in her voice.

"And I's uh the star, that twinkle in his eyes," Joan added, nearly bringing Clora Lee to tears.

Before Clora Lee had a chance to digest what Dew Dap's little family had said, Joan picked up the bundle, and headed for the fire with it. But when Clora Lee saw what Joan was about to do, she grabbed the girl, with hopes, of talking some sense into her.

"You's let me go," Joan shouted.

"I's uh do no such thing," Clora Lee replied. "I's uh ain't gon let ya burn this stuff, fo you's look at it."

"I's done told her, I's uh ain't want it."

"But you's don't know what it is."

"And I's uh don't care," Joan said, as she tried her best to pull the bundle free from Clora Lee's grasp.

"Na Joan, I's uh don't like Effie, no more then I's like a polecat. But I's uh ain't gon let you's burn this stuff, fo you's look at it," Clora Lee argued.

"Then you's keep it," Joan shouted as she released the bundle, and headed for the woodshed.

Clora Lee cut Joan off, before she could enter the small dying structure. "Na Joan, I's done see'd ha them boys look at ya, when you's got them fine dresses on. Na after what you's done said, I's uh think, Dew Dap should see ya in them fine dresses to, twinkle."

No matter how hard she tried, Clora Lee couldn't stop herself from smiling, as she stood waiting for Joan to open her mouth. But Joan had no intentions of helping a friend, who was fighting a losing battle. And Joan wasn't doing any better, as she stood with her mouth, just a twisting and turning, while trying to out last Clora Lee. But then like two little girls playing dare, they both took to laughing at the same time.

"What you laughing at?" Clora Lee asked through her laughter.

"I's uh laughing at you," Joan said laughing. "Na why you's laughing?"

Clora Lee answered the girl with one word, "Twinkle."

Standing up straight, with her hands propped up on her hips, Joan said, "I's uh can be twinkle, if n I's want."

"You's already is." Clora Lee laughed, as she pointed to the two nice size melons, Joan carried around for breast.

After pushing her chest out further then it already sat, Joan shook her breast proudly. And the girls may not have noticed it, but in her strange unpredictable way, Effie had given them another reason to laugh.

That evening, as Joan and Clora Lee took the girls for their walk, they appeared to be closer then ever. With Joan holding Madeline's left hand, and Clora Lee gripping the little girl's right, the two young teens, lifted the little Night Sunshine up in the air every few steps. For it was a sight of pure happiness, and everyone saw it, including Mrs. Arnold, as she stood in the window with her two love girls.

"Weee," Joan said, as she and Clora Lee took Madeline for another ride through the air.

"I's uh tell ya, Joan. I's uh glad, you's my friend," Clora Lee said smiling.

"I's uh reckon, Jeremiah was right," Joan replied.

"Bout what?" Clora Lee asked, looking puzzled.

"Fo he's left, he's said, I's uh should get to know ya, cause we's part of uh plan."

"What plan?"

"I's uh don't know, but he's was always talking to Effie bout something, when he's was teaching me to read and write."

"He's teach you's ha to read and write?" Clora Lee asked, as if she didn't hear her friend correctly.

"Every time he's teach you," Joan replied, leaving Clora Lee speechless.

Clora Lee became rather quiet, as she and Joan took Madeline for another ride through the air. And as they brought the soon to be five year old back down to earth, an old female who was sitting on a bench behind the mansion, called out to Joan. Even though Clora Lee knew the old female, she couldn't recall a single time, when they had ever spoken to each other.

"Ha you's doing, child?" the old female asked, as she came up on the girls.

"I's uh just fine," Joan replied.

"Child, I's uh tell ya, na. We's house slaves, took you's to be gone from here, when the Misses chunk ya out," the old female said, which started Clora Lee to thinking.

"Well me and my girls uh be just fine, as long as we's got Dew Dap and our friends," Joan replied, looking at Clora Lee.

"I's uh reckon so, cause I's hear that young n, follow ya round, like a calf do its ma," the old female said, as she tried to touch Madeline.

But being that the little girl didn't know the old female, she quickly ducked behind Joan.

"You's ain't got no call to be scared, Dumpling," Joan said, caressing Madeline to her body.

"She's don't like nobody but Joan, and Sally," Bessie said, as she stared at the old female.

"Bessie," Joan said softly.

"Well I's reckon, she's right," Clora Lee said, as she rushed to the aid, of little Miss. Sunshine.

Feeling she had done something wrong, Bessie put her head down in shame. But Joan wasn't about to let her big little helper stay sad. So kneeling down, Joan wrapped her arms around Bessie with the tenderness that was meant for an angel.

"I's uh gon cry, if n my little helper don't smile," Joan said sadly.

After putting on a perfect performance, while pretending to cry, Joan sparked a joyful reaction out of Bessie.

"I's uh smiling," Bessie said, while sporting a big bright smile.

Joan ended her performance, and immediately began to kiss Bessie wildly on the jaw, neck, and forehead. And with the sudden show of affection, Bessie had no other choice but to start laughing. And when Joan tickled her big little helper, Bessie wiggled like a fish on dry land. But before Madeline could join in on the fun, Effie sent her voice roaring across the yard.

"What are you doing?" Effie shouted, as if she was mad at the old female.

"I's uh gotta go, child," the old female whispered, then shuffled off in the direction of the backdoor.

Clora Lee stared at her grandmother, as if she were a vile creature, cast out of heaven on a cold dark night. Down to earth she fell, with only one purpose. To make every slave's life a living Hell, which made Clora Lee, look upon Effie with abhorrence.

"Come on Joan, we's gotta go," Clora Lee said, as she thought about doing the unspeakable.

Knowing that Clora Lee had ill feelings for her grandmother, Joan took the girls, and hastily led them away. Yet Clora Lee on the other hand, moved rather slowly, while never losing sight of Effie and the old female. For the girl, was waiting to see what would be the aging female's fate.

"You's can come on, Effie ain't gon hurt her none," Joan said.

"Ha you's know?"

"I's uh can't tell ya," Joan said, as though she had something to fear.

In an instant, Clora Lee felt something ripped through her insides. "Wait!" Clora Lee shouted, as she turned and ran toward the back door.

"Clora Lee, you's come back here," Joan yelled.

But Clora Lee didn't stop, as she went right on running, until her eyes gave way to Effie escorting the old female through the backdoor.

"Come on, Clora Lee, we's gotta go," Joan said, tugging on the girl's arm.

But Clora Lee wasn't about to leave, until she found out what Effie was trying to hide. Even if that meant, she had to stand in the shadow of the large house all night, then so be it. Yet Nelson had other plans for his niece. For the often disappearing one, appeared out of no where, to grab Clora Lee and dart off with her.

"What was that," Mrs. Arnold asked.

"Just two slaves, fighting over a couple of worms, ma'am," Effie said, then led the old female away.

When Clora Lee finally got her feet back on the ground, she quickly made an attempt to return to the mansion, but Nelson grabbed her. But Clora Lee wasn't about to let Nelson, or anyone else stop her, from finding out what Effie was trying to hide. So like the hell cat that she was, the girl took to fighting her uncle, even though he never raised a hand to defend himself.

"Na you's listen to me, Clora Lee. You's can't make it hard for her. The Misses uh kill her, and old Mae too. And she's uh kill Cowayne, and Sistah," Nelson said calmly, but with a sense of desperation in his voice.

"Is she's Effie ma?" Clora Lee shouted.

"You's keep yo's voice down," Joan said softly.

"She's ain't nothing but an old slave," Nelson replied.

"We's ain't slaves, no mo," Clora Lee shouted, while ignoring Joan's warning.

"Clora Lee, we's friends, ain't we?" Joan asked.

Clora Lee found herself looking at the girl, as if they were bitter enemies again. But the look on Joan's face, told Clora Lee something was seriously wrong, so she nodded her head yes, and waited to see where the question would take them.

"Then I's uh give ya my word. If n we's ever leave here, I's uh gon tell ya, who's she is. Na you's gotta stop, fo the Misses kill her," Joan cried.

Feeling she was about to do more harm then good, Clora Lee became a totally different person, which prompted Nelson to slowly release her. But Nelson wasn't quite ready to trust the teens on their own, so he sought the help, of two perfect little angels.

"You's girls, gon be all right," Nelson asked Bessie and Madeline.

"Uh hu," Bessie said, bringing a smile to Nelson's face.

Knelling down, Nelson said, "I's uh want you's two, to keep ya eyes on them young ns for me."

"We's will," Bessie replied, as if she and Madeline were up for the task.

"Good, cause I's uh gotta go," Nelson replied.

When Nelson was gone, Joan and the girls walked Clora Lee to the female shed. There she saw Dew Dap sitting with Pleasant, Cowayne, and Matthew. Joan walked over and leaned up against Dew Dap, while Madeline crawled up in his lap. And knowing that his girls loved him, the boy didn't say a word, as he just gave Joan a look of approval. And as they went about listening to Sistah give another stellar performance, Joan started picking in Dew Dap' hair, which made all eyes fall on her. But Joan's attention quickly went to

Bessie, who had taken a seat on the ground next to Matthew. And right away, the teen began to think like a mother, as she worried for Bessie's young fragile heart.

With her head resting on old Mae's shoulder, Clora Lee started crying. For her day had been long and hard, which made the young off breed female ask herself, was life truly worth all of its troubles?

"What's ailing ya, child?" old Mae whispered, as she gave Clora Lee a gentle jolt with her large arm.

"I's uh all right," the girl whispered in return.

"Then why's you's crying?"

Clora Lee cast her eyes on Joan and Dew Dap, sending the old female in the wrong direction.

"Child, ya'll got pleanty nough time for that," old Mae whispered with a smile.

Clora Lee gave old Mae a kiss on the jaw, right before returning her eyes to the fire, as she enjoyed a slow end to a disturbing day.

The next morning, Clora Lee found herself, tied to a much bigger problem then the one she had went to bed with. From the moment the girl opened her eyes, all she heard was Matthew. For the little boy had started in on his big sister, and didn't let up. And as Clora Lee washed her face, Matthew was right there, begging like a hungry hound. And when the girl went about skinning the three coons, that were to be their breakfast, Matthew was still on his job. And by the time Clora Lee had gotten down to roast the coons over an open fire, she was well in to praying. For her little brother had no intentions of letting up, as he went on and on, for that which his big sister could not give him?

By the time Matthew took to eating, it didn't take Clora Lee long, to figure out why her prayers were never answered. For the little boy was able to pull off breathing, begging, and eating at the same time. It had to be the greatest achievement known to mankind, as Sistah, old Mae, and Isabella, laughed all through breakfast. And when Joan and the girls showed up, Matthew acted as though Bessie was a total stranger, as he continued to beg his sister to no end.

Finding herself trapped by Matthew's begging, Clora Lee took to walking, hoping it would obtain her a little peace and quiet. Yet peace never came, as Matthew followed his big sister step for step, even though she did her best to ignore him.

"You's stop talking to me, and I's mean it," Clora Lee shouted.

But Matthew went right on asking Clora Lee the very same question, the girl had been hearing all morning long. And when Clora Lee saw Cowayne coming toward them, she couldn't remember a happier sighting of the boy.

"Cowayne, tell Clora Lee to let me go with ya," Matthew cried.

"Matthew, you's ain't got no call, to ask Cowayne to make me do nothing," Clora Lee said, as she no longer shouted.

"I's uh can't take ya na, but I's uh gon take ya later, when me and Dew Dap go check our traps," Cowayne said.

"Can he's take me Clora Lee, can he?" Matthew begged.

"If n you's leave me be," Clora Lee said, looking at Cowayne in fear.

"You's gone watch over Joan, and them girls for Dew Dap," Cowayne said to Matthew, hoping the chore would keep the little titan out of Clora Lee's hair.

After watching Matthew run off with a happy heart, Cowayne asked Clora Lee why she was looking so fearful.

"I's uh ain't gon be with ya," Clora Lee said, looking as if she wanted to cry.

"Na Lee, you's knows, I's uh gon be with Dew Dap."

Cowayne knew their problem ran deeper then the mere fact, of who was going to be with him. For Clora Lee, it had everything to do with the two of them being apart. In the pass five years, the two had become inseparable, and Clora Lee didn't see any reason for the sudden change. And as she stood over Cowayne, stroking his face with her hand, Clora Lee could feel her body start to tingle. Then like a lightning bug flashing its glowing light, the teen saw herself standing in front of Cowayne, the way she had seen Mrs. Arnold stand before Jonathan on many occasions. And the thought of Cowayne doing such a thing to her, started Clora Lee's body to moisten.

"I's uh gotta go, Lee" Cowayne said, as he stood up.

Even though Clora Lee didn't understand why Cowayne was dead set on getting every bullet off of that stupid wagon, she still supported him. And as she sashayed toward the female shed, with a troubling look on her face, Clora Lee changed her mind, and headed for Joan. For she felt her and Joan should stay close to each other, in case something should happen to their boys. Yet Clora Lee didn't know what she would do, if darkness came over the plantation, and neither Dew Dap nor Cowayne had made it home. And how could she tell Joan, Dew Dap would not be coming back, just because Cowayne wanted to get some stupid bullets. The young teen could only hope for the best, as she came upon the woodshed.

"I's uh reckon, you's gon work, till we's put you's up yonder, with old Pete," Clora Lee said, as Joan was smack dab in the middle of her daily routine.

The forever working female, was washing the cloths, her little family had worn the day before. And Joan was bent over the leaky wooden tube, just a rubbing and splashing, like she was enjoying herself.

"Joan, if n you's ain't the washing-est female I's ever come across," Clora Lee said, standing next to Madeline.

"Well we's ain't got clothing like the Misses, and her young ns do," Joan stated proudly.

"Well I's reckon, we's all can't lie around like fat hogs, neither," Clora Lee replied, hoping to get a smile out of her friend.

"Na Clora Lee, you's knows, that ain't no way, for you's to go round talking bout ya Misses and her young ns," Joan said, while giving Clora Lee the smile, she had been waiting for.

"Well I's uh just hush my mouth, then," Clora Lee said, as she to, sported a big bright smile.

"And I's uh reckon, it uh be uh good thing, fo's that fat hog hears ya," Joan said, looking at Clora Lee.

It didn't take the girls long to start laughing at themselves, thus bringing Clora Lee's sadness to an end.

"Joan, I's uh reckon, I's can't do no wrong, when I's with ya," Clora Lee said after calming down.

"Na Clora Lee, what kind uh friend I's uh be, if n I's uh let ya do wrong?"

Clora Lee didn't answer Joan, as she took to admiring the wonderful job, the little stump, had done with Madeline's hair. And Clora Lee would have went right on admiring, the beautiful work, if it were not for Joan redirecting her attention.

"You's see what I's uh done to they's puppets?" Joan asked.

"I's uh don't know ha you's do it," Clora Lee said, as she took a look at Madeline's hand puppet.

"I's uh making my dumplings a D-O-L-L," Joan said, keeping the girls clueless to their up coming gift.

Clora Lee nearly fell flat on her face, when she heard Joan spell the word, doll. "Ha you's knows ha to spell?"

"Na Clora Lee, I's uh reckon, you's don't listen to nothing I's say," Joan snapped, as she stopped her washing. "I's uh told ya yesterday, Jeremiah taught me, just like he's taught you."

Clora Lee didn't totally believe Joan, and she had a good enough reason. Even though the two females hadn't been hanging together that long, she knew from the look on Joan's face, the teen was hiding something. So with that something on her mind, Clora Lee went and stood next to her friend before speaking again.

"Why Jeremiah, teach ya ha to spell?" Clora Lee asked.

"Cause he's taught me to read. But we's still don't know ha to spell Cowayne."

"Ha you's knows bout that?"

"Cause I's heard, Jeremiah talking bout it."

"With who?"

"I's uh can't tell ya."

"Well you's better tell me, fo I's uh go to that house, and tell the Misses, you's call her a hog," Clora Lee said.

"Well I's uh reckon, if n you's aiming to get ya self kill, then me and the girls, uh watch ya," Joan said, as her and Clora Lee wrung out a cotton sack dress.

"Na Joan, ha we's gon be best friends, if n you's gon let me go get myself kill?" Clora Lee grunted, as they tried to squeeze every drop of water, out of the homemade dress.

"We's is, and I's uh ain't gon let ya go wrong. But if n you's dead set on being one of the Misses girls, then I's uh ain't got no call to stop ya," Joan said, after shaking the dress out.

"Oh Misses. Oh Misses," Clora Lee said, as she strutted over to a tree, and laid the dress across one of its branches.

"Na girl, you's come over here, and sit beside ya Misses," Joan said, doing her best to imitate Mrs. Arnold.

The two friends couldn't do nothing but laugh, as they realized how silly Mrs. Arnold and her two slave girls were. And neither Clora Lee nor Joan could see them selves, living such a make believe life, in a world of cruelty and pain. Nor could either of the teens, be as loyal, as Mrs. Arnold's girls. And if Clora Lee had her way, Mrs. Arnold would be just as dead, as that old stinking Reb, she killed.

After a morning of working and having fun, Clora Lee and Joan spotted their reasons for living. And Joan, who was already steaming, didn't care if the boys were returning with enough food, to feed the whole plantation for days. For Dew Dap looked a sight, which made Joan madder then Hell, and that old Devil himself. But as for Clora Lee, all she could do was shake her head, being that Matthew had both Dew Dap and Cowayne beat. For the little boy had the catch of the day, thrown over his shoulder, as if he were a happy go lucky wanderer. Yet Clora Lee couldn't understand why Matthew of all people, was carrying the fish, seeing how he hated water, far worst then any cat.

"Na you's see why I's uh wash every day?" Joan asked.

"I's uh reckon, you's uh be washing tomorrow to," Clora Lee replied angrily.

"Clora Lee. Clora Lee. You's should uh see'd me. I's uh pull um in, all by myself," Matthew boasted, as he ran toward his big sister.

"Don't you's come near me, and I's uh mean it," Clora Lee shouted, as she hid behind Joan.

"Clora Lee, if n you's don't get from behind me, I's uh gon hold ya, so Matthew can hug ya," Joan yelled, as she tried her best, to shake free of the girl.

Bessie, who had always seen the sight of Matthew as a wonderful thing, was left without any reason to smile. For the little girl stood close to Joan and Clora Lee, hoping the boy would just go away.

"You's stink," Bessie said to Matthew.

"Na dumpling, we's don't talk bad to um, when theys come home like that. We's don't talk to um uh tall," Joan said, then led the girls in doing an about face.

"Joan, if n we's ain't go out and get dirty, then what we's gon eat?" Dew Dap asked, as he stood looking at the back of his female's head.

"Na Dew Dap, don't you's go getting riled with me, cause we's knows ya'll gotta go out, so we can cook. But na you's gotta go down to that there creek," Joan said, looking over her shoulder at the teen.

"Joan I's knows, I's gotta wash," Dew Dap replied, giving the girls a reason to look at each other.

"Matthew, you's go take them fish over to that there barn, and tell Pleasant, theys for them house slaves. Then you's come back here, so you's can go down to that creek with Cowayne and Dew Dap," Clora Lee said, as she waited for the little dirt king to start complaining.

But no sooner then his big sister finished talking, Matthew took off running, while leaving the word, okay, echoing joyfully in the wind. And for Clora Lee to see her little brother so eager to take a bath, she could have beaten her own bottom, for not letting him go with Cowayne much sooner.

"Come on, Cowayne, lets go tie our critters up, so we's can get down to that old creek," Dew Dap said, as he started for the back wall of the woodshed.

Cowayne gave Clora Lee the four gutted coons, and left her once again, without saying a word. And the look on Clora Lee's face, told Joan, her friend was in need of a bit of help.

"He's can't wait forever," Joan said.

"Ha you's knows, we's ain't did it already?" Clora Lee grumbled, as she kept her back to Joan.

"Cause we's ain't talk about it."

"You's ain't tell me."

"I's uh told ya, when I's uh told my ma, and you's knows I's did."

"Well I's uh still, don't know ha you's do it."

"Na you's done see'd the Misses do it enough, to know ha to do it," Joan snapped, after yanking Clora Lee around.

"Joan, I's tell ya the truth. You's bout the slipperiest fish ever caught," Clora Lee said of the girl's reply.

"Na I's uh done told ya, it hurt, but you's uh get use to it."

"Is you's, use to it?" Clora Lee asked, looking at Joan.

"Well I's uh reckon, my day coming, when I's uh ain't gotta worry bout waking up my girls," Joan replied.

Even though she didn't know a thing about the sexual part of love, Clora Lee couldn't help but to wonder what the girls had to do with Joan getting use to the pain. And for that reason, Clora Lee looked at her friend, with a great deal of skepticisms. For Clora Lee didn't hear Madeline and Bessie saying they were hurting, because Joan was hurting. And that thing, about it feel so good, you can't feel the pain, until its over, wasn't a good sell for Clora Lee either. For the teen had spent too many nights, hearing her mother and Ella cry out in pain, from Big Willie's violent grunting. And if Joan were to tell her that lie again, she would surely ask the little stick of dynamite about Mrs. Arnold and Jonathan. That should be proof enough, that no female ever get use to a male's grunting. For Clora Lee, it had to be love, to make the female go through so much pain, for a whole lot of nothing. Be it love for the male, or loving what he can do for her. But what ever the reason, if it wasn't a fair exchange, then one of the two was coming up short, and Clora Lee knew she would never do that to Cowayne.

That evening after finishing her walk with Joan and the girls, Clora Lee found a bit of comfort, in ending her day with Cowayne. The two sat in their favorite evening spot, staring out at the darkness, as if it held some great magical secret to the troubled world, which they found them selves in. Yet there was no secret to solving what was troubling the two young lovers, as they sat on the fence without saying a word.

Feeling she had to do something to break their silence, Clora Lee placed her left hand in front of Cowayne's eyes. But when Cowayne didn't respond to her playful act, Clora Lee began to slowly move her hand closer to the boy's face, until it touched his nose. Still Cowayne didn't speak, as he continued to sit in silence. A silence, Clora Lee knew she had to break, one way or the other. And Clora Lee felt old Mae had the best trick, for what was ailing her lover. So with her thumb and index finger, Clora Lee squeezed Cowayne's nose, cutting off his breathing, as she waited for him to breath out of his mouth.

"What you's doing?" Cowayne asked, before taking a breath.

"Who you's thinking bout?"

Cowayne smiled a suspicious smile, as he turned his head to keep from laughing. But if the teen thought he could avoid answering Clora Lee with such a primitive tactic, then the poor boy didn't know a thing about females. With her right arm wrapped around his head,

Clora Lee squeezed as hard as she could, with hopes, of forcing the teen to surrender. But it was safe to say, Clora Lee knew what was about to happen next. Cowayne tipped her backward, causing the girl to scream out.

"Cowayne, you's bet not make us fall," Clora Lee shouted after her loud scream.

With his arms holding Clora Lee tightly, Cowayne jumped, thus landing them both safely on the ground. But through the whole ordeal, Clora Lee went right on holding on to his head. And with their feet flat on the ground, Clora Lee did her best to apply even more pressure, as she held his head trapped between her arm and right breast.

"You's had enough?" Clora Lee asked joyfully.

Cowayne had long recognized the opportunity that came from being trapped in such a welcome position. Yet the polite young male never thought of taking advantage of the situation, until he heard the off beat question. With his head only needing to be adjusted slightly, Cowayne quickly maneuvered it to suit, what he saw as a fruit begging to be plucked. And as he came face to face with her right breast, Cowayne began to nibble away at its nipple.

"You's stop," Clora Lee shouted, as she took to slapping Cowayne on the head.

After quickly covering up, Cowayne allowed Clora Lee to slap him at will, as he laughed while moving about. And Clora Lee never let up, as she stayed with him every step of the way. Then out of the blue, Cowayne sent the cat and mouse game in a different direction. And with the cards in his hand, it was Cowayne's turn to try and force Clora Lee in to a submission. Yet Clora Lee wasn't about to let her friend know how good his little act made her feel.

"What you's got, in yo's pocket?" Clora Lee asked, as she found herself trapped in the warm embrace.

Seeing that Clora Lee was about to use her hand to seek out the hidden object, Cowayne moved away just before she got the chance to touch his firmly erected cock.

"What you's hiding from me?" Clora Lee asked, as if she didn't know what Cowayne had to offer her.

"Nothing," he replied with a smile.

"Then you let me see it."

Cowayne stood confused, seeing that he didn't know how to react to the girl's demand. But Clora Lee wasn't about to let her friend figure out his next move. For Cowayne had gotten his quick feel, and Clora Lee was hoping she could do the same.

"Cowayne, you's come back here," Clora Lee said, as she chased after him.

With speed being Cowayne's biggest advantage over his Lee, it had to be obvious, how she was able to catch him so easily. And once Clora Lee got her left arm around Cowayne's waist, she ran her free hand in his right pocket. There, she found a few specks of lint, and a nice size hole. A hole, which allowed Clora Lee free access, to the silky skin, that covered his extreamly hard club.

"I's uh wanna see it," she said, holding on to the severely erected cock.

"You's done see'd it."

"I's uh wanna see it again," Clora Lee cried, as she started for the buttons on Cowayne's pants.

Before Clora Lee could get to that which she was seeking, they heard a familiar voice roar across the night air. And along with Sistah's voice, came another disappointment. It was as if the words, Clora Lee, you's come here, was created just so the two lovers could live their lives at the door step of heartache and misery.

Chapter 18

No More Rooster

After her night in the dark with Cowayne, Clora Lee found herself burden with Sistah for nine long days. No matter the time of day or night, Clora Lee couldn't move or turn around without stumbling over Sistah. There was no escaping the angry motherly figure. For even when Clora Lee took her evening stroll with Joan and the girls, Sistah was there. And no matter how hard Clora Lee tried, Sistah stuck to her like a leech, and that nearly drove the teen crazy. But Sistah was determined to make sure Clora Lee kept her promise, even if it meant turning the two of them in to enemies.

On the tenth day of Sistah's around the clock guard duty, the misfortunate female went about her business. For Clora Lee had safely obtained her monthly, which made Sistah one happy female. And to enjoy her happiness, Sistah went straight to the old barn, where she spent the whole day with Pleasant.

With her body temporarily unfit for Cowayne, Clora Lee sat in the doorway of the female shed, cramping, as if she were the one who had eaten that stupid apple. And when Matthew paid her a visit, Clora Lee was as grouchy, as a hungry bear. But the boy was far too young, to know anything about his sister's problem, as he tried to strike up a conversation with her.

"Why you's ain't gone with Cowayne?" Matthew asked.

Agitated by her position, Clora Lee responded in kind. "When you's gon stop asking so many questions?" she growled.

Before the little boy could drop his head in sadness, old Mae spoke up. For the old slave was sitting in her usual spot, pretending to be asleep. But knowing Clora Lee didn't mean any harm, old Mae felt it would be wise, to set the matter straight.

"Come here, Matthew," the old female said softly.

After taking a few steps, Matthew found himself in old Mae's arms, receiving a loving hug.

"You's member, I's told ya, females sometime get as bad, as uh dog on uh bone?" old Mae asked.

"Uh huh," Matthew replied, nodding his head, but still looking sad.

"Clora Lee gon be like that old dog, for a spell, so you's run alone, and let her get some rest," old Mae said, as she hugged the little boy.

Even though Matthew was willing to do as the old female said, he still couldn't bring himself to raise his head. For the boy wanted so much, to be able to hang out with his big sister, no matter the price he had to pay for such a privilege. And seeing her brother in such a sad state, Clora Lee set her problem aside, with hopes of cheering him up.

"Matthew," she called out softly.

"Huh," Matthew replied, turning around.

"Come here," Clora Lee said, just as soft as old Mae.

Matthew walked over to his big sister just as slow, as he was walking away. But when he finally made it to Clora Lee, she took her hand and gently raised his head.

"You's wanna know uh secret?" Clora Lee asked, in the sweetest of tones.

"Uh huh."

"We's gon be alright."

"We's is?"

"Uh huh, and you's gon grow up to be a good looking fellow. And all the girls gon come round me, so theys can look at ya," Clora Lee said with a smile.

"I's uh ain't gon be with no girls, I's uh gon be checking traps with Cowayne," Matthew cried with all honesty.

Old Mae and Clora Lee smiled, knowing the little boy's life was going to change, whether he wanted it to or not. And the way Clora Lee handled the situation, made old Mae proud, seeing how the teen had filled her mother's shoes with ease.

"Come on, we's gotta go find Cowayne," Clora Lee said, as she stood up.

After giving old Mae a hug, the sister and brother set out to find the third member of their group, before he ultimately found them. And as old Mae watched the children, as they walked away, she knew Clora Lee was right. They were going to be just fine, and she didn't have to worry about their future any more, which set the old female's mind at ease.

When Clora Lee and Matthew found Cowayne, the three of them went to visit Joan and Dew Dap. They found Joan cleaning the wood shed, while Dew Dap was skinning a coon. As for the girls, they were playing joyfully with their hand puppets.

"Joan, I's uh reckon, we's gotta tie ya down, to stop ya from working," Clora Lee said, as she brought her feet to a stop.

"I's uh done told her, she's gotta get some rest," Dew Dap barked, as he went on skinning the coon.

"Na Dew Dap, ya'll ain't gon bother me, cause I's uh got work to do," Joan said, while stopping just long enough, to wipe the sweat from her forehead.

"Don't worry, Clora Lee, I's uh gon sit on her," Dew Dap said, as he looked over his shoulder at Joan.

"You's ain't gon do no such thing, cause my girls ain't gon let ya. Ain't that right, girls?" Joan asked with a smile.

With the girls giving credence to Joan's statement, Dew Dap knew he didn't have a chance in Hell, of carrying out his threat. And Clora Lee, who started the whole thing, was enjoying the girls abandoning their brother for the greater good. And someday, when they are fine young ladies, Dew Dap will thank her, for bringing Joan into their lives, Clora Lee thought to her self.

Later that night, Dew Dap saw the affects of Joan's self impose work ethics. For when he awaken to take the girls out, Dew Dap found it hard to get Joan to open her eyes.

"Joan," he whispered.

With Joan being in a deep sleep from months of working until reaching exhaustion, Dew Dap was unable to wake her up. But the concerned young male knew if they didn't take the girls out, Joan would be angry with herself in the morning. So with the helpful female well being on his mind, Dew Dap took a deep breath, then gathered up his sisters, and took them out by himself.

After laying his sisters back down, and closing the door, Dew Dap resumed his spot next to Joan. And with his cold nose on the girl's forehead, Dew Dap gave her a light kiss, before drifting back off to sleep.

The next morning when Dew Dap left the woodshed, he was hoping Joan would go on sleeping until around mid morning. But when he and Cowayne made it back, Dew Dap found Joan hard at work, plaiting Madeline's hair.

"What I's told ya," Dew Dap said, as he and Cowayne caught sight of the little work uh lot.

"I's uh reckon, she's want them girls to be pretty."

"But she's ain't got enough sleep, to do a bird," Dew Dap cried with concern.

"You's gotta learn, when female's get uh notion to do some thing, theys gotta see it through, even if n it kill um," Cowayne said, before he disappeared, leaving Dew Dap to deal with his problem.

"Joan, I's uh thought you's was gon be sleep," Dew Dap said, as he tied the coon to the woodshed.

"Ha I's uh gon sleep, when that old rooster, crowing like theys ain't no tomorrow?"

"But you's ain't get enough sleep."

Hearing the firmness in her brother's voice, Madeline laid up against Joan, as if she were afraid. And being the motherly figure that she was, Joan knelt down and gave her little dumpling a great big hug.

"Na don't you's be worrying, cause Dew Dap ain't gon hurt me none, cause he's loves me," Joan said, making the girls laugh.

"I's uh loves ya?" Dew Dap asked, as he knelt down in front of Joan.

While stroking his face, Joan gave her heart stopping reply, "And I's uh gon be the only female, you's ever love."

In the most submissive manner, any male could surrender him self to a female, Dew Dap rested his large head upon her chest. And even though the boy didn't know the white man's true meaning for love, he knew Joan had given him another reason for waking up in the morning. Yet Dew Dap didn't know how to stop that old rooster from crowing. But as the boy could hear the beating of Joan's heart, he prayed for that old rooster to never crow again. And by the time Joan had gracefully kissed the wool on his head, he was determined to stop that old rooster from disturbing the only female he would ever love.

The next morning when Joan opened her eyes, she quickly went into a state of panic. Her girls were gone, and that sent Joan's heart to racing. She quickly made it to her knees, and in a state of fear, the girl pushed the old woodshed door open so hard, it slammed against the outer wall. But to Joan's surprise, the sun hit her like a charging bull. And along with the sudden burst of light, came a moment of temporary blindness. But Joan could hear her girls laughing, which told the motherly figure, they were all right. And by the time her eyes had adjusted to the sun light, Madeline was the first thing she saw.

"You's was sleeping," the little night sunshine said smiling.

"I's was sleeping?" Joan asked playfully.

"Uh huh," Madeline said, as she nodded her head, while leaning to one side.

After watching Madeline balance herself on one leg, Joan stepped out in to the late morning sun light to singing birds, and an abundance of life. And as she took to looking around the yard, Joan was hoping for a sign that would help her to determine the time of day. But after noticing a few house slaves walking about, as if they were a group of lonely lost sheep, the girl was still at a lost. So with no idea of the time, Joan scooped Madeline up in her arms, which brought her face to face with the woodshed. And noticing that the shadow was still on the west side of their sleeping quarters, the girl knew the day was still on the topside of high noon.

"Why you's ain't wake me up?" Joan asked, after walking over to where Dew Dap was sitting.

"Cause you's was sleeping."

"I's uh was sleeping, cause I's uh ain't hear that old rooster," Joan said, never looking at their fire.

"Cause he's ain't crow," Dew Dap said, never raising his head.

"I's uh reckon, he's tired to," Joan replied, while rubbing her nose against Madeline's face.

"He's over the fire," Madeline said, then laid her head on Joan, as if she had spoken out of turn.

"Who's over the fire," Joan asked.

"That old rooster," Bessie said, confirming Madeline's statement.

After walking over to the fire, Joan couldn't help but to notice that the rooster was slowly roasting, as if it were waiting for her to eat it. But the girl never touched the poor bird, as she took to looking at Dew Dap with a smile, while walking back to where he was sitting. And no sooner than she reached him, Joan placed Madeline on a stool, right before kneeling down in front of her brave dark skin knight.

"You's do that for me?" she asked.

"He's ain't let you's get no sleep," Dew Dap said, as he held a shameful look on his face.

Joan threw her arms around Dew Dap and gave him a great big kiss. A kiss, that threw Bessie and Madeline in to another one of their laughing spells. But Joan didn't care about their girls laughing, being that she had her very own hero.

"What you's girls, laughing at?" Joan asked when she and Dew Dap broke their kiss.

"You," Bessie and Madeline said simultaneously.

Like the good motherly figure that she always displayed, Joan left Dew Dap to go play with her girls. And with both of the girls in her grasp, Joan went from one to the other, tickling them with her nose. For every time Joan would attempt to put her nose on the side of their necks, the girls would laugh with a great deal of joy, shouting to the world, they were happy.

"What my dumplings eat?" Joan asked, as the girls tried to catch their breath.

"Berries," Bessie laughed.

"I's hungry," Madeline cried, as she laid her head on Joan.

"Dew Dap, you's ain't feed my babies?"

"We's was waiting for you."

"Well we's gon eat that old rooster," Joan said, still holding on to the girls.

After getting her girls back to smiling, Joan sought to feed her family. And being from the house, Joan knew quite a few things about the proper way to live. So the motherly figure led her girls over to the pail of water, which she had covered with a cut from an old cotton sack. There, she poured some water on the girls hands, and watched over them, as they rubbed their tiny paws together. And after wetting a rag she cut from an old shirt, Joan washed their faces, and dried their hands. But knowing her job wasn't complete, Joan told Dew Dap to wash up as well, while she took care of the knife.

By the time Joan had removed their breakfast from over the fire, Bessie was handing Madeline one of the two freshly washed pans. With one hand under Bessie's pan for support, Joan carefully placed the rooster in it. Then she and the girls escorted the well done crower over to where Dew Dap was sitting. But before the boy was allowed to put the knife to their breakfast, Joan said her final goodbye to that old pesky rooster.

"Bye, bye Mr. Rooster," Joan said, then joined the girls in a moment of laughter.

Joan and her girls were all smiles, as they came up on the female shed, chewing like a trio of happy critters. And her mother was already sitting on a bench, directly across from old Mae, exactly where Joan knew she would be. As for Sistah, the misguided one was sitting in the doorway of the female shed, sewing on what she called a pair of long johns for Pleasant. But the unfortunate female couldn't get anyone to believe the murdered piece of cloth, would never be anything more, then just a waste of time. And poor sex starved Clora Lee, was plaiting old Mae's hair, which like Isabella, and the other females, were laughing at Sistah's sad attempt at sewing.

"Morning," Joan said, as she went and stood against the shed, after placing the girls next to her mother.

And while leaning against the wall, Joan appeared to be preoccupied with the two expecting females. She also took a good long look at the young girl, who was nursing a toddler. Yet for some strange reason, Joan didn't see the little half breed in the same manner that she saw Clora Lee. For the child was born of cruelty. And the poor child would be forever cursed by the soldiers, who had their way with his mother. For unlike Clora Lee, the little boy would never know its father, or his father's father. And to Joan, that meant everything. For she wanted Dew Dap to father all of her children, so their grandchildren can know where they came from.

"Ain't it uh shame, ha that old rooster up and died," Isabella said, looking at Madeline and her chicken wings.

With her concentration broken, Joan mumbled, mum huh, while still chewing.

"I's uh wonder, ha it died," Isabella said, giving Joan the impression, she was asking her a question.

"I's uh reckon, he's done crowed himself to death," Joan said with a flair of sass in her voice.

"Well I's uh reckon, it ain't gon crow no mo," Clora Lee said, looking at Joan with a smile.

"Then I's uh reckon, we's gon sleep, till we's get up, if n no body ain't round here talking," Joan said, cutting her eyes at Isabella.

The females could tell the girls knew something about that old rooster, no longer being among the living. And the way the two girls took to staring at her, reinforced Isabella's belief. Yet if Sally, Sistah or old Mae didn't get the girls to talk, then the female knew better then to press the issue, being that Joan had begun to act a lot like her new found friend.

Feeling she had closed the book on Isabella, Joan directed her attention, where it would do the most good. "What you's fighting, Sistah?" she asked.

"Herself," old Mae said, causing the air to fill with laughter.

"Ouch! Mae you's stop talking bout me, cause you's making me stick myself," Sistah complained.

"You's was gon stick ya self any ha, so don't you's be putting it on me."

"Well I's uh ain't gon sew um, na," Sistah said, as she tossed the long johns on the floor of the female shed.

"I's uh reckon, Pleasant gon be mighty happy," old Mae said, sparking another round of laughter.

But Clora Lee wasn't about to let Sistah suffer long, as she quickly rushed to the unfortunate female's rescue.

"Well I's reckon, Dew Dap ain't gotta tie ya down no mo?" Clora Lee said to Joan.

With her mind solely on enjoying the plantation's last bird, Joan ignored Clora Lee, as she went right on eating. And when Clora Lee beckoned her to come closer, Joan slid toward her friend, as if the two were about to hatch, some seninster plan against the other females.

"We's gon be all right, when we's leave here," Clora Lee whispered.

"I's uh know," Joan whispered back with a smile.

"You's talked to Dew Dap?"

"I's uh ain't gotta talk to him," Joan whispered with confidence.

Clora Lee eyes went toward the sky, as her head wobbled from side to side. Then like a good friend, Clora Lee pointed to Joan's feet and smiled. Yet Clora Lee didn't end up with the last word, as Joan started everyone to laughing, when she said, Cowayne had some pretty good kicking feet as well.

"Ya ma gon go with us," Clora Lee whispered, while everyone went on laughing.

"What she's gon stay here for?" Joan whispered, while glancing at her mother.

"Mae, what them girls whispering bout," Sally asked the old female.

"Child, I's uh can't hear them young ns, with my old ears."

After hearing the mother of her son answer Sally, Sistah smacked her lips, and fold her arms while pouting, as she turned away from the old female. And as she sat clearly out of the old female's sight, Sistah began to silently mock the mother of her beloved son, as she drew her own share of laughter.

"Na Sistah, you's stop mocking me, cause you's knows, you's ain't saying uh thing."

"Mae, you's ain't see'd me, mocking ya. And you's knows what them girls talking bout, but I's uh got my eyes on missy," Sistah said, as she cut her eyes at Clora Lee.

"Well you's keep watching that child, cause theys got females watching Pleasant," old Mae said, winking at Sally.

"Na Mae, you's stop saying that, cause you's knows, ain't nobody watching Pleasant," Sistah said with a touch of fear.

"Fine then, you's gon watch that child, cause I's ain't gon tell ya no mo," old Mae said, as she winked her eye once more.

"Then I's uh ain't gon talk to ya no mo. And I's uh gon tell Cowayne, not to talk to ya," Sistah said, as she pouted.

With Sistah already declaring a war of silence on her, old Mae pretended to cry, as the other females played along.

"Mae you's stop that crying," Sistah said firmly, after a few of the females, pretended to weep for their old friend.

"I's uh can't help it, cause you's ain't gon talk to me, no mo," old Mae said, as if she were truly crying.

"Mae, I's uh done told ya, to hush that crying," Sistah said, as she sprung to her feet.

"She can't help it, Sistah, cause she's ain't got nobody to talk to her," Sally said with a straight face.

Seeing that Sistah had fallen for Sally's deception, better than a stumbling drunk, old Mae faked her crying even harder. And as the old female did her best to lure Sistah closer, the misfortunate one acted as if she smelled a rat. Yet old Mae went right on crying, knowing that it was tugging at Sistah's hesitation, like an old slave, trying to get its master's mule up and working. But the often bumbling female wasn't about to move, before making sure, she wasn't falling for another one of old Mae's tricks. And as she looked at the other females, all Sistah got, was a bunch of sad looking faces. And with old Mae faking harder then ever, Sistah had no other choice, but except the fact that her friend was truly crying.

With her arms stretched wide, Sistah attempted to give old Mae a comforting hug. But the warm hearted female was taking on the role, of a turtle befriending an alligator. For when the old female got hold of Sistah's dress, she held it with all her might. And like all trapped animals, Sistah tried her best to break free, but there was no way she could escape the old slave's grip. And once the old female had gotten her massive arms around the plantation's trouble maker, there was no letting go. And when old Mae was able to get Sistah across her lap, everyone laughed, while anticipating what was to come next.

"Ouch Mae," Sistah shouted, after feeling a firm slap on her rear end. "Ouch Mae, you's stop," Sistah cried, as the second lick struck her bottom.

"You's not talking to me, and I's uh can't hear ya," old Mae said, while shooting Sally a third wink.

The females couldn't help from laughing at Sistah, seeing that she always fell for the same old trick. And when the children who were playing off to the side, came running over to take in the sight, Sistah begged old Mae to stop. But the old female went right on spanking her friend, as the children jumped for joy.

"Na you's gone in yonder, and stop meddling folks," old Mae said, pointing to the female shed.

"I's uh ain't going no where," Sistah shouted, while rubbing her ass.

Knowing that Sistah was unpredictable, as any creature God had ever created, the females waited for her to get violent with old Mae. But when Sistah was done ridding her rear end of its pain, she did just the opposite. For the female that was getting stranger with each passing day, sat on the ground at old Mae's feet. And with her head on the old female's thigh, she talked about telling Pleasant.

"You's gon give me time to leave, fo you's tell him?" old Mae asked.

"No," Sistah replied softly.

"You's mad at me to Sistah?" Sally asked.

"I's uh mad at all uh ya," Sistah said with her head still on old Mae's thigh.

"Na you's hush that kind uh talk, and go to sleep," old Mae said, as she stroked one of Sistah plaits.

"I's ain't sleepy," Sistah said, while looking up at her friend.

At that very moment, Sally saw the mother and daughter connection she learned about, the night Duval first laid eyes on her. And as Sally was itching to tell old Mae, Sistah was her daughter, Effie appeared out of nowhere. For the female was like a haunting ghost, from the other side of life, not knowing which way to go. And the way Effie held her eyes on Sally, it made the ex-slave wonder, if the infamous one was reading her mind.

"You's looking for me?" Sally asked, as she noticed Effie had diverted her attention to Joan.

One look from Effie, told Sally to shut up, and stay out of her way. And Sally had no intentions of upsetting Mrs. Arnold second in command, as she went back to sewing without saying another word. But before Effie could return to spying Joan, Clora Lee had finished plaiting old Mae's hair, and was ready to move on.

"You's ready?" Clora Lee said to Joan, as she no longer wanted to be around the females.

"Come on girls," Joan said, as she laid Sistah's long johns down.

While ignoring Joan for a brief moment to stare at the long johns, Effie quickly caught everyone's attention. And when Sistah grabbed the sewing, that not even Joan could help, Effie eyes immediately went back to the little stitching queen.

"You's gon fix um," Sistah shouted to Joan.

Looking back, Joan said, "I's uh gotta fire by the woodshed, we's uh fix um there."

Joan's response put the females in the most awkward position. For the females did their best to keep from laughing in the presence of Effie. But old Mae didn't try to hold back her laughter, as she let it out, just before giving Sistah another wisecrack.

"I's uh reckon, Pleasant ain't gon be cold, if n you's burn um, after he's put um on," old Mae shouted to Joan.

"Na Mae, you's cut that out," Joan said, while laughing, as her and Clora Lee went right on walking.

And old Mae went right on laughing, as Effie took to amusing herself in a totally different manner. For the royal house slave stood terrorizing Sally, with her forever present, unemotional stare.

When the girls finally brought their stroll to an end, they were standing behind the old barn. And if anyone would have asked them, the two had no intentions of denying, they were waiting for Cowayne and Dew Dap to return. Yet neither, appeared to be worried about their precious provider, as they carried on a conversation, while Bessie and Madeline chased after Matthew.

"When you's gon tell me, who's that old female is?" Clora Lee asked, as Joan stared at her girls, while they tried their best to catch Matthew.

"She's ain't nobody."

"Then why Nelson said, the Misses was gon kill Mae and Cowayne?"

"Cause the Misses, don't like house slaves talking to us, cause we's filthy animals. And we's ain't want her to be sleeping out in the cold," Joan said, still watching her girls.

"Oh," Clora Lee said. "I's uh reckon, Jonathan ain't filthy," she mumbled, after pausing for a moment.

"Cause she's clean him," Joan replied, while moving her head back and forward with her mouth open.

Knowing what her friend was insinuating, Clora Lee couldn't do nothing but look at the girl, as if she were shocked. But deep down inside, Clora Lee knew one day, the both of them would be doing the very same thing for Cowayne and Dew Dap. And if it were not for Sistah, Clora Lee knew she would have given it to Cowayne that night in the dark.

"You's ever do that to Dew Dap?" Clora Lee asked, while waiting for her friend to say no.

"Na Clora Lee, you's knows I's did," Joan confessed.

"What he's say?" Clora Lee asked, with a gleam in her eye.

"Ooo. Ooo. Oh Joan. Oh Joan. Ooo."

Joan spoke softly, so the girls and Matthew wouldn't hear her. But with Clora Lee laughing louder then that old rooster use to crow, the children quickly became intrigued with the teens conversation. But the teen couldn't help her self, with the way Joan was carrying on. And the pint size female had Dew Dap's reaction down to an art, and was milking it like a calf on a fat tit. For if there was one thing Joan could do just as good as work a needle and thread, it had to be her ability to make people laugh. And for that, those in the house would forever miss the little female, who often made them laugh.

"Ha it feel, when you's do it?" Clora Lee begged, through her laughter.

"You's keep yo's voice down," Joan whispered.

"I's sorry, but I's uh can't help it."

"I's uh reckon, he's feel mighty good," Joan said, avoiding the question.

But Clora Lee wasn't about to let Joan get away with such a lame answer, as she desperately wanted to know every single detail. "I's uh talking bout you," she whispered.

Joan looked at the children playing, then back at Clora Lee. She took a deep breath and let it out, as if it were going to help her speak. "Well I's feel good, knowing that I's made him feel good," she said, with the most serious look on her face.

"Ha it feel in ya mouth?"

Joan could tell by the look in the gril's eyes, her questions, were going to have questions. And knowing that her friend wasn't going to let up, Joan took another deep breath, and thought real hard before speaking.

"Well I's uh reckon, his skin is the softest thing, I's ever felt. But its bout the hardest thing I's uh ever had in my mouth, that I's can recall," she went on, while studying Clora Lee's reaction. "And when he's did his business, it was full of salt," Joan said, as if she could still taste the boy's salty seeds in her mouth.

"Salt," Clora Lee said loudly.

"Clora Lee, if you don't keep yo's voice down, I's uh ain't gon tell ya nothing no mo," Joan whispered, as she gave Clora Lee a slap on the arm.

"I's uh can't help it," Clora Lee said, repeating the first answer, she had given the girl.

"You's uh help it, if n I's uh hit ya uh might harder," Joan said, as she no longer wanted to discuss the matter any further.

"Why it taste like salt?"

"Ha you's want me to know, I's uh ain't the good Lord?"

"Well I's uh reckon, if n you's know ha to do it, then I's uh should know ha to do it to," Clora Lee said, as if her words would make it so.

Joan didn't know what to say, to such a statement, as she sat trying to figure Clora Lee out. The way Joan saw it. Clora Lee had been with Cowayne long enough to know everything about him, including his likes and dislikes. So the female couldn't see why Clora Lee was allowing one little love act, to take total control of her past, present and future.

"Clora Lee," Joan said, staring at the ground.

"What?" Clora Lee replied.

"Cowayne gon be happy, no matter ha you's do it.

"I's uh reckon," Clora Lee said, looking at the girl's mouth.

"Well you's can march up to that there house, and ask the Misses, if n you's gotta mind to," Joan said with a serious look on her face.

Clora Lee cut her eyes at Joan, then without saying a word, she softly looked away. And as the little stump started to laugh, Clora Lee fell in to a deep thought. A thought, that dragged the teen beyond deep, to a disappearing realm, where she wondered blindly in her own mind. That is, until something brought Clora Lee back to life.

Back from her state of euphoria, Clora Lee found Madeline playing with her leg. The little girl was trying to attach an old ring she had found behind the barn, on to Clora Lee's ankle. And even though Madeline didn't know how the toll of captivity worked, she definitely knew where it was suppose to be placed. And as Clora Lee watched Madeline, she went to thinking again. In order for the slaves to truly be free, they needed to rid themselves of their rings.

"Come on," Clora Lee said, while scooping Madeline up, and running with the little girl.

"Bessie, come here, dumpling," Joan shouted, as she watched Clora Lee do her best to run with Madeline.

When Joan got Bessie, the two took off behind Clora Lee, as if something was dreadfully wrong. Yet Joan couldn't help but to wonder, what had gotten in to her friend?

"Clora Lee, where we's going?" Joan shouted, as she ran at Bessie's pace.

"To find Cowayne," Clora Lee shouted.

The girls found Cowayne and Dew Dap gathering grass for the horses and cows that was being held behind the pigpen.

"You's girls come to help?" Dew Dap laughed.

"Can we's help?" Bessie asked Joan.

After taking one look in Bessie's eyes, Joan couldn't bring herself to tell the adorable little pumpkin no. "You's gon wash up, fo you's go to sleep," Joan said with a sweetness.

Bessie quickly stated that she would, just before running off to go help her brother. But as for Madeline, the little dumpling wasn't about to go anywhere without Joan. So with her tiny hand clinging to Joan's index finger, Madeline escorted her acting mother through the tall grass.

"I's uh reckon, we's might as well help um," Clora Lee said, being that she was the only one standing still.

As Clora Lee and Joan joined in on the grass pulling project, Matthew showed up laughing and breathing hard. And from the look on his face, Clora Lee was willing to wager another twenty years in slavery, the boy had been fighting. And the way he was laughing, gave proof to the fact, Matthew had once again, gotten the best of his victim.

"What you's do?" Clora Lee asked, as Matthew went straight to pulling grass.

"I's uh ain't do nothing," Matthew replied, as he tried to wipe the smile from his face.

Clora Lee had too much on her mind, to press Matthew for the truth, as she tried to show Joan the proper way to pull grass. But something told the girl, before the day was out, she would have some female running up to her or Sistah, yapping, about how Matthew had beaten up on her son. And Clora Lee knew they had only Pleasant to blame, for Matthew's superiority over the other little boys on the plantation. For if it were not for Pleasant teaching Matthew, the true art of African fighting, they would not be burden with all of the complants that followed such a strange gift.

"Why we's pulling grass any ha?" Joan asked.

"You's uh see," Cowayne said smiling.

After nearly an hour of pulling grass, it was time to sneak the precious cargo pass the mansion. And with Mrs. Arnold spending most of her time staring out a window or two, both Cowayne and Clora Lee knew they had to be extra careful. So while Cowayne, Dew Dap, and Matthew, struggled with the sack of grass, the girls went ahead, deeming themselves the scouting party. And once they got the boys safely pass the woods, Clora Lee took a different course of action.

"We's gotta take the girls to ya ma," Clora Lee said looking at Joan.

"Why?" the girl asked, wondering what Clora Lee was up to.

"I's uh wanna go," Bessie said, looking up at Joan.

By the time Bessie had asked Joan for the impossible, Clora Lee was already leading them in the direction of the female shed. And no matter how much Bessie begged, or Joan questioned her, Clora Lee went right on walking.

"Ma, can you's watch the girls for me?" Joan asked, as Bessie began to cry.

"Child, them young ns ain't gon let you go from here," old Mae said, as she watched Madeline hold onto Joan for dear life.

"Come on na dumplings, I's uh coming right back," Joan said, as she was faced with both of her girls crying.

"Ya'll want some berries, don't ya," Clora Lee asked the girls.

Clora Lee's statement quickly drew a sour look from Joan. For the duck high female never lied to her girls, and she didn't feel anyone else should be doing it either. But like always, Joan picked the time and the place, to handle her unwanted problems. And when the time was right, Joan had a few choice words for her friend.

"We's gon get um," Clora Lee said, looking at Joan with all honesty. "But ya'll gotta stay here, cause you's might get bit by a snake. Or a spider," Clora Lee said, after seeing Joan's reaction to the word snake.

When Joan had finally gotten the girls to quiet down, she wiped their tears, and gave both of them a kiss, followed by a great big hug, before leaving. And after seeing Joan in action, Clora Lee clearly understood why the girls didn't want the little stump to get two steps out of her undergarments. For Joan was giving the girls far too much attention.

When Joan and Clora Lee were clearly away from the girls, the stick of dynamite didn't waste any time in cutting loose.

"I's uh don't take kindly, to lying to my girls," Joan said, with a serious look on her face.

"I's uh telling ya the truth, but you's gotta believe me, we gon get um some berries," Clora Lee said, as she put her arm around Joan's shoulder.

"Na Clora Lee, the way them house slaves picking berries, where we's gon find some berries?"

"You's ever see'd them house slaves go cross that there fence? No. Na you's gotta trust me, if n we's gon be friends," Clora Lee said, as if she really needed the girl to be her friend.

"I's uh reckon, we's uh bout the only ones that uh go," Joan stated, seeing the teen's logic.

"Nelson go's cross it, cause we's done see'd him uh time or two. Ain't they's bout the prettiest things you'd ever see'd?" Clora Lee asked, as they came upon the horses and two cows.

"Who they's for," Joan asked, while looking at the animals rather strangely.

"They's ours," Clora Lee said proudly. "That one there is mine," she said, pointing to the Roan.

"He's beautiful," Joan said, of the gray and white spotted horse.

"We's gon need um, when we's leave here," Cowayne said, as he watched Matthew get Dew Dap familiar with the animals.

"But we's don't knows ha to ride no horse," Joan said, stating the obvious.

"They's gon show us ha to ride," Dew Dap replied, as he stroked one of the horses with a brush, Matthew found behind the smoke house.

"But what we's gon do bout my girls?" Joan asked with fear in her voice.

With Joan in his arms, Dew Dap assured the acting mother, their girls would be all right.

While everyone was thinking about leaving the Big A, Clora Lee was thinking of a more pressing issue. She wanted the rings off of Pleasant, Sistah, and old Mae's legs, and the teen didn't want to wait another minute. For they were free, and Clora Lee felt they should look free, as well as feel free. And as long as her friends wore the mark of slavery, then it was safe to say, none of them were truly free.

"Cowayne," Clora Lee shouted.

"What?"

"I's uh want them there rings, off of ya ma, and Sistah, and Pleasant."

"Why?" Dew Dap asked.

"Cause they's free," Joan replied with a touch of brass, as she answered for her friend.

With Clora Lee, Joan, Dew Dap, and Matthew close behind him, Cowayne went charging toward the blacksmith shed. And when the five future travelers reached the blacksmith shop, they went straight up to Pleasant. Yet it was Cowayne, who knelt down and studied their friend's ring.

"What you's doing?" Pleasant asked.

"He's trying to see ha we's gon get yo's ring off," Clora Lee said, nearly shouting.

"Boy, you's can't take that there thing off me," Pleasant cried.

"But you's ain't no slave, no mo," Clora Lee said, as she hung on to Pleasant's arm.

"I's uh don't care, theys put them there things on us for life. And theys aiming for um to be there, till I's die," Pleasant said with a mountain of fear in his voice.

"But Mr. Lincoln said, we's ain't gotta wear um no mo," Joan said, as if she were some kind of store front lawyer.

Pleasant studied Joan's face for a moment, then like the children wanted him to, he went to look for something that would help the youngsters set him free. And when Pleasant found two files on a shelf, he was hesitant to give the boys their ex-master's tools. But both Dew Dap and Cowayne, quickly took hold of a file, before Pleasant could reiterate his opposition to their task.

"Come on Joan, we's gotta go get Sistah and yo's ma," Clora Lee shouted, as she darted out of the blacksmith shed.

As Pleasant and Sistah sat together for the first time without their rings, neither knew what to say. Yet it was obvious, the two former slaves were thinking about something, which had everything to do with that wretched tool of captivity. For the two was thinking of the day, when they received, the wretched thing. They remembered how it burned like Hell, for better then an hour. But what Pleasant remembered the most about the ring, is how it turned a proud and brave son, in to a fearful creature.

When Pleasant and Sistah saw the children again, they were dragging their feet, and looking sad. And as Matthew cried, Pleasant was forced to ask what was wrong with the boy.

"We's can't get my ma ring off," Cowayne said sadly.

"Come here," Sistah said to her three babies.

With the three children in her arms, Sistah tried to sing their troubles away. But with or without the ring, Sistah knew her old friend had been free, long before the war had ever started. And the female had no doubt in her mind, when the day old Mae meet the white man's God, she will still be free.

Chapter 19

No Return

On a bright sunny day, one full week after a bad storm tore through the territory, Cowayne sat under the giant magnolia tree. And beneath the large tree, Cowayne peered out at Nelson, who was resting his elbows on the very first table, Pleasant made all by him self. And as the teen watched Nelson looking in at him, Cowayne knew he would have been totally invisible to anyone else. For the large green leaves covered the boy like a tent, making it impossible for the average person to see him. But Nelson was far from being average. For he could appear and disappear at will, which was why Cowayne knew the often mysterious male saw him.

As Cowayne and Nelson played their game of cat and bigger cat, they heard a ruckus coming from out by the front gate. And while Nelson stood perfectly still, Cowayne scurried from beneath the tree, as he came to the conclusion, the soldiers were back. And seeing that he didn't have enough time to get to their pistols, Cowayne ran to the side of the mansion to peep things out. But when the youngster got to see what all the fuss was about, he couldn't believe his eyes. The freed slaves were cheering Mr. Arnold's return from the war. And the way they carried on, told the boy, the fools cared not for the freedom, Mr. Lincoln had given them.

After getting an eye full of those who Clora Lee had him to feed, Cowayne felt sick. And as he stood ready to puke, from the sight of those worthless chunks of flesh and bones, as they groveled over their master like a pack of dark nappy head hounds, the boy had to spit. And just like a pack of dogs, they couldn't keep still, as the human dogs moved about, while wagging their invisible tails. Yet Cowayne paid them no mind, as he tried to spot Jeremiah. But all Cowayne saw, was Mr. Arnold, sitting lifeless in a chair with wheels on it. And the way his once powerful master sat slumped over, Cowayne could have sworn the man was dead. But the white man's well being was not something Cowayne would ever concern himself with. For the teen was hoping that Jeremiah was in the large house, making sure everything was right for his former master. But when he saw a few more house slaves bolt out of the front door, the youngster sought to rid him self of the awful sight.

"What you's looking for, boy," Nelson asked, as Cowayne started to walk away.

"I's uh was looking for Jeremiah," Cowayne said, staring deep in to Nelson's eyes.

"He's ain't coming back," Nelson replied, keeping his eyes fixed on the ungrateful slaves, as they rejoiced.

"Ha you's know?"

"Cause I's uh been here watching that there gate all morning," Nelson said, as he was back to looking at Cowayne.

But some how, Cowayne knew Nelson was lying, as the mysterious one studied his reaction with a bold strangeness.

"You's ain't do no such thing," Cowayne said, knowing Nelson couldn't have been watching him, and the gate at the same time.

Cowayne was smart, but he had a lot to learn about Nelson, and his nearly unlimited capabilities. For on a number of occasions, Nelson stood in plain sight of the adventurous teen, yet Cowayne, nor Clora Lee, ever caught sight of him. And if Cowayne knew that Nelson could die, and rise again, he would no longer contradict the mysterious ex-slave, no matter what he said.

"Na ha you's knows what I's been doing?" Nelson asked, just before walking away.

"Cause I's uh was watching ya."

"Why you's watching me?" Nelson asked, as he continued on his way.

"Cause you's was watching me," Cowayne shouted angrily. "I's uh saw ya, watching me," he shouted, after seeing that Nelson had no intentions of entertaining their conversation.

The still wanted to be slaves, rejoicing exploded, dragging Cowayne's attention back to where it started. And as the teen watched a clean dress slave push Mr. Arnold up to the front porch, he got a touch of Nelson's capabilities.

"I's uh reckon, you's mad, na," Nelson said, as he stood directly behind Cowayne.

Cowayne spun around to find the one he thought was gone, standing about ten feet from him. But the boy could have sworn he felt Nelson breath on his ear.

"You's scared, boy?"

"I's uh ain't scared of nothing."

"You's better be scared, cause he's hate ya, and he's hate Sistah. And some day, he's gon hate Sally, and he's gon hate Joan," Nelson said harshly. "And he's may can't talk, but he's can write. And he's uh write ya'll death, if n ya'll don't leave here," Nelson said, with anger and fear.

Cowayne didn't care about Nelson's sudden interest in his well being. But as for Sistah, that made the teen fighting mad. "He ain't gon do Sistah nothing," the teen spat.

After giving Nelson his little self assured statement, Cowayne attempted to leave the mysterious one behind. But like always, Nelson was one step ahead of the boy. With his hands gripping Cowayne's arms at the elbows, Nelson held the teen trapped against the side of the large house. And even though Cowayne stood just as tall as Nelson, he couldn't seem to free himself from the strange hold.

"You's think he's gon let ya have Clora Lee? Do ya? Na you's listen to me. You's get off this here plantation, and you's get off of it, why you's can," Nelson said, then slung Cowayne to the side, and started in the direction of the female shed.

Feeling that Nelson had gone a tad too far, Cowayne quickly sought to defend his honor. But just before he went to strike, the mysterious one spun around, as they both heard Clora Lee calling out for Cowayne. And knowing that Clora Lee was calling him, so the two of them could go see Jeremiah together, Cowayne was being forced to make a choice.

"You's better go to her," Nelson said, with a sympathetic look in his eyes.

As Nelson sadly walked away, Cowayne knew he had to do something, but the poor boy didn't have a clue of what that something was going to be. And with Clora Lee closing in on him fast, Cowayne did the first thing that popped in his head.

"Help me lord," Cowayne mumbled, while grabbing Clora Lee, as she came up on him.

Cowayne never had much use for the white man's God, or his words. But the boy knew Sistah lived by the God, she had never seen, or heard speak. And one day when he asked her why she prayed to a person no one had ever seen, the boy stood confused by the words, he will always help you, when you truly need it. And from where Cowayne stood, he needed God's help, like his love needed Clora Lee. So without giving the mysterious God existence much thought, Cowayne held on to Clora Lee with more love, then any male had ever possessed.

"You's let me go, cause I's uh gotta go see Jeremiah," Clora Lee shouted, as she tried her best to break free.

With his voice cracking, Cowayne tried to say what his fear wouldn't let him. And as he tried to tell Clora Lee, her great grandfather was never coming home, Cowayne could feel his world turning black.

"He's is to," Clora Lee shouted, as she tried to squeeze out of Cowayne's grasp. "Cowayne if n you's don't let me go, I's uh gon whop you's good," she said laughing, thinking that her friend was playing.

"Lee, Jeremiah ain't come back," Cowayne said as a tear ran from his eye.

With his words yet to register in Clora Lee's head, Cowayne held on to her even tighter. But Clora Lee was determined to break free, as she continued to struggle like a fish on a line.

"Cowayne, I's uh ain't playing, na you's let me go."

But Cowayne knew he couldn't do what his Lee asked of him. For the first time in his life, Cowayne had Clora Lee close to his body, yet he didn't feel invincible. In fact, the young male felt helpless and weak, as he waited for God's help to come raining down on him like a summer shower. And as he hoped the invisible man was there, Cowayne tried one more time to break through Clora Lee's wall of excitement.

"Lee, Jeremiah, ain't never coming back," Cowayne said, as his body shook with fear.

The harsh words, finally hit their mark, as they tore deep in to the heart of Clora Lee's soul. And like her great grandfather, the girl wanted so much to be dead. For life had struck Clora Lee far worst then she could have ever imagined. And that was why the girl cried out the word, no, just before falling lifeless in Cowayne's arms.

With the weight of the world crashing down on Clora Lee, the two young lovers found themselves on the ground, with no chance of rising. And as Cowayne was impelled to hold his Lee as she cried for her great grandfather, Nelson words stayed on his mind. And even though Cowayne didn't like Nelson, he couldn't stop wondering, why old Pete's son, wanted him to care about Sally and Joan.

"Why," Clora Lee cried, as she pulled on Cowayne's shirt, hoping to release the pain that dwelled deep with in her body.

"What's wrong with Clora Lee," Matthew asked, as he ran up.

"Not now Matthew," Cowayne replied, hating to turn the boy away.

"Matthew," Clora Lee cried, while holding her hand out to her little brother.

Seeing Clora Lee wiggling her fingers, Matthew knelt down, and before he knew it, the boy found himself trapped in his sister's weeping grasp. And on any other day, Matthew would have been trying to pry himself free. But seeing that Clora Lee needed him, Matthew was more then willing to allow him self to be held like a baby. For Matthew loved Clora Lee more then anyone, and just like Cowayne, the little boy never wanted to see his big sister unhappy. So like the faithful little brother that he was, Matthew laid in her arms without an ounce of regret.

After what seem like forever, Clora Lee brought her crying to an end, leaving nothing but the birds singing to fill the air. And with the weight of Clora Lee and Matthew weighing in on him, Cowayne could feel the numbness tingling through his legs, like a mess of little bugs eating at them, as if they were rotting flesh. Yet the unsung hero didn't make any attempt to move, as he went right on comforting his friends.

"Why you's was crying," Matthew asked Clora Lee, as he studied her eyes with the curiosity, that could only be found in a little boy.

Clora Lee sat up, thus giving Cowayne's legs a much need break. And after seeing his sister sit up, Matthew did the same, leaving the blood starved legs to shout with joy. And with his legs enjoying their new state of freedom, Cowayne laid back and waited for Clora Lee to answer Matthew's question.

"Cause I's sad," Clora Lee said, as she wiped her tears from Matthew's face.

"Why," Matthew asked.

"Cause Jeremiah is dead. You's member Jeremiah, don't ya?"

"I's uh think so," the little boy replied honestly.

"Jeremiah is Effie pa, and Effie is Ethel ma. So that make Jeremiah our great grandpa," Clora Lee explained.

"Why Effie don't play with us, like Sally play with Madeline and Bessie?" Matthew asked sadly.

Clora Lee hesitated before speaking, knowing that the boy cared greatly for their grandmother. "Cause we's ain't gon never play with her," she said strongly.

"But she's our grandma," Matthew cried.

"Na you's listen to me," Clora Lee said angrily.

"Lee," Cowayne mumbled.

But Clora Lee went right on yelling at Matthew, as if she no longer felt the pain of their lost. "I's uh said, we's ain't gon talk to her, and I's uh mean it."

"Lee," Cowayne said a little louder.

"What?" Clora Lee snapped.

"You's ain't gotta holler to at him."

"I's uh sorry," Clora Lee said, hugging her little brother.

With his eyes on Cowayne, as if to say thank you, Matthew accepted the warm hug. Yet something in the little boy, said he still wanted an answer to his question. For Matthew wanted his question answered, like he wanted to laugh and play with their grandmother. And Matthew wanted the long talks, which grandmothers often have with their grandchildren. And he also wanted his friends to see him running toward her, calling out, grandma, grandma, as if she were the best grandmother in the whole world. But being that Clora Lee had spoken, Matthew knew his yearning for Effie and her love would never be his for the taking.

When Clora Lee felt better, she told Matthew all there was to know about Jeremiah. How he taught her to read and write. And how she spent long days with him, learning how to count, as well as add and subtract, and even multiply. On that day, Matthew heard about how Jeremiah prepared them for a future, that he knew would surely come. And as they stood at the threshold of that very future, Matthew felt a sense of pride, brought about by the slave name Jeremiah. And the little boy would surely carry that pride with him, until the day he would be no more. But Matthew would make it a family tradition, not to let his great grandfather's teaching fall by the waist side. For just like his big sister, the little boy vowed to teach his children and his grandchildren how to read and write. But first, Matthew had to learn how to do those things himself.

When Matthew little history lesson was over, the three got up and took a long walk around the main yard. But Cowayne could see that Matthew wasn't the same, as he appeared to be preoccupied with the mansion. For the little boy couldn't seem to take his eyes off of the giant dirty white house, as it stood short of its legacy. The poor place hadn't had a washing in years. And those back steps that led to the backdoor needed fixing. The place was going down, and no one could say different. But Matthew didn't see all of the mansion's problems, as he just went right on staring at the house, knowing that Effie was somewhere behind its walls.

"What wrong, Mae?" Clora Lee asked, as the three of them stopped to check on the old female.

As old Mae sat in her favorite spot, picking at her fingers, she told Clora Lee to take Matthew for a walk, so she could have a word with Cowayne.

"But we's just had uh walk," Matthew squawked.

"Come on," Clora Lee said, as she held her little brother by the arm.

"But I's uh wanna stay with Cowayne."

"You's hush, fo I's whop ya one," Clora Lee barked.

"And I's uh gon tell Cowayne," Matthew cried, as if the teen was their father.

"That poor child thinks plenty much of ya," old Mae said, while still picking at her fingers.

"Lee ain't gon hit him none."

"I's uh knows that, child. But that don't stop that boy from loving ya like uh pa. Na you's gotta take him from here, fo masa Arnold put them there rings back on Sistah, and Sally, and Pleasant. And you's young ns ain't never had them God forsaking things, so ha ya'll gon make it?" old Mae asked her son.

"We's ain't slaves no mo, ma."

"Boy, as long as masa Arnold got breath in his body, we's gon be his slaves, no matter what them white folks say," old Mae said, with her face covered in fear.

"You's ain't gotta worry, ma, cause we's leaving here."

Hearing her son speak with a dying determination, the old female thought to give him a bit of advice. "And don't you's go telling them others, cause theys uh run tell it, show's I's sitting here."

"I's uh ain't gon tell no body," Cowayne said, knowing that his mother had been talking to Nelson.

"Good, na you's run along, and let ya old ma get her rest," old Mae said, as she laid her back against the female shed.

Walking away from his mother, Cowayne set out to find Clora Lee, so the two of them could make a few changes to their plan. For after hearing his mother's warning, Cowayne felt they had no other choice, but to move their time of departure up a few weeks.

"Come on Lee, we's gotta talk," Cowayne said, as he found her and Matthew sitting in front of the woodshed with Joan.

Seeing that she had just made up her mind about giving sewing a try, Clora Lee wondered what could be all that important. And as she glared at Matthew running just fast enough to stay one step out of Bessie's reach, Clora Lee had to smile. For the teen saw the two children, as her and Cowayne reborn. Yet Clora Lee knew Bessie and Matthew were truly cutting their own path to something special.

After finishing what turned out to be a very brief talk with Cowayne, Clora Lee tried to get back to her sewing. But as she did so, the girl held a puzzling look on her face. A look which made Sally and Joan feel that something was bothering the young female.

"You's all right?" Sally asked.

"He's worried bout his ma," Clora Lee said, while picking up on Sally's concern.

Having a good deal of trust in Sally, Clora Lee felt the female would surely keep a secret, if she wanted her to. But Cowayne said, for her not to tell any one, and that meant Sally, as well as Sistah. For Clora Lee and Cowayne's love was built on trust, and neither would ever do anything to damage their basic foundation. Yet Clora Lee couldn't help but to wonder, what type of sign the Arnolds could possibly give them, which would say it was safe to make their move.

For ten long days, Clora Lee waited and watched, as Cowayne stayed close to the plantation and his mother. And with the laziness of an old hound, Cowayne laid under the large magnolia tree, watching the mansion like a leprechaun, keeping his eyes on its gold. Yet on the morning of the eleventh day, Clora Lee suggested they watch the large house from their old favorite place. And like always, Cowayne felt his Lee had a good idea. But the boy was reluctant to go any where near their favorite tree. For the tree, was much too close, to the house, and far too dangerous for the two of them, with Mr. Arnold being back home.

"Come on," Clora Lee said, as she leaped to her feet.

Cowayne stared at Clora Lee's hand, and then he turned his eyes to the butt print, she left lingering on the army blanket. And at that very moment, everything in Cowayne's heart, told him it was a bad idea, yet he never knew his Lee to be wrong about any thing. So with his fear still haunting him like a bad dream, Cowayne took hold of Clora Lee's hand, and just like that, the two were walking head on in to danger.

When the teens finally made it in their tree, Clora Lee and Cowayne saw the most shocking thing, they had ever seen. As Mr. Arnold sat in his wheelchair beside the bed, the teens could not believe their eyes. And even though his face, still held the same dead expression, the two ex-slaves felt the man appeared to be a tad bit sadder then usual. But Mr. Arnold, sad face, wasn't the thing that nearly threw the teens from the tree. In fact, Cowayne and Clora Lee enjoyed seeing the once feared slave owner, suffer a fate, far worst then death. Yet his suffering, had to be far worst, then anything the Devil could dream up on his best day. And no matter how evil their former master had been in the past, Cowayne felt no man born of a woman, should be forced to suffer such a horrible fate.

While the teens watched Mrs. Arnold's mouth, as it went up and down on Jonathan's dick, their hearts began to grieve for Mr. Arnold. For the helpless man, had no other choice, but to watch, as his wife gave pleasure to her most beloved slave. And when Mrs. Arnold's mouth left Jonathan's dick, she got up on her hands and knees, directly in front of her husband. Then with the help of her girls, Jonathan's dick found its way between Mrs. Arnold's sweet pink walls. And oh how Mrs. Arnold carried on, as Jonathan worked her like she was a slave in night rotation.

"Where is your slave bitch, now?" Mrs. Arnold shouted, after screaming from the pain of Jonathan stabbing his dick, deep into her juicy wet cut.

And when Clora Lee heard Mrs. Arnold's question, she knew right away, the woman was talking about her grandmother. Yet the young female didn't have time to think about Effie, when the girls were leaning Mr. Arnold forward, so their Misses could slap his face. And oh what a slap it was, as Mrs. Arnold tried to rid herself of the pain she no longer had to hide. For all of the years that her husband laid with slaves, and the many white women he came across, Mrs. Arnold slapped him with a hate like no other. Yet the sound of Mrs. Arnold's crashing blow didn't bring the teens any pleasure, even though they hated the broken man far more than his wife ever could.

But if the teens thought Mrs. Arnold's slapping of her husband was the worst of the worst, then they were sadly mistaken. For when Jonathan started his drive toward what the teens took to be another common explosion, they were treated to something different. As usual, Mrs. Arnold used her mouth to catch Jonathan's salty seeds, yet she didn't share it with her girls. Instead, Mrs. Arnold spat the load in her husband's face. And seeing such a thing, Clora Lee and Cowayne felt the insult was a gift, sent straight from the depths of Hell. Yet Mrs. Arnold was far from being finished, as she took to smearing the semen and spit mixture all over her husband's face, before returning to milking Jonathan's dick like a common whore. And between her sucking and sapping on the dark hunk of flesh and muscle, the woman laughed a wicket laugh. A laugh that said, Hell was born in a woman, and there, is where it will live for all eternity.

Feeling they had seen more then enough, Cowayne gave the signal for the two of them to start their descent. And once their feet touched solid ground, the two didn't stop, until they reached the new barn. And in the loft of that faded barn, Clora Lee and Cowayne got down to laying out the next four days of their young lives.

After hearing their little plan, Clora Lee strongly opposed, to what she took to be a fool hearted mission. For it wasn't as if Cowayne was going out to check on a few traps down by the creek. They were talking about going further then either of them had ever traveled before. And Cowayne wanted to do it all by himself, without her to back him up.

"What if n you's run in to another stinking Reb?" Clora Lee asked, with both fear and anger.

"Then I's uh tell him to take uh washing," Cowayne joked.

But Clora Lee didn't find anything funny, as she struck Cowayne on the shoulder. The young female was scared out of her mind, and there was nothing she could do about it. For Clora Lee knew the trip had to be made, in order for them to safely leave that old plantation. But with Cowayne wanting to go it alone, had to be the craziest thing he every thought about doing.

"I's uh ask Joan, if n Dew Dap can go with ya," Clora Lee said, hoping Cowayne would change his mind and take her instead.

"No," Cowayne replied franticly.

"Why?"

"Cause you's gon need him, to help ya with them traps. And don't you's forget to take ya guns and some bullets."

Clora Lee put her head down to keep Cowayne from seeing her face. But Cowayne knew his Lee, so he just laid back and waited for the girl to lay her head in his chest. And when his friend did just as he expected, Cowayne felt her tears. But the boy remembered the last time, he and Clora Lee were faced with her crying. And remembering the day well, he wasn't about to go down that road again.

After spending everyday of her life with Cowayne, Clora Lee didn't see any reason to change their routine. For the teen always thought it would be better to die with her friend, rather then live one day without him. But with the boy she loved, having her to face the fact, that the two of them may not die as one, clutched in each other's arms, the girl felt an emptiness take over her body. And as Clora Lee laid on Cowayne, wishing the Blue Coats would have blown that stupid pecan tree straight to Hell, she thought about beating her own ass, for suggesting they watch the house from their tower.

"Come on Lee, let's go check on Matthew," Cowayne said with a smile, as he tried to cheer her up.

As Cowayne sat up, Clora Lee pounced on him, thus sending the poor boy crashing back down to the floor. And with her body on top of his, Clora Lee stared in to Cowayne's eyes, with both good and bad intentions. For Clora Lee knew if Cowayne didn't make it back, she would have lost him, without the two of them ever making love. And Clora Lee couldn't see that happening, knowing how much she wanted to share her body with him. So while feeling she didn't have a moment to lose, Clora Lee sat up, and started to take her Union soldier shirt off.

"What you's doing?" Cowayne asked with a smile.

"I's uh gon be yo's Mrs. Arnold," Clora Lee said, as her light brown face lit up.

After taking hold of Clora Lee's hands, Cowayne reminded her with a reluctant sadness, the two of them were going to do it, when they leave the plantation.

"But what if n you's don't come back?" Clora Lee cried as she tried to get another button lose.

Cowayne pulled Clora Lee back down on top of him, right before rolling her over. And while on top of her, he asked his friend, if she didn't want him back?

"If n you's say that again, I's uh gon get up from here, and give you's a good whopping," Clora Lee yelled, not seeing the humor in his joke.

"Then I's uh reckon, I's uh be coming back," Cowayne laughed.

Clora Lee turned her head, as if to say she was mad. But Cowayne on the other hand, took it to be the perfect time, to rub his nose on her neck.

"You's stop, cause you's tickling me," Clora Lee said, with a seductive laugh.

Hearing Clora Lee laugh, had Cowayne moving in for the kill, as his sleeping dick began to stiffen. And as Clora Lee went on with the deceptive laugh, she wrapped her legs around his waist. Then like a crab, Clora Lee used her pretty light brown legs to draw Cowayne closer, hoping to get him excited enough to change his mind. And as the erected dick provided Clora Lee with a selfish way of having sex, she sucked his neck, while rushing to a satisfying explosion.

"What you's up to na?"

With Cowayne's question dancing in her ears, Clora Lee knew her lover didn't know enough about females, to know that she had gotten just enough satisfaction, to carry her over for the next few days. For Isabella's little joke about rubbing sex, had proven to be useful after all, Clora lee thought to her self, as she smiled.

"I's uh can wait," Clora Lee said, as she ran her tongue in Cowayne's mouth, for a much needed kiss.

"But I's uh wanna do it," Cowayne whispered, after breaking the kiss.

"Well, we's gotta take our clothes off," Clora Lee said, realizing her little trick, had worked far better then she thought it would.

The two sat up, knowing it was finally their time. And neither would forget their first time, as they went to take their clothes off. But then like always, their ears shouted, things were not be as they wished them to be. For the frustrated teens heard Joan, calling out Clora Lee's name, as if she were that old rooster, hatched from a different egg.

"I's uh see'd um come in here," Joan said, as she looked around the new barn.

"I's uh reckon, theys done went some where else," Dew Dap said, looking up at the loft.

Even though Clora Lee and Cowayne knew they didn't have a moment to lose, the two still silently laughed, while buttoning their shirts. And as the young lovers were once again, being forced to wait, Clora Lee felt it would be a good thing for Dew Dap and

Joan to see them coming down from the loft. But the teen quickly changed her mind, when she heard Sistah telling Matthew to check the loft. And when Clora Lee and Cowayne heard Matthew say okay, as if he were happy to do Sistah's bidding, the two knew they were in trouble. But as always, her female instincts came to the rescue. And it did so, before the little Benedict Arnold could make his way up the ladder.

"Theys sleeping," Matthew shouted, as his climb came to an end.

"Matthew, what you's doing," Cowayne asked, as he sat up, looking sleepy.

"Cowayne, if n you and Clora Lee don't get down from that there loft, I's uh gon take a stick to the both uh ya," Sistah bellowed.

Clora Lee sat up, hoping to fool Sistah as well, yet her performance didn't work any better.

"Don't you's play with me missy, cause I's ain't for it," Sistah barked. "Na you's come on down here."

Cowayne leaped to the ground, while Clora Lee took the safe, but the long way down. But either way, Clora Lee knew Sistah would still be waiting, no matter how long she took to set her feet back on solid ground. And just for the hell of it, Clora Lee made a point of taking a snail's pace down the short ladder.

"You's hurry up, missy," Sistah said firmly.

With only three rungs left, Clora Lee closed her eyes and jumped to the barn's floor, as if she was leaping to her death. And for Clora Lee, a face off with Sistah could easily be seen as a brush with death. Yet gravity acted as if it wanted the girl dead, as it appeared to pull her feet to the earth much faster then usual. And when the teen's feet hit the dirt floor, she could feel her heart stop beating, as if to say, you are on your own with this one.

"If n you's two sleepy, then you's can sleep in the female shed," Sistah said, as she took the two by the hand.

With Dew Dap, Joan, Matthew, Bessie, and Madeline behind them, Sistah marched Clora Lee and Cowayne from the barn. And like soldiers in the Union army, Sistah marched her brigade toward the female shed.

"Hup two, hup two, hup two," Sistah bellowed, as she led her little soldiers across the yard.

While marching her way to the female shed, Clora Lee saw Effie coming out the backdoor of the dirty white house with a pail of water. The once preferred house slave, went over to a tree, and dumped the water on the ground. Right away, Clora Lee felt a sense of satisfaction, from her grandmother's sudden fall from grace. Yet the teen couldn't bring her self to smile or laugh, as she marched onward with her friends.

The next morning, long before the sun was due to make its grand apperance, Cowayne and Clora Lee stood at the fence, just yards from the large magnolia tree. And with a small pouch that Sally made from a Cotton sack in his hand, Cowayne tried to assure Clora Lee he would be all right. The teen also did his best, not to look at her, as the two of them went over their plan, for what he took to be the one hundred time.

"Don't forget to take Dew Dap and Matthew with ya," Cowayne said, as he kept his eyes on the ground.

"You's got enough bullets?" Clora Lee asked.

"I's uh got some in my pockets," Cowayne replied, as he patted his pockets without ever looking up.

"You's look at me." Clora Lee whispered sadly.

Cowayne raised his head, and stared deep in to Clora Lee eyes. The teens have always been able to say more with their eyes, then any amount of words ever spoken between the two of them. And standing in the dark, wasn't going to be any different, as Clora Lee eyes shouted, take me with you. But Cowayne's eyes were full of fear and pain. For he was afraid, some white man would get the ups on him, leaving Clora Lee to be victimize in the worst way. And Cowayne also felt a sense of pain, which came from the sight, of seeing his Lee looking sad.

"I's uh gotta go," the boy grumbled.

Clora Lee threw her arms around his neck, and held Cowayne with all the love she wished to give him. "You's come back to me, cause I's uh love ya," she whispered softly.

"I's uh hear ya, Lee."

Before the soft responce could caress the darkness, Clora Lee was stroking his chest with her left hand, while she kept her right arm around the teen's neck. For the young female was hoping they could finish what Sistah had rudely interrupted. So with full control of her lover's right hand, Clora Lee placed it, on one of God's gifts to man. And even though Cowayne didn't squeeze her left breast, Clora Lee still sighed peacefully, as if the boy was easing his firm erected cock, through her virgin walls. And as her desperate need for attention rose, Clora Lee moved his hand down toward that little piece of Heaven on earth. And she could feel the juices spewing from her body, as if it was preparing it's self for a feast.

"Lee, I's uh gotta go," Cowayne mumbled, as if the words, was the only English he could speak.

Clora Lee sighed with a disturbing disappointment, as she watched Cowayne back away from her. "Sistah sleeping," she whispered.

"But I's uh gotta get started, fo the sun come up," Cowayne said, as he went to go over the fence. "And you's make sure Matthew show Joan and Dew Dap how to ride them horses good, cause theys ain't ride um in uh spell," he continued.

Clora Lee didn't bother to answer Cowayne, as she held on to him with a love, far greater then anything selfish. And with the tears rolling down her cheek, Cowayne could see the pain, his leaving was causing, the one true love he would ever have.

"Lee, I's uh coming back," Cowayne said, as he tried to free himself from her dying grip.

"You's better," Clora Lee said through her crying.

Knowing that she had to let the love of her life go out into the world on his own, Clora Lee grabbed Cowayne, and kissed him with a violent passion, that was meant for death. And with her tears all over his face, Cowayne couldn't help but to accept the salty kiss, even though he knew time wasn't on his side.

"I's uh gotta go, Lee," Cowayne said, as he could see his friend was getting tired of hearing the five words.

With her heart filled with sadness, Clora Lee watched as Cowayne disappeared into the darkness. Then like a woman left to grow old, with only memories for comfort, Clora Lee made her way back to the female shed. And being stricken with sadness, the teen didn't even bother to check to see if Pleasant was awake. For Clora Lee just kept right on walking, as if her acting father wasn't even there. And when she made it to the female shed, Clora Lee stood in the doorway looking out at the darkness, knowing it held all that she loved.

When Clora Lee finally made it back down on the floor next to Sistah, she was pretty sure her months of practicing had paid off. For the girl was willing to bet, her departing and return went unnoticed, compared to the last time she tried such a thing. But if the teen had paid more attention to her departure, as well as her sad return, she would have known better. For both times, the teen was clearly seen by Sistah, old Mae, and above all, Pleasant. Yet at that very moment, Clora Lee didn't care, as she said a prayer for her lover's safe return.

Chapter 20

Cowayne Is Missing

Clora Lee was still lying on the floor, long after all of the other females had left the shed. For her mind was totally consumed with thoughts of Cowayne, as she found herself clinging to the cool floor, staring at the ceiling. But when Matthew's little head invaded the doorway, Clora Lee knew it was time for her to get up.

"You's ain't sleeping," Matthew cried out with a smile. But being that the thought of Cowayne, was weighing heavy on her mind, Clora Lee sat up and stretched, as if she were wore out from sleeping all night. But the young female didn't sleep a wink, as she worried about her Cowayne. And as Clora Lee stared at the four walls that surrounded her, for the first time, she realized the house of captivity was also a fortress. And the teen knew that Cowayne didn't have such a place to protect him, as he tracked through the white man's world.

After standing up, and taking another long stretch, as if she really needed it, Clora Lee was ready to leave the shed. And like an old horse leaving its barn for the corral, Clora Lee slowly made her way to the door.

"You's ready, to go check on Joan and them girls?" she asked Matthew, while standing in the doorway.

After Matthew nodded his head with out saying a word, Clora Lee closed the door to tidy herself up a bit. And when the door came open again, Clora Lee stood in the doorway, covered with a pair of Union pants and a black shirt. The shirt had a couple of bullet holes in it, which told everyone, the man that once wore the garment, didn't need it any more. Yet that didn't matter to the ex-slaves, being that the girl had something to call her own.

"We's going and sit with Joan uh spell," Clora Lee said, as she avoided eye contact with Sistah and old Mae.

"Where's that Cowayne?" Sistah asked, after Clora Lee had made an attempt to walk away.

"I's uh reckon, he's checking them traps," Clora Lee replied, before her and Matthew went back to walking.

Sistah looked at old Mae, only to find the old female was already looking at her. And the two must have been thinking the same thing, because they both held the same confused, yet frighten expression. And old Mae had already begun to pick at her fingers, which told Sistah, she was scared about something. Yet both of Cowayne's mothers didn't know what to say, as they allowed Clora Lee to go about her business.

"I's uh ain't tell Sistah, Cowayne was gone, huh Clora Lee," Matthew said, when they were well away from the female shed.

"No, and we's ain't gon tell her," Clora Lee said, hugging the little bug catcher, as they went to get her guns.

With breakfast in their bellies, Matthew and Clora Lee set out to show Dew Dap and Joan, everything they knew about horses.

And while Clora Lee fought to get Joan in a pair of trousers, Matthew tried to get Dew Dap reacquainted with saddling a horse. But with Mr. Arnold being back, Dew Dap was about as skittish, as a mess of hens, running from a stray dog. For the teen couldn't stop looking over his shoulder, fearing their former master, would come rolling up in his wheelchair, raring to give him a good taste of the whip. So while slowly approaching the horse, Matthew was holding, Dew Dap tripped, thus causing the animal to rise up on its back legs, taking Matthew with it. And as Matthew held on to the bridle for dear life, he wondered what had gotten into Dew Dap.

The sight of Matthew dangling from the horse, as she and Joan walked out of the barn, sent Clora Lee screaming like a white woman, running from a band of Indians. And as Clora Lee ran toward the horse, screaming as if Matthew had died, she could see Cowayne running from an army of Rebs. Yet no sooner then Matthew's feet were safely back on the ground, Clora Lee grabbed him with a force unlike no other. She then, began to shake the boy, as if he were one of Joan's well made ragdolls.

"You's gon kill him," Joan yelled, as she took hold of Matthew.

Realizing what she had done, Clora Lee dropped to her knees, and cried like a baby, while telling Matthew, she was sorry. And oh how the words, and the tears came pouring out Clora Lee, like milk from an over turned pail.

Knowing that the whole thing was his fault, Dew Dap went over and placed the blanket back on the horse. He then grabbed the saddle, and started for the animal, while asking Clora Lee what he had to do next. The crying teen pulled her self together, and told Dew Dap what he already knew. And after the first horse was perfectly saddled, Clora Lee proceeded to direct the teen through saddling the second animal, as if the boy had never done the task before.

With Matthew thinking the hardest part was behind him, the boy was ready to find out how much Dew Dap and Joan remembered, after being away from the animals for eleven long days. But there was still one problem left. How was Matthew going to get Joan on her horse? For Joan, was just a tad bit taller then Matthew, and far less nimble. And the pants that Joan wore with regret, wasn't helping the girl any. For the breeches were far too tight, for Joan to raise her short, but nicely shaped legs. And the way Joan saw it, the only thing the pants were good for, was exciting Dew Dap, as he couldn't seem to take his eyes off of the girl.

"Clora Lee, I's uh told ya, these breeches, was too tight," Joan bellowed.

"What you's want me to do, you's knows, you's can't wear none of them others?" Clora Lee replied.

"And I's uh can't wear these," Joan confessed.

Dew Dap went over and took hold of Joan thighs, and lifted her high in the air.

"Dew Dap, if n you's don't put me down, my dumplings ain't gon know ya, when I's uh get down," Joan shouted.

But by the time Joan had finished shouting, she was sitting on the horse looking at Clora Lee. Speechless but not blind, Joan read the look on Clora Lee's face for all that it said. And the pretty dark brown skin female knew she was in for an ear full, during their evening stroll. Yet Joan couldn't take her eyes off of Clora Lee, for fearing that she would end up looking at Dew Dap. And if the tiny teen were to do such a thing, she knew Clora Lee would manipulate it, until the dead Rebs had themselves a victory celebration. So with that in mind, Joan just rolled her eyes, and turned her head, leaving Clora Lee to continue their silent conversation all by herself.

After riding the horse for better then an hour, Joan found herself nearly crawling back to her girls, sore ass and all. And having Clora Lee beside her every step of the way, Joan's ears were being rubbed raw as well.

"Na see, Joan, I's uh told ya, them there breeches was good," Clora Lee laughed.

"Clora Lee, don't you's start that again," Joan cried, as she walked like a young virgin, who had been fucked all night by an old mule dick man.

"Na Joan, I's uh ain't doing no such thing. I's uh just saying, ha Dew Dap was looking at ya. If n you's knows like I's knows, you's ain't gon go in that woodshed tonight."

"Na Clora Lee, I's uh done told ya, to quit bother me." Joan said, as they rounded the far right corner of the female shed.

Hearing Joan's voice, Madeline was up and running in the teen's direction, as her and Clora Lee entered the little girl's sight. And Madeline hit Joan so fast, the duck high female, didn't have time to put her hands out. Nor did Joan have the time to tell her little dumpling, that she was nursing a very sore ass. For Joan was trapped, as the other females, quickly jumped to the wrong conclusion.

"Child them foots, show nough got you's walking mighty poorly, this morning," Sistah said, as Joan hobbled along in the tight pants.

Rather then take a seat on the bench next to Bessie, Joan leaned up against the female shed, as she tried to ignore the other females laughing at Sistah's meddling. And with Madeline showing her all the love in the world, Joan knew her suffering was for a good cause. And no amount of teasing was going to stop Joan from doing the best for her girls.

"I's uh told her, not to go in that woodshed, tonight," Clora Lee said smiling.

"You's just wait, till Cowayne get hold uh ya, then you's do all yo's yapping," Joan said softly, while looking down on Madeline.

A silence came over the air, as the females took to looking at Clora Lee. Yet she couldn't bring her self to think about the females, nor their eyes, as her thoughts ran back to that painful place. She wondered how far Cowayne had traveled, and if he was all right. Clora Lee wondered if he was tired, and how many times had he stopped to take a break. With out saying a word, Clora Lee walked off, as if she were lost and alone, staggering mindlessly across some God forsaken desert.

The females looked at each other, as if some great miracle had taken place. They had never seen anyone stop Clora Lee so easily before, and with such a small statement. But Joan wasn't quite sure of her victory, as she stood thinking about what had taken place back at the corral. And if Joan wasn't sure there was some thing wrong with her friend back at the corral, she was thrown head first into the fact, that Clora Lee had a very serious problem. So with Sally watching the girls again, Joan went after Clora Lee, hoping to find out what was wrong. And when she caught up with Clora Lee under the pecan tree, Joan couldn't help but to wonder, what was wrong with the girl.

"What's ailing ya?" Joan asked, after placing an arm around Clora Lee, who was sobbing like a baby. And when Clora Lee couldn't bring herself to answer the question, Joan tried it again. "Is you's gon have uh baby?" the little stump asked.

Clora Lee shook her head no, as she went right on crying, with no regards for her self respect. And even with the house slaves standing in the windows, the teen still couldn't stop her tears from falling like rain drops on a stormy night. But when Effie came out of the backdoor, Joan had no other choice, but to escort Clora Lee across the yard in the direction of the woodshed.

"Na Clora Lee, you's tell me, what in the world is wrong with ya," Joan said firmly, as the two stood in front of the woodshed.

"Co, Co, Cowayne," Clora Lee forced out of her mouth.

After thinking for a moment, Joan realized, she hadn't seen the rambling teen all morning. "Where is Cowayne?" she asked.

"He, he, he's gone," Clora Lee said, right before braking out in to tears once again.

With Joan misinterpretating the facts, accompanied by Dew Dap's bad timing, as Clora Lee went on crying, made for a disastrous situation. And as the unsuspecting male walked up with their knife in one hand, and his spear in the other, Joan set her internal fire to blazing.

"I's uh tell ya, Dew Dap. If n you's leave me and my girls, we's ain't gon never speak to ya, as long as you's live," Joan yelled.

"Joan I's uh ain't gon go no where."

"I's uh reckon, Cowayne done said the same thing, but he's done up and left Clora Lee here with his ma."

Seeing that Joan had already made up her mind, Dew Dap eased over to the woodshed and sat in the doorway. The young male was learning fast, and he knew there would be no winning with Joan. For the duck high female had to speak her mind, before she would be willing to listen to anything he had to say.

"Cause if n you's think, you's gon tell us, you's ain't gon leave us, then up and go, we's gon be right with ya," Joan yelled, as she began to cry.

With every word Pleasant told him, still fresh in his head, Dew Dap tried his best to keep quiet. But seeing that Joan was yelling at him for no reason, Dew Dap rose to his feet, and stabbed the spear in the ground.

"Na you's look uh here, Joan. Cowayne ain't bit mo up and left Clora Lee, no more then I's uh done left you. Na you's hush that fuss, cause you's making Clora Lee cry," Dew Dap said without shouting.

"Then why's she crying," Joan asked.

"I's uh don't know. You's females, uh cry, when you's laughing."

"Na Dew Dap, you's done told me, you's ain't gon use that kind uh talk with me, and I's uh ain't gon take it," Joan said, standing back on her legs. "And while you's playing, with yo's stick, you's need to tell Clora Lee, where Cowayne done run off to."

"He, he, he's gone to mark the trail," Clora Lee cried.

"Na Clora Lee, if n you's knows where he's is, what you's crying for?" Joan asked with more then just a touch of anger in her voice.

"Cause I's uh not with him."

"Aw Clora Lee, you's can't go everywhere Cowayne go," Joan said with a softness.

Dew Dap was at a total lost, as he stood looking at Joan. For the poor boy didn't know what to make of the young female. She was ready to rip his head off for nothing at all, but when it came down to Clora Lee, the little tornado was as calm as a new born baby. And feeling he had seen enough, Dew Dap grabbed his spear and started to walk off, which turned out to be a big mistake.

"Dew Dap, if n you's don't get back here, I's uh gon take that there spear, and put it on yo's bottom," Joan yelled, as she held Clora Lee in her arms.

Feeling he didn't need to hear any more yapping, Dew Dap stuck the spear in the ground, and retook his seat in the doorway. As for Joan, she went back to dealing with Clora Lee, like the girl was some helpless blind person.

"Na Clora Lee, you's listen to me. You's knows, Cowayne loves ya. And you's knows he's loves ya, like he's loves his ma, and his... Sistah, and I's uh done told ya that."

Joan had to catch herself, before she made the mistake of saying sister, rather then Sistah. For the last thing the girl wanted to do at that point in their friendship, was to be the reason for Clora Lee losing Cowayne, Sistah, and old Mae, all in one swoop. For that, would definitely make her and Clora Lee mortal enemies again, and Joan didn't want to lose her best friend. But most of all, Joan didn't want to bring old Mae any harm. For Sally had always told her daughter, how if it were not for old Mae, they would be in Heaven, singing with the angels. And as much as Joan hated slavery, she hated the thought of being dead even more.

"Na Clora Lee, you's stop that there crying, cause you's knows Cowayne is coming back for ya," Joan said, as she gave the girl a firm shaking.

"I's uh know, but I's scared," Clora Lee cried.

"Well if n that, don't beat sleeping with uh polecat. Na Clora Lee, you and Cowayne ain't never been scared of nothing, and I's uh knows it. Na you's get up from that there stool, and you's stop that crying, cause we's gotta cook Mae and them young ns something to eat," Joan shouted, as she walked away from Clora Lee.

No matter what Joan said, Clora Lee went right on crying. And feeling she had just about enough of her friend's whining, Joan was ready to take a different approach, to solving their problem. For the little tight breeches wearing female grabbed her broom, and gave Clora Lee a firm lick on the shoulder.

"Ooouch," Clora Lee cried.

"If n you's don't want me to hit ya again, you's better stop that crying, and I's mean it," Joan said holding the broom, as if she was ready to give Clora Lee another good lick.

Clora Lee rubbed her arm for a moment, before standing up. And knowing how Joan felt about her girls and their things, Clora Lee bent over to pick up Bessie's hand puppet, which she mistakenly knocked off of the bench. And when Clora Lee's butt was high in the air, Joan took full advantage of the generous offering. For the stump size female gave Clora Lee a solid lick, right where it would do the most good.

"Ooouch Joan," Clora Lee cried, as she grabbed her ass.

"That's for making me worry for nothing."

"Dew Dap, you's make Joan stop hitting me," Clora Lee cried, looking for a little help.

"Dew Dap ain't gon do no such thing, na you's get my dumpling puppet."

"Ha I's uh gon get it, when you's gon hit me?"

"Na Clora Lee, I's uh done hit ya, ain't I?"

Taking Joan at her word, Clora Lee reached for the puppet, and once again, she received a good swat on the ass.

"Ooouch, Joan, you's said, you's ain't gon hit me," Clora Lee yelled.

"I's uh ain't said, no such thing. I's uh said, I's uh done hit ya. Na you's get my baby puppet."

"I's uh ain't, till you's put that there broom down," Clora Lee said, as if she were back to her old self again.

"I's uh gon hit ya again, if n you's don't get my dumpling puppet," Joan said, as she still held the broom in a threatening manner.

Seeing that Clora Lee wasn't going to budge, until she got rid of that old broom, Joan threw the thing without ever looking or thinking. And Dew Dap, who had made the mistake of sitting with his head down, didn't see the broom coming. But when the dirty old sweeper landed in his lap, Dew Dap leaped to his feet, spitting dirt and dust, as if he was made of it.

"Na you's get my baby puppet," Joan said, as she moved closer to Clora Lee.

Believing that the threat of being struck was a thing of the past, Clora Lee reached for the puppet like before, only to find out, Joan was more then willing to use her hand, to get at the root of their problem. Yet Joan's attempt to make Clora Lee suffer, came back to haunt her as well.

"Joan!" Clora Lee cried out, as she came up with the hand puppet.

But when Clora Lee caught sight of Joan, she had to laugh. The little ball of fire was holding her hand as if it were broken.

"You's gotta spit on it," Clora Lee said, as she was more then willing to help her friend with the solution.

"Clora Lee," Joan screamed, as she pulled her hand from the line of fire, and quickly called out for Dew Dap.

But when the girls turned their eyes to the woodshed, Dew Dap was no where to be seen, giving the two females causes to laugh. And the two laughed so hard, they nearly cried. But Clora Lee knew it was a laugh, she truly needed. And the warm hearted laugh, made the girl forget about her troubles for a few minutes.

The next morning when Clora Lee opened her eyes, she found Sistah standing over her. And even though the sun had yet to call for a new day, old Mae was already sitting on her stump, and that made the teen feel, Sistah had been given the right of passage. But the girl wasn't about to panic, as she got up off of the floor, expecting to be attacked. And when Sistah didn't strike her, Clora Lee looked around at the other females. Some were awake, while the other was still sleeping. And those who had awaken early, held a certain sense of fear in their eyes. A fear that made Clora Lee start for the door, but she never made it. And as Sistah held her with a dying grip, Clora Lee tried her best to break free.

"You's let me go," Clora Lee cried out in fear.

After Sistah did as Clora Lee asked, the girl ran out into the darkness. Filled with fear, Clora Lee began to look around, as if she was losing her mind. And no one could blame the girl, being that Cowayne was out among the white man, with out a soul to help him.

"What you's looking for, child?" old Mae asked.

Something inside of Clora Lee told her not to answer the old female, as she continued to look about the yard. And when Sistah emerged from the female shed, more determined then ever, Clora Lee was on her knees, fighting back the tears that were sure to come.

"Na you tell me, where my boy is," Sistah said standing over the girl.

After hearing Clora Lee give her the same answer, she heard the day before, Sistah pulled her dress up a bit, and knelt down in front of the teen. And while looking at the child she had grown to love, Sistah reiterated her question with a touch of force. And like a storm cloud rolling in from the north, Clora Lee heard the words, where is my baby? In a flash, Clora Lee could hear Joan's voice, rumbling through her head, like a thousand horses running down hill. And as the big little voice shouted, get up, and don't you's cry, Clora Lee rose to her feet, feeling stronger then ever.

With her confidence back from its time among the dead, Clora Lee told Sistah, she was going to look for her friend. But the misfortunate female wasn't buying it, as she darted out in front of the girl, preventing her from walking away.

"Don't you be lying to me, missy, cause I's knows, you's ain't gon go do no such thing," Sistah growled.

"I's is, if n you's let me," Clora Lee said, standing her ground, as her Arnold's blood came rising up, as if the broken man was back on his feet, standing tall.

"Na Sistah, you's leave that child be, so she's can go get Cowayne, so I's uh can get my morning sugar," old Mae said, looking at Clora Lee.

Sistah politely moved out of the way, daring Clora Lee to leave and come back with her son. But Clora Lee hesitated before moving, as she tried to figure a way out of the trap, the old female had laid for her. And as Clora Lee started to move her feet, she hoped to come up with an idea that would get Cowayne through one more day.

When Clora Lee was gone, Sistah mumbled with a fear, only a mother could feel. "Mae, that child, ain't gon come back with my boy," she said, as the tears began to fall from her eyes.

"You's knows it, and I's knows it, but she's gon tell us something," old Mae said, as she also felt Sistah's pain.

"I's uh gotta good mind, to take a stick to her," Sistah cried angrily.

"You's ain't gon do that child no such thing, cause Cowayne is gon be all right," old Mae said, as if she wasn't telling Sistah something.

"But Mae, my boy could be dead out there."

"Out where?" old Mae asked, as she stood unaware, of the way Sistah had spoken.

And even though Sistah had spoken as clear as the Misses, she still couldn't bring herself to answer the old female, who had given her the child that she so desperately loved. For the misfortunate female, could only think of her precious son, as she began to weep from a heavy heart.

"Come here," old Mae said to Sistah.

But Sistah was too torn by the absence of her son, to satisfy the old female's request. For the misfortunate female started backing away, while shaking her head, no longer wanting to be apart of their friendship. And as the tears ran down her face, Sistah walked away feeling, she was the blame for her child not being there. And for the first time in her disturbing existence, Sistah felt like a worthless mother, worthy of death, and all of the horror that came along with it. For Sistah wanted so much to die, just to be with her child, even if it meant burning in Hell's eternal flame, for all eternity.

"You's come here, Sistah," old Mae shouted in a state of panic, as she watched the female, slowly make a move toward the fence.

Sistah turned around and stared at old Mae for a moment, before making her way back to the friend, which had given birth, to their beloved son. But by the time Sistah had reached old Mae, she was bellowing like crazy. And no amount of hugging was going to comfort Sistah, if it wasn't coming from her son.

"Na Sistah, you's stop yo's worrying, cause he's gon come back here with uh arm full of rabbits," old Mae said, as she held the female in her arms.

"I's uh don't want no rabbits, I's uh want my boy," Sistah cried.

Old Mae tried to be strong for the both of them, but when she felt Sistah's tears on her face, the old female fell apart. The two were crying, as if Cowayne was lying up on that hill with old Pete. And their tears were a sure sign, that the two mothers were preparing themselves for the worst. Yet as Sistah went on believing that her son was dead, the old female prayed to the Lord above, for the boy to make it back in one piece.

By the time Clora Lee had made it to the old barn, and changed into a pair of pants and a shirt, Dew Dap was at the door, softly calling out her name. And a moment later, Clora Lee emerged from the barn, ready to go check the traps.

"Where's Matthew?" Dew Dap asked.

"He's sleeping," Clora Lee replied, still holding to her look of sadness, brought about by Sistah's pain.

"But Cowayne told him to help us."

"Cowayne ain't here, na come on, so we's can get back fo Sistah come looking for us," Clora Lee said, as she started for the fence.

When Clora Lee and Dew Dap had made it over the fence, Matthew came running their way with a full head of steam. And the little titan was shouting for them to wait, while charging toward the fence like a run away train.

"If n you's don't hush that yelling, Sistah gon hear ya," Clora Lee whispered.

"She with Mae, crying," Matthew said, as he squeezed through the middle and bottom plank of the fence.

"Well you's gon wake Mr. Arnold, and he's gon cut ya head off," Clora Lee said, while running the index finger of her right hand across the back of Matthew's neck.

"He's ain't gon do no such thing, cause he's can't walk."

Clora Lee grabbed Matthew by the collar, as she and Dew Dap rushed off with him. For the last thing the girl needed, was another encounter with Sistah, knowing she couldn't produce Cowayne, no matter how bad the angry mother wanted her son.

As the sun came up over the mountains, Clora Lee stood watch, as Matthew and Dew Dap checked their next to last trap.

"Hurry up," Clora Lee said softly, as she held a suspicious look in her eyes.

"Why?" Matthew asked.

"You's hush, and do as I's say," Clora Lee whispered nervously, as she stared across the creek.

"What's wrong?" Dew Dap asked, as he took on the look of an extremely nervous individual.

"Leave it," Clora Lee said, as she began to back away from the edge of the water, while still looking across the creek.

With the sudden change in their routine, Matthew slipped and fell in the water, just as he released the trap. And to the little boy's misfortune, the trap gave way, catching his foot like a coon.

"Get him free," Clora Lee shouted, as if Dew Dap wasn't already trying to free the boy from the well made trap. "Cut it," she said strongly, while spotting a group of white men riding toward them.

When Dew Dap saw what Clora Lee was looking at, he panic. And with his hands shaking like a drunk, in a desperate need of a drink, the boy mistakenly dropped the knife.

"You's pick up that knife, and cut that damn rope," Clora Lee spat, as if she were Mr. Arnold in the flesh.

Knowing Clora Lee had the pistol, Cowayne use to shoot the doe, Dew Dap quickly settled down. And with the knife back in his hand, Dew Dap cut the rope, right before scooping Matthew out of the water.

"You's get him back to that woodshed," Clora Lee barked, as she placed her back up against a tree.

"You's can't stay here," Dew Dap said, as he did his best to hold Matthew.

But Matthew was clawing and kicking, as he tried with all his might to break free, while crying out for Clora Lee.

"Matthew, you's mind me, and gone back to that woodshed," Clora Lee growled, as she prepared herself for the fight which had death written all over it.

As her hands disappeared beneath the faded blue Union shirt, Clora Lee did her best to block Matthew out of her mind. For the girl knew she would be giving the white men a big advantage, if she were to allow herself to be affected, by Matthew and his childish antics. So with her head in the fight, Clora Lee steadied herself, and quickly mapped out a strategy. And after watching several battles near that same body of water, Clora Lee knew her opponents were riding in to a big disadvantage. For the girl knew, when the white men horses hit the water, she was coming up shooting.

But just before the white men reached the creek, Clora Lee was thrown for a loop. For she heard one of the men shout, don't let them boy's get away. And that left Clora Lee with a very serious problem. The teen was being forced to make a decision, she cared not to make. But in no time at all, the female was back to thinking. And by the time the white men horses hit the water, they got an unwelcome surprise. For when Clora Lee brought her hands from beneath the faded union shirt, they held the two pearl handle pistols. And the teen didn't hesitate, as she took to firing the fancy weapons at will.

By the time Clora Lee had fired three shots from the pistol in her left hand, and five from the gun she held firmly with the right, the four white men bodies were in the water. But Clora Lee didn't have time to celebrate the fact, that she had killed four white men without ever allowing them get off a single shot. For Matthew had broken away from Dew Dap, and was charging toward her, not knowing, he was running head first into a tornado. For Clora Lee spun around, while raising her right leg just in time to catch Matthew in the chest with it, thus sending the poor boy crashing to the ground.

"Stay!" Clora Lee shouted, as she held the pistol in her right hand on Matthew. But the pistol in Clora Lee's left hand was cocked, and ready to fire upon anything, that had enough life left in it, to crawl out of the water. And her cross arm stance, told Dew Dap, what her and Cowayne had been doing all those years.

"I's uh gon tell…."

Before Matthew could get the word Sistah out of his mouth, Clora Lee had placed her left foot under the poor boy's chin. And with her foot applying just enough pressure to keep Matthew from speaking, Clora Lee eyes commanded him to be quiet. And as the three ex-slaves watched one of the white men crawl from the water, Clora Lee took to reloading her pistols.

With the pistols reloaded, Clora Lee walked over to the crawling man, as if she were dying to be her grandfather. And what Matthew saw his sister do without a ounce of hesitation, told him, he wouldn't be telling anyone, anything. For Clora Lee placed four bullets in the back of the white man's head, thus putting an end to his ex-slave hunting career.

"Tell your God, we ain't slaves no mo," Clora Lee shouted to the dead man. "Get up" she barked at Matthew, while walking toward him.

Matthew stood up looking scared, as if he thought his sister was going to shoot him as well. And the way Clora Lee reloaded the pistol, with every step she took, gave Dew Dap the same impression.

"Get them horses," Clora Lee said to Dew Dap, while staring at Matthew.

The large teen, ran down to the creek, and quickly gathered up the horses, before making a hastily return with the animals. And Clora Lee quickly took one of the horses and tied it to the tail of another, as she told Matthew, to get his butt in a saddle. And when her little brother was clearly seated on a horse, Clora Lee gave him the critters, along with a hateful stare. Then with the arrogance of a woman born to kill, Clora Lee swung up on a horse without ever placing her foot in the stirrup.

"Go," Clora Lee shouted, as she gave her horse a good thump. "And you's hurry up and get back to that corral," she said angrily, causing the little boy to ride as fast, as he could.

When Clora Lee and Dew Dap made it behind the pig pin, they found Matthew waiting for them. And after quickly dismounting, and giving the horses to Matthew, Clora Lee rushed off to the blacksmith shop.

Arriving at the blacksmith shop, Clora Lee found Sistah there. Yet the last thing, the teen needed at that time, was to deal with Sistah over something she didn't know anything about. So Clora Lee quickly ran to the back of the shop, and hid her pistols. Then like a white woman on an evening stroll, the teen took the long way to the female shed, hoping old Mae wouldn't ask her about Cowayne, or the shooting she may have heard.

When Clora Lee made it to the female shed, she took a seat in the doorway, and waited for old Mae to start in on her. But to her surprise, old Mae didn't say a word, as she just sat on the stump, looking worried, while picking at her fingers. And that made the teen feel worst then ever, as she felt like crying.

"You's gave them critters, to Sistah?" old Mae asked, when she got around to speaking.

The untimely question caught Clora Lee off guard, as she had prepared herself to talk about Cowayne, and his absence.

"Uh huh," Clora Lee said, as she broke down in to tears.

"Child, what you's crying for," old Mae asked, as if she didn't already know.

There was nothing to happen on the Big A plantation, that the old female didn't know about. For old Mae had eyes and ears in the strangest places, but the old female wasn't going to tell Clora Lee that, as she watched the girl shake her head no. And like Sistah, old Mae knew that Clora Lee was crying over Cowayne, and his absence.

"You's come here," old Mae said, as the girl's crying got stronger.

Clora Lee got up and went over to old Mae, knowing she couldn't tell the birth mother of her friend the truth. Yet she stood next to the kind hearted female, dying for her to make things right. And when old Mae wrapped her large arm around Clora Lee, the teen appeared to feel a little better. But when the old female began to rock Clora Lee ever so lightly, she threw the teen for a whirl. For Clora Lee got the chance to hear something, only fourteen of the old slave's sixteen children were privilege to hear. The old female started to hum. And her humming was just as soft, and as sweet as Sistah's could ever be. And when Clora Lee tried to pull back, so she could look the plantation's oldest picker in the eye, old Mae held on to her a little tighter.

"Na don't you's be worrying, bout that Cowayne, cause he's ain't out yonder by him self," old Mae said, looking up in the sky.

Looking at the near toothless smile, Clora Lee wondered how the old female could be doing such a thing, when they hadn't heard from Cowayne in nearly two days. Yet Clora Lee knew old Mae believed in the white man's God, just as much as Sistah. But God, or no God, this was Cowayne, and Clora Lee was only going to believe her eyes. And until Cowayne came back to her, Clora Lee had no intentions of trusting God, or anyone else.

"Na Clora Lee, you's knows I's uh can't do no humming," old Mae said, after singing a bit of the old song Duval had taught Sistah. "And don't you's be telling folk, I's uh can hum, cause theys knows better," old Mae went on.

Clora Lee wondered why the old female would want to hide a voice, that was just as good, or maybe better then Sistah's. Yet before Clora Lee could contradict her statement, old Mae took to humming again. But the old female didn't hum long. For old Mae gave Clora Lee just enough to see her through the day, before sending the teen on her way.

Knowing that Sistah was still out there, Clora Lee hated to leave the protection awarded her, from standing next to the old female. But the girl knew she couldn't go on avoiding Sistah, seeing that they both had to sleep in the same shed together.

"You's heard that there shooting?" old Mae asked, as Clora Lee started to walk away.

Clora Lee stopped in her tracks, but didn't turn around. "Uh huh," she replied, while shuffling off rather quickly.

Clora Lee knew she had to hurry up and find Joan, before Sistah got the notion to look for the little ant. And knowing that old Mae heard her shooting, Clora Lee was pretty darn sure Sistah did as well. That was why Clora Lee found herself trotting toward the woodshed like some scared slave. For the teen had no doubt in her mind, if Sistah got a hold of Joan, the little work a lot, was going to talk faster then Matthew on a rainy day.

When Clora Lee reached the woodshed, she didn't know whether to breathe a sigh of relief, or fall into a complete state of panic. Neither Joan nor Sistah were any where in sight, and that meant the two could have been together. Clora Lee ran up to the broken down building, and peeped in the door, without speaking to Sally or the girls.

"She's gone some where with Dew Dap," Sally said, as she poured some water on the coon that was slowly roasting over an open fire.

Sally's words, gave Clora Lee the chance to regroup, and ask the female, if she had seen Sistah.

"She's come through here right fo you's did, asking for Joan," Sally replied, as she watched Bessie thread a needle.

Sally might as well, had taken a giant needle, and ran it deep into Clora Lee's heart. For her words had hit the teen where it hurt. And with Cowayne out there by himself, Clora Lee felt she was already doing enough hurting.

Seeing that Clora Lee was looking lost, Sally sought to try and clear the girl's head. "I's uh told her, the same thing I's told you. She's went that uh way with Dew Dap," Sally said, pointing in the direction of the pigpen.

Clora Lee took off like a scared cat, as she tried to make it to the former house slave, before Sistah got a hold of her. And poor Dew Dap would be just as bad as Matthew, if Sistah started in on him, Clora Lee thought to herself, as she took to the brush. And seeing that Sally had given Sistah far too much information, the girl could feel her goose cooking over a blazing fire. So that was why she found herself creeping through the thick brush from the back side of the pigpen, while hearing Sistah bellowing like a mad cow.

"I's knows, ya'll know where my boy is, but ya'll ain't gotta tell me nothing uh tall," Sistah yelled, as she stormed away crying.

Clora Lee stayed hid, until she was absolutely sure, Sistah wasn't up to one of her tricks. Then, and only then, did the teen emerge from the brush, wondering why she had ever doubted her friends?

"You's just missed Sistah," Joan said, as Matthew led her and Dew Dap's horses around the pigpen.

"And she's awful mad," Matthew said, looking scared. "Is she's gon give you's uh beating?" the little boy asked.

"No," Clora Lee replied, looking worried. "What she said bout our horses?"

"Nothing," Dew Dap mumbled. "I's uh reckon, Cowayne uh be back tomorrow," he went on to say, while trying to maintain his balance.

"Where's Pleasant?" Clora Lee asked.

"He done rode his horse," Matthew said, while starting to run with the animals.

"Matthew, I's uh done told ya, not to do that," Joan said, as her voice bounced, as much as her breast.

Clora Lee smiled as she took Joan's horse from Matthew, and led the animal around the pen. But it didn't take Clora Lee long, before she was up on the animal with the girl, taking her friend faster and faster.

"Clora Lee, I's uh gon whop you's good, when we's get off this here horse," Joan said, giving her best friend another reason to laugh.

"You's member, you's hit with that old broom?"

"And I's uh gon hit ya, again," Joan shouted.

With Joan's statement waiting to become a reality, she and Clora Lee knew they were truly the best of friends. And with their friendship being one of the best ever, the girls knew no amount of broom whopping, was going to tear them apart.

Chapter 21

Leaving the Big A

The next morning, Cowayne strolled across the main yard, long before the sun launched its attack on the nightly sky. And as the six coons, and one possum he had tied to a branch, made enough noise to wake the dead, the teen knew he wasn't going to surprise anyone. Yet Cowayne didn't seem to care, as he pulled the branch with a small piece of rope. And despite the animals voicing their opposition to the way they were being treated, judge Cowayne wasn't in the mood for dealing with complaints of any kind. Instead, the boy just wanted something to eat, along with a few hours of sleep.

"Morning," Cowayne said to Clora Lee, Matthew, and Dew Dap, as they came to investigate the racket.

But the critters complaining didn't just wake the dead. For the animals also had half of the plantation stretching and yawning, as if it was high noon. But when Sistah saw what was causing the disturbance, she was on her feet and out of the door faster then a bad boy's spit. And in no time flat, Sistah was charging toward Cowayne like a bolt of lightning.

"Where you's been?" Sistah yelled, as she tried to kiss her baby, and talk at the same time.

Even though Clora Lee wanted to be the first person to hold Cowayne in her arms, she politely relinquished the right away to the boy's favorite mother.

"Don't you's ever leave me again," Sistah said, as she tried to kiss every inch of the boy's face.

"I's uh ain't go no where," Cowayne said, unaware that Sistah knew he had left the plantation.

Before Sistah knew it, she had slapped Cowayne in the chest. "Don't you lie to me, I's uh ain't sleep a wink. And I's knows, you's done left here," Sistah said angrily.

After receiving his very first lick from Sistah, Cowayne didn't know how to respond to such an act. But with the tears falling from her eyes, he couldn't bring himself to tell another lie, even if it was going to be a better one. And the boy's mind quickly fell on the day, when Mrs. Arnold had beaten him. He remembered how Sistah cried at his feet. And she cried that whole night as well, while holding him in her arms, as if he were still an infant. A lump came up in Cowayne's throat, as he searched for the right words that would make his special mother feel better.

"I's uh sorry, Sistah, but I's uh had to go, to prove I's strong," Cowayne said, remembering Pleasant had told him, he and his village were taken by the slave traders, as they celebrated his successful transformation to adult hood.

"And I's uh sorry, I's uh hit ya," Sistah said through her crying.

"You's can hit me again, if n you's want, cause I's uh yo's baby," Cowayne replied.

"You's, my baby. You's, my baby," Sistah shouted, as she rocked her son from side to side.

Even though old Mae knew Mr. Arnold was a dead man, too evil to die, she still appeared to be worried about something. And as the old female stood in the doorway of the crumbling shed, she watched, as Sistah showed Cowayne all the love in the world. And just like Sistah, there were tears running down the old female's face, yet no one noticed old Mae as she cried. For they were all marveling over the attention Sistah was giving her baby, which left the old female feeling like a defunct outcast.

After allowing Cowayne to eat more then his share of their breakfast, both Clora Lee and Sistah sent him to the old barn for a bit of sleep. And while Sistah spent the whole morning, expressing her joy over Cowayne's return, Clora Lee sat outside of the old barn with her pistols. For Clora Lee was standing guard over what she deemed to be her own. And as she did so, the girl fully understood, the plantation had become a very hostel place for the teen. But if Mr. Arnold or anyone else saw fit to harm her Cowayne, they would face the same fate, as that old Reb.

When Cowayne had finally opened his eyes from a long nap, he and Clora Lee got down to covering the next two days of their lives. The two had to make sure everything was just right, before going out into the white man's world.

"You's see'd any white men," Clora Lee asked, as she appeared to be sad.

"I's uh see'd um, but theys ain't see'd me," the boy said, as he stared across the yard."

Clora Lee laid her head on Cowayne's shoulder without saying another word, as she ran her hand inside of his. And when Clora Lee took notice of how his hands had grown over the years, she had to smile. For she knew the two of them weren't just growing older, they were also growing up. And if Cowayne were white, he would be considered a man, worthy of a woman, and a family. But Clora Lee little experience from the day before, told her it was unlikely, they would be welcomed with open arms, in the white man's world.

"You's had any trouble?" Cowayne asked.

"Na do I's uh look, like I's had trouble?" Clora Lee replied, as she studied his face.

Like all females, when faced with a troubled question, Clora Lee gave Cowayne a gray answer. An answer, that could never be seen as a lie, nor would anyone ever be able to dispute its truth. And women from all four corners of the earth, as well as the center, have mastered such a craft since the beginning of time. And no matter how long the earth will continue to turn, women everywhere, will forever be masters of their craft. Yet Clora Lee knew her Cowayne was going to see the four new horses, and she would be force to tell him the plain truth.

"What you's thinking bout?" Cowayne asked, as the girl appeared to be miles away.

"Na I's uh ain't thinking uh tall," Clora Lee said, as she laid her head against his dark brown face. "What I's uh gon think about ya for?" Clora Lee went on, before kissing his ear.

Clora Lee was becoming a master in her own right, as she went on manipulating their conversation. For the teen didn't want to tell Cowayne about their little skirmish with the white men, for fearing he wouldn't want to leave the plantation. And the last thing Clora Lee wanted for the two of them, was to stay on the Big A, knowing that Cowayne would forever be in danger. So the way Clora Lee saw it, Cowayne didn't need to know about yesterday for the time being, no more then he needed to know right away, that his mother could sing just as good as Sistah.

By the time the two realized it, they were on the ground wrestling like two puppies at play. And like always, Cowayne allowed Clora Lee to get the best of him.

"You's surrender?" Clora Lee asked, as she sat on Cowayne's midsection.

"No," Cowayne said firmly.

"Then I's uh speck, I's uh gotta beat ya, like them Blue Coats beat them Rebs," Clora Lee said, right before Cowayne rolled her over.

Feeling she was in a better position to make Cowayne surrender, Clora Lee wrapped her legs around the boy and went to work. "Na, do ya surrender?" she laughed, while moving her body against Cowayne's firm erection.

And when Cowayne collapsed, Clora Lee proudly accepted his action as a yes, even though she knew the out come from the very start. And Clora Lee knew she would also get a touch of satisfaction from what they were doing. So that was why she found great pleasure, in torturing the boy with sweet kisses, while working her pelvic to another dry climax.

With a fist full of Cowayne's hair in her hand, Clora Lee pulled his head back and said, "I's uh had enough, na you's get up."

With Cowayne, feeling he was one kiss away from Clora Lee's gates, the teen didn't see any reason to stop. Yet Clora Lee needed her lover to stop, as her breathing told him, she was ready to go all the way. And all the way, was where Cowayne saw fit to take his Lee, as he proceeded to squeeze her breast, as she sucked on his neck with a great deal of passion. A passion that was so strong, it had Clora Lee feeling like a bird, free falling from the top of a cloud. And with Cowayne going for the buttons on her shirt, Clora Lee had begun to fear the fast moving fall. And by the time Cowayne had made the first button a casualty, Clora Lee knew she was in a situation, which left the captor, at the mercy of the captive.

"I's uh surrender," she whispered, hoping to regain control of her body and mind.

But like a mouse being stalked by a cat, Clora Lee didn't see a way out of her dilemma. And just like the mouse, every move Clora Lee made, appeared to take her virginity one step closer to a quick demise. But with hopes of saving the life of their promise, the teen tried to slide her body from beneath the danger. Yet before Clora Lee could make her great escape, she found herself with a much bigger problem. For the teen had come to realize, all of the buttons on her shirt were undone. But that was only half of Clora Lee's problem. For by the time, she took to chewing on her bottom lip, Clora Lee could feel the warmth of Cowayne's mouth on her breast. And with all of his squeezing and nibbling, Clora Lee nearly lost her mind. Yet as she laid half way between satisfaction and disappointment, Clora Lee was well on her way, to entertaining the thought of giving in to their burning desires. But some how the teen knew that would be a bad thing, with everyone depending on the two of them.

"You's get up," Clora Lee cried, as if she didn't really mean it.

And with Cowayne not listening, the girl didn't know what to do. But with her purse crying out for the real thing, Clora Lee knew she had to make her point a little clearer.

"You's get up na, and I's mean it," she said, as her voice came back like a strong wind.

"Lee, if n I's get up, I's uh ain't talking to ya no mo," Cowayne said, with the most serious look on his face.

Clora Lee closed her eyes, before speaking. "If n you's wanna go back on our word, then you's go right ahead, but I's uh ain't gon help ya none," she mumbled, as a tear ran down the side of her face.

As Clora Lee laid stretch out with her eyes closed, she could feel Cowayne's pitiful dark brown eyes up on her. But the girl knew all too well, the danger that would come from looking into those beautiful puppy dog eyes. For they had controlled her from the day she was born. And Clora Lee knew they would continue to do so, until she was no more among the living. And the teen knew they were waiting for her to raise those pretty light brown eyelids of hers. But Clora Lee weren't about to do such a thing, as she stuck to her guns.

Seeing that Clora Lee was dead set on disappointing him one more time, Cowayne rolled off of her, with the intentions of never mounting the girl again, even if she begged him to.

"You's mad at me," Clora Lee asked, after making it to her feet.

But the girl could have asked the question a thousand times, and she still would not have gotten an answer. For Cowayne was dead set on staying silent. And even though his silence, left Clora Lee hanging over the cliff of disaster, she still held to her faith, he would not seek out another. So with the chill of their painful victory covering them like a blanket, Clora Lee sought to give her friend some time to himself.

"I's uh gon go by Sistah," she mumbled, while walking away.

When Clora Lee was gone, Cowayne laid back and gazed up at the white clouds in the sky. And while the fluffy white patchs, helped to make the clear blue sky, take on the look of a quilt, Mrs. Arnold often used to cover her bed, Cowayne stared at a pattern, which clearly resembled a large horse. And while studying the figure, the boy wished he was still out marking the trail. For if he was still out in the white man's world, Clora Lee wouldn't be sad, nor would he be frustrated. Yet the teen knew the white man's world, would be nothing without his Lee. So Cowayne just sat wondering why he and Clora Lee made that stupid agreement in the first place. But then it occurred to the teen. For Clora Lee had offered her body to him, the morning he left to go mark the trail, and he respectfully refused, just so they wouldn't break their word. Cowayne closed his eyes, and thought of all the wonderful things he saw, while marching across the land, the Indians once called their home.

After two days of resting and planning, Cowayne and Clora Lee were ready to take their family and friends to what they hoped would be a better life.

"I's uh don't see it," Matthew hollered to Clora Lee from beneath the mansion.

"You's keep yo's voice down," Clora lee said softly. "Na you go over yonder, where I's uh done told ya."

Matthew moved toward the front of the mansion, in the direction where Clora Lee had pointed. "Wow," he said in a state of aw.

"You's got it?" Clora Lee asked.

"No, I's uh see uh frog, and it's uh big un."

"If n you's don't get over yonder and look for my thing, I's uh gon leave ya here," Clora Lee yelled softly.

"I's uh got it," Matthew shouted, giving his sister cause to wonder, if he was talking about the frog, or that which he went under the large house to get.

When Matthew made it to her, Clora Lee took the object and wrapped it in a piece of cloth, then the two made a bee line for the woodshed.

"What is it," Matthew asked, as the two hurried pass Effie without speaking.

"You's turn around," Clora Lee said, to Matthew, who was looking over his shoulder at their grandmother.

Matthew did as he was told, but the little boy was smiling, as if he had seen something funny.

When Clora Lee and Matthew made it to the woodshed, they got with the rest of the group, so they could go get old Mae.

"Ha ya ma, gon walk all that way," Pleasant asked.

"We's got uh wagon," Cowayne replied, speaking of the wagon, which held the bullets.

"Well I's uh hope, you's gon take her stump, cause she's ain't gon go without it," Pleasant said, as he spoke rather fast.

Like everyone else, Pleasant was nervous. But to Cowayne and Clora Lee, it was just another adventure, and they were ready to take it on with no regrets.

"Come on ma, we's ready to go," Cowayne said, as he and his group found old Mae sitting in the doorway of the female shed.

"Boy, yo's old ma, is too tired, and too old, to go anywhere this here fine day," old Mae said, as her voice sounded weaker then ever.

"But ma, you's can't stay here," Cowayne cried.

"You's come here Sistah," old Mae said, with her large arms stretched out.

Sistah went and knelt down next to old Mae with a gentle sadness. She then laid her head on the old female's large bosom, no longer wanting to leave the plantation.

"You's look funny in them breeches," old Mae said after letting out a light chuckle.

"Mae, why you's laughing at me?" Sistah asked, as she cried like a baby.

"Na you's hush that crying, Honey Bee," old Mae said as the tears, began to fall from her eyes as well.

"I's uh ain't, no honey bee," Sistah mumbled like a little girl.

"You's my Honey Bee," old Mae replied, as she stroked one of Sistah's plaits.

Joan stood in a state of shock, wondering when her mother had told old Mae about Sistah. But one look at her mother, told the female, Sally was just as shocked, as she was. Duval, Joan thought to herself, as she stared at Clora Lee, who was crying.

"You's come here Cowayne," old Mae said to the son, she lost to Sistah, three days after his birth.

With both Cowayne and Sistah in her arms, old Mae spoke decisively. "Na boy, don't you's leave ya Sistah here, you's hear me."

"Mae, I's uh ain't gon leave ya," Sistah said crying.

"Na you's hear me, and you's hear me good. You's gotta leave her, cause that old masa, got it in for ya, and he's ain't gon stop, till he's get ya."

"Mae, I's uh don't care bout that old masa, no mo. And I's uh don't care bout the Misses, neither," Sistah said, as a river of tears ran down her face.

Old Mae went back to her old trusted friend. She looked up at Pleasant, and let her teary eyes do all of the talking. And hearing the old female loud and clear, Pleasant spoke back to her with a simple nod. And with the understanding that Pleasant was going to take Sistah from that God forsaken plantation, even if he had to drag her, the old female felt at ease. And when old Mae called Sally to her, the little female wondered what the old slave wanted.

"Na you's help Cowayne take care of my Honey Bee, cause she's took care of you," old Mae said, as Sally rested on her, between Cowayne and Sistah.

Sally quickly said okay, not wanting to tell the old female, she earned every bit of the food Clora Lee had given her, by sewing those pouches. Yet Sally just listened, as old Mae told her, not to let Sistah stick herself anymore.

"Na Clora Lee, I's uh want ya'll to take Isabella with ya," old Mae said.

"No Mae, I's uh ain't gon go out yonder. I's uh ain't gon go, cause them white folks out yonder," Isabella said with fear, then took off running.

"Ma, we's can't take her, if n she's don't wanna go," Cowayne replied, while looking at Sistah.

"You's ain't gon say bye to me, Matthew?" old Mae asked.

"Uh huh," Matthew replied, as he threw himself between Cowayne and Sally.

"You's don't stand there Clora Lee," old Mae cried.

Clora Lee went over and found just enough of the old female to lay her head on. And with every one but Pleasant touching her, old Mae cried the tears of a loving mother, worthy of love. Yet there was one, she didn't call up on, knowing one day, the child would be there to guide her little family well.

"I's uh ain't gon leave ya, ma," Cowayne cried.

"Na you's hush that talk, cause you's gotta take Sistah and Sally from here, cause masa Arnold ain't dead," old Mae said, still crying. "And the Misses got it in for Joan," she went on.

Joan lowered her head, as she heard Matthew say he wasn't going to let their ex-master kill his Sistah.

"Na you's see, why you's gotta leave? Cause if n you's stay here, he's gon kill Matthew to," old Mae said crying. "And what you's, gon do bout Clora Lee? You's want her to die? Cause if n masa Arnold kill Matthew, she's gon make him kill her, and you's knows it."

Old Mae was pleading her case, hoping Sistah and Cowayne would see the danger that would surely come, from the two of them staying on that old plantation. But old Mae could have gone on talking, until there was cotton growing back in the fields, she once worked so well. For Sistah wasn't going to leave her, and the plantation's oldest picker, knew there was no way to change the dysfunctional mother's mind. So with that being her only problem, old Mae focused all of her energy on the one person, the misfortunate female could never live without. For the old slave knew if she could get Cowayne to leave, Sistah would surely follow him.

"I's uh go, ma, if n you's tell me, who's my pa is," Cowayne said, as he wiped the tears from his eyes.

"Child, I's uh don't know what you's wanna know that for," old Mae replied.

"I's uh gotta know, ma," Cowayne said with a mountain of sincerity.

Even though her son was born in to a life of slavery, he was no different then any other child. And just like every child that was, and always will be born of a woman, Cowayne had the same desperate need, to know who fathered him.

"I's uh was put with two no count slaves," old Mae mumbled, as she gazed up at the sky. "One of um was Thomas, and the other was that old Lewis. Na you's take which ever one you's want," old Mae said, as she looked at Joan.

"I's uh take um both," Cowayne said. "When you hear bout me, theys gon be calling me, Thomas Lewis," the teen spat proudly, as he held his mother with sixteen full years of love.

"Na you's gon, and take Jonathan with ya," old Mae said, no longer crying.

Hearing a name he had grown to hate, Cowayne stood back, and looked at his mother with a strangeness, which told her, he wanted no part of the Misses boy. Making sure he took Sistah from the Big A, the boy understood. Leaving her behind was hard, yet he could force himself to do it. But to take Jonathan with them, both he and Clora Lee felt that was asking far too much. Yet Cowayne agreed to do as his mother asked, while making eye contact with Clora Lee. And Clora Lee had that I don't know look on her face, which told Cowayne, she was just as surprised as he was. But if the one she loved, agreed to take Jonathan with them, then Clora Lee was willing to accept the task. But if that low down snake were to try anything, he would surely die, Clora Lee vowed in silence, as she stared at old Mae.

"Sally gon need somebody," old Mae said, looking at the female, who didn't like the idea, no more then the two teens.

Poor Sally couldn't understand why her old friend would do such a thing. If old Mae wanted to give her a male to deal with, she could have at least picked one that knew how to treat a female. What about Joan's father, or even Nelson. Sally liked Nelson, and she had thought about asking Clora Lee, if it was okay to bring him along. Yet old Mae had given her to a good for nothing dog, who wasn't even worthy of a pig's love, the pretty little ex-house slave thought to herself.

"Pleasant you's get my Honey Bee," old Mae said, as she held Sistah, with what strength she had left.

"Mae I's uh done told ya, I's uh ain't gon leave ya," Sistah cried, as she continued to hold on to the old female.

Old Mae uttered those special words which she said to Pleasant on his first day, as well as to her babies, on the night they were born. "Gorr goal lu di na balch," old Mae said, as she ran her hand over Sistah's head.

Pleasant took hold of Sistah, but he couldn't get her arms from around old Mae's massive right leg. And no matter how hard he tried, Sistah continued to hold on to old Mae for dear life. But then like a flash of light, Nelson ran in and grabbed Sistah. And while bending over Sistah as if he wanted to kiss her, Nelson blew something green out of his mouth, and the misfortunate female immediately went limp. The mysterious one then scooped Sistah up and ran toward the fence, with Clora Lee and Cowayne dead on his heels.

"You's stop um," old Mae shouted to Pleasant, after calling out to her son, and getting no response.

After giving old Mae a quick kiss on the fore head, knowing it would be the last time he would ever see her, Pleasant went to do his friend one last favor.

"You's put her down," Cowayne said" as he and Clora Lee flanked her uncle.

With his back to the fence, Nelson slowly lowered the still unconscious Sistah to the ground. And as he could feel her feet touching the earth, Nelson admired Clora Lee and Cowayne's attack method. Yet the mysterious one knew he didn't want to hurt Cowayne or his niece.

"You's ain't got much time, boy," Nelson said, looking at Clora Lee.

Nelson wasn't watching Clora Lee, because he felt she was the more dangerous of the two. For Nelson knew Cowayne well enough to know, if he were to let Sistah fall, the teen would rather die, before allowing his mother to hit the ground. For Nelson knew as long as he held on to Sistah, Cowayne was under his control, which meant Clora Lee was left to launch an attack all by herself.

"Na Clora Lee, ya'll stop," Pleasant said, as he tried to keep the children from doing something they would soon regret.

"He's done something to Sistah," Cowayne shouted.

"She's ain't nothing but sleep," Pleasant said, as he stood in front of Nelson and Sistah.

"He's ain't got no call, to spit in her face," the boy yelled.

"Na boy, you's ain't got much time, fo it be dark, and them white folks gon be out looking for ya'll," Nelson said, still looking at Clora Lee.

"What you's know bout white folk, you's ain't never been no where but on this old plantation," Clora Lee yelled.

Nelson laughed, as he tapped Sistah in the face. And no sooner then the misfortunate female, opened her eyes, she started calling out for old Mae once again. But when Sistah realized she was nowhere near the crumbling shed, the fight for old Mae started all over again.

"You's let her go," Cowayne yelled.

"You's keep yo's voice down," Pleasant said, as he also tried to hold Sistah.

"He's ain't got no call, to spit that stuff in her face," Clora Lee barked, repeating Cowayne's earlier statement.

"If n you's say we's leaving, then we's better be on our way," Pleasant said, as he held on to Sistah.

Cowayne took one last look at his mother, knowing that Pleasant was right. Yet the teen couldn't bring him self to move, as his eyes fell on Clora Lee. The girl was crying, as she tried her best to hold Matthew, who had to be fighting harder then Sistah, as he struggled to break free. And at that very moment, Cowayne wondered if their desire, to leave the plantations, was worth all the pain it was causing.

Then like a Rebel soldier, refusing to leave his fallen comrade, Cowayne scooped Matthew up and put him over the fence. But the little boy showed his disapproval, by trying to slide back through the middle and bottom slack. And seeing that Matthew wasn't going to stop, Cowayne had no other choice but to call on Clora Lee for help.

"Come on Lee, you's gotta hold Matthew," he said.

Clora Lee climbed over the fence, and took hold of Matthew, as the little boy continued to struggle for what he took to be a good cause. And Cowayne couldn't help but to feel sorry for Matthew, as he was left with the impossible task, of trying to get control of Sistah.

"Sistah, you's gotta stop fighting," the teen said crying.

"I's uh ain't gon leave Mae," Sistah bellowed.

"I's uh don't wanna leave her, but we's gotta, cause we's gotta go."

Faced with the thought of losing her only child, Sistah was forced to rethink the situation. And seeing that her baby needed comforting, Sistah stopped fighting and took hold of him. And if Pleasant thought Sistah and Cowyane favored each other before, then after seeing the two ex-slaves crying, he was totally convinced they had something in common.

"I's uh don't wanna leave her, Sistah, but we's gotta," Cowayne said, as he couldn't stop himself from crying.

"I's uh know," Sistah replied, while wiping the tears from both of their faces.

With Sistah and Cowayne ready to go, Pleasant signaled the others to get over the fence. And like a small group of sheep, trying to make their way along an icy path, one by one, the ex-slaves began to cross over the fence. Dew Dap put Joan over the fence first, then handed her Bessie and Madeline. With all that she had, Sally pulled herself over the fence in her union breeches, more then ready to bid the Big A Plantation goodbye. And the four ex-slaves who were invited to join Clora Lee and Cowayne's little expedition, climbed over the fence, wondering if they had made the right choice. For the two males and two females weren't sure, what to make of Sistah and Cowayne's reluctance to leave old Mae behind.

"I's uh gotta get Jonathan," Cowayne said, as he held Sistah's hands in his.

"We's don't want him," Clora Lee growled.

Cowayne couldn't agree more, as he started to go over the fence, just before Sistah stopped him.

"You go get that boy, like Mae told you," Sistah said, then climbed over the fence.

There it was again, Clora Lee thought to herself. Sistah was acting like a normal female, and Clora Lee was determined to find out how she could travel between the two worlds so easily. Yet Clora Lee knew the Big A plantation, wasn't the place to draw Sistah's little trick out in to the open. So with Dew Dap holding Matthew, Clora Lee took a seat in the cool grass, and waited for Cowayne to return with that no count, good for nothing lap dog.

When Cowayne found Jonathan, the newly unwanted member of their traveling party, was sitting out by the old pecan tree looking at Obdi. The once faithful house slave was running across the yard with a crowbar, as though he had to be somewhere fast. And as Cowayne drew closer to Jonathan, he saw that forever disgusting smile, and wondered what his mother was thinking, when she asked him to do such a thing. For if Jonathan could find humor in Obdi's sense of urgency, then the Misses special slave, wasn't someone Cowayne wanted with him, nor their group.

"You's ready?" Cowayne asked, as he stopped about five feet from Jonathan.

Jonathan got up, as he continued to watch Obdi run toward the front gate with the crowbar. And when he was finished dusting his pants off, Jonathan took to sizing Cowayne up, before moving a muscle.

When Cowayne and Jonathan reached the rest of the group, everyone stood up except for Sally. For the female that was the exact same age as Sistah, sat looking at Jonathan, as if he were something a person would get on the bottom of their shoes, while tracking through a cow pasture. And she would have went on looking at Jonathan that way, if it were not for Dew Dap, reaching his hand out to help her up.

"Thank ya," Sally said, after making it to her feet.

With everyone ready to go, Cowayne and Clora Lee led their group toward the wooded area. And as Matthew reluctantly marched toward the brush, he tried to take one last look at old Mae, but no sooner then the boy turned his head to steal a quick peep, Clora Lee spun him around like a top, thus making everything a blur.

"You's can come from behind that shed, na," old Mae said softly.

Effie stepped from behind the wall, sobbing as if she was made of tears. And while walking toward old Mae, Effie held her hand against her face, the same way Clora Lee did, the day she came home crying.

"Na Effie, you's knows, you's gon be with them young ns, so you's stop that there crying," old Mae said.

"I know Mae, but I'm scared," Effie said, as she continued to cry.

"Na you's ain't got no call to be scared, ain't nothing gon happen to ya out yonder."

"I don't think I'm going to make it."

"Na you's hush that kind uh talk, cause you's knows, you's can walk from here to yonder, so you's ain't got no call to be scared of nothing," old Mae said, as she held Effie in a motherly embrace. "Na we's got work to do, cause you's gotta be ready, when Honey Bee, boy come back for ya."

There was no mistaking it, for both old Mae and Effie knew, Sistah was Beatrice.

As Obdi and Nelson struggled to move the stump, that old Mae spent nearly a life time sitting on, Effie took a straight razor and a tin cup out of her apron. And with the cup resting against old Mae's left hand, Effie went to work. And as the blood flowed from the old female, she began to hum ever so softly, while watching her children head out to find freedom. For they were the last of the old slave's sixteen babies, that were born in to a world of hatred and abuse. But the old female was getting the chance to see them walk away from a world she must die in. And by the time her children had made it over the last hill, the old slave known as Mae, was no more.

Sistah stopped, as everyone continued down the hill, while they made their way toward the brush. And looking back, Sistah acted as though a chill had come over her from a slight breeze, even though there wasn't a spec of wind blowing anywhere. Yet Sistah wasn't the only one to feel the chilling effect, being that Cowayne had felt it as well. There was something seriously wrong, and the old slave's children knew it. And as Sistah started to run back up the hill, Sally caught a funny feeling out of the blue. But Cowayne could only stop one of them, so he grabbed Sistah. Yet the misfortunate female, wasn't about to let anyone stop her from getting back to old Mae, as she took to fighting Cowayne with an anger so strong, it could have moved mountains. For Sistah was determine to get back to old Mae, even if it meant she had to hurt her baby to do it.

"You's let me go, cause Mae need me," Sistah shouted.

"I's uh can't let ya go back," Cowayne said, as he took to crying, while absorbing every blow Sistah laid on his head and face.

"You's let me go," Sistah cried, as Cowayne grabbed her hands.

"You's stop, Sistah," Sally said crying, while looking back toward the main yard.

Despite hearing Sally's direct order, Sistah went right on fighting, until the short female took hold of her nose. And as Sally held Sistah's nose, she told Cowayne to get up. But having a feeling, that Sally was going to need more then a simple tug on Sistah's nose, to get control of the situation, Cowayne was reluctant to do as the short female asked.

"You's get off of her, or I's gon grab yo nose to," Sally said as she cried, without knowing why. "Na you's get up, so we's can go," she said to Sistah, after Cowayne had released his lone remaining mother.

"You's hear yo's singing? Cowayne asked Sistah, as they started back to walking.

"I's uh hear it, but I's ain't singing," Sistah replied through her crying.

"Then I's uh reckon, you's need to keep walking," Sally said, never acknowledging, nor denying that she heard the singing as well.

But Clora Lee didn't hear any singing, yet she was willing to bet Cowayne and Sistah did. And the young quarter breed female knew they had to be hearing old Mae. Some how, Clora Lee felt old Mae humming to her, was no accident, as she was beginning to think the old female had planned for her to hear the soft melody for some reason, that would surely come to light one day. For the old female knew better then anyone, if she were to tell Sistah and Cowayne of the humming, they both would believe her. Yet Clora Lee found it hard to believe the look on Joan's face, as she wondered if the little stump was hearing the humming as well.

Chapter 22

Bad Tradition

After pushing everyone hard, to make up for the lost time, Clora Lee and Cowayne reached their first marker, just before night fall.

"YOU'S GON BE ALRIGHT?" Cowayne asked Clora Lee.
"You's get them horses, cause we's tired uh walking," Clora Lee said, as she could feel Jonathan's eyes gripping her body, like an extra layer of skin.

"You's member, you's gotta be up at first light," Cowayne said, as he, Matthew, and Pleasant started back for the plantation.

Cowayne didn't have to tell Dew Dap, he was leaving Clora Lee and Sistah under his care. For the two boys had made such an agreement, long before either of them knew, they would ever be leaving the plantation. And knowing such a thing, Dew Dap would never let his friend down, no matter what life laid upon his shoulders.

That night, while Mr. Arnold and his family ate their evening meal, Effie stood against the wall behind him. She watched, as one of Mrs. Arnold's girls, fed the sad broken man, as if he were a child.

"Did either of you girls, see Jonathan, today?" Mrs. Arnold asked.

"No Misses," the girls replied, like a pair of skinny black cats.

Then all at once, the third generation Aaron J. Arnold started coughing. Before Mrs. Arnold could ask her son if anything was wrong, she and her baby daughter started coughing as well. Then Mrs. Arnold's two love slaves took to gagging, like a couple of geese, or two cats, choking on the same fur ball.

With everyone gagging except for Christine and her father, Effie slowly made her way toward the table. And when the once preferred house slave came to a stop, she was standing directly behind her former master.

"I don't have to tell you, your wife has been sleeping with a filthy slave," Effie said, with her face pressed up against Mr. Arnold's. And as she looked at Christine, Effie spoke with a slithering tone. "But your little girl there, I am not allowed to harm a hair on her head," she went on to say, with a deadly tone.

"What you's do?" Christine screamed.

"Now why would I do anything?" Effie asked. "You see that little girl of yours. She is going to have Jonathan's baby. One that will look like your daughter, and grand-daughter, and that is why you don't see her spitting up Mae's potion," Effie said with a smile, as Christine shouted for her to shut up.

But Effie went right on talking, while everyone except for Mr. Arnold and Christine were spewing green vomit, as if they were a group of human volcanos. For Effie had used old Mae's blood, along with the root, Nelson and Obdi got from beneath the old slave's favorite stump, to make a deadly fast killing poison. A poison that was violently killing Mr. Arnold's family, and there was nothing the man could do about it, being that Jeremiah had sealed his fate, shortly before the war had ended.

"I am going to tell everyone, what you have done, and they are going to burn you alive," Christine yelled, as she stood crying.

"And what are you going to tell them, when they see that child crawl out of your belly? And what are you going to do, when they kill it, before casting you down to the whores?" Effie shouted, as she eyed Christine with a vile disturbing stare.

Christine violently pushed her chair back from the table, as if she wanted to charge the former house slave. And as the pregnant young female stood clinching a knife in her hand, she couldn't find the nerve to move toward the one who was killing her family. But when her eyes fell on little Aaron Arnold lying on the floor, shaking like a fish in a basket, something snapped in Christine. And by the time her mother was no longer among the living, Christine was already fleeing the death and vomit, as she ran from the room, and out of the house.

Left all alone with the master who fathered her only child, Effie sought to get her revenge. And with a fist full of Mr. Arnold's ungroomed hair in her hand, Effie snatched his head back. Then with a slow cunningness, she placed a knife to his throat, but stopped short of killing the once powerful man. For Effie just stood enjoying the pleading look in Mr. Arnold's eyes, as the two blue balls were begging to die. And seeing such a thing, made Effie laughed a sinister laugh, while using the knife to scrap the tears from the white man's face.

Leaning over Mr. Arnold's shoulder, Effie whispered, "old Mae got something special for you down in Hell."

Then like a lantern being blown out just before bed time, Mr. Arnold's world went black.

That night, as Clora Lee slept close to Sistah, Jonathan snuck over and tried to touch her breast. But having no intentions of trusting the Misses boy, Clora Lee played possum, as she watched over the rest of the group. And no sooner then Jonathan went to enjoy him self, Clora Lee quickly clawed his face, causing him to scream, as if he were a female.

"I's uh kill ya, if n you's ever touch me," Clora Lee shouted, causing the rest of the group to spring to their feet.

One of the boys charged Jonathan, but he was much too small, and too slow to take on the bigger male. And when Dew Dap started for Jonathan, Clora Lee quickly stopped him.

"But we's can't let him do that," Dew Dap argued, knowing he could take Jonathan with ease.

"He's right," Sistah said, confirming the teen's statement.

Knowing Jonathan like she did, Clora Lee pulled one of her pistols, and said, "You's drop that knife."

Holding to that snake like smile, Jonathan slowly came out of his pocket, with a medium size knife. And after giving Dew Dap a fearful look, Jonathan tossed the knife on the ground.

"When Cowayne get back, we's gon handle ya," Clora Lee said, as she was determine to make the male pay for his mistake.

But Jonathan didn't appear to be scared, as he stood looking at Clora Lee with that ever present sneaky grin, that he wore like it was made just for him. But the ex-slave knew he was no match for Dew Dap, so he was glad Clora Lee wanted Cowayne to handle the situation. Yet Jonathan felt it would be better for him to leave the group, rather then face the fire that was sure to come from Pleasant, after he easily defeats Cowayne.

"I's uh going back to the plantation," Jonathan said, as he started to walk away.

"If n you's take one more step, I's uh gon kill ya," Clora Lee barked, as if she wished the house boy would take her threat lightly.

Like the fool that he was, Jonathan smiled, while taking that one more step with a touch of arrogance. But Jonathan's arrogance quickly faded, as Clora Lee's smoking gun, sent his body collapsing to the ground like a fallen tree.

The next morning at the crack of dawn, Effie, Obdi, and Nelson were hard at work. As for Mr. Arnold, he laid naked on the floor of the female shed, with old Mae's dead bare body on top of him. And from the missing skin off of her back, it was safe to say, the three had a hard time getting old Mae over to Mr. Arnold. Yet the three ex-slaves stood both out of breath and proud of their accomplishment, as they were ready to send Mr. Arnold where he belong. And as Effie stood outside of the strange drawing that circled old Mae and Mr. Arnold, she said goodbye to the man.

"Hell is from where you came, and Hell is where Mae will strike you down," Effie said angrily, as she watched Mr. Arnold struggled to breathe. Then with a tormenting sass, Effie spoke like a good slave. "Masa, masa, old Mae had a young n, living in yo's house."

After taking the burning torch from Obdi and dropping it in the circle, Effie emerged from the female shed, as the flames rapidly over took the rotting structure. Yet Effie wasn't scared of the fire, or the damage it was doing, as she went stood next to Nelson and Obdi. And flanked by the two males, who were holding musket rifles, while they stood with pistols in their belts, Effie wore a satisfying look on her face. For it was the same look, she often displayed, while watching Clora Lee learn how to read and right.

"Look," Obdi said, as he pointed the musket rifle in his right hand, toward the group of white men charging through the front gate on horse back.

"Give me that," Effie said, taking the rifles from Obdi's hands. "Put them pistols on the ground, and get out of here," she shouted.

"But Mae told us not to leave ya," Nelson said.

"Get out of here, before Jonathan gets his hands on Sally," Effie shouted, as she gave Nelson a letter, she had taken from her bosom.

Nelson immediately gave the letter to Obdi, and told him to go and follow the signs, that the two of them had talked about. And as Obdi headed for the back fence, he heard Effie shouting something about telling Clora Lee, she had Mrs. Arnold's riding crop, to get her to trust him. But Obdi wasn't thinking about trust or anything else, as he ran with all his might. But unlike Pleasant, Obdi couldn't run with the ring, he was charged to wear. Yet the ex-slave ran just the same, as he headed for the fence.

Believing the two slaves they were about to face, didn't have the nerve to pull a trigger, nor the ability to shoot straight, the white men charged on. But when Effie fired, and one of their comrade's fell from his horse, the white men knew they were in for a fight. And by the time they were able to raise their weapons, Effie had sent another white man falling to the ground. And Effie had fired all four rifles, by the time she had taken a bullet.

"I guess that little bitch, won't be keeping her slave baby after all," Effie said, as she took another bullet. "Run," Effie shouted to Nelson, as she fired her last shot, hitting nothing but air.

By the time Nelson got up to run, it was too late. A bullet caught him in the small of his back. Then another pierced his head. And as Nelson went down, a musket ball tore through his right leg, putting an end to the ex-slave's life. The mysterious one died, without ever revealing to Cowayne and Clora Lee, he was the shadow they often felt in their presence.

Not knowing that Mr. Arnold was dead, nor having any knowledge of his previous condition, the men dared to damage the once pretty white fence, in pursuit of Obdi. And being left with only one choice, the riders headed back for the front gate, hoping to catch the ex-slave before noon, so they could get back to their drinking.

"What theys call that town, where we's gon find freedom?" Pleasant asked the boy, who had begun to call himself Thomas Lewis.

"I's uh reckon, you's just named it," Thomas Lewis said, as they finished untying the horses.

"Na Cowayne, you's knows, I's ain't gon be naming nothing here bouts."

"I's uh done told my ma, I's uh gon be Thomas Lewis, and I's uh reckon, I's uh gotta be," Thomas Lewis said, thinking about the shooting they just heard.

"Well Thomas Lewis, you's tell me, ha I's done name uh town, and I's uh ain't never see'd it," Pleasant said, repeating himself.

"That's why's you's named it," Thomas Lewis replied, as they mounted their horses. "Na we's gotta get back to Lee," he went on, while giving the horse a taste of his heels.

As Thomas Lewis, Pleasant, and Matthew struck out with the horses and two cows, he noticed that his little friend wasn't talking much. In fact, Matthew hadn't said a word, since they left the plantation. Nor did the little boy seem to be excited about their trip. Not even the sight of that old large moose, which sent everyone running, could make Matthew speak a word. But Thomas Lewis did notice one thing about Matthew. For he continuously kept his eyes on the sky over the main yard, and that made the teen look as well.

"I's reckon, theys cook like Dew Dap," Thomas Lewis said, of the black smoke that was clouding the sky over the main yard.

Knowing he wasn't telling the truth, Thomas Lewis sent his eyes toward Pleasant. Yet Pleasant didn't say a word, as he to, held a look that Thomas Lewis had never seen before.

"I's uh reckon, its time to move on," Pleasant said, as he tried to ride a little faster.

Before the three could make it to the spot where Clora Lee and Cowayne often entered the brush, they heard more gunfire, and it was far too close for Thomas Lewis liking. Then a short while later, the three heard another shot, as they began to ride even faster.

"What about them cows?" Pleasant barked, as the animals couldn't keep up with the horses.

But the cows were the last thing on Thomas Lewis mind, as another shot rumbled out of the brush.

"Obdi," Matthew shouted, after taking a look over his shoulder, to see where the shooting was coming from.

Thomas Lewis turned just in time, to see the white men riding out of the brush in hot pursuit of the ex-slave.

"Matthew, you's get in that there brush, and take Pleasant with ya," Thomas Lewis said, as he gave the extra horses to the boy.

With time being of the essence, Thomas Lewis turned his horse without slowing the animal down. And as he rode toward Obdi, Thomas Lewis reached in the saddlebag, and came out with one of his pistols. And after bringing his horse to a stop, Thomas Lewis fired two quick shots, killing a white man with each.

Seeing that the teen had the ability to shoot, just as good as Effie, the two remaining white men felt it would be better for them, to abandon their mission, and head back to town. So with their horses heading in the opposite direction, the men rode as if they desperately wanted to see many more tomorrows. But their change of heart came a little too late, seeing that Thomas Lewis had already made up his mind. For Thomas Lewis fired three more shots, sending the men falling from their horses.

With the battle over, Obdi fell to the ground exhausted.

"Get up," Thomas Lewis said, as his horse stood over the former house slave.

"Theys killed Effie and Nelson," Obdi said, as he tried to catch his breath.

"What about my ma?" Thomas Lewis growled.

"She's dead," Obdi said, still gasping for air.

"You's let um kill my ma?" Thomas Lewis shouted, pointing his pistol at Obdi.

"No," Obdi said, falling back down to his knees. "She's was buried this morning, just fo theys come through that front gate," he went on, without telling the teen how his mother died.

"What you's doing out here?" Thomas Lewis asked, as he took to reloading his pistol.

"Nelson told me bout ya markers. He's said if n I's uh follow um, then I's uh catch up with ya."

"You's lie," Thomas Lewis shouted, as he finished loading his pistol, which gave Obdi six ways to meet the white man's God.

"You's hold up, Cowayne," Pleasant said, as he rode up.

"I's uh name Thomas Lewis, na."

"Well Thomas Lewis, ya ma, had Nelson following ya. Na you's can leave him here, but I's uh ain't gon let ya kill him."

"You's can go back to that house," Thomas Lewis growled.

"Nelson said, the first born son of his pa King, gotta help us," Obdi mumbled, looking at Pleasant.

"Tie him to that horse," Pleasant said angrily, as he pointed to the animal closest to Obdi.

Getting off of his horse, Thomas Lewis could see in Pleasant's eyes, the same look he held on the day he wished to kill Big Willie. Yet Thomas Lewis didn't understand why his friend would want to do such a thing to Obdi. And what was Obdi mumbling about? For Pleasant had never told him of any such King, nor his son. Thomas Lewis was getting tired of everybody hiding things from him, as if he were still a slave.

"Ha long Nelson been following me," Thomas Lewis asked, as he finished tying Obdi to the saddle, and gathering up the dead men horses.

Seeing that Pleasant wasn't going to utter a word, Obdi sought to tell the teen what he wanted to know. "He's see'd Clora Lee kill that Rebel soldier, the day he's was choking ya," the ex-house slave said, as Thomas Lewis got on his horse.

To make sure Obdi didn't do any more talking, Pleasant told Thomas Lewis, they would talk about it later, as the three set out to catch up with Matthew. And even though Obdi had a lot more to tell the teen, but the look on Pleasant's face, told him to keep his mouth shut.

When Thomas Lewis and Pleasant caught up with Matthew, the little boy was following the trail like a true Indian. For the way they left and returned to the plantation, was the exact same way Matthew took the horses, trying to get back to his sister. But Thomas Lewis rode on the out side of the brush, knowing that Matthew knew what to do.

"You's, trying to leave me?" Thomas Lewis asked, as Matthew led the horses out in to the open.

"Why you's tied him up?" Matthew asked, as he looked at Obdi wrapped in rope.

"Cause he's don't know ha to ride," Thomas Lewis replied with a smile.

By the time Thomas Lewis reached the spot where Clora Lee and the others were to be waiting, no one was there. Yet he noticed the signs, she had left for him to follow.

"Why she's ain't here?" Matthew asked.

"I's uh reckon, she's ain't wanna stop," Thomas Lewis replied, as he held a nervous look on his face.

But Pleasant wasn't buying it, seeing that the two young lovers lived by their word. And their old friend knew it wasn't like the girl, to change something, the two of them had already agreed on.

"Theys ain't far," Pleasant said, looking at the ground after riding for better than an hour.

"What you's doing?" Thomas Lewis chuckled.

"You's ever track a lion?" Pleasant asked the teen.

"Na Pleasant, you's knows I's uh ain't never see'd no lion."

"Then you's don't know much bout tracking," Pleasant replied with a smile.

"Pleasant and his pa killed uh elephant, and ate him," Obdi bragged.

"Then I's uh gon tell Lee, you's called her a lion."

"Na Co…. I's mean Thomas Lewis, I's uh ain't said no such thing, na did I's Pleasant?" Obdi cried, not wanting to anger Clora Lee.

"I's uh gon get Clora Lee to make him take uh washing, two times uh day, for that one," Pleasant said.

"Na that's good for ya," Matthew laughed.

Hearing Matthew's voice, Clora Lee marched a hobbling Jonathan out of the brush at gun point, with the ex-slaves behind her.

And seeing such a thing, even Obdi knew something was seriously wrong.

"What he's do?" Thomas Lewis barked.

"He's tried to take Clora Lee," Sistah said with a whole lot of anger in her voice.

"Matthew, you's get everybody on theys horse," Thomas Lewis said, as he dismounted.

"But we's can't ride," one of the four new comers said.

"Pleasant, you's tie um on theys horse," Thomas Lewis spat.

"You's ain't gon do no such thing, and I's uh mean it," Sistah snapped. "We gon take our time, and we gon get there, when we get there," she went on.

Once again, Clora Lee saw that side of Sistah, she was dying to understand. That side, which made Clora Lee feel like she was going crazy. But being that they were away from the plantation, Clora Lee was determined more then ever, to find the answer to Sistah's mind boggling double life. And Clora Lee knew she would have her answer, before they reach their destination, even if she had to fight the female to get it.

"I's uh can't ride good enough to carry my dumpling," Joan said, as she held her horse.

"Give her to me," Sistah said, as she swung her body up on a mare with no saddle.

After everyone had mounted a horse, and was on their way, Sistah stayed behind. She was there only to give Thomas Lewis a word of caution. A word, that sealed Clora Lee's belief, while striking a chord for what was to come.

With Madeline sitting on the horse in front of her, Sistah leaned forward and said, "Mae ain't here, so I's uh ya ma na. But I's uh tell ya this, Thomas Lewis. Mae ain't like us killing our own, and I's uh don't like it either. Now what ever you do him, you do him. But don't you kill him, or you will answer to me. You's hear me?" Sistah snarled, as her voice traveled between two different ways of speaking.

"I's uh hear ya, Honey Bee," Thomas Lewis said with out smiling.

Sistah cut her eyes at Thomas Lewis, as he went on staring at Jonathan with a burning hatred. Yet Sistah was hoping he saw her venomous glance, as it shot through the air like a cannon ball fired across a ship's bow. And Sistah was hoping he would take heed to her warning, as she and Madeline rode off to join the others.

While Thomas Lewis and Jonathan stood staring at each other, Clora Lee watched, as Pleasant and Matthew lead their friends up a hill. And as her and Thomas Lewis were baffled by Sistah's ability to ride a horse, they stayed focused on the task at hand. For Jonathan had to be dealt with, and dealt with accordingly, in order for the teens to move on.

"I's uh reckon, I's uh gotta fight the both uh ya," Jonathan said, never taking his eyes off of Thomas Lewis.

"You's stay out of it, Lee," Thomas Lewis said, as he took off his shirt.

When Jonathan saw the knife Thomas Lewis had hidden in his pants, the crafty twenty something ex-slave pulled a knife out of his boot. And seeing the knife, Clora Lee charged her horse up on him, but Thomas Lewis quickly waved his friend off.

"I's uh reckon, she's gon shoot me, when I's uh kill ya," Jonathan said, as he held that disgusting grin.

"I's uh shoot ya na, if n I's want," Clora Lee shouted.

"Give him ya word, Lee."

"I's uh do no such thing," Clora Lee said, aiming her cocked pistol at the Misses boy.

"Lee," Thomas Lewis said strongly, yet with love.

"If n you's dead, it won't matter, if n I's uh keep it."

"You's uh keep it."

No matter what the love of her life said, all Clora Lee gave the Misses boy, was a cold hard Arnold stare. For she just spat on the ground, then backed her horse away, while staring at the Misses bed boy, with an evil eye, which told him, he was just as good as dead.

Seeing that the fight was on, Thomas Lewis prepared him self for what was to come. So with his knees slightly bent, and leaning forward, Thomas Lewis slowly moved toward Jonathan. And while still holding his slick slave smile, Jonathan flipped his knife from hand to hand, as if he was waiting for Thomas Lewis to make the first move. And the way Thomas Lewis saw it, he wasn't about to let Jonathan wait long. Using the old Indian trick, Broken Branch had shown him, Thomas Lewis went to swing his knife at Jonathan, and acted as though he lost his balance. Like the fool he was, Jonathan bit on the deception, and found himself with a cut on the right arm.

"Who you's gon kill na," Clora Lee barked with a smile.

"I's uh see, you's been practicing," Jonathan said, after taking a look at his arm.

The two moved clockwise in their invisible circle, until Thomas Lewis quickly reversed his motion. And when Jonathan tried to correct his movement, Thomas Lewis jumped at him, causing the smiling one to stumble backward.

"Come on Lee, let's go," Thomas Lewis said, as he turned his back to Jonathan.

Unaware, that Thomas Lewis was setting him up for his next move, Jonathan rushed to his feet, and charged after the teen. But Thomas Lewis quickly turned around and leaped for the smiling one. Yet Jonathan acted as if he were waiting for such a move, and tossed some dirt and grass in Thomas Lewis's face.

"Lee, my eyes. My eyes, Lee," Thomas Lewis shouted, as he held his hand, on the bridge of his nose.

Thinking he had the upper hand, Jonathan rushed Thomas Lewis, and found he had been fooled once again. For Thomas Lewis flipped Jonathan, sending the foolish ex-slave for a short ride. And when Jonathan's body hit the ground with a thump, Thomas Lewis was on top of him, before he had a chance to recover. And being the only one with a knife, Thomas Lewis was more then willing to use it. But Jonathan had no desire to face the sharp blade, as he immediately took to fighting back. And fight, Jonathan did, until he found himself sitting on top Thomas Lewis. But once again, Jonathan was his own worst enemy. For the Misses boy, sat straight up, while trying to pry the knife from Thomas Lewis's hand. But what Jonathan didn't know, the adventurous teen was willing to teach him. So faster then a cat can lick its paw, Thomas Lewis raised his leg, and took the foolish ex-slave down, thus reversing their positions. And sitting on top of Jonathan, Thomas Lewis had no intentions of making the same mistake.

With both hands on the knife, Thomas Lewis laid his weight in on the no longer smiling jackal. But if Jonathan would have asked the first Indian he saw, the warrior would have told him, it was all part of the teen's next move. And what a next move it was. For when

Thomas Louis felt Jonathan's arms getting weak, he slammed their hands off to the side, sending himself crashing forward. And when the Misses former sex boy grunted, Thomas Lewis knew his head butt was administered perfectly. And knowing that the fight was over, Thomas Lewis saw fit to silence Jonathan once and for all. So with the speed of a fly, Thomas Lewis had his razor sharp blade in Jonathan mouth, cutting away at the love slave's tongue.

"You's can go back to ya Misses, cause we's don't want ya with us," Thomas Lewis said, as he wiped the blood from his knife, on Jonathan's shirt.

"Who you's kill? You's ain't killed spit," Clora Lee shouted, just before spitting on Jonathan, as Thomas Lewis got on his horse.

The two looked at Jonathan, feeling it was for the last time, as they gave their horses a swift kick. And at that very moment, Clora Lee and Thomas Lewis rode off, knowing they were truly putting the Big A Plantation behind them.

Sistah was riding along side the two young females, when Pleasant called for her to take a look. Looking over her shoulder, Sistah was able to see Thomas Lewis and Clora Lee riding down a hill like two gangbusters. It was the most beautiful thing Sistah and Pleasant had ever seen. The way Thomas Lewis and Clora Lee rode side by side, as they had lived every day of their young lives. And something told Sistah, they would ride to their death the same way. But at that very moment, Sistah couldn't bring herself to think about death, and all of the pain that went along with it. For the often misguided female was much too proud of her babies, to bring herself to think of something as ugly, as death. And if death knew what was good for it, then the ugly child from Hell, would surely stay away from Sistah's children.

Chapter 23

The Truth

That night, as Clora Lee and Thomas Lewis took a bath together in a creek, she kissed him as the two of them stood naked beneath the stars. And while kissing him, Clora Lee ran her hand down from Thomas Lewis chest, to his hard throbbing club.

"I's uh reckon, you's do got big foots," Clora Lee said smiling.

"Ha you's know?" Thomas Lewis asked, as he had no idea of what Clora Lee was talking about?

"Cause it's big."

"Ha you's knows it's big?"

Clora Lee bit her bottom lip, as she stood with her legs open, while inserting Thomas Lewis strong erection between her virgin lips. And the look in her eyes, told Thomas Lewis of the pain she was feeling. But Clora Lee didn't stop, until he had broken through her virgin walls. And with her arms around his neck, Clora Lee rode him to a quick exploding climax. But the teen was not a lone, as her high piercing squeal, told Thomas Lewis, he was neither too late, nor too early for her timing.

"I's uh wanna do it again," Clora Lee said, as she washed herself.

But Clora Lee didn't have to ask Thomas Lewis twice, being that he was already playing with her pussy, as she stood bent over washing those pretty light brown legs of hers.

"Don't you's worry, you's gon get more of that there, then you's can handle," she said, with the most seductive smile.

And seeing such a smile, told Thomas Lewis, he would be getting just as much loving, as the next male.

"What you's, gon do bout Sistah?"

"Yo's Sistah, ain't gon stop, what I's uh gon give ya. I's uh gon give ya, everything uh female can give her man," Clora Lee said.

"Na Lee, you's knows white folks don't want no slave, to be call no man."

"Theys give us babies. And theys women folk, got mo slaves babies hid or dead, then theys got cotton in theys fields. So I's uh ain't gon pay no mind, to what them old devils want," Clora Lee said angrily. "Na if n you's finish playing with that, we's need to wash, so we's can get some sleep."

"I's uh never see'd you's look so pretty, before," Thomas Lewis whispered, while rubbing Clora Lee's ass.

Long before the sun signaled a new day, Thomas Lewis had his eyes opened in the most arousing way. With her naked body wrapped in an old union blanket, Clora Lee gently rode Thomas Lewis sleep hard erection as his ears heard her whisper wake up. And Thomas Lewis didn't disappoint his Lee, as he took hold of her breast.

"I's uh just getting what's mind," Clora Lee said, as she stared down at the suspicious look in Thomas Lewis eyes.

With her lover no longer caught off guard, Clora Lee knew she had to hurry up and get her good feeling, before the pain came knocking again. So with her body laying flat on Thomas Lewis, Clora Lee humped until she let out a soft cry of satisfaction. And to her benefit, Clora Lee had made Thomas Lewis cum, just as fast as she did. But Clora Lee was determined to feel the pain, as she sat up straight and rode Thomas Lewis, as his dick slowly shrunk inside of her body. And as she felt his seeds running around inside of her, Clora Lee softly said Cowayne, making it the last time that she would ever call him by the name, which Sistah had given him.

After laying down longer then she had intended, Clora Lee sat up on Thomas Lewis and asked the pivotal question, "You's surrender?"

"I's surrender," Thomas Lewis said with a smile.

When Clora Lee was done kissing Thomas Lewis more times then she could count, the beautifully shaped teen got up and went to the creek. There she washed herself, thinking solely of having babies. But then like a bad dream, Clora Lee thought about Jonathan. For she felt leaving him alive, would some day come back to haunt them, and the girl hated the thought with a fearful burning passion.

"You's wake up," Clora Lee said, while shaking Thomas Lewis with her foot.

Thomas Lewis opened his eyes to an early morning sky. And seeing Clora Lee standing over him, the first thing to catch his eyes, were her clean clothes. He then found himself, focusing his eyes on the gun belt, which made Clora Lee's breeches look even better. And the way Thomas Lewis saw it, the guns looked a lot better on his Lee, then they did on the dead white man.

"You's get up, and go down to that there creek, and get cleaned up," Clora Lee said, as she sat his things on the blanket.

Thomas Lewis ran down to the creek like a man on fire, smiling all the way there. He was no longer frustrated, nor did he feel left out. For the teen had no doubt, his feeling of complete and utter joy, would never change. Some how, Thomas Lewis knew it would last for the rest of their lives. They were free, and on their way. He was in love, and making love. For there was nothing else, the poor boy could bring himself to want, as his feet hit the cold water.

While Thomas Lewis was in the creek, Clora Lee went to have her talk with Sistah. And on her way to the strange acting female, she spotted Obdi sitting on the ground looking lost.

"Clora Lee," Obdi called out softly.

Clora Lee rested her left hand on its gun, and walked over to where Obdi was sitting. She stood over him, waiting for the former house slave to say what was on his mind.

"Ya grandma told Nelson to give ya this, but he's gave it to me, cause he's stayed to help her," Obdi said sadly, as he gave Clora Lee the letter. "She's also said, you's had that," Obdi mumbled, pointing at Mrs. Arnold's riding crop.

"She's ain't knowed nothing, you's just wanna to stay with us," Clora Lee grumbled, as she stared at the letter.

Knowing that he didn't have anything to lose, Obdi stood up, to say what he had to say. "I's uh ain't gotta stay, but ya grandma know'd bout that Rebel soldier you's kill. And I's uh told her and Mae bout them men, you's kill, while Cowayne was gone," he said with pride.

"You's ain't see'd nothing," Clora Lee said angrily.

"Then I's uh speck, I's ain't," Obdi replied, then sat back down, leaving Clora Lee to go have her talk with Sistah.

When Clora Lee finally reached Sistah, the female was sitting on the ground, explaining how things were going to be, when they reach their new home. And as Clora Lee stood listening to Sistah, she saw it again. For Sistah was speaking without a flaw in her voice, and that told the teen, it was time for the two of them to have their one on one show down. And Clora Lee knew she had to do it, before Sistah's perfect demeanor ran back into its hiding place.

"Sistah, we's gotta talk," Clora Lee said, looking at her friend.

"Can it wait?" Sistah asked, as if she had no intentions of changing again.

Clora Lee didn't trouble herself, with the perfectly stated question. For the teen just walked off, knowing the strange acting female would follow her.

"Is there something wrong?" Sistah asked, when they came to a stop.

"Ha you's do that?" Clora Lee asked.

"Do what?" Sistah asked in return, putting the burden back on the teen.

"Back there with Jonathan, you's ain't had nothing wrong with ya. You's talk like you's was no different then me or Joan, or Sally. And some time, you's talk like you's white folks. Ha you's do it?"

Sistah sat on the ground looking sad. She looked as if some one had come to her with news of Thomas Lewis passing. The way she looked when Obdi said old Mae was dead.

"You's better sit down," Sistah said, looking up at Clora Lee.

And when the teen who waited for ever, to lose her virginity sat on the ground, Sistah took a deep breath. And after holding it for what appeared to be a lifetime, the mysterious female slowly released the air from her body.

"Fo I's uh come to the Big A, I's uh was own by some good white folks," Sistah said. "Well I can say the wife and the daughters were good," Sistah went on, as she began to pick at the green grass that rested in front of her.

"Then why you's looking sad?" Clora Lee asked, as she noticed how Sistah's speech bounced back and forth, from poor to good, as if it had a mind of its own.

"Cause I's uh did a bad thing," Sistah said sadly. "One night while the lady of the house was sleeping, her husband came in our room, and he's took me."

"That's what masas do," Clora Lee said, as the thought of slavery, still made her angry.

"But the Misses said, he's was never to come in our room," Sistah mumbled, while starting to cry.

"But he's was the masa. And the masas do's what theys want. And theys go in the slaves rooms, and take which ever one theys want."

"It wasn't a slave room," Sistah cried. "It was for me and Sara. And we's ain't never had to worry bout him, or none of them others. We was the Misses little girls."

"You's can't be the Misses little girl," Clora Lee said firmly, while trying to get her friend to understand the realization of slavery.

Sistah didn't say a word for nearly a minute, as she rocked back and forward, leaving Clora Lee to wonder. She wondered what Sistah could have possibly done, to make her act so crazy over some slave hating white folks. But Clora Lee didn't speak a word, as she just waited for Sistah to go on with her story.

"And that night, he's come in our room, and when I's woke up, he's was putting a rag in my mouth. He's, took off my undergarments, and got on top of me, and he's hurt me awful bad," Sistah said, as the snot began to run from her nose. "And when he's left, I's uh took off my gown, and I's uh put it on Sara. I's uh ain't wanna do it, but I's uh wanted the Misses to kill him, like she said, she would. She said, she uh kill him, if n he's do her Sara, like he's did her other girls," Sistah said crying. "That's why I was in the room with her, so I could tell the Misses, if n he's come in there."

"What did you do?" Clora Lee asked firmly.

"I's uh ain't mean it, Clora Lee, I's swear, I's uh ain't mean it," Sistah said, as she cried harder.

"I's uh knows you's ain't mean it, but you's gotta tell me, what you's do?"

"I's uh put the rag in her mouth, and I's uh got a stick, and I's uh did her like he did me. But she still made too much racket, so I's uh put the pillow on her face, and she stop moving. So I waited until morning, then I's uh ran and got the Misses. When she see'd Sara, she's ran out of the room, and she's killed him, just like she said she would. She killed him. She killed him, before he could get out of bed."

By the time Clora Lee realized the girl was not a normal child, Sistah was banging her forehead on the ground, repeating the words, God for give me, until the teen didn't want to hear it anymore. But from where Clora Lee stood, the white man got what was coming to him. And as for the little girl, she was just another white female, who had no idea, she owned a slave.

"So she's sold you to the Big A?" Clora Lee asked.

"No. She said, she was taking me back, where she got me from," Sistah said, as she continued to pound her head on the ground.

"Well it ain't much we's can do bout it na, so you's get up and stop that there crying," Clora Lee said, as she began to look at the letter from Effie.

But Clora Lee knew if the shoe were on the other foot, Sistah wouldn't hesitate to find a way to comfort her. So Clora Lee scooted over to Sistah, and put her arms around the only true mother she ever had, and the two hugged each other tightly.

"Come on, we's gotta go see bout them others," Clora Lee said, as she helped Sistah to her feet.

When Sally saw Sistah crying, she quickly assumed the female was still crying over old Mae.

"Sistah I's uh gotta tell ya something."

Still crying, Sistah looked at Sally, wondering how much more her poor crumbling heart could take. And just as Sally was about to speak, Thomas Lewis walked up and stood next to Clora Lee, who was still holding on to Sistah.

"I's uh reckon, you's need to hear it, just as much as Sistah," Sally said of Thomas Lewis. "That night, Duval came to see masa Arnold bout ya ma keeping ya, masa Arnold told him, Mae was Sistah ma too."

While Sistah went back to crying on Clora Lee's shoulder, Thomas Lewis looked at Pleasant. The faithful friend hunched his shoulders, signaling, he didn't know a thing about the twisted situation.

"Why you's ain't tell us, when we's was on the plantation?" Clora Lee asked.

"Cause masa Arnold told the Misses, to kill um, if n theys find out," Joan said.

"Mae knowed Sistah was her baby, that's why she's called her Honey Bee. Masa Arnold told Duval, Mae called her that, when she's was a baby," Sally said.

"You's knows her real name?" Pleasant asked.

"Beatrice," Sally said, looking at Sistah.

"I's uh reckon, you's do look like Sistah," Pleasant joked, looking at Thomas Lewis.

Sistah started laughing through her tears, as she reached out for Thomas Lewis. And like the good son that he had always been, Thomas Lewis went to his sister, giving Clora Lee the chance to read her letter from Effie.

While hoping for a little privacy, Clora Lee drifted off to herself, just before tearing open the letter. But for some reason, Clora Lee was reluctant to read her grandmother's words. For the teen had known for a long time, Effie could read and write, yet she had never seen her grandmothers do either. And for years, Clora Lee wanted to know what her grandmother's handwriting looked like. So as she stood glossing over each and every letter, as they formed their words, Clora Lee silently read Effie's only gift to her. And the more Clora Lee read, the more her past had become that of a troublesome burden. A burden that weighed in on the girl's soul like a millstone, dragging it down into the depths of darkness, where there is no forgiveness.

My Dearest Clora Lee:
If you are reading this letter, then my fear of not joining you has come true. But I know I am leaving you in good hands, just like Mae knew Cowayne would be alright with you and Beatrice by his side. You are a good girl, with a good heart, and I know you will do good things in the white man's world, so take care. And every now and then, give Matthew a wink for me. He loves to smile at a winking eye. And when you tell Cowayne Sistah real name is Beatrice, tell him, his name come from a turtle down in Louisiana, and that is why Jeremiah could not spell it.
Love: Grandmother

Clora Lee gently folded the letter and placed it in her shirt. She then gazed up at the sky, as her tears began to fall like the raindrops, which fell on the night that she was born. For the poor teen couldn't believe how wrong she had been about her grandmother. And all the ill things she said and did against Effie came rushing forward, to beat Clora Lee relentlessly, causing the teen to drop to her knees. There, she wished time could be turned back, just as easily, as it constantly moved forward. But time would not allow such a thing, preventing Clora Lee from ever obtaining her grandmother's forgiveness. A forgiveness that was desperately needed, in order for the teen to move on with the new life, Effie had awarded them.

When the group was ready to continue on with their journey, Pleasant gave Thomas Lewis the knife Duval had once worn with pride. And after taking the knife, Thomas Lewis placed it on his left gun belt, while catching Pleasant off guard.

"You's ain't tell me, how long Nelson been watching me."

"From the day, Sistah left ya with Ella, na can we go?"

"Is you's really the son of uh King?" Clora Lee asked.

"I's uh reckon, Thomas Lewis tells ya everything," Pleasant said, looking at the ground. "I's uh ain't nothing but uh slave, that ain't no slave, no mo," Pleasant mumbled after pausing for a moment.

"You's had a castle?" Bessie asked.

"We uh talk later," Beatrice said, bringing the matter to an end.

"What was them words, my ma said, fo we's left?" Thomas Lewis asked.

"Be strong, and you will survive," Matthew blurted out.

"Ha you's know?"

"Cause Mae told me," Matthew said, as if the words were given to him, for safe keeping.

As they rode westward, Clora Lee gave Matthew the wink, Effie wrote about in her letter.

"She's told ya," Matthew shouted through a big bright smile, as Bessie sat behind him, on that old gray horse.

At that very moment, everyone felt what ever the future held for them, they would face it head on, with a full head of steam. And even though they were leaving the Big A, for a world filled with uncertainty, the ex-slaves had no idea, the old plantation held one last secret, which may stay hidden for all eternity.

THE END

CPSIA information can be obtained at www.ICGtesting.com
Printed in the USA
244232LV00002BB/1/P